CW01512032

SOME OF US
ARE LIARS

Also by Fiona Cummins

Rattle
The Collector
The Neighbour
When I Was Ten
Into the Dark
All of Us Are Broken

SOME OF US ARE LIARS

FIONA CUMMINS

MACMILLAN

First published 2025 by Macmillan
an imprint of Pan Macmillan
The Smithson, 6 Briset Street, London ECIM 5NR
EU representative: Macmillan Publishers Ireland Ltd, 1st Floor,
The Liffey Trust Centre, 117–126 Sheriff Street Upper,
Dublin 1, DO1 YC43
Associated companies throughout the world
www.panmacmillan.com

ISBN 978-1-0350-1300-5 HB
ISBN 978-1-0350-1301-2 TPB

1 3 5 7 9 8 6 4 2

A CIP catalogue record for this book is available from the British Library.

Typeset by Palimpsest Book Production Ltd, Falkirk, Stirlingshire
Printed and bound by CPI Group (UK) Ltd, Croydon, CR0 4YY

Visit **www.panmacmillan.com** to read more about all our books
and to buy them. You will also find features, author interviews and
news of any author events, and you can sign up for e-newsletters
so that you're always first to hear about our new releases.

For Keely Buckle, the sister I never had

Next morning I went up into the room. Snowdrops
And candles soothed the bedside; I saw him
For the first time in six weeks. Paler now,

Wearing a poppy bruise on his left temple,
He lay in the four-foot box as in his cot.
No gaudy scars, the bumper knocked him clear.

A four-foot box, a foot for every year.

– Seamus Heaney, 'Mid-Term Break'

PRESS ASSOCIATION (PA) Breaking news

MIDTOWN-ON-SEA – 18 NOVEMBER 2023 – ESSEX Police has confirmed that an arrest was made this morning following an eleven-month investigation into the murder of one of its officers, Detective Constable Douglas Lynch.

The police officer was found dead at his home in December last year, with his wrists and ankles bound and multiple facial lacerations consistent with a seagull attack. A post-mortem revealed that DC Lynch, who had a phobia of birds, died from heart failure induced by fear.

This is a breaking news story. More to follow.

PROLOGUE

Wednesday, 27 September 2023

Saul

The call came on a sultry night when it seemed as though summer would last forever and winter was a lifetime away.

Saul Anguish was gathering marsh samphire, cutting through the succulent stems with the edge of a blade. A wisp of snipes was wading through the wetlands, their bills probing the mud for insects, the striped crown of their feathers illuminated by the dying rays of sunlight.

It was from a number he didn't recognize, but the young man had been primed to expect it. He placed the vivid stalks into his cloth bag and kicked at the crusted edges of the salt-soaked earth, watching colours bleed from the sky.

The voice was male and authoritative. The last time Saul had heard it was a few weeks earlier, when he'd received a commendation for outstanding bravery from its owner, the Chief Constable of Essex Police.

Lauded for the brilliance of his tactical thinking and his unparalleled courage in saving the life of a young boy, Saul, with few friends and no family to celebrate his success, had slipped away from the ceremony as soon as the official photographs had been taken.

But the Chief Constable had not forgotten the sharp-eyed detective with his gift for policing and the secrets in his heart.

He offered Saul a choice. He did not have to accept the assignment. He understood if it put him in a difficult position among his fellow officers, if going off-book didn't conform to his personal code of ethics, if he was unable to operate alone and under the radar. If lying for the greater good went against his principles. But he'd come highly recommended by his former inspector, whose opinion, despite his fall from grace, was still widely respected.

At twenty-six, Saul was too cynical to believe that choice in this scenario was anything other than illusory. A part of him was surprised by the call, a forensic trail connecting them both, but he understood that no one rose to such a senior rank without mastering the art of plausible deniability. If he declined, he could kiss goodbye to his promising career. But that wasn't the reason he agreed to the request.

When the Chief Constable had told him that he was authorizing him – unofficially, of course – to quietly investigate a suspected killer operating from inside the force, a bad apple rotting – *infecting* – their revered institution in plain sight, he'd given him a name.

It was a name Saul recognized.

A name that terrified him.

But knowledge was not only power. It was a weapon.

ASSOCIATED PRESS (AP) Advisory notice

MIDTOWN-ON-SEA – 22 JULY 2024 – THE Emmy-Award-winning actress Winter Kellaway will give evidence at Midtown Crown Court this week as part of the gross negligence manslaughter proceedings involving her four-year-old nephew, Teddy Miller.

Witnesses expected to take the stand during the two-week trial include investigating officer Detective Constable Saul Anguish, as well as Jen Miller, Teddy's mother, and the boy's older sister, Iris Miller.

NOW
Monday, 22 July 2024

Jen

Some days are full of motion. A man on the morning train spills his coffee on her coat and dries it with tissues and over-blown apologies. During her dash to St John's for afternoon pick-up, a pre-schooler on a scooter careens into the back of her legs, laddering her almost new tights. When dusk falls, the wind commands the trees to dance, to twist and bend and bow. As she runs hard and fast through the night-time streets, her hair whips around her face and she concentrates on the sound of her footsteps, trying to outpace the past.

Some days are still. *She* is still. Even the act of breathing is an effort, a chore she can barely persuade herself to complete. She doesn't rise from her bed in the morning. She doesn't shower or turn on the radio or make a cup of coffee. Instead she listens to the murmured voices of her husband, cajoling their daughter to eat her cereal, and her daughter, not questioning why her mother is in bed, but whether she'll still be there at the end of the day. Like yesterday. And the day before.

As the front door slams behind them, as the sounds of their conversation drift away, the house holds its breath again, silence pushing down on her chest. Her arms are resting by her sides, her legs unmoving against the sheets. She tells herself if she waits just a moment longer, he will come.

But the minutes liquefy into hours, and shadows creep across the bedroom wall, swallowing up the light. However long she waits, the outcome is always the same. No small boy burrowing beneath her duvet; no plump fingers, sticky with jam, smoothing her hair from her face and planting kisses on her forehead; no trips to the swimming pool or jumping in puddles or racing each other to the swings and the slide.

No Teddy.

And some days, like today, are both. She is up and dressed before sunrise. But she doesn't turn on the television or the radio because she knows the airwaves will be full of analysis and discussion, photographs of her family and judgement disguised as opinion.

She cannot stomach these 'experts', these so-called talking heads. Their sombre faces and authoritative declarations of how and what she must be feeling sicken her. It is their good fortune to have no experience of what it means to be a part of her family, members of an exclusive club no sane person wants to belong to.

She stands at the window overlooking the bay and watches the fishing boats bring in their catch, the crawl of the sun from sea line to sky. A moment of serenity before the forthcoming storm.

Her daughter is staying with friends for a few days; her husband is – where? She doesn't know and he hasn't told her. She is certain only of one thing. He won't be watching from the public gallery when the trial begins.

As soon as she steps out of the front door, photographers cluster around the gate at the end of the path. One of them shouts out, a rough appeal, 'Head up, love. Can you look this way?' But she doesn't lift her head. It's a story to them, all in a day's work. To her, it's the remnants of a life that grief has all but destroyed.

The taxi's engine is running. A journalist – she's seen him before, both here and on television – is waiting by its passenger door. A cameraman films her as she walks briskly towards the kerb. She won't challenge them because their response is always delivered with the same pigeon-chested belligerence. *The pavement's a public space. We're allowed to be here.*

She presses her lips together and opens the taxi's rear door. Eyes down. Zero engagement.

'Have you spoken to your sister since that day, Mrs Miller?' The journalist's accent is northern, nasal. When she doesn't reply, he tries again with the kind of faux intimacy she despises. 'Jen? How are things with your parents? Can you tell our viewers what it—'

She slams the door and his words are cut off. She breathes out and fastens her seatbelt with trembling hands.

'Midtown Crown Court?' She hears the question mark in the driver's voice and knows he's asking for more than a confirmation of her destination. Even now, she is unused to the curiosity of strangers.

'Yes.' She doesn't elaborate, but even if she was in the mood for conversation, her voice sounds scratchy with nerves and emotion.

He catches her eye in the rear-view mirror. 'Tough day

ahead.' His tone is sympathetic. It's clear he's recognized her. She nods because it's not his fault and she doesn't want to be rude. When they pull up outside the court, she fumbles for her purse but he shakes his head. 'No charge.'

At this act of kindness, a rush of heat spreads across her chest and she blinks back tears.

Outside the courthouse, a phalanx of photographers lies in wait. They haven't noticed her yet but they will. As soon as she steps from the safety of the cab.

Her phone vibrates with a message. It's David Jarvis, the prosecution barrister, short and to the point: *How are things?* He doesn't care about her feelings, though. There's a subtext here and it's as clear to her as the cloudless sky above. *Are you still coming?*

Eight months and four days ago, her son – her Teddy – was taken from her in an act of reckless stupidity by her sister.

If Jen appears in the witness box today, she will condemn that sister to a life behind bars and a child to a future without a mother. Her parents – almost broken by the tragic events of last year – will lose their daughter as well as their grandson. But if she does not, her husband will divorce her and seek full custody of their surviving child. As things stand, he will probably win.

The taxi driver looks at the waiting photographers and back at her, a gentleness to his voice that softens his accent, half Albanian, half estuary vowels and glottal stops. 'Shall I drive around the block a couple of times?'

She offers him a ghost of a smile, grateful for his understanding, his display of compassion.

They drive away from the court building, following the curve of the bay. The traffic is light on this July morning, signalling the start of the summer holidays, but it's only a brief postponement. Crowds will arrive later in the day, swarming Midtown-on-Sea's pretty streets and artisan cafes. In the distance, the beach is dotted with a handful of early sunseekers. By lunchtime, it will be packed.

Memory throws her back to the afternoon of the accident on the cusp of autumn and winter, that same bright sand dulled by the rising tide, the gunmetal wash of the estuary and the patches of fog that hung in the air like nebulae. Teddy's laughter carried on the wind. Her parents, her sisters' families and her own, friends and colleagues, gathered for a joyous celebration that tipped into tragedy of the most searing and irreversible kind.

'Are you ready to go back to the courthouse?' The taxi driver interrupts her thoughts. A simple question. Except it's not so simple after all.

Because Jen Miller doesn't know whether to tell the truth. Or to take her daughter and run.

PART ONE

BEFORE

1

Thursday, 16 November 2023

Saul

When the fog rolled in from the bay, it was impossible to tell where the sea ended and the land began. This was pertinent to the detective Saul Anguish because he was marooned in a kayak in the middle of a greyness that swallowed everything.

It had come on without warning, in the way that coastal fog sometimes does. A change in air temperature, pushed inland by the wind. Some of the fishermen called it fret, but Saul had another name for it. The darkening. While it gave the illusion of light, it switched off the senses, made him feel disorientated and vulnerable, especially on open water. It was so thick he could not see beyond the bow of the vessel.

He cursed, the clouds of moisture cold against his face. He'd checked the weather forecast before he'd left, but there had been no signs until he'd found himself ambushed by stealth. He couldn't call for help. Mobile phone coverage here was patchy at best. Saul had overheard the fishermen grumbling as they brought in their nets, ringing hotels and restaurants to hustle for orders as soon as they landed on the jetty, but often too late, at a disadvantage to their competitors who'd trawled the waters further along the coast.

The foghorn let out a groan. Saul lifted his head and scanned his surroundings, a flicker of unease stirring within him. He had only the vaguest sense of where he was, the fog transforming the seascape he had come to know intimately into a monochrome canvas. All around him, he could hear the rhythm of the waves, gaining in power and intensity as the wind swept in from the east. He listened for the cry of the gulls, seeking a connection to the natural world, to other living things, and glanced upwards. He'd read somewhere that seabirds fly above fog, using the sun to navigate. But there was nothing inside this murk except him.

He bent, his hair damp in the November chill, and squared his shoulders. From memory, the marina was in a north-westerly direction. He felt in his pocket for the brass compass he'd acquired from the house of a murder victim in the spring of the previous year, her initials engraved across its back.

As soon as he'd seen it, he'd had to have it. It gave him a rush to use it out here on the waves, knowing it had once belonged to her. He ran a thumb across the inscription and wondered if she'd ever done the same. Her name had been Evelyn Parker. She was fifty-eight. The streaks of egg yolk from her breakfast had barely dried on her plate when she was strangled by her husband for having the audacity to undercook his bacon.

Although a gifted detective, Saul hid many secrets. One of them was his compulsion to collect mementoes from every crime scene he attended, intimate treasures that had belonged to the dead and spoke to the darkness within him.

He confirmed his nautical position and put the compass away.

Saul's arms moved at a steady tempo, his paddles carving through the spume. A year ago, he'd never been in a kayak, but after being shot and badly injured by a pair of spree killers at a hotel in Scotland, he'd been undergoing intensive rehabilitation. The scars that the young couple had left on him were more than physical. But the detective was determined to mend his body, if not his mind, and part of that included strengthening the muscles in his back. Blue had suggested sea-kayaking and Saul, seduced by the challenge of mastering an unfamiliar skill in a place he loved, had fallen hard.

That first time, it had felt like a riot to his senses. A robust wind, tempered by the tentative rays of spring sunshine, had exhilarated him in ways he hadn't felt for months. But it had been difficult, in the beginning. Frustratingly so. His deltoids and hamstrings, weakened by lack of exercise, had burned from effort. And when the instructor had guided the kayak back to shore, Saul had stumbled across the wet sand, reaching for his cane, a shadow of the man he'd been.

But, as the seasons turned, as he bought his own kayak and took her out every day, his physique transformed, becoming stronger, leaner. The softness of his post-injury body hardened to match his damaged heart, scarred by everything he'd seen and done. He pushed himself until his mind emptied, and all he could focus on was the movement of his arms, that repetitive rise and slice. He learned how to ride the tides, and to read the weather, and what to do if his kayak was swamped or capsized. Early morning, if those tides allowed, he would drag himself from the coastguard's lookout, his cottage on the promontory of a cliff, while the rest of the world slept, and he would be alone, at the mercy of the gods of sea and sky.

The deeds of his past still taunted him as he lay, open-eyed and heartsore, in the quiet hours of the night, but while his mind was active, the intense physicality of being on open water wearied him, and sometimes he lost himself to the luxury of sleep.

On those nights when sleep eluded him, he would rise in the hours before dawn and sift through the paperwork he'd begun to assemble as part of the Chief Constable's off-the-record investigation, the call logs and CCTV footage, and scraps of evidence he'd gathered himself. To avoid suspicion, his work was conducted in the hours around his own duties, in those shadowy between-times when he was alone.

While he did not like the liar that duplicity had made of him, he recognized its necessity. It was a long game, one of skill and strategy, and Saul was determined to win it. But like any game, the power balance could shift at any time, and he could not afford to make costly mistakes.

A sound caught his attention, as if something was breaking the surface of the waves. He stilled for a minute, catching his breath, allowing his kayak to drift. Above the pump of his heart, he heard a rhythmic splashing, like a seal he'd once seen by the wharf.

Through the grey cloak of the fog, a small rowing boat came into view. Its occupant had her back to him, but he could tell it was a woman, resting the handles of the oars in her lap. He opened his mouth to call to her, to warn her about a nearby rocky outcrop that had torn a hole in the hull of many unsuspecting vessels in this corner of the bay, but she'd picked up the oars again and was moving at a determined clip across the water.

Something about the urgency of her movement piqued Saul's curiosity, and he angled his kayak in her direction, keeping his paddles loose and still.

When the woman came into view again, she was much closer. The wind had begun to strengthen, thinning the fog, and she was clearly visible, although she hadn't noticed him yet. She placed her oars in the bottom of the boat and reached down to retrieve an item from a plastic bag. Saul frowned, unsure if the drifting clouds of fret were playing tricks on his vision. He inched his kayak towards her, his movements quiet and discreet.

In her right hand she was holding a white dress with a large print of a rose at its breast. Saul was no expert, but if he'd been forced to make a guess, he'd have said it belonged to a child. The wind ran through it, and it moved, like the ghost of a past he could not know and didn't understand.

The woman half stood, and the boat lurched, knocking her off balance. Heart in mouth, Saul watched her steady herself. The dress had capped sleeves and was full-skirted, embroidered with a handful of blue and yellow flowers. A summer dress. A promise.

The woman held it close to her for a few seconds, and then tossed it into the sea. As she lifted her head, she caught sight of Saul. Shocked, she turned away from him, obscuring her face. But it was too late. He'd already seen her.

As quickly as she'd arrived, she was gone, rowing hard and fast across the waves in the direction of the marina and the expensive waterfront estates. Saul considered following her, but could not find a reason to do so. Instead, he found himself peering into the choppy waves, wondering why she'd gone to the effort of disposing of it in this way, and what had caused her to commit such a final and deliberate act.

It didn't take him long to find it. In a quirk of fortune, the dress had snagged on the rocky outcrop he'd intended to warn her about, and the ebb and flow of the water made the fabric billow, as if it was a living thing. A cog whirred in Saul's mind, a mechanical click and grind. For reasons he could not articulate, he wished to take ownership of that dress, an instinct he would not interrogate but had come to trust.

It was only when he drew close enough to touch it that Saul realized it was not a rose at its breast at all, but the faded bloom of a bloodstain.

2

Jen

The doorbell rang, three sharp blasts. Jen Miller murmured an expletive-ridden plea to a higher power that the noise had not woken her exhausted younger sister or six-day-old niece and hurried to answer it.

Winter – dressed in a calf-length pastel pink fur coat and oversized sunglasses – was standing on the doorstep, arms outstretched. Her outfit might have looked ridiculous on some women, but not Winter.

The eldest of the three sisters – and an actor of international stature – Winter was used to commanding attention. From her early teens, she had ticked all the boxes of what many consider to be conventional beauty: she was tall and slender with the kind of striking good looks that saw her front international modelling campaigns for several high-end fashion houses. A motorist had once crashed his car into a telephone box because he'd been distracted by the sight of her on the way to the beach, dressed in a metallic high-neck bodysuit and cut-off shorts. Even before she was famous, she was always served first in a bar or

19

given the best table at a restaurant. Beauty was a powerful currency.

It would have been easy to hate her, but her generosity, both materially and of spirit, saved her from ruin. But she wasn't without flaws. Despite her genetic advantages, she was prone to jealousy and could be judgemental, and she still sucked her thumb, although the newspapers didn't know that. Her real name was Deborah, but that was too pedestrian, so everyone, including her own family, had called her by her professional moniker for years.

'It's perfect,' she said, shrugging off her coat, rain clinging to the artificial fibres like teardrops. She pushed an extravagantly beribboned box full of cakes at Jen. 'Absolutely bloody perfect.'

Jen, an advertising copywriter, exhaled in relief and flashed her sister an appreciative smile. She had a work deadline in three hours that she couldn't miss and a meal to prepare, plus she needed to collect Teddy from nursery and Iris from school. She didn't have time to disappear down to the waterfront and check if the event planners had pulled off a miracle. The cakes looked delicious. She promised herself she wouldn't eat one unless her dress zipped up at tomorrow's final fitting.

Winter wandered into the hallway, chucked her faux fur over the newel post at the bottom of the stairs and kissed her sister on both cheeks. Her perfume tickled Jen's nose. It was sophisticated. Expensive. Like everything about her.

A pull of longing surprised the younger woman. Winter, stylish in a cashmere jumper and tailored trousers, was widely recognized for her talents, fêted by their extended family and her army of fans, responsible for no one but herself. Who was Jen? A mother. Wife. Sister. Daughter. Of course she was, and she was proud to be those things. But as she glanced down at her faded jeans and her cardigan that had lost its shape several washes ago, she couldn't remember what it was to be *herself*, independent of the wants and desires of others.

Winter removed her sunglasses, the gold designer logo glinting against her manicured fingernails. In a moment of cattiness, Jen wondered why she'd bothered to wear them when the weather outside was so damp and grey, but she chided herself for such an uncharitable thought. Her sister was a celebrity. It came with the territory.

'You're not going to believe it when you see it. It's *insane*.' Winter pulled out her phone to show Jen some photographs, enthusiasm bubbling from her like the champagne she always drank. She was right. The transformation was breathtaking. Unreal.

Not for the first time, Jen was filled with gratitude that Winter had offered to project-manage the party to end all parties. It wasn't that she didn't want to celebrate her recent marriage to Phil, or their parents' golden wedding anniversary, or Alyssa's forthcoming fortieth, but with two young children and a flourishing business, even the idea of organizing such a lavish affair had felt exhausting.

When Winter stepped up and proposed that she not only lend them her vast beachside estate but pay for the celebrations as her gift to them all, Jen had bitten her hand off. Alyssa had been pregnant at the time and Jen knew from experience that early motherhood was all-consuming, so neither sister wanted to impose further pressure on her. Then Winter, often away from home for months at a time, had checked her schedule and confirmed she had a six-week break, starting in November, and everything had fallen into place.

'Are you sure?' Alyssa and Jen had asked this question in unison when Winter had outlined her plan. Their elder sister had replied by drawing them into a hug, as she'd done since they were little girls. The Kellaway sisters. *All for one and one for all.*

Winter had just wrapped filming on a television series that would net her more money than either of her siblings had made in the last twenty years combined. It was an eye-watering sum that had seen Jen choke on her mouthful of wine when Winter had mentioned it over lunch a few months earlier during a rare day off, a casual addendum to Jen's own grumblings about the cost-of-living crisis and the rise in energy prices. But she was generous to a fault, Jen couldn't deny that.

Eight years ago, when Iris was born, Winter had gifted Jen a million pounds to help her and Phil buy the house of their dreams. It was a ridiculous amount of money – far too much, Jen had protested – but Winter was not married, did not want children and insisted that her sisters share in her own good fortune. 'It will go to you or your kiddos when I die. What's the difference if you have some of it now?' She'd presented Alyssa with the same amount, and the youngest of the sisters had used it to buy a house a few doors down from Jen, which meant all three of them now lived within a two-mile radius of each other.

'When do Mum and Dad arrive?'

Jen pretended to consider this for a minute, but as the organized one of the trio, the date and time were etched into her mind, her desk diary and her Google calendar. Less than twenty-four hours from now. 'Tomorrow afternoon.'

Winter clapped her hands together, her beautiful face creased into a smile. 'This is going to be the greatest weekend of our lives.'

Jen grinned at her sister, but not for the reasons that Winter thought. Not surprisingly, the eldest Kellaway daughter had always demonstrated a taste for the hyperbolic. Still, even if it wasn't going to be quite the greatest weekend of Jen's life, she shared the sentiment that it was likely to be one of her most memorable, if nothing else.

3

Alyssa

Alyssa, the youngest of the Kellaway sisters, opened one sticky eye. She could see the fading light through the tall sash window, Jen's sewing machine, a froth of fabric spilling from it, and a mug of tea that had cooled yet again before she'd found time to drink it. A trickle of drool had seeped from the corner of her mouth onto the sofa cushion, and the skin on her face felt crumpled when she touched it, which reminded her of the pile of ironing in the laundry basket at home.

The baby was still asleep. Mercifully. No one had warned her it would be like this. The constant demands for milk. The crying. Oh lord, the crying. She wanted to weep herself from the sheer exhaustion of feeding a newborn every two hours. Federico was next to useless. How he managed to snore through their daughter's high-pitched wails was beyond her. Even thinking about it made her bristle with resentment.

She sat upright, her body still tender from the violence of birth. Hers had been an easy labour with no interventions, and she was physically fit and had recovered well. But every now and then, she was reminded that childbirth was an act of extreme brutality.

From the sitting room, she could pick out the voices of Jen and Winter, discussing The Party. Alyssa adored them both, but she'd never felt less like attending a party in her life. It wasn't their fault that baby Claudia had arrived three weeks early. But Alyssa still looked six months pregnant. Nothing fitted her. At least, not any of her decent clothes, just those shapeless garments that magnified all the parts of her that she wanted to hide. Technically, she could wear the glitzy maternity dress she'd bought last month for the occasion, but it no longer sat right on her soft, leaking body.

That morning, when she'd stopped for a coffee – decaffeinated, naturally, although she'd longed to order her usual macchiato – one of the cafe staff had asked her when she was due. Even though she was pushing a pram with Claudia tucked inside it. Bloody cheek.

And then Claudia had started screaming, and she'd struggled with her takeaway cup and the pram, and trying to hold her baby, to comfort them both, and an elderly woman with sunken, over-rouged cheeks had pursed her lips and said was it any surprise the baby was unsettled if her mother was drinking caffeine, and Alyssa had snapped at her for making assumptions and cried all the way to Jen's house.

The baby made a noise. Barely a mewl. Alyssa dragged herself over to the Moses basket that had last belonged to Teddy but had now been repurposed for the newest member of the family. It was impossible to believe that her sturdy nephew had once been small enough to fit inside it. Her mind flitted to earlier that day, her own tear-stained arrival, and the boy's hot hand tugging her upstairs to his room, excited to show off his new racing-car bed.

'Come and see, Auntie Lyssa.'

She'd been irritated, desperate for five minutes to herself to eat something – anything – while Jen cuddled the baby, but Teddy didn't understand that and she'd snapped at him too. 'For heaven's sake. In a minute, OK?' At his crestfallen face, she'd felt a stab of guilt and relented, allowing herself to be commandeered by a small boy when all she'd wanted was some chocolate and a weep on her sister's shoulder.

Jen, practical, loving, had said to Teddy in a quiet voice that his aunt was a bit tired because new babies need lots of looking after, and then she'd persuaded Alyssa to turn on the television while she walked Teddy up to pre-school – and Claudia too, if Alyssa didn't mind them taking her out for a stroll. She'd made her sister beans on toast before they left, and insisted Alyssa stay at their house for the rest of the day, and for dinner. 'Spaghetti carbonara, your favourite.'

Alyssa had wanted to fall upon her with gratitude, but she didn't have the energy for that, and instead had collapsed onto the sofa, feet tucked beneath her, and had nodded off at some point, exhausted by her early start. While she was sleeping, Jen must have returned from dropping Teddy at his afternoon session and put Claudia down for a nap.

The baby mewled again.

Her eyes were closed but her mouth opened up like a rosebud, searching for her mother's breast. Alyssa lifted her from the basket and studied her screwed-up face, searching for signs, as she'd done from the moment she was born.

The maternity unit had been quiet, the rainy night keeping away all but those in active labour. Federico had dropped her at the entrance of Midtown's hospital – 'You'll be ages,' he'd said, confident, a touch dismissive, 'I'll catch you up' – and she'd walked alone, pausing with each contraction, down a long corridor to the lift that took her up to the third floor, wondering whose idea it had been to make life for pregnant women as difficult as possible.

Her labour had been swift. Federico had barely made it, taking his time to park the car and then dropping by the hospital's all-night cafeteria for a slice of cake and a cup of tea. 'I didn't have time for dinner.' His voice had risen a notch with each word of self-justification. 'I needed *something* to keep me going.'

The midwife had rung his mobile phone four times before he'd answered. When he'd appeared at Alyssa's bedside, out of breath and with crumbs around his mouth, the baby was crowning. He'd thrust a packet of shortbread fingers at his fiancée and shouted words of encouragement that made her want to swear. Six minutes later, greasy with vernix and amniotic fluid, she was in Alyssa's arms.

Her hair was dark, like her mother's. Her eyes were brown, like Federico's. But in the hollow of her spine, her newborn daughter had a birthmark in the shape of a cat's eye.

Like him.

4

Hannah

The girl with the bunches ran at full pelt down the lane by the Safeway supermarket and across the field that led back to her house.

The sun had baked the earth until the mud had dried in clots that scraped the skin off her knees when she fell and the boys from school caught up with her to claim their prize.

She didn't like playing the kissing game. Daniel tasted of the snot that streamed in a thick line from his nostrils to the cupid's bow of his lips. Miss McGovern instructed him to blow his nose at least three times a day, but it was never enough.

At playtime, when the class lined up by the crates, he would lick the slug trail away with the tip of his tongue, but it was always back by the time she'd pierced the foil lid of the small glass bottle and forced down her milk through a straw. For the rest of the morning, her hands smelled sour, especially on days as hot as this one when condensation collected on the outside of the glass, and the milk was warm

28

and on the brink of turning, and she watched Daniel's face with grim fascination as the snot continued its endless descent.

But there would be no kiss chase today. Miss McGovern had asked her to wait while she wrote out a reply to her mother, who'd sent in a note querying why the teacher had not corrected her daughter's spelling and punctuation errors.

Dear Mrs Matthews,

Hannah's handwriting was so beautifully neat it seemed a shame to sully it with my red pen. Her mastery of the fountain pen is most impressive. But your point is noted for future consideration.

Yours, Sandra McGovern

As soon as she was let out of school, she had flown through the gates, past the ice-cream van, through the alleyway and across the field. Sweat trickled down her forehead, stinging her eyes, and she rubbed it away, wiping her damp palms on the white cotton fabric of her summer dress. She was late, and her mother would be cross because they were supposed to be going to British Home Stores to buy swimming costumes for their trip to Bognor Regis, and her father was going to meet them there as soon as he'd finished work at the electrics factory, and she and her siblings might be allowed to have sausages, chips and beans, washed down with that fizzy blackcurrant that made their noses tingle.

They didn't go out for dinner very often. Only on birthdays, and sometimes to the carvery on Mother's Day, and to the fancy Beefeater with its *comp-li-ment-ary* bread rolls and salad bar because it only cost one pound, and her brother had to pretend he was younger than twelve, even though it made his ears redden with shame because he was taller than their mother now.

At the far end of the field, which was overlooked by five or six houses but otherwise deserted, the girl paused to catch her breath. At the weekend, she and her friends had found the fraying remnants of one of their school's ties and a single black patent shoe with a strap and buckle. They had scared themselves silly with stories about a bad man who stole children and fed them to the black panther he kept in a cage in the concrete yard at the back of his house.

The panther was not a figment of her imagination, but a fact. Even though the law had changed and it was now illegal to keep such exotic animals as household pets without a licence, it was regularly flouted.

Occasionally, on her walk to school, the girl heard the snarl of the big cat, and, terrified it would escape, would run past it and not stop running until she was through the gates and hanging her bag on her peg. On the days she was feeling brave, usually when one of the two sets of twins in her class walked home with her, she would persuade them to give her a leg-up and peer over the wall.

The panther, sleek and watchful, would pace the cage that was too small for it, and she would shiver with that heady combination of fear and excitement until the animal lunged at the rickety wire mesh that contained it, making her jump, and all of them would run off, screaming and laughing.

This was at the forefront of her mind because that afternoon, the whole of the fourth year juniors had watched a video recording of the previous day's episode of *John Craven's Newsround*. The black panther had escaped – or was deliberately released, her father muttered darkly – and a BBC television crew had filmed a segment in her home town, interviewing neighbours and shopkeepers, including her friend Michelle Duncan's parents, who owned the caravan park where an *e-visc-er-ated* deer carcass had been found on the seventh hole of the crazy golf course. The 'c' was silent, Miss McGovern had explained, pursing her lips, when Hannah had asked what it meant. 'To disembowel, dear. All internal organs removed.'

The girl licked her lips, thirsty. She would be home in less than five minutes, but she unscrewed the lid of her flask and poured the last remaining drops of orange squash into the blue plastic cup. At ten years old, she was embarrassed by the flask's peeling edges and childish design. Three years ago, she had loved Holly Hobbie with all of her heart, but now, like her friends, she preferred Care Bears. She had asked for a matching lunchbox set for her birthday but her father had said it was a waste of money when her flask was still serviceable, and an old ice-cream tub was plenty good enough for her fish-paste sandwiches and crisps.

As she placed the cup back on top of the thermos, a flicker of movement at the far end of the field caught her eye. She stilled, flask in hand, unzipped school bag by her feet, mouth open. Catching flies, as her mother would say.

She watched the shadow as it moved through the long grass, disappearing and reappearing. She couldn't think of the word to describe it, but it reminded her of Grandma's curtains, swaying in the summer breeze.

The sun beat down from a cloudless sky. There was a stillness to the afternoon, a sense of this small corner of Hannah's world holding its breath. A bluebottle circled her head with an irritating drone before landing on her arm, but she didn't flick it away as she usually might. Her gaze was fixed on the progress of the dark shape, which seemed both erratic and purposeful. She wondered what it could be.

After a minute or so, it emerged from the undergrowth and she had her answer. Too big for a domestic cat. Too *sin-ew-y* to be a dog. Her heart thumped against her ribs, and she bent to retrieve her school bag, never taking her eyes from the wild animal at the far end of the field.

A pair of larks spiralled skywards in a burst of song, and the panther lifted its head and looked at her with its amber eyes. She ran.

5

Winter

Winter Kellaway had a personal assistant, a personal trainer, a personal chef and a personal stylist. She had a housekeeper and her own make-up artist, a business manager, a publicist and an agent, and fans in all corners of the globe. But she didn't have children, or a spouse, and now, not even a lover.

It wasn't that she didn't crave these things. In her quiet moments, when the pace of her professional life stilled, as it occasionally did, she yearned for them.

But the man she might have built a life with was married and wouldn't leave his family – wouldn't even *pretend* to consider it – and she wasn't the type of woman to settle for scraps. She loved him, in her way, but a part of her despised him too, for his lack of moral fibre. She wasn't proud of her own behaviour either. He had a public profile, a wife at home, two children. Better for them all if she walked away.

A set of never-to-be-repeated circumstances had led them to spend a single drunken night together before her conscience and his shame had forced them both to break it off. If news of their brief liaison ever leaked, the fallout would be catastrophic: Winter's career, her celebrity status, her *reputation*, would be destroyed in a matter of hours. In all scenarios, the woman, eternally cast as home-wrecker, was at best a temptress and at worst a whore.

Because of this, Winter's family – her sisters, her nieces and nephews, and her parents – had become the lynchpin of her life. Although her filming commitments saw her travel extensively, and she was often away from home for months at a time, those closest to her provided the love and stability she needed to survive in an industry as ruthless as hers. Of course she had friends. All famous people did. But most of them were star-fuckers and hangers-on, or employees paid to like her. She wasn't naive. Some hoped the gloss of celebrity might rub off on them and some hoped for the opposite, a slip-up worthy of a photograph or video that could be sold to the tabloid press.

Every now and then, she forged a bond with a fellow actor, who understood the pressures of the job in a way her family could not; but, like her, they were often filming in far-flung locations for long periods, and without careful nurturing, the shoots of those tentative friendships withered and died.

She was still in touch with a handful of school friends from her pre-fame days, but they were busy with their own families, and the closeness that blossomed from shared experiences eluded her. Her routine of first-class air travel, red-carpet premieres and designer clothes was too far removed from the Year 6 WhatsApp group chat about SATs and secondary schools. But that was OK. She was living the life she had chosen. And she had her sisters.

The radio was on, and Jen was boiling spaghetti for the carbonara. Winter didn't eat pasta. Or cream. Limited cheese. No processed meat. But her sister sometimes forgot that. It wasn't that she didn't enjoy them, but armchair critics could be cruel. One summer, she had relaxed her healthy eating regimen and the comments about her body had been so vitriolic she'd vowed never to do that again. She took a restrained sip of her white wine, picked up a knife and began chopping tomatoes for the salad.

Jen let out a shriek and turned up the radio. A familiar song was playing, a nineties anthem: the soundtrack of their youth.

She grabbed Winter's hand and pulled her into the centre of the kitchen, both of them laughing, cheeks flushed with alcohol.

'Remember when we used to know all the moves?' Jen was twisting her feet into a complicated series of dance steps. Winter felt a rush of affection. Her sister looked ridiculous in her oversized slipper boots and skinny jeans. And at least ten years younger than she actually was. Naturally pretty and blessed with good skin. Jen took a mouthful of wine, closed her eyes and shimmied her hips. 'And what about that time you bunked off school with your mates to get your album signed?'

Winter laughed and swayed in time to the music. 'The police removed us from the queue and carted us back to school. Mum went ballistic.'

Alyssa appeared in the doorway of the kitchen, a patch of dried baby sick on her shoulder and a grin on her face. 'I haven't heard this song in ages.'

Jen held up the wine bottle and a glass. 'Drink?'

Alyssa bit her lip. She hadn't touched a drop of alcohol during her pregnancy, and now she was breastfeeding, but Winter could tell that tonight she was tempted. 'Go on, then. A tiny one. With soda water.'

The music played on. The women reached for each other, as they'd done as girls, holding hands and singing along, loud and raucous. The kitchen – the hub of Jen's home – was filled with the love and laughter that comes from trust and familiarity and kinship.

'Mummy,' said a small voice into the melee. 'You're being noisy.'

Standing in the kitchen with his thumb in his mouth was Teddy, hair sticking up and one pyjama trouser halfway up his leg. Iris, his big sister, was holding his other hand, a stern expression on her face. 'We can't go to sleep.'

Jen rushed towards them and planted a kiss on the top of each of their heads. 'Sorry, Mr Ted,' said Winter, using the family's affectionate nickname for the little boy. She crouched next to him and pulled him in for a hug.

Teddy took his thumb out of his mouth and leaned into her. 'Your singing is very bad, Auntie Winter.'

'That's rude.' Iris poked him in the ribs.

But Winter, who was used to fawning and compliments, laughed harder than his observation deserved. 'Thank you, Teddy. I appreciate your honesty.'

Iris peered around the kitchen. 'Where's baby Claudia?'

'Sleeping like a baby,' said Alyssa, 'which is a ridiculous expression when you think about it because babies never sleep for long.'

The eight-year-old shot her mother a hopeful look. 'Are you going to have another baby, Mummy?'

Jen gave a snort of mirth. 'No, sweetheart.'

'But why not? Please, Mummy. Please. I really want a baby brother or sister.'

'And I really want you to go to bed.'

When the children were settled back upstairs, and Alyssa

had checked on the baby, the women gathered at the table. Jen's pasta was delicious and nourishing, and even Winter, who had restricted herself to a bowl of salad without dressing, couldn't resist a few forkfuls.

'Are you scared about tomorrow night?' Winter winked at her middle sister.

Jen crossed her eyes in return, their favoured call and response since childhood. 'I don't think so.' She drew out that last vowel sound. 'Should I be?'

Alyssa leaned forward, her elbows on the table. 'Be afraid. Be very afraid.' She and Winter shared a conspiratorial glance.

Jen put down her glass and narrowed her eyes. 'You promised.'

'We promised not to embarrass you,' said Winter.

'Yes,' said Alyssa, 'although it depends on your definition of embarrassment, I suppose.'

'I didn't want a hen do, remember?' Jen spun the slender silver band on her ring finger. 'I'm already married.'

'It's not a hen do,' said Winter.

Alyssa chimed in. 'It's a celebration. Because we couldn't let the momentous occasion of your marriage pass without a' – she cocked her thumb and fingertip until they were almost touching – 'little gathering of your nearest and dearest.'

'But we're already having a party on Saturday,' said Jen.

'Yes, but this is Friday night.' Winter reached across the table and took her sister's hand. 'And that party's for Mum and Dad too. And Alyssa. This is just for you. Some of the guests are already in town. You don't have to worry about a thing. It will be fun, trust me.'

Neither Winter nor Alyssa had shared with Jen how disappointed they'd been to discover she and Phil had eloped without any of the family present except for Iris and Teddy.

It had seemed churlish to complain when she had been elated, floating in a bubble of post-wedding euphoria. But both sisters had felt stung that Jen – the first of the Kellaway girls to marry – had chosen to do so without them. Since they were small, they'd talked about how they would be each other's bridesmaids. While they recognized it was Jen's choice and should be respected, it had served as a painful reminder that her primary loyalty was no longer to them.

The front door slammed. Phil stumbled into the kitchen, followed by Federico and a wave of alcohol fumes. A thin wail rose from the sitting room.

'Fuck's sake.' Alyssa muttered it under her breath, but Winter caught her expression of irritation and said what her sister wouldn't. 'Keep it down, lads. You've woken up Claudia.'

'Good evening, ladies.' Phil gave them an unfocused grin. At the centre of his lips was the tell-tale stain that suggested he was currently one fifth human and four fifths red wine. Winter topped up her glass. Jen kissed him on the cheek.

'I take it you had a good afternoon.'

Phil folded himself into one of the kitchen chairs, his limbs loose from too much alcohol. 'It was' – he eyed Federico – 'magnificent.'

Federico grabbed an empty plate and began to load pasta and salad onto it. '*I* was magnificent, you mean.'

Winter and Jen exchanged a glance, a sisterly shorthand that didn't need words: why was their brother-in-law more interested in filling his face than saying hello to his fiancée and infant daughter?

Phil helped himself to a beer from the fridge and held out his hand to Jen. When she took it in her own, he kissed the back of it and reached for a slice of garlicky flatbread. 'You were, my friend.'

Federico and Phil had worked together for ten years. Federico, handsome, and with an edginess that appealed to both men and women, was a music producer whose star was in rapid ascendancy. The last two years had been a whirlwind of touring, collaboration and hours in the recording studio. Phil, his manager, was in charge of negotiation, contracts, royalties, sponsorship, licensing and merchandising. If Fed was the face of their collaboration, the creative energy, Phil was the money man with a talent for spotting lucrative opportunities. While the former was a darling of the music press, the latter, sharp-suited and serious, was regularly profiled in the financial pages. Best friends. Business partners. A formidable team.

Alyssa appeared in the kitchen, holding Claudia. The baby's face was red and sweaty from crying. Federico dropped his fork against the plate with a clatter and held out his arms. 'Give her to me.'

His girlfriend held the baby a bit closer to her chest. 'When you've sobered up.'

A shadow of disappointment crossed Federico's face. 'Come on, Alyssa. I haven't seen her all day.'

'Whose fault is that?'

Alyssa spun around and left the room. Federico started to rise from his chair but Phil laid a hand on his arm. 'Leave it, mate. She's tired, and you've been out all day while she's stuck at home with a newborn. It's hard work.'

Winter sipped her wine and gave Federico a level look. 'Are you planning on taking any paternity leave?'

'We're so busy at work it's ridiculous.' Federico turned his attention back to his food. 'This is a pivotal moment in my career.'

Jen sat back down at the table, resting her chin on her

steepled hands. Her voice was soft, non-judgemental. 'She needs you too.'

Winter glanced at Phil but his expression was neutral. She waited for him to back his wife. To back his sister-in-law. He'd always been at great pains to insist he was a feminist. But he said nothing. Irritation flared inside her but she forced herself to dampen it down. The party was forty-two hours away. She didn't want family tensions to derail the celebrations.

'I'll go,' she said, expecting Alyssa's boyfriend to take the hint. But Federico shovelled in his pasta and did not reply.

The sitting room was in darkness, the bloated moon hidden by cloud. The earlier fog had lifted but the night air held an opaque quality. Alyssa stood at the window overlooking the garden, her baby nestled against the crook of her neck, a tiny human comma.

'He wasn't always a prick.'

'I know. But he's adjusting, like you. Parenthood doesn't come automatically to some men. Or women.'

'Yes, but I don't have the luxury of ignoring her, do I? One of us has got to look after Claudia. I can't swan off to work or go down the pub.' Tears glistened in Alyssa's eyes.

Winter drew her younger sister towards her into a hug. Alyssa could be spiky at times, occasionally haughty, and, as the baby of the family, she was used to getting her own way. But Winter loved her so. She felt in her pocket and pulled out a small square box. 'For you.'

'What is it?' Alyssa gave a tremulous smile. 'I don't have a gift for you, sorry.'

'I wasn't expecting anything. This is for you. I know I'm not at home very often, but I want you to know I'm always with you.'

A thin diamond-studded pendant with three entwined circles at its heart lay on the plush flocking. Winter pulled down the front of her top to reveal a matching chain. 'I've got one too, and one for Jen.'

'It's beautiful. Thank you. Can you put it on for me?'

Winter placed the chain around her sister's neck and fastened the clasp. 'Family always.'

Alyssa slipped her hand into Winter's and squeezed it. 'Family always.'

Winter's recollection of her childhood was muddied by memories of her parents and siblings. As the eldest – almost eight years separated them – she couldn't remember the day Alyssa was born, but, standing in the sitting room, the feel of her sister's hand in hers and watching the clouds cross the moon, she was struck by a vivid flashback to the summer she was thirteen and Alyssa was five.

Winter's father had suggested a tent in the garden for a sleepover with her friends. Alyssa, who at the time had been obsessed by Winter in the way only younger sisters could be, begged to be allowed to join them, but her request had been denied. She'd been put to bed at the usual time with a story and a kiss, but refused to go to sleep, and occasionally, one of Winter's friends pointed up at the small figure gazing down on the fun from her bedroom window.

At midnight, when the girls were scaring each other with tales of a disfigured man with a bladed glove and fedora who crept into their nightmares to kill them, Winter had caught the sound of singing, a high-pitched sound that was barely audible, like the breath of a ghost. It stirred a memory in her, something primal and dark.

She had clutched at her nearest friend, and pressed a finger to her lips. Each girl had nudged the next until the tent was silent and the only sound from the garden was the rustle of leaves and that quiet voice. Even now, the distinctive smell of canvas threw her back to that night, the fear and surprise of it, that lullaby about mamas and mockingbirds.

Winter, egged on by her friends, crawled across the groundsheet in her pyjamas. She remembered a twig digging into her knee and the feel of the night air on her face, cool and fresh. Her eyes took a moment to adjust from the torch-light inside the tent to the textured darkness outside and the shape of the bushes and trees, which felt like a threat now that daylight had fled. The house – at the distant end of the garden – was in darkness, except for a light shining at the back door.

Winter glanced around her, up the garden, away from the house and her friends in the tent, and towards the apple tree. A pale flash captured her attention, a nightdress and silver limbs against the backdrop of midnight. A slight form, sitting cross-legged among the windfalls, the scent of fermentation hanging on the breeze.

She was singing the same two lines over and over again, borrowed from that lullaby their mother used to sing, and when she saw Winter, she smiled, her teeth gleaming in the darkness.

'Why aren't you in bed? Mum and Dad will kill you if they find you out here.'

The expression on Alyssa's face changed, as if shutters had been pulled across it. 'Everyone's sleeping.'

'What are you *doing*?'

'Protecting you.'

Her voice was high and clear in the night. Alyssa, five years old. Chestnut curls. Rounded cheeks. But then, as now, Winter glimpsed the vulnerability in her eyes, a fleeting fear that made her feel something uncomfortable, like stumbling across a secret by accident or uncovering a truth that should remain buried. At thirteen, she did not want to interrogate this fear. She knew its origins, and it had no place in the sweet-smelling garden on a summer's night. She swallowed down her feelings and did what her parents would expect of her.

'You need to go back inside now.'

If she'd anticipated resistance from Alyssa, it didn't happen. Her little sister was docile, accepting of her fate. Her nightdress, which hung off one shoulder and grazed the tops of her knees, was damp from the grass, and her eyes were hollows in her face. From their vantage point at the far end of the garden, both sisters paused to watch the silhouettes of Winter's friends inside the tent, backlit by their torches, shadow figures from another realm. Mesmerized by the shape of them as they moved in the darkness, their bodies made fluid and mysterious.

'Do you ever get scared?' Alyssa spoke so quietly, Winter had to bend down to catch her words.

'Yes. Of Mum finding all the uneaten fruit and vegetables that are rotting in my school bag.' She grinned at her sister to show she was joking. But Alyssa did not smile back.

'I do.'

Winter put an arm around the girl's shoulder. 'There's nothing to be scared of, OK? Mum and Dad, and Jen and me, we'll keep you safe.'

But Alyssa let out the tiniest of sighs.

A breeze rustled the leaves and made Winter shiver. They were still standing amidst the piles of fallen apples, and Winter wondered what had happened to the wasps she'd seen gorging on them that afternoon, bad-tempered from an excess of fermented sugar, too drunk to fly. Tucked safely in their nest, she decided, which is where Alyssa ought to be.

She turned to her then, to tell her that she couldn't stay outside a minute longer, that it was late – too late – for a five-year-old to be awake, and that she must never leave the house again without their parents' knowledge or permission.

Above their heads, the clouds parted to reveal the moon in all her glory and two bats swooped between the trees, too swift to leave anything but a whisper of wings in their wake.

She smiled down at her sister. Alyssa did not smile back but her eyes were wide and her lower lip trembled, a baby still. In that moment, there was a fragility to her that undid Winter, a glimpse of vulnerability that would prove to be the hallmark of her life. Even as a teenager, it loosened something inside her, made her bend towards her sister as a mother might. She smoothed the curls from Alyssa's forehead and dropped a kiss there. 'Come on.'

It was only when Winter reached for her little sister's hand to lead her back to bed that she noticed Alyssa was gripping a kitchen knife so tightly her knuckles were white, its blade glinting in the cold light.

6

Friday, 17 November 2023

Blue

The airport was surprisingly busy for the early hours of a freezing November morning. Dr Clover March – Lucky to her sister, Blue to the detective Saul Anguish – felt more than a twinge of envy towards the travellers heading abroad in search of winter sun.

But today wasn't about holidays. It was about goodbyes.

A gifted forensic linguist on a permanent secondment to Essex Police via the National Crime Agency Major Crime Investigative Support section, and sometime lover to Saul, the young woman with hair the colour of a summer sky swallowed down the lump in her throat and forced a brightness she didn't feel. 'When will you be home?'

Her elder sister Macy was patting her pockets, searching for her passport, and when she found it, brandished it with a triumphant *ta-da*. 'Hard to say. A year, probably. If the job goes well.'

'Are you nervous?'

'If living with strangers in a remote corner of the Amazon rainforest researching wild monkeys with virtually no mobile

45

phone signal and basic facilities is a nerve-wracking prospect, then yes.' She grinned, a flash of teeth. 'Other than that, I'm fine.'

She shouldered her rucksack and pulled Blue into a hug, murmuring into her ear. 'Will you be OK? I can stay if you want me to. It's not too late to cancel everything.'

Blue freed herself from her sister's arms. 'Of course I don't want you to cancel.'

'I mean it.' Macy placed her hands on Blue's shoulders and tried to catch her eye, but Blue wouldn't look at her. 'You've been through so much, and—'

'Stop.' It sounded harsher than she'd intended, but Blue didn't want to talk about that now. She noted, not for the first time, that her sister could never bring herself to use the word. *Rape.* So ugly. Like she was.

'Have you thought any more about counselling? I can email you some suggestions, if you'd like. It's important not to let it fester—'

'I said stop,' Blue snapped at her, raising her voice.

Macy held up her hands in mock surrender and mumbled an apology. An awkward silence hung between them. After thirty seconds or so, she eyed her younger sister. 'Did I mention the amazing desserts? *Picarones* are the Peruvian equivalent to doughnuts, apparently, but they taste even better.'

A smile played around the corners of Blue's mouth. 'Will you bring me some back?'

'Consider it done.'

Not wanting her irritation to sour their goodbye, Blue hugged her again, squeezing her as tightly as Macy's rucksack allowed. Although this was a dream opportunity for her sister, a conservation scientist who was beginning to make a name for herself, she'd be counting the days until her return. The sisters spent much of their spare time together, and although it wasn't the first extended work trip that Macy had taken, it was the longest by some stretch.

'I suppose I'd better go. I've got to fight my way through security and I don't want to miss my flight.' She stroked Blue's cheek. 'I'll miss you.'

'If I get a chance to fly out and visit, I will.'

'Promise?'

'Promise.'

A last goodbye, an exchange of 'I love you's, and then she was gone, disappearing through the throng of passengers into the departures hall to catch a flight that would take her 6,000 miles away to South America.

Blue trudged back to the train station through the terminal building, overwhelmed by a numbing flatness.

A year without her sister seemed an impossible prospect. Macy had warned her that contact would be intermittent at best. It would feel strange to go from messaging each other several times a day to weeks without news.

In the time it took her to get back to her flat in Midtown-on-Sea, the pre-dawn darkness had given way to the same grey fog as the previous day. As she walked up from the station through a dampness that enclosed everything, she glanced behind her, a familiar pricking sensation at the back of the neck.

She hadn't mentioned it to anyone, not her sister or Saul, in case they thought it was a trick of her overactive imagination, especially since the attack, but in recent weeks, she'd come to the uncomfortable realization that she was being watched.

7

Friday, 17 November 2023

Winter

Winter sat on the toilet seat with her knickers – white cotton, nothing fancy – around her thighs. Sometimes, when she lost out on a part to a rival she envied, she forced herself to remember that even the most beautiful and talented women were reduced to this most basic of bodily functions. She examined the smooth plastic stick, shook the end and capped it. Winter didn't swear often, but if she did, expletives would be falling from her mouth like last night's rain.

She studied the mole on the inside of her thigh. Her legs were lightly tanned, just the right side of muscular. All that time in her home gym was paying off. When she was younger, she used to wonder how it was that some girls had flawless limbs while hers were glow-in-the-dark pale and peppered with follicles that looked like strawberry seeds. Now she was older, she knew the answer. Genetics. Money. Someone to teach them about fake tan and razor burn.

It was early. Too early. But she'd woken to a room filled with deep blue shadows, the kind that precede the slide into dawn, her heart beating a full military tattoo in her chest.

How long was it now? Two months, possibly three? She'd been so busy with work and planning this party that she'd lost track of her dates. She'd tried to go back to sleep, but the thought buried itself in her brain, playing on a loop until she'd levered herself out of bed, fear driving her downstairs to dig out her diary. Even though the rest of the world was obsessed by technology, Winter preferred to write things down.

She'd flicked back through the pages, seeking out the neat lower-case letter she marked on the paper each month. 'P' for pain in the arse. For period. And now, in the still of the sunrise, for panic.

Her finger stopped on a date in mid-September. Her head spun. Two months ago.

But it could be stress, right? That was a possibility. The tension levels on the set of her last job had been stratospheric, especially when one of the producers walked out mid-shoot. Or it could be from not eating enough. Since she'd hit her forties, she'd noticed her jeans becoming tighter and had been strict about watching her weight. Fluctuating hormones could cause irregularities too. In any case, she was too old to have a baby, wasn't she? It was highly unlikely she'd fall pregnant naturally. Women her age never did. Except for that woman in her magazine a year older than she was who'd done exactly that.

She'd checked the security cameras for any lurking photographers, slipped on her coat over her pyjamas, tucked her hair into a beanie and driven to the all-night supermarket in the next town, using the self-service checkout to pay for a selection of pregnancy tests.

And now here she was at 5 a.m., waiting to discover her fate.

Her fingers itched to call Jen, but it was too early. Of the three sisters, Jen was the calm and practical one. She would know what to do. But it was Jen's special weekend, she couldn't do that to her. And this was complicated. Whatever the result, she would keep it to herself for now.

Winter placed the capped test on the shelf without looking at it. She would make herself a cup of coffee before she checked the result. After all, if she *was* pregnant, a few extra minutes wasn't going to make much of a difference now. And hadn't her sisters given up caffeine? And alcohol? She shuddered at the prospect of that.

Tying her silk robe around her waist, she wandered out of the bathroom, her fingers trailing against the polished wood of the galleried landing, and went downstairs. Even now, three years after she'd moved in, Winter couldn't believe that she – an ordinary girl from the suburbs – lived here.

The Beach House. Ten thousand square feet of unadulterated luxury on the Essex coast, with easy access to London and the airports. Marble floors that gleamed under a chandelier that cost more than a house on one of Midtown's exclusive wooded estates. Six bedrooms, all en suite. A state-of-the art kitchen with a ceiling-height aquarium bursting with tropical fish. A cinema room. Three separate living areas. A media hub. A temperature-controlled walk-in wine storage room. Home gym and pool. A long private driveway that snaked down to the main house, protected by cameras and electronic gates. Two guest cottages, hidden within the grounds like a fairy tale, and Winter Kellaway was its queen.

While she loved the master bedroom with its abundant soft furnishings, bespoke eight-foot bed and a dressing room the size of her first flat, the sitting room was her sanctuary. Full-sized glass windows ran the length of the property, overlooking the private beach and the bay beyond, filling it with natural light.

A plush oversized sofa in dove grey, big enough to seat ten, dominated the space, and a piano stood by sliding doors that opened onto a vast stone terrace that looked across the expanse of water. The party planners had flown in dozens of specially cultivated sakura trees, and strung them with tiny lights, and the result was a paradise of serenity and cherry blossom. Even in the thinning darkness, Winter could pick out the shape of the fragile pink flowers. Hester, who was in charge of design, had assured her client the blooms would not fall before the wedding.

Later today, the decorators would arrive to put the finishing touches to Winter's spectacular outside light display, and the cavernous marquee that loomed by the rose garden, over-looking the sea. On Saturday morning, the florists would get to work at first light, and caterers would arrive with platters of seafood and champagne, and a specially constructed chocolate river for the dozens of children due to attend.

Winter drank her coffee in the stillness, savouring its rich smokiness. Then she washed up her mug and put it back in the cupboard. Unlike her sisters, Winter thrived on order. She was the kind of woman who packed her holiday suitcase two weeks in advance and stored her designer handbags in breathable dust protectors. Briefly, she considered breakfast, but recognized that as the form of procrastination it was.

Much as it frightened her, it was time to confront the truth.

In the bathroom, she glanced at herself in the mirror. Her face looked tired, her jawline beginning to soften, and her hair was finer than it used to be. She had five, possibly ten years left, if she was lucky. It was messed up when she thought about it. She had been fêted for her youth and beauty, the latter a genetic quirk of fate beyond her control; but ageing, despite the treatments, the expensive creams and serums and surgeries, was beyond her control too, and no one praised her for that. The wind was changing, yes; older women were being championed on screen in a way they hadn't been a decade earlier, but the wheels turned slowly in her industry. A baby would put a bomb under everything.

She examined her feelings on motherhood in the way a tongue might probe the hole left by an excavated tooth. She loved children, especially her nieces and nephew. But she had no desire to be a single parent, even though her wealth – which already funded a housekeeper, laundry service and gardener – would ease the inevitable upheaval. She'd admired the make-up artist on the previous week's shoot for a glossy supplement, who was bringing up two-year-old twins on her own, but that life wasn't for Winter. She wanted the husband, the dog and the white picket fence.

But what if this is your last chance? You wanted children once, remember.

Pregnant or not, she needed to know.

Taking a deep breath, Winter closed her fingers around the test stick and flipped it over, eyes reading and rereading the small window as if that might change the result. But there was no denying it. Winter – actor, sister, aunt, liar – was about to inhabit her newest role.

Mother-to-be.

8

Jen

*Clean the bathrooms, change the spare bed, vacuum, do a quick
supermarket shop for Mum and Dad, pack an overnight bag for
Iris, manicure, pedicure, facial, pick up dress, confirm the hotel
reservation for next week, drink a large bottle of gin . . .*

Jen turned over in bed, pulling the duvet up to her chin,
and ran the to-do list through her head one more time. It
wasn't light yet, but she knew she would struggle to get back
to sleep. She closed her eyes, her body still tired from the
previous night – Federico and Winter hadn't left until past
midnight, despite her rather obvious yawns – but her brain
was urging her to get up and out of bed. She could go for
a run and make a start on the bathrooms before the children
stirred.

Downstairs, she made herself a cup of herbal tea and
stretched her legs, trying to wake the muscles up. She
wondered what her sisters had planned for tonight, and the
butterflies in her stomach took flight. Getting married again
in front of all her family and friends had seemed like a good
idea when it was six months away. But Jen should never

53

have let them railroad her. Winter was the brightest star in the galaxy, while she was more of a black hole, content to hide in the shadows and let others shine.

Still, marrying Phil was all she'd ever wanted. She'd known him since primary school, playing tag in the playground and pinching his crisps. He'd sent her a Valentine's card once, a cartoon he'd drawn by hand and coloured in with felt-tip pens, and she had held his hand at the leavers' disco, blushing as they danced together for the last song of the night, but, as often happens, they'd grown up and apart, moving to different secondary schools, and then countries.

It wasn't until Phil, who'd spent several years living in the United States, returned to Midtown-on-Sea that their childish romance blossomed into adult love. She'd been drinking coffee at the cafe her friend owned, and working on a business idea she'd had, trying to make the numbers work. He'd walked in, suntanned and smiling, and recognized her immediately. The cafe had been packed, and he'd asked if he could sit at her table. She was busy, frazzled, groaning inwardly, but she'd pasted on an expression of welcome, and coffee had turned into lunch, and the previous twenty years had melted away.

He hadn't left her side after that, moving into her flat within a month. She smiled to herself as she remembered the way he'd looked at her that first night they'd spent together, a mixture of knee-weakening intensity and 'Hey, hello, I've found you again at last.' No other man had looked at her like that before, and he was still doing it, even after all these years. Last night had been no exception.

'What the hell is going on with Federico?' She was putting cream on her face, smoothing it into the lines that had settled into her skin, seemingly overnight. Phil had stood behind her, his arms around her waist. 'He's a bit immature, that's all. He needs to grow up.'

She'd turned on him, the embers of her anger reigniting. 'He'd better do it quickly. Alyssa can't manage it all on her own.' Her eyes narrowed. 'Why didn't you say anything earlier?'

Phil pulled her towards him, as he'd done countless times before. She'd been stiff, a little resistant, and so he didn't force her into his embrace, but stroked the back of her hand instead. 'I was trying to keep the peace. I didn't think it would help Alyssa or Federico if we all piled into him, especially as he was so drunk. He'll feel bad about it in the morning.'

'If he remembers.'

Phil had laughed. 'He'll remember. Because I'll be reminding him.'

She'd softened then, moving closer. His hand traced the dip of her waist, the curve of her hip. He bent to her, and they kissed for a few moments, familiar with the shape of each other's mouths, the rhythm of their passion, an intimacy they'd repeated a thousand times before, but that still felt fresh. He'd tasted of wine and garlic. Even after two children, their attraction to each other remained undimmed, their physical relationship a potent reflection of the deep emotional connection they shared. Jen was naturally private, and although she confided in her sisters about some matters – the children, her work, the fact she sometimes wet herself when she laughed – she did not talk about Phil. He was hers alone.

'I don't know what I'd do without you,' he'd said, nuzzling into her neck. And it was true. Sometimes the thought of losing Phil made her pause for a minute, breathless. He was sewn into her life, every part of it. He loved her sisters too, and they loved him, especially Alyssa. He was the brother they'd never had. The idea of existing without him was unthinkable. Impossible. Happily, he felt the same way.

Tomorrow, they would celebrate that love – the start of the rest of their life – in the most public of settings, in front of all their friends and family.

Jen filled a water bottle from the tap and was tying up the laces of her trainers when a small noise made her turn around.

Teddy was standing by the table, dressed in his pre-school uniform and clutching a stuffed dinosaur in one hand and a train in the other.

She ruffled his hair. 'It's six o'clock, sweetheart. Too early for you to be up. But I'm impressed you dressed yourself.'

'I did it last night, I did. Before bed. Put my jammies on over the top. Can I watch cartoons now?'

It was efficient, if nothing else, Jen thought, admiring his time-saving logic. She'd banned television in the mornings because he took so long to get ready, but his four-year-old brain had come up with a clever solution.

'Shall I tuck you back into bed for a bit? Otherwise you're going to be tired for your sleepover tonight with Grandpa.'

'I don't want to.'

'Go back to bed? Or have a sleepover?'

His lower lip stuck out. 'Sleepover. I want to stay with you.'

'Your aunties have arranged a special dinner for me.'

'Why?'

'Remember when you, me, Daddy and Iris went to that beautiful house in Scotland?'

'With the swimming pool?'

'Yes, and you carried the rings for Daddy.'

'You got married.'

'That's right. It was just the four of us. But this is a celebration with all our friends and family.'

'That's tomorrow.'

'Yes, but tonight is a special dinner for the girls.'

He pouted. 'Is Iris going? Not fair.'

'No.'

'But she's a girl.'

'I meant my friends, and Auntie Alyssa and Auntie Winter, and Grandma. Iris is spending the night at Calypso's.'

'What about me?' Teddy pulled at a loose thread on the cuff of his sweater.

'You're spending the night here with Grandpa, remember?'

'Why can't I stay with Daddy?'

'Because he's going out with some of his friends and Uncle Fed.'

The little boy waited a beat. 'I *have* to come with you, Mummy.'

'Why?'

'Because there's a monster in my cupboard with sharp teeth and scratchy claws, and a tail with spikes.'

She let out a belly laugh and ruffled his hair again. The teachers at his pre-school often praised him for his vivid imagination. 'How about you and I have a special day out next weekend instead?'

He nodded then, mollified, and asked for a second time if he could watch cartoons. She sighed, seeing her early-morning run get swallowed up by childcare and chores.

'If you want to. But keep the volume down. Daddy and Iris are still asleep.'

Teddy zoomed off to the sitting room, and she smiled at

his energy, even at this early hour. She untied her trainers and took a sip of her cooling tea.

'Mama?'

Teddy was back in the kitchen again, a sweet smile on his face. 'Will you come and watch them with me?'

His expression was so hopeful that she almost relented, but she had to get everything ready for the arrival of her parents, as well as ticking off all the other jobs on her list.

'I'm sorry, sweetheart, I can't at the moment. But I promise I'll watch as many cartoons as you want once the party's out of the way, OK?'

'OK.' His voice was flat but he didn't challenge her.

In the days that followed, Jen would come to bitterly regret that decision, wishing, as she often did, for just a few more minutes with her son. But, in that moment, her head filled with a thousand other things, she'd had no sense of the tragedy that lay ahead.

By the time Phil appeared in the kitchen a couple of hours later, she'd cleared up the dirty dishes from the previous night's dinner, cleaned the downstairs bathroom, put fresh linen on the spare bed, made a shopping list and laid the table for breakfast.

'Are you still free to drop the children off?' She grinned at her husband, feeling a rush of excitement at the prospect of the next forty-eight hours.

He shook his head, eyes glued to his phone screen. 'Sorry, I can't. There's a crisis at work. Fucking Federico.' Phil opened the drawer, hunting for his keys.

'What's happened now? I thought you'd booked the day off.'

'I did, but this won't wait.'

She followed him into the hallway and watched him put

on his coat, lace up his boots. Teddy wandered after them and tugged on his mother's T-shirt. 'Is it breakfast yet? Can I have toast?'

She shushed him, asking him to hold on a minute, but while she was fielding further requests for juice and a banana, and whether he could have waffles instead of toast, the front door slammed. Jen opened it again, calling down the path. 'What about your suit? Shall I pick it up for you?'

But Phil, walking briskly, was too far away to hear.

'Where's Daddy going?' Teddy wrapped his arms around his mother's thighs and squeezed her as tightly as he could manage. She pulled him closer, thinking how much he'd grown. 'Is he going to see Auntie Lyssa again?'

She laughed before she could stop herself. 'What do you mean, *again?*'

'He visits her house a lot.'

'I think you might be getting a bit muddled up, sweetheart.'

'Am not.'

'She came here yesterday, remember? We took baby Claudia for a walk. They stayed for tea.'

'Not yesterday.' He stared at his mother crossly, as if she was being deliberately obtuse. 'On Monday. And the day I go swimming.'

She frowned, uncertain of herself in the face of his conviction. 'How do you know that?'

'I can see from my bedroom window. Can I have maple syrup with my waffles?'

She followed her four-year-old into the kitchen and poured him some milk. As she mixed up the batter for his breakfast, she kept her voice light. 'But Uncle Fed is there too, I expect.'

Teddy took a long drink and put down his glass, a white

moustache above his top lip. He picked at the bowl of raspberries, popping one of the plump fruits into his mouth.

'Silly Mummy. Daddy watches until Uncle Fed goes out.'

'Don't tell fibs, Teddy.' Her tone was sharp. Teddy's overactive imagination would get him into serious trouble one day. Her husband had many flaws, but he was neither a liar nor a cheat.

This time, her son did not argue back, but picked up his bowl and walked quietly from the room.

9

Hannah

When their father was sacked from selling life insurance policies for the Prudential, his brother got him work as a security guard at the paper mill. But he kept falling asleep on night shifts, and when a gang ransacked the premises and stole thousands of toilet rolls from under his nose, he was sacked from that job too. Eventually, after months of hand-to-mouth living, the family was forced to move where his new employment had taken him, which was a small town in the West Midlands.

They'd only been able to afford a rental because his salary at the electrics factory was half his previous earnings, but Hannah liked their new two-up two-down. It had a gas fire and an *avo-ca-do* toilet and a smoked glass table in the kitchen.

Her two brothers shared a room, while her two-and-a-half-year-old sister spent every night in a too-small cot that Hannah could touch with her fingers from her own narrow bed, but she didn't mind. She liked listening to the baby talk herself to sleep, and to the soft babble of her early-morning chatter. Their parents slept on a sofa in the front room that turned into a bed. It was magic, according to her mother, and even though she smiled when she said it, Hannah thought she looked sad. She always looked sad. When she couldn't sleep, Hannah would listen to the furious arguments between them, back and forth over the same thing they had argued about for the last six months.

'Why did she make a complaint if you didn't do anything?'

'Because she's a malicious cow who wanted to get me into trouble.'

'But why would she want to get you into trouble? If you didn't do anything?'

'I told you. Because she's a psycho.'

Round and round they went until Hannah put her pillow over her head and waited for the front door to slam because her father refused to have an argument he couldn't win. Sometimes he came back in the middle of the night, drunk and shouting, but mostly he wouldn't come home until the morning while the children were eating their breakfast, and he stumbled into bed, bleary-eyed and morose.

Hannah had settled well into her new school because she was bright and quick-witted and could easily manage the work. For the most part, she liked her classmates, but when one of the girls teased her for having socks that were grey with grubbiness, an anger that made her stomach burn took hold.

She chased the girl to the wooded end of the playground, out of sight of the dinner ladies, and wrestled her into the dirt, rubbing muddy dust into the girl's pristine white socks edged with ribbon. Then she smacked her around the cheek with a ruler. The crack it made sent the sparrows flying upwards, and it left behind a livid streak, but although the girl cried, she did not tell their teacher. Most importantly, she didn't bother Hannah again.

Hannah bent to pull up her sock, which had slid down to her ankle because the elastic had gone, still breathing heavily from her run. She glanced over her shoulder, half convinced the panther had chased her, but the street was empty. It had rained almost every day at the start of the month, but now the weather had turned, baking the earth.

Which was why her house looked odd, she realized. Every other house in the cul-de-sac had its windows open, except Hannah's. Even the top ones were closed, which was unusual as her mother liked the feel of fresh air rushing through, especially in the heat.

Perhaps her mother was waiting for her in the car with her siblings, impatient and ready to leave. She turned to scan the road, but their Morris Marina, with its scratched paintwork and lumpy seats, was empty. Hannah's gaze travelled beyond it, and she stilled, winded. Parked behind their mother's rust bucket was the old butcher's van their father had bought from the scrap merchant a few weeks ago and now used for work. If he was home this early, it could only mean bad news.

She re-shouldered her school bag and jumped over the broken paving slabs towards the front door. Her skin felt itchy, as if an army of ants was crawling all over her, but even if she hadn't bitten her nails to the quick, she resisted the urge to scratch. Her father had walloped her the last time she'd done that – 'You look like you've got scabies, dirty girl' – and perforated her eardrum.

She hesitated, hovering her finger over the bell before bending down and retrieving the spare key from beneath the iron foot-scraper. Her mother or one of her brothers usually opened the door with a smile and a plate of custard creams, but it remained shut.

Something felt off, but she wasn't sure what it was. She hesitated, contemplating running back to school and Miss McGovern, but not knowing what to say when she got there stopped her. With a growing sense of unease, she unlocked the door and stepped inside.

10

Saul

The smell of turpentine transformed the coastguard's lookout into an artist's studio. Saul picked up his brush and painted a delicate trail of red from the back of the thumb-sized wooden chair he'd upholstered himself, across a square of pale carpet he'd purloined from a skip and towards the bath he'd bought in a job lot of doll's house furniture.

As crime scene tableaux went, it was chillingly perfect.

With precision, he dabbed the tip of his paintbrush on the tiny silver taps and smudged the enamel on the side of the bath with his index finger until he was satisfied. He leaned back in his seat, surveying his handiwork. He breathed in, inhaling the oils and thinner, the lingering acridity making his eyes water. It was almost an exact replica of 27 Grosvenor Place.

Eighteen months ago, Detective Constable Saul Anguish and his team had been dispatched to a flat at the tattered edges of town after one of the most harrowing 999 calls in living memory of the Murder Club, their unofficial name for Midtown's Major Crime team.

Even the call handler, many years of experience under her belt, had faltered as the woman had begged for her life. Her screams – the grind of a power drill against her temple – and then her silence had proved profoundly disturbing.

Her long-term boyfriend had attacked her from behind while she was reading in the armchair in their bedroom. He'd then dragged her, bleeding and almost dead, by her hair to the bath, where he'd stripped her and poured nitric acid over her face and body, and then he'd disappeared.

With no way to neutralize the acid, it had dissolved the top two layers of her skin, the tips of her eyelashes and her mouth by the time the police had arrived. Bone took much longer to corrode, but signs of damage were present in the post-mortem examination that took place the following morning. Her boyfriend had not doused her in acid to hide evidence of her body. He'd targeted every part of her – her eyes and lips and breasts – that a lover had complimented in the secret messages he'd discovered on her mobile phone.

With tenderness, Saul placed a matchstick figure in the miniature bath and glued fine strands to its head. The detective had fashioned a cap of brown hair, which he'd cut from the victim as she'd lain in situ. Her killer was still on the run. But the police would find him. Saul was counting the days until he was fit enough to rejoin the Murder Club. In the meantime, he made it his business to keep up to speed on every fresh case of unnatural death.

Saul rose from the table by the window in the spare bedroom and carried the tableau to a small cubbyhole hidden behind a door. In years gone by, it had served as sleeping quarters for live-in staff, but Saul used it as a place to dry and display his macabre creations. The lock and deadbolt were useful, but he knew he would need to find a new home for them soon. He would always be a collector. But his work for the Chief Constable had shown him it wasn't safe here any longer.

Downstairs, in the thin light of afternoon, Saul set two plates on the kitchen table and stirred the pan of curry he had made from scratch. His mouth watered. Blue had stopped eating lately, anxiety squatting in the pit of her stomach. Both of them were scheduled a rest day today, and he'd invited her to lunch, convinced he could tempt her into consuming at least a few mouthfuls. Steamed rice. Naan. Some vegetable samosas from the deli in town.

On cue, she walked past the sitting-room window, shoulders hunched in the gloom, and he went to let her in. Two years on, his stomach still contracted with an intoxicating combination of nerves and desire whenever he saw her. If truth be told, he had loved her from the moment they'd met, both young and inexperienced, starting new jobs at Midtown Police on the same day.

Even before she spoke, he could tell she was upset. Although he'd never met her sister, he knew how close they were, and what saying goodbye would have cost her.

He held out his arms, but she sidestepped him. 'I can't stay long.'

'Have something to eat, at least.'

She didn't answer, but sat at the table, which he took as a sign of assent. Saul had never asked questions of Blue – she'd told him once that she'd found this trait one of his most attractive – and so he did not talk, but let her gather herself in silence.

He stole glances at her while he served up their food. Her hair was greasy and the shadows beneath her eyes told him that she hadn't slept again. It made him ache to know she was denied such relief, but he had seen her struggles for himself.

Despite her narcolepsy, a medical condition that stole wakefulness from her without warning during the day, her nights were plagued by insomnia, fragmented sleep and dreams so vivid she cried out, afraid. He knew why, although they never spoke of it. Her fate was tied to Saul's, and their shared history was a burden she struggled to carry.

She did not feel guilty for the revenge they had executed on her rapist, a police officer by the name of Douglas Lynch. She had told Saul that herself. But she regretted it. The vulnerabilities it had exposed tormented her. She could not bear the touch of strangers. As for Saul, the sexual pull, the *fire*, that had existed between them now threatened to engulf her, to incinerate everything, and she ran from its heat, frightened by it.

The young forensic linguist, sarcastic and clever, had become a hollow-eyed wraith, but when Saul had tried to raise it, she batted away his concerns. 'As if you can talk,' she'd say, and remind him that DC Saul Anguish, the detective who couldn't cry, sometimes wept in his sleep.

11

Friday, 17 November 2023

Alyssa

The baby was crying again. Alyssa, swimming up through the thick porridge of sleep, waited to see if Federico would magically transform into the kind of father who leapt into action, swooping his daughter from the Moses basket by her side of the bed and soothing her back to sleep before bringing his girlfriend a cup of tea. But it turned out that magic didn't exist in the real world.

She pulled the baby to her left breast, shifting at that still-unfamiliar sensation of let-down, that odd pricking feeling, as she prepared to feed. As her eyes adjusted to the gloom, she realized it was much later than usual, the curtains muffling the daylight. Federico's side of the bed was empty.

She gave a heavy sigh. In the early days of their relationship, he would nuzzle into her, whispering farewells between butterfly kisses, reluctant to leave the sanctuary of their bed and only tearing himself away when it had got so late he'd had to rush through his shower and run for the train. The memory of that made her heart sing. But now he raced into his day, away from her, their home, without a backward glance.

When she had met him that first time at a rock festival in Italy, he'd been a shy young man with a passion for music, a guitar case slung across his body. She'd watched him dancing, oblivious to the crowds around him, unselfconscious, and with a rhythm she found mesmerizing. She wasn't looking for a relationship. After what had happened with Dante – what was it with her and men with Italian names? – she had allowed her heart to freeze, resistant to all efforts at warmth. But there was something about him that touched her, and that block of ice had begun to thaw at the edges.

When the song had finished, he'd turned in her direction and caught her staring. 'Hey.'

She'd stuttered, her mouth drying, suddenly painfully shy. She pushed her fringe out of her eyes. 'Hi.'

He'd come to stand beside her then. Almost too close. She could smell his sweat, a kind of earthy sweetness. It made her blush, to think of pressing her face against his skin and inhaling him, like an animal might do, and she was confused by her attraction to him, that instinct towards baseness with a man she didn't know. He was British, he told her, the son of Italian migrants on a brief visit home to their mother country.

'How long are you here for?' A boring question, but it was all she could think of to say.

'Long enough.' He'd smiled, making eye contact and holding her gaze. 'What about you?'

'Until the day after tomorrow. My friend's supposed to be here too, but her father's ill and she had to fly home. She insisted I stay, but' – she gave a shrug that conveyed the loneliness of being by herself in an unfamiliar place – 'it's not the same without her.'

Federico had smiled that lazy smile of his, the one she'd fallen for as a twenty-something, but now, as an exhausted mother pushing forty, incensed her. She remembered that first night as clearly as if it had just happened, instead of eighteen years ago.

'Dinner or drugs?'

She'd leaned forward, thinking she'd misheard him. 'Sorry?'

'I can only afford one. Which would you prefer?'

She'd chosen dinner because she was hungry and she wasn't a party girl like Winter, who, only the previous week, had gleefully offered to share with her sisters the half a dozen bottles of extra-strength prescription drugs she'd brought home after filming her first major series in the United States.

It hadn't been a proper dinner in a restaurant. Instead, they'd eaten thin slices of pizza topped with prosciutto and rocket from one of the concession stands, washed down with bottles of ice-cold Peroni. As the sky had darkened and music filled the air, they'd shared cannoli stuffed with sweet ricotta and candied fruits, and he'd kissed the icing sugar from her lips.

'Do you have a job?' he'd said later, back at his tent, their legs entwined.

She'd propped herself up on one elbow, her body sticky with heat. 'I write interviews for a music magazine.'

'You're kidding me,' he'd said, his eyes sparking fire. 'Which one?'

The biggest and best, she could have said. One that had flown her halfway around the world to sprawl across emperor-sized beds in luxury hotel rooms for half an hour with the band *du jour*, or to spend two weeks on a tour bus across America's Deep South for an in-depth profile piece that later won her a prestigious award, or had introduced her to a drummer called Dante, who'd broken her heart.

But she didn't. She waved a hand, as if to say it wasn't important. 'You probably haven't heard of it.'

'Did you get free tickets to the festival?' His eyes widened. 'What about backstage passes?'

She shrugged, not convinced it was the time to tell him she was here as the VIP guest of one of the major record labels, and had spent most of the day rubbing shoulders with rock stars and over-eager publicists. 'Perks of the job.'

'I'm a musician,' he'd said, giving her a quarter-grin that squeezed her insides. 'No one knows my name yet, but one day they will.'

She'd smiled then, but it was the polite smile she reserved for young men on the periphery of the industry, desperate for a break that never came. She saw them every day. Thousands of hopefuls, all chasing dreams that would turn to dust. At times, it felt like the magazine received demos from them all.

But she'd underestimated his determination, his persistence and his talent. Six months after they'd begun dating, he'd moved to London – and then into her flat. And now, all these years later, Federico's time had finally come. Things had moved rapidly in the last twelve months. With Phil's business smarts and her fiancé's creativity and charisma, as well as money-can't-buy exposure in the form of Instagram accounts belonging to Winter and her celebrity friends, he was teetering on the edge of global success.

Never mind that he had a new baby.

Never mind that he had a girlfriend who'd stupidly allowed her own pretty damn successful career to slide while his had flourished.

He was obsessed with feeding the beast of social media, of building his brand, of becoming someone else, a public persona she did not recognize. With that came an arrogance – a belief in his own hype – she'd never noticed in him before. And there was nothing she could do about it.

It wasn't so bad for Jen. Although he was acquiring fame in his own right, Phil didn't travel to all the gigs, just the high-profile ones. And her children were older, more self-sufficient than this squirming newborn, who was apparently her sole responsibility. Even Teddy could dress himself now.

As for Winter, she was thrilled by Fed's success. The two of them had bonded over the pressures of life in the spotlight, although Winter was considerably more famous than her soon-to-be brother-in-law. Alyssa had noticed them giggling together last night at Jen and Phil's house, and it had struck her with the force of a hammer blow that he hadn't laughed like that with her for a long time.

Alyssa fed the baby and went downstairs. She couldn't be bothered to get dressed. Federico's coffee cup was on the worktop, a heat ring marking the expensive polished wood. She considered the day ahead: a manicure and pedicure with her sisters in the afternoon, and Jen's special dinner. She'd promised Winter she'd help her devise some party games, but her elder sister hadn't messaged her yet and, for complicated reasons, she didn't feel like being the one to initiate contact.

A soft knock on the back door. Her stomach turned over in anticipation. 'Come in.'

Phil strode into the kitchen. His hair looked as if it had just been cut, and he was clean-shaven and smelled of expensive cologne. His clothes were stylish and pressed, and his nails were neatly trimmed. A vision of pre-wedding perfection.

Alyssa was aware of her faded pyjamas and the patch of dried baby sick on her shoulder. She remembered, too late and with a flush of heat, that she wasn't wearing a bra. Her brother-in-law handed her a see-through plastic beaker of freshly squeezed orange juice with a straw through its lid and an almond croissant from the deli-cum-bakery down the road. 'I bet you haven't eaten yet.' He peered at her. 'You look exhausted.'

She tipped her head forward, hiding a rush of confusion behind her fringe, deflecting his concern with a weak attempt at humour: 'And you look like you've been manscaped to within an inch of your life.'

He let out a burst of laughter. 'I have. Even my nostril hairs have been tidied up, see?' He leaned backwards to show her.

She grimaced, swallowing a mouthful of the juice, savouring its pulpy sweetness. 'I believe you. I don't need to see the proof.' Her stomach rumbled and she became aware of her hunger, a ravenous, demanding mistress. She tore open the paper bag and took a bite of the croissant, pastry flakes fluttering to their resting place on her chest. 'God, this is good.'

The baby, who was sitting in her rocker, started to fuss. Without waiting to be asked, Phil swept down and lifted Claudia into his arms. 'Who's a beautiful girl, then?'

'Phil . . .'

He smiled at the child in a way that made Alyssa catch her breath. Why couldn't Fed be more like him? 'Yes?'

'Don't say that.'

He was crestfallen. 'Sorry. I didn't mean anything by it. Jen's always telling me I shouldn't define Iris by the way she looks. I should say she's clever or funny or kind instead.'

'You're a good father.' The croissant felt dry in her mouth, the richness of the almond paste curdling on her tongue. She let the remaining half drop back into the paper bag, shiny with grease spots. 'Have you told Jen yet?'

He shifted his position until Claudia was pressed against his left shoulder, his opposite hand rubbing her back. 'Not yet.'

'You promised you would.'

'I know. But the wedding's tomorrow. It's not the right moment.'

'*I* can't do it.'

'We could tell her together, if you wanted to.'

'No.'

Embarrassment coloured her cheeks. It made her petty and cruel. 'Give her to me.' She held out her arms for her daughter, not bothering to conceal her impatience. With a gentleness that belied his solid build, Phil handed the baby back and Alyssa enfolded the tiny body in her own, refusing to look at him. 'She needs to know.'

'And she will, I promise. But let me do it my way, and in my own time. It's going to come as a huge shock, isn't it? Let's give her this weekend, at least.'

She softened then, knowing he was right, and plucked a piece of lint from his jacket. 'Where's Fed?'

Phil shifted on the spot, pulling his mobile phone from his pocket and scrolling through it to avoid her scrutiny, as focused as a laser-guided missile. 'Not sure.'

'He's not working, then?' She answered her own question. 'Obviously not, as you're here.'

'I've got no idea where he is. We'd planned to do a bit of work this morning, but I said I'd be late because I had errands to run. He said he had somewhere else to be, but

I didn't ask him about it and he didn't tell me, I'm afraid.' He rubbed his nose twice with the heel of his hand. 'That's all I know.'

Alyssa inhaled the sweetness of her baby's head, but didn't probe any further. She had all the information she required. An old university friend, now a professor in kinesics, had come to stay a few months ago, and had been persuaded into joining her fiancé and brother-in-law for their monthly poker night.

When her friend had returned home, drunk and exuberant, he'd waved a wad of cash in her face. 'Candy from a baby.'

She'd laughed, shaking her head at him. 'What do you mean?'

'Your brother-in-law. Gave himself away every time.'

She stared at him blankly. 'You've lost me.'

'I probably should have warned them I'm an expert in body language, but I was having way too much fun to do that.'

Each time he'd rubbed his nose, her friend explained, her brother-in-law had given himself away without realizing it. Because Phil Miller had a tell when he lied.

12

Friday, 17 November 2023

Saul

Night was beginning its crawl across the sky, staking its claim. One by one, lights came on in the windows of several homes on the street, beacons of warmth in the encroaching darkness.

The detective had been monitoring the flat for almost two months, but this was the first time he had noticed a police officer in its vicinity. Plain clothes. Unobtrusive. But Saul identified him by his try-hard efforts to blend in, his unnatural state of vigilance and his brogues. The shoes almost always gave them away.

He slid further into the seat of his car. It was important that he was not seen. Although he knew many of the police officers based at Midtown-on-Sea by sight, he did not recognize this one. He held up his phone and took a surreptitious photograph, cursing the lack of flash. The image was blurred and lacking in clarity.

The streets were Friday-night busy, even though rain made the pavements gleam, and Saul watched revellers ducking into pubs and restaurants, full of weekend good humour despite the weather. He had hoped to spend his afternoon – the *night*, if truth be told – with Blue, but she had left the coastguard's lookout not long after lunch, disappearing into the grey and unrelenting drizzle. 'I'm behind on paperwork,' she'd said, pecking his cheek, but she wouldn't meet his eye.

He could tell she was distracted, but he didn't know why. He wanted her to stay, but he didn't know how to ask that either. Instead he said nothing, choosing to spend these empty hours on an unofficial surveillance operation that held no guarantee of results.

He eyed the police officer again. Was he another rotting apple in the barrel? Or something worse? It was too early to tell. Saul held his breath as the man, who was carrying a pizza box, walked up to the suspect's front door, hesitated, and then pressed one of the bells belonging to the communal block of flats. And then another. After a minute or two, someone buzzed him in.

Saul might lack experience, but he knew how police bureaucracy worked. As the Chief Constable had explained in that single communication, if the suspect *was* arrested, it would be as a result of an extensive investigation undertaken by the Kent arm of the Serious Crime Directorate. There was a protocol. Official channels. Everything above board. But the Chief Constable had wanted to gather his own intelligence too. He needed to know how far the rot had spread. And Saul was determined to find out who this man was.

He would watch and wait; no harm in that. He knew how to pass the time.

Without taking his eyes off that front door, Saul dialled Blue. Her phone rang for what felt like forever, and he was just about to hang up when she picked up, sounding breathless. Music was playing in the background, a dreamy electronic beat.

'Hello.'

'Are you OK?'

'God, yes. Sorry. I was in the bath.'

He didn't know what else to say. She was independent. Fiercely so. He couldn't share his compulsion to check on her, to make sure she was safe. If she'd stayed the night, it's likely he'd have confided in her about this secret operation, but the timing had been all wrong. She'd been quiet, lost in thought, and he'd persuaded himself to wait. He regretted that now. He wanted to talk it through with her, but face to face. A part of him willed her to invite him over, but he wasn't sure if that was a good idea.

'I didn't mean to interrupt you.'

She'd turned the music down. He wondered, suddenly, if someone was with her. As far as he was concerned, their relationship was exclusive, but they didn't discuss it. He wasn't interested in other women. He loved her. But he'd never said those words out loud and neither had she. Perhaps he should have done. While he could not bear to confront this possibility, he sensed that she was pulling away from him.

'You didn't.' A silence.

'Are you going out tonight?' He hated himself for saying it, for asking questions of her when that had never been his style. He'd been on his own for so long that he'd got used to the loneliness. Until her.

She laughed out loud. 'No way. I had an early start, remember? I'm going to put my pyjamas on, finish my paperwork and probably fall asleep on the sofa.'

He exhaled, oddly relieved. 'Sounds relaxing.'

He paused to see if she would suggest a late-night drink or make plans with him for tomorrow, but she did neither, and his pride would not allow him to ask. Her voice was soft, but final. 'Goodnight, Saul.'

A worm of anxiety burrowed its way through his stomach and settled in his chest. He missed her as soon as she was gone. Perhaps she would call him in the morning. He hated himself for wanting it so much.

The rain continued to fall. Saul sat in his car, watching the flat until the night grew silent. At some point he must have nodded off, and when he awoke, stiff and chilled, the light in its window had gone out.

He swore under his breath, wondering what he might have missed and if it had been important. Even the street lamps were in darkness now, and the fog had rolled in again from the bay, obscuring everything. Saul drove home along the back roads, past the church and skirting the salt marshes, until he reached the coastguard's lookout, his cottage on the promontory of a cliff.

There was no light at the window here or warm body waiting for him. The heating had switched itself off hours ago and the air inside the ancient stone building was frigid, his breath coming in clouds.

In the lonely stillness of the night, Saul climbed into bed. It felt cold and empty, and, as he waited for sleep to claim him, he tried not to see it as a premonition of his future.

13

Hannah

What struck her first was the silence. No background burble from the television or radio. No sounds of laughing or arguing or crying from her siblings, or singing from her mother, who often belted out hymns as she did the house-work, a throwback to the Sunday school days of her childhood.

Perhaps they'd got bored waiting for her to come home and gone to the park instead. It wouldn't have been the first time. But then she noticed a pan of potatoes on the hob.

Hannah's immediate reaction was disappointment. No sausages and chips for tea then. But it was quickly followed by that creeping sense of unease again. Her mother would never have gone out and left the gas on. She was paranoid about household accidents, banning the use of candles and insisting they turn off every plug socket when they weren't in use. Hannah turned off the flame. The pan had almost boiled dry.

She called out for her mother – once, twice – but there was no reply. In the kitchen, her sister's crayons and colouring books were spread across the table, and she almost tripped over her youngest brother's toy cars, scattered across the lino. The cutlery drawer was open, but there was no sign of any of them.

Her father's work boots were by the back door, side by side, next to a coil of rope. The sight of them made her feel sick and, again, she considered running all the way back to school. But the thought of the escaped panther and what she would say when she got there stopped her in her tracks.

With growing trepidation, Hannah climbed the stairs to the bedrooms. She pushed gently against her brothers' door, and then froze.

The two boys were huddled in the same bed, arms around each other, eyes shut. Both of them were bleeding from the head and neither was moving. The eldest – Michael – was clutching a silver-coloured plastic knight's shield, as if to protect his brother.

Her mother was sprawled across the bedroom floor, still as a statue. One of her slippers had come off, and Hannah stared at her painted toes, encased in skin-coloured tights. Her mind drifted. She didn't like those tights. Their bland smoothness made her think of shop-floor dummies.

She crouched down next to her mother. Helen was lying on her stomach, arms raised above her, face resting on her left cheek. Hannah had helped her try out a home perming kit the previous week because she couldn't afford a hairdresser, but now the tight curls at the back of her head were dark and matted.

She whispered to her mother and poked her gently, but her mother didn't move.

Hannah felt a great wave of grief rising inside her. It was the same panicked feeling as that time she'd gone to the beach and swum out too far. The current had been stronger and choppier than she'd expected, dragging her under, the seawater burning her nose and the back of her throat and stinging her eyes. She'd flailed in the water until a teenage lifeguard had yanked her to safety by the straps of her bathing suit.

She didn't know what to do next. She screwed up her eyes and tried to think. What would Nancy Drew do? Call the police? An ambulance? Tell an adult?

She scrolled through the few adults she knew in their new home town. Tony and Lorraine from next door, who always saved their orange Revels for Hannah and her siblings. Miss McGovern. Her father. At the thought of him, the ants began their crawl again. Where was he? And more importantly, where was her little sister?

'I'll be back in a bit, I promise.' She didn't want to leave her mother and brothers, but she knew she must. In the hallway, she stood on the small square of brown carpet at the top of the staircase. Her bedroom door was closed. It was never closed.

Her legs were trembling, but Hannah didn't know how to stop them from doing that. The same thing sometimes happened after she'd been in a running race at school or when she hadn't had any breakfast and had been too busy playing Sticky Glue with her friends to eat her lunch, but this felt different. She couldn't make the feeling go away.

But her love for her sister outweighed any fear she felt for herself.

She opened the bedroom door.

Her father was standing in the centre of their room, his back to her. He had a hammer hanging loosely in his right hand, but that didn't frighten her because he'd used the same hammer to nail her netball hoop to the wall at the weekend. In that beat of time, it still felt benign.

Until he swung around to face her.

He was wearing overalls and they had stains all over them. His face held a blankness that made her breath catch. The lenses of his glasses had spatters of blood on them.

She backed away.

He took a step towards her.

A whimper caused both of them to pause in their tracks. A face, eyes wide and full of tears, peered out at Hannah from under the cot. There was a dark smear on her yellow T-shirt.

'Come out from there.'

Her sister looked at Hannah. Hannah shook her head. *No.*

Her father roared the command again. Her sister started to cry, to crawl forward on her hands and knees. Hannah hesitated, torn in two. She could run for help now. She was fast. Faster than her father, who smoked and ate too much. But if she left her sister alone, she might not see her again.

'Girls are full of trouble.' Her father dragged the baby out by her wrist. She was screaming now, trying to squirm out of his grasp. 'Shut the fuck up.' He raised the hammer. The air was ripe, swollen. Hannah could smell that her sister's nappy needed to be changed.

She tried to distract him, smiling through the threat of tears. 'Why are you home so early?'

Her father's gaze was unfocused. He reeked of whisky. 'Let me go, haven't they? Bastards.'

The baby continued to cry. She wasn't really a baby, but they all called her that. Her cheeks had the polished-apple look of a child that had worked herself into hysteria.

'Come in here. And close the door behind you.' He shook the baby so hard that her teeth clacked together and she screamed even louder. 'Shut up, you little fuck.'

Hannah did as he said and held out her arms for her sister. 'Let me change her. She'll stop crying then.' It was a gamble, an act of desperation. She couldn't bear to think about what her father had planned for them, but she needed to focus, to find a way to divert him.

He swung the hammer in a lazy arc. 'I know a way to stop her crying.'

Hannah calculated the gap between where she stood and the doorway. In theory, she could run with the baby in her arms, but it would slow their progress.

Her father eyed her in a way that suggested he had guessed what she was thinking and that he would rather deal with Hannah first.

He let go of the baby and allowed her to run to Hannah. Then he positioned himself by the bedroom door.

Hannah hoisted her sister onto the changing table by her cot. She smoothed her damp hair from her forehead and crooned in her ear. 'Stop crying. Hannah's here.' She held her close until the juddering sobs slowed into occasional hiccups.

With practised fingers, she stripped the towelling nappy off her sister, cleaned her and smothered her with cream. Her father was looking out of the window and muttering to himself. Hannah picked up the safety pin and ran her thumb across its point. She bent over her sister, her voice low. 'When I say so, go and knock for Lorraine with the orange sweeties, do you think you can do that?'

The baby nodded. Hannah made a show of sprinkling talcum powder on her sister's bottom, pulled up her shorts and leaned over her soft cheek, a whisper disguised as a kiss. 'Clever girl. Can you reach the front door handle? You can, can't you?' She pressed a finger to her lips. Her sister nodded again, eyes wide. 'Don't tell Daddy. Just do it when I say, OK? Run as fast as you can.'

She lifted her sister off the changing mat, placed her on the floor and turned to face their father.

'Can I get a drink please? I'm thirsty.'

His response was to swing the hammer at Hannah. It didn't connect, but she screamed from the shock of it and the baby started to cry again. He took a step closer to them both, a manic light in his eyes.

Hannah lunged forward and drove the tip of the safety pin into his groin with as much force as she could muster. 'Now, baby. Run.'

Lacking the logic of an older child, her sister did not run around her father but through his splayed legs. Hannah groaned as he bent down and grabbed a fistful of the two-and-a-half-year-old's T-shirt, lifting her off the floor, her bare feet kicking like a frantic insect.

Panicked, Hannah glanced around the room, snatched up the bottle of talc and flung it in her father's eyes. He dropped her sister onto the carpet and rubbed at the chalky powder, anger pulsing from every pore of his body, still grasping the hammer. He lunged at Hannah, and as she turned to run from him, he grabbed one of her bunches and jerked it hard, stopping her in her tracks. A bolt of pain shot through her.

The baby scrambled to her feet and glanced at her elder sister, uncertain.

'Run.'

Hannah watched her trot through the door, the fat parcel of her nappy the last thing to disappear from view. Her father loomed above her, that blank expression on his face wiping all traces of the man she knew. She closed her eyes and visualized her mother's smile.

In the distance, she could hear the baby, clumsy and crying, clambering down the stairs backwards. Even at her young age, it was clear her sister sensed the danger she was in, but she lacked the concentration to remain focused on her escape. She heard the girl stop and shout for her mother, for Hannah and their brothers, but when no one replied, she continued her lumbering descent.

Hannah willed her onwards. Held her breath into the silence, terrified her father would give chase. She had almost given up hope when she heard footsteps padding across the wooden floor. The sound of a kitchen chair being dragged across the hallway to the front door.

She remembered all those sleepy mornings in her bed, reading stories of woodland animals lost in a snowstorm, and princesses fighting dragons, the warm solidity of her sister's body leaning into hers, the milky sourness of her breath. Or the times they had played in the scrubby patch of garden, make-believe games with mud pies and leaves, stirring their creations with a stick.

'What the fuck is that little bitch doing?' Her father came to from his reverie and started towards the bedroom door. Without thinking, Hannah flung herself forward and grabbed at his arm to stall him.

He was so close she could smell her mother's blood on his overalls. Furious, he threw her off. She cowered, braced for his attack, but even then, in the face of his ire, she was still listening.

Finally, above the thump of her fear and her father's heavy breathing, there it was.

The click of the mortice lock.

The front door slammed and Hannah felt something in her heart loosen and soar. It didn't matter that she was about to face the same fate as her mother and brothers. Her sister, for whom she would sacrifice her own life, even at the tender age of ten, was safe.

She didn't see the first blow coming. After that, she felt nothing at all.

14

Friday, 17 November 2023

Winter

The restaurant was lit up with Friday night magic, full of chatter and laughter. Winter was hit by its damp warmth as she pushed her way through the doors, windows running with condensation from the heat of all those bodies and its marriage with the chill night air outside.

She had commandeered the entire restaurant for Jen's special night. Experience had taught her that even a private room and a plateful of food was not enough to deter the most dedicated of autograph-hunters. On one memorable occasion, a drunk woman had crawled beneath their table for a dare in the middle of a family meal. The woman – Winter's 'biggest fan', apparently – had tried to stand up, but in doing so had lost her balance, grabbed hold of the tablecloth, and brought it – and lunch for nine – crashing down onto the floor. Winter had been forced to throw away the shoes she'd been wearing that day, the mint green silk stained with red wine. Iris had cried.

She blinked away the memory and drank in the scene. Jen was already there, cocktail in hand and surrounded by friends, her face flushed with pleasure and the social pressure of being the centre of attention. She waved at Winter, the curve of a quarter-smile accentuating her cheekbones. Of all the sisters, she was the one who liked to hang back, interested but shy. To Winter, though, she appeared uncharacteristically relaxed, and she patted her past self on the back for making an excellent decision. Her sister deserved to enjoy herself.

'Winter!' Her mother's voice was loud but warm above the hubbub of the restaurant. She felt herself enveloped in a hug. Carol Kellaway released her daughter and took a step back, holding her at arm's length. Her breath smelled of alcohol. 'You're too thin, darling.'

Winter thought about the pregnancy test she'd taken that morning and resisted making a sarcastic quip. Her mother would know soon enough. *But only if you keep the baby.* That voice in her head reminded her there was still a decision to be made.

She changed the subject. 'Have you seen Alyssa yet?'

Her mother's face clouded. 'I've called her several times over the past week, but she hasn't picked up. I'm worried about her, to be honest. New motherhood can be challenging. Dad and I offered to come and stay for a bit, but she didn't want us to.'

Winter was surprised, although she hid it. That was not the impression Alyssa had given her. At all. She recalled a conversation they'd had a few days earlier, Alyssa, tired and emotional, weeping for her mother.

'Perhaps you should try again.'

Her mother took a mouthful of her gin and tonic, her forehead creased. 'I will, I promise. She's coming tonight, though, isn't she?' Her eyes held a familiar glassiness that suggested this wasn't her first drink.

'She should be here by now, but I can't see her.' Winter

90

scanned the room again, but there was no sign of her sister or her newborn niece.

Carol squeezed her eldest daughter's hand. 'You're a good girl, paying for all this.'

'Hardly a girl.'

Her mother laughed, finished her drink and signalled at a waiter to bring her another. 'Sorry, I forget you're all grown women these days. I miss the times when the three of you used to follow me around everywhere and fought over who got to hold my hand.'

Winter grinned at her mother's wistful expression, and leaned into her, inhaling the scent of her perfume, a constant of her childhood. Carol Kellaway, resistant to even minor changes, had worn the same one for forty years. 'We'll always need you, Mum.'

She thought for a minute, aware, perhaps for the first time in her life, of what it might have been like for her mother. 'It must have been hard for you, having three young children, and a job, and a husband who refused to cook.'

'Believe it or not, your dad has now learned how to heat up a tin of beans.' Her mother's mouth collapsed into laughter. 'Although he still burns the toast.' She reached out and squeezed Winter's hand, her eyes soft with memories. 'It was worth it, love. Every single minute.'

Winter gave her mother a gentle nudge with her shoulder. 'Even when Alyssa was being naughty?'

This was familiar territory, as comfortable as the childhood bed Winter still slept in whenever she returned to her parents' home. The folklore of family, so ingrained over the years that no one thought to challenge it anymore: Winter was the creative one; Jen, the sensible sister; and Alyssa, the youngest, was spoilt and misbehaved.

But her mother didn't smile as she usually did. Instead, she took a large swallow of her newly replenished drink, her face serious. 'It wasn't easy for her.'

'What, being the baby of the family and treated like a princess?' Winter forced a snort of laughter to disguise the bitterness that ambushed her occasionally when she remembered the special treatment Alyssa had received when they were growing up. 'It wasn't easy for any of us.'

As women, their bond was unbreakable, but as young siblings, their rivalries had been more complicated than even their mother and father had realized. Jen had always been the easy-going one, and although Winter and Alyssa would willingly die for one another, they had often competed for the affections of both their parents and their middle sister.

'Come on now, Winter.' Her mother's tone was mild but the rebuke was apparent. 'It wasn't like that. We treated all of you in the same way.'

Winter knew she should stay quiet, especially tonight, but the hurt she'd carried as a teenager burst from her, surprising them both. 'What about her gorgeous bedroom, and the horse-riding lessons, and the ballet tuition, and the puppy, and whatever else she asked for? No wonder she finds real life hard as an adult when she's used to having things handed to her on a plate.'

'You didn't want those things.' Her mother's voice was even, but she took another slug of her drink. 'We offered them to you. We offered you *everything*.' She waited a moment, as if considering whether to comment further. 'But Alyssa always needed a bit more from us than you and Jen did.'

In truth, Winter had known that. Most of the time she'd understood it, and had been glad that Geoff and Carol were so generous and loving, but every now and then, it had enraged her. She had been unable to articulate her own feelings of inadequacy, which were heightened by the fuss that everyone made of the youngest Kellaway sister.

She thought of the jealous pinches she'd sometimes given Alyssa when no one else was around. Alyssa had never been one to tell tales, but her eyes had filled with tears, silent and reproachful. Jen had been much more accepting of the fuss her parents had made of their youngest sibling, shrugging it off with typical equanimity, but then she'd always been the kindest of the three sisters and, with eleven months separating them, had more in common with Alyssa than Winter, although she was close to them both.

'In any case, it's all worked out in the end, hasn't it?' Her mother drained her drink and sucked on the lemon wedge, wincing at its sharpness. 'You have more now than you could ever have hoped for.'

'Because I've worked damn hard for it.'

'Nobody's saying you didn't, my darling.' She placed her empty glass on a nearby table and reached for Winter's hand. 'Dad and I are so proud of you and everything you've achieved. Your strength of character. Your determination. Your desire to succeed.' Her voice was low, full of compassion and difficult to hear above the hubbub of the restaurant. She stumbled, swaying on her feet, and it dawned on Winter that her mother was edging towards drunkenness. 'Listen, your dad and I were thinking that perhaps it's time to talk to Jen about—'

A woman with a sleek bob and wearing a dress printed with pineapples touched Winter lightly on the elbow. 'I'm so sorry to interrupt, but the manager's asking for you. He wants everyone to take their seats as soon as possible. He's fussing about the food being overcooked.'

In the whirl of activity that followed, Winter and her mother were separated by a tidal sweep of friends and family, by platters of Italian antipasti and bowls of gleaming olives and carafes of expensive wine, by daft games that Jen's work colleagues had secretly organized, and funny stories about the happy couple, and their conversation was forgotten.

When Alyssa finally arrived, an hour late, full of apologies, dark circles beneath her eyes and the baby tucked into a sling, Winter's irritation had long since been soothed by delicious food and bonhomie, and she was ambushed by a rush of affection for her youngest sister.

She beckoned to her from across the restaurant, pointing to the chair next to her. 'I saved you a seat,' she said, piling garlic prawns and salad onto Alyssa's plate, and pouring her half a glass of white wine and waving away her protestations. 'I know you're breastfeeding, but it's only a drop.' And the sisters had chattered about the next day's wedding, and how Jen would make such a gorgeous bride, and they both dropped soft kisses on Claudia's head, who did not stir.

At the end of the evening, when the guests had said their *thank you*s and *goodnight*s and *see you tomorrow*s, the Kellaway women were the only ones left in the restaurant. Jen, flushed and beautiful, tipsy from champagne cocktails and the outpouring of love and affection, threw her arms around Winter.

'Thank you for the most perfect night.'

Alyssa, baby still strapped to her chest, drifted towards them, tucking herself into Jen's embrace and snaking an arm around Winter's waist, as she'd done since she was a young girl. Carol stood behind Alyssa and placed her arms around them all, always the mother hen, no matter their age.

They told each other how much they loved each other, and in that moment, one of those sweet snapshots in time where the feeling becomes the memory that overrides all else, each woman was buoyed up by a sense of belonging, a profound understanding that no matter what else happened in life, they were the lucky ones, blessed with the love and security of family.

Winter didn't know then – none of them did – that in twenty-four hours' time, the Kellaway clan – loving, tight-knit, unbreakable – would be ripped apart by events that no one could have foreseen. That the bonds that had tethered them to each other, the foundations that had sustained them throughout the years, were flimsy as a house of straw, blown away on the wind.

PART TWO

THE DAY OF THE PARTY

15

Jen

It was still dark when Jen opened her eyes, convinced Teddy had cried out for her. She was halfway out of bed, the morning air chill against her skin, before she remembered she was not at home, but in the guest cottage on Winter's estate, and she was getting married – again – that afternoon.

She buried herself beneath the covers and stretched out her toes – freshly pedicured with Candy Rain – luxuriating in the rarity of clean sheets *and* a lie-in. She wondered if her children were awake yet.

Iris would be tired today, overstimulated from the excitement of staying at Calypso's house and their much-anticipated midnight feast. The practical part of her knew she should have cancelled the sleepover so that Iris had an early night, but she couldn't bear the idea of disappointing two eight-year-old girls. And it had been kind of Calypso's mother to offer.

She glanced at the clock on her bedside table. Five o'clock. She imagined a sleepy-eyed Teddy climbing out of his new racing-car bed, thumb plugging his mouth and padding into her parents' room, asking for milk and cartoons. Carol had insisted on taking care of the children. 'Every bride needs to enjoy the night before her wedding, darling. Dad will look after Teddy, and we'll get Iris ready when she gets home. You just concentrate on yourselves.'

Phil had been reluctant, though. When Iris was a toddler, her grandmother had popped to the bakery for a loaf of bread, and had left her alone and asleep in the nursery. On the spur of the moment, Phil had nipped home for lunch. His daughter's screams could be heard from halfway down the street, and he'd found her red-faced and sweaty, gripping the bars of her cot. Two minutes later, an unapologetic Carol had sauntered up the path, swinging her shopping basket and swatting away his concern. 'No harm done, dear. Everyone does it.'

When she'd arrived home from work and her husband had recounted the story, Jen had been mortified by her mother's behaviour. Furious too. But the passing years had dulled the sharp edges of her shame and anger, as well as her memory of that day, and because her parents now lived abroad in rural France, she'd welcomed the opportunity for them to spend some one-on-one time with their grandchildren.

'I don't think so,' said Phil, when Jen had first mooted the idea a few weeks ago. 'Your mother can't be trusted.'

'That's not fair.' A flush had painted her cheeks, as it often did when she defended her parents to Phil, but she kept her voice calm, not wanting to argue. 'It happened a long time ago and she thought she was doing the right thing by leaving Iris to sleep, remember? I'm almost certain she wouldn't do it again.'

Phil had rolled his eyes. '*Almost?* Do you want to take that risk?'

'You find someone to look after the children then.' The

words were out of her mouth before she could stop them, but she'd meant it. Perhaps she shouldn't have snapped at him, but it irritated her that all childcare arrangements were somehow her responsibility by default.

He'd blurted out a couple of names – one of the friendlier school mums and his sister – but Jen, arms folded, had stood her ground. 'Already tried them.'

When she'd suggested he might like to cancel his stag do and help out the morning of their wedding instead, he'd had a change of heart and conceded that his in-laws were the best option after all.

Jen often struggled to ask for help, even though she was the first to offer it. For this reason, she had made the arrangements with her parents before she'd even checked with Phil because it meant she didn't have to prevail on the hospitality of others or perform that dutiful dance of offering to return the favour and pretending to mean it.

In any case, most of her friends had been at last night's dinner, celebrating with her, so it made sense for her father to watch over Teddy, and for her mother to get the children changed into their wedding finery, ready for this afternoon's party. They were all due at the cottage later anyway. She couldn't wait.

At that thought, it felt like a dozen champagne bottles were popping in her stomach. She glanced at her wedding dress, hanging in a plastic bag on the back of the door. She hadn't intended to buy anything new, convinced that one of the many dresses in her wardrobe would do the trick, but Winter had insisted, taking her into London to visit bridal boutiques and paying for the elegant silk and lace designer sheath that Jen had eventually chosen.

'Try it on,' Winter had encouraged Jen when she'd noticed

her taking a surreptitious peek at the price tag. 'You'll thank me for it later, I promise.'

Jen had resisted, knowing it was out of her financial league, but Winter would not listen, and when she had slid the wedding dress over her head, her treacherous heart had skipped a beat.

Gazing at herself in the mirror, Jen, a middle-aged mother of two with crow's feet, a smattering of grey hairs and a pouchy stomach, couldn't quite believe she was the same woman who'd arrived in oversized jeans and a bobbly jumper from Next. The colour warmed her skin and the material skimmed her body in all the right places. She had never before owned a dress that made her feel like this.

She'd emerged from the changing room in a swish of ivory to gasps from the staff and a slow whistle from Winter, who'd said, 'Knew it. You must buy it, Jen. You look sensational.'

'I don't know. It's so expensive.'

But Winter had dismissed her protestations with a wave of her hand. 'I'll buy it for you.'

Jen had flushed, embarrassed. Sometimes it felt like Winter used her vast wealth to buy not only material possessions, but her family's affection. She drew her elder sister to one side, conscious of the staff pretending not to listen. 'I can't let you do that. You're already spending a fortune on the party.'

'How about I get it for you as an early Christmas present?'

'Christmas is four months away.'

Winter had grinned. 'Perfect timing.'

Jen had shifted awkwardly, reluctant to abuse her sister's generosity. Her gaze flicked back to the mirror, tempted but undecided.

'You do look beautiful, dear.' The sales assistant was

carrying a froth of tulle and lace over her arm. 'And I don't say that to everyone.'

In the end, Winter had solved the problem by paying for the dress – and shoes, veil and wedding underwear – without Jen's knowledge while she was getting changed. By the time she'd pulled on her jeans, laced up her trainers and become boring Mrs Miller again, a selection of beribboned bags was resting on the counter and Winter's diary was open, waiting to agree with Jen a date for her first fitting.

The lunch that Jen bought afterwards to say thank you had felt paltry by comparison.

Jen closed her eyes, willing herself back to sleep, but it was no use. Several years of early starts had ruined her ability to lie in for hours, as she'd done as a young woman. She'd been looking forward to a child-free morning, the indulgence of a leisurely breakfast and being pampered by a make-up artist and hair stylist with her sisters by her side, but now, in the quiet darkness of Winter's cottage, she missed Iris and Teddy.

She rolled over, trying to get comfortable, but she was wide awake. She wondered if her mother would remember to warm Teddy's milk – even though he was no longer a baby, he still liked it heated through on these chilly mornings – and if he'd be a good boy about having his bath. And Iris's hair was so curly. Had she reminded her mother that she didn't need to wash it? It had taken Jen countless tear-stained bath times with her daughter to perfect the art of combing it through, and thinking ahead, as always, she'd washed it on Thursday night, so it would be clean and manageable for today.

A longing to cuddle her children overwhelmed her. She chastised herself for being daft, overly sentimental. It had only been a few hours since she'd last seen them, and they would be here later, when Carol arrived to have her make-up done. But Jen had wanted to be a mother for as long as she could remember. When those well-meaning but dull relatives who frequented family gatherings had asked each of the sisters what they wanted to be, Winter would say famous, Alyssa would smile dreamily until the conversation had moved on and Jen would stuff a cushion up her jumper and cradle her fake bump.

She slipped out of bed and pulled on a clean pair of gym leggings and a sweatshirt, the underfloor heating sending a pulse of warmth through her body. It was still early. She could nip over to her house, say good morning to Teddy, welcome Iris home from Calypso's, and be back here by the time the hair stylist arrived.

The guest cottage earmarked for the bride-to-be boasted the most scenic views of the bay, but on this cold November morning, it was impossible to see further than a couple of paces ahead. A dense wall of fog obscured everything, transforming the landscaped gardens into nothingness. Beyond the grounds of Winter's estate, Jen could hear the push and pull of a restless tide, and the groan of the foghorn, eerie and rhythmic, alerting vessels to the rocky coastline.

She shivered, the air damp against her skin and hair. If the cottage was a haven, warm and comfortable, being outside was akin to a slap across the face.

Jen began to make her way across the lawn, trainers crunching against the frozen grass, each blade tinged with rime. Her breath formed clouds in the morning gloom. Teddy called that 'dragon's smoke' and it made her smile to think of him screaming in delighted terror as she chased him through the park, pretending she would eat him up. She'd forgotten to wear gloves and she rubbed her hands together. It was much colder than she'd anticipated and she whispered a prayer to the wedding gods that the fog would lift by the afternoon.

The formal gardens on Winter's estate were divided into neat geometric patterns and included a large vegetable patch that supplied the kitchen, an orchard with various types of fruit trees, a rose garden and a wide bank of rhododendron bushes. By the water fountain, there was a maze made from seven-foot yew hedges that Teddy and Iris had got lost in more than once.

It was rare and impressively beautiful, a country estate with extensive grounds, sea views and a vast house at its heart, but Jen had always believed the number of rooms was irrelevant: a home-owner, however wealthy and talented, could only sleep in one room at a time.

Although the fog made it difficult to see where she was going, Jen was familiar with the footpaths that criss-crossed the lawns and found her way to a dome-roofed pergola at the apex of the ornamental pond, a stone's throw from Winter's property.

She glanced upwards, noticing the glow of a lamp emanating from her eldest sister's bedroom. It was un-usually early for Winter to be awake, and she hesitated, not sure if she should stop by the main house to say good morning before she headed off or let her sister be.

While she was deciding what to do next, a rush of footsteps – running hard and fast through the undergrowth – caught her attention. It was not the measured rhythm of a jogger, but the aggressive, desperate pace of someone in a hurry. She spun around, her heart jumping at this intrusion in the pre-dawn hush, but all she could see through the fog was the vague outline of trees and bushes.

The footsteps grew closer.

She froze, and listened through the murk, trying to get a sense of which direction the sounds were coming from, but it was no use. Slowly, she rotated clockwise, alert and watchful, her arms raised in a defensive position, body pricking with adrenaline.

A blur of noise and movement crashed through the trees behind her, and by the time she'd turned towards its source, blinded by the weather, they'd set off running again, feet pounding against the mulch and fallen leaves. Before she'd even had a chance to properly register that she might be in danger, the intruder had disappeared into the fog, and was gone in less than a couple of seconds.

Torn, Jen considered giving chase. She was a fast runner, but this person had a head start and it was impossible to see where they'd gone in this greyed-out nothingness. And what if they were violent? *Violent*. A pretty word with such ugly connotations.

A scenario – dark and terrible – unspooled in her mind. Could it be a crazed fan? Had they tried – or, worse, *succeeded* in – breaking into her sister's home? Was Winter . . . ? She did not allow herself to form the words, even in her mind.

She turned then and sprinted back towards the house, all thoughts of seeing her children forgotten. The air was frigid against her flushed cheeks. She knew what could happen to celebrities, especially female ones.

Last week, she'd watched a documentary about the unsolved murder of a high-profile television presenter, deliberately mown down by an unidentified driver on her way to work. And a friend had told her about another famous woman – a media darling and mother of five – who'd been forced to leave her job for the safety of her family after credible threats of rape and abduction were uncovered by police.

A lamp illuminated Winter's front door, a tasteful construction made from wood and glass. Jen pressed her fingertip to the biometric keypad and it opened with a click. When Winter had first moved here, she'd invited both her sisters to be part of her inner sanctum, so they could access the house in the event of an emergency. Jen stepped inside the vestibule and pumped the handle of the interior door, surprised to discover it was unlocked. A frisson of fear ran through her. This was unlike her security-conscious sister.

She called out her eldest sibling's name. Once. And, more sharply, a second time.

Silence.

She walked forward, her trainers echoing slightly as she passed through the unlocked interior door into the cavernous hallway. Everything was tidy and in its place. Vases of calla lilies and blush-coloured roses covered every surface, interspersed with lush garlands of greenery. The florist and her team had descended the previous night because there was so much to do during these last few hours before the wedding. Their skill was evident in the artistry of the arrangements, and the scent was heavenly.

Winter had suggested serving post-ceremony drinks in this part of the house, and Jen could see the fire was already laid in the huge fireplace that dominated the space. Gleaming champagne flutes on silver trays were already waiting atop a makeshift bar that a specialist team had built a couple of days ago.

Dotted at strategic points around the hallway was a selection of oversized glass lanterns containing white pillar candles, waiting to be lit. It looked like a scene from a magazine shoot: 'At home with Winter Kellaway'.

Except the star of the show was still unaccounted for.

Jen kicked off her trainers – the wooden floors had been freshly polished and she didn't want to track mud across them – and stood, uncertain, in the centre of the hall. Above the silence, she heard a distant – but familiar – voice coming from upstairs. With trepidation, she climbed the staircase.

Winter was sitting on a bed, dressed in high-necked silk pyjamas and a matching robe. Music was playing. She leaned over, closed her eyes and kissed the shirtless man lying next to her. While she was lost in that moment of intimacy, his free hand, hanging down the side of the bed, groped for her handbag and withdrew a sheaf of papers. He glanced at them, his face darkening, and pushed her away.

'When were you going to tell me?'

'Tonight, I promise. It's just—'

The man struck Winter in the face with a closed fist. As it made contact with her nose, a sickening crunch echoed around the bedroom, and Winter fell back onto the bed, blood spraying from her in a scarlet arc.

Jen picked up the remote control and switched off the home cinema system. *The Enemy Within*, Winter's most recent film. In her view, it was one of her sister's weakest, and the reviewers had unanimously agreed, but Jen would never have dared to vocalize that.

Winter did not take criticism well, especially from her family. Jen didn't blame her. Being judged all the time must be soul-destroying – it was one of the reasons Winter refused to do nude scenes – and she knew her sister depended on the supportive nature of their tight-knit unit. But she wondered which vicious newspaper critic had prompted

Winter to torment herself by rewatching this particular film on this particular morning.

Where *was* she? As Jen tried to put herself in her sister's shoes, an idea so obvious occurred to her that she berated herself for not thinking of it sooner.

She raced back downstairs, through the open-plan living area towards the rear of the house, and made her way to Winter's safe room, a hidden space beneath the second stair-case that few people knew about, which had been installed to protect her in the event of a home invasion. The family was not allowed to call it a panic room as that upset their mother, but that's what it was. A place to lose one's shit.

She banged on the smooth surface of the mahogany door that concealed reinforced steel beneath it. 'Winter, are you in there?'

Her sister's muffled reply could be heard from inside. 'Jen? Is that you?'

'Yes. Open the door.'

'Has he gone? The intruder? Has he gone?' Jen could hear the thread of panic in her sister's voice as she repeated the question.

'Yes, it looks that way.'

Jen heard the beep of the security panel followed by the clunk of a deadbolt. The door slid open. Winter, pale as a ghost, was standing by a chair in the safe room, a canister in her right hand. The security expert had warned her against keeping lethal weapons like knives or guns inside because, if the safe room was breached, they could be used against her, but she seemed so vulnerable with only pepper spray for protection. Jen went to her, gently removing the aerosol, and gave her a hug.

A bank of closed-circuit television screens played on a

loop, alternating between the back of the house, the extensive gardens, the security gates and the front door. When the safe-room locking mechanism was activated from the inside, as it had been on this occasion, the security system automatically dialled the emergency services. Police would be here within minutes.

'Did you see him?'

Jen shook her head, her expression grave. 'No, but whoever it was ran past me.'

'Was it . . . ?' Winter couldn't bring herself to articulate his name.

Silence. It stretched between them, an absence of words that said everything. 'I don't know. It could have been.'

Winter closed her eyes, her body trembling. In the early-morning quiet, Jen remembered the obsessive fan who had smashed his way into Winter's house all those years ago. A loner with a penchant for famous women, he had scaled the garden wall and broken a downstairs window to gain access. Winter had woken to a stranger in her bedroom with a knife at her throat.

That encounter had left Winter with a deep-seated fear of history repeating itself.

As any victim of crime would attest, a horrific ordeal leaves its scars, both physically and mentally.

It was no surprise that Winter had locked herself in her panic room at the merest hint of an intruder.

She was a woman who lived alone.

And, if the intent had been to cause her serious harm, it wouldn't be the first time that someone had tried to kill her.

16

Saturday, 18 November 2023

Saul

Saul missed the Murder Club. After last year's injuries, he'd been moved to lighter duties, but they did not provide the intellectual rigour that sustained him, or feed the dark compulsions that drove him. He longed to lose himself in the silt of humanity, to pan for the glimpses of gold that would help him unravel the depravity of killers like the acid attacker or Evelyn Parker's husband. His cases were often dull with so much paperwork that his mind drifted, and he dreamed of escaping the bureaucracy of it all.

It was supposed to be his weekend off, but he could not settle. After a couple of hours of restless sleep, he'd woken to the cries of the kittiwakes, the only sound in the silence of his cottage. The screen of his phone remained dark – no messages or calls from Blue – and he was too proud to break first. Pride was his weakness, but even though he recognized that in himself, he did not act on this self-knowledge, but let the hurt fester inside. After an early walk across the salt marshes, instead of heading back to the coastguard's lookout, he'd found himself at the police station to finish off some admin and to occupy his mind.

The duty sergeant, sipping coffee behind the front-desk window, was surprised to see him. 'Can't keep you away. Haven't you got anything better to do on a Saturday?'

He was joking, of course. But Saul didn't bother to answer because there was too much painful truth in that question, so instead he raised a hand and wandered upstairs into the warren of rooms.

Because it was the weekend, it was quiet, a state of affairs he welcomed. He sat at an empty desk, switched on his computer and tried not to think about the forensic linguist who had captured his heart.

His phone buzzed with a message, startling him. He read it, his heart thumping. And then, pride forgotten, he rang Blue's number. Once. Twice. But she didn't answer. Three times. Four. He willed her to pick up his call because he dared not leave a message or send one, and it was imperative he spoke to her. He cursed under his breath, uncertain how to proceed.

Detective Inspector Elena Nunn materialized by the side of his desk, making him jump, and he slipped his phone into his pocket. He swore she was the most soft-footed officer he'd ever worked with. She was older than him, but not by much. Six or seven years, perhaps less. She grinned at him, a dimple in one cheek. He didn't know her well, but he liked her. She was no-nonsense but fair. And smart. If anyone had to replace his former DI, Angus O'Neill, he was glad it was her.

'Are you free, Saul?'

He thought about explaining it was his day off and that he needed to leave due to an unexpected emergency, but it was complicated. She did not suffer fools gladly, but he couldn't tell her why he had to go. A part of him knew that if he wanted to advance his career, he needed to impress her. And if he got rid of her quickly, he could try to reach Blue again.

'Yes, what do you need, boss?'

'Do you know who Winter Kellaway is?'

Saul considered the question. He'd always been uninterested in celebrity and its trappings. He was not on social media. He did not scour online gossip sites, or read newspapers filled with tittle-tattle. He did not care about their love affairs or divorces, their drug problems or secret rehab programmes, their pregnancies, holidays, home renovations and all the other minutiae of their so-called private lives. Strip away wealth, the country homes and supercars, expensive clothing and jewellery, and they bled in exactly the same way as the homeless who begged for charity on the streets of Midtown.

That said, Winter Kellaway had managed to infiltrate even *his* consciousness. 'The actress?'

'They call women actors these days.' Her tone was amused. 'But yes, that's her.'

'She lives on the country estate that edges the bay.'

'In a fuck-off mansion called The Beach House, yes. Listen, the panic button in her safe room was activated earlier today after an intruder breached the property. Initial reports from the officers who responded suggest everything is quiet now, but the Chief Constable is a friend of the family and keen to avoid uncomfortable headlines, especially if this leaks, as I'm sure it will. For the sake of appearances, he's asked me to send a couple of officers down there to take a statement and to provide a bit of visibility and reassurance. You up for the job?'

It sounded like his idea of hell, but he couldn't exactly say no. 'Sure.'

DI Nunn rubbed her hands together. 'Excellent. I'll send DC Hunter with you. Do you know him?'

'No.'

'This will be your chance to remedy that.' She flashed another grin and was gone.

DC Isaac Hunter reminded Saul of a clockwork toy that had been wound up until the torsion spring was close to breaking point, and then let loose in a burst of power. He had a puppyish energy that was both irritating and disarming. He bounded over to Saul in the station car park and offered him a fizzy sweet from the half-empty bag. When Saul shook his head, Isaac crammed three sour cherries into his own mouth, licked the sugar off his lips and stuffed the packet back into his pocket.

'Do you want to drive or shall I?'

'You can,' said Saul, partly because he wanted to get the measure of the new detective constable, partly in case Blue called him back, and partly because he feared what more sugar might do to the young man.

DC Hunter was the same age as Saul, and in one of those twists of fate, they discovered they shared a birthday. But the similarities between them stopped there. On the drive to the Kellaway property, Isaac chatted about his secondary school (private), his university (Cambridge) and his parents (rich). Saul did not mention his patchwork schooling, his alcoholic mother or his violent father.

'We can get some lunch together later, if you want to. When we've finished here, I mean.' Isaac's tone was friendly.

But Saul, preoccupied by Blue's continuing silence, did not want to be friends. 'No thanks.'

114

The black-painted metal gates that enclosed Winter Kellaway's estate were open when they arrived. This struck Saul as odd, given the earlier security breach, but then he noticed a stream of vehicles arriving: a florist's van; several catering trucks; a woman with a video recorder in her hand and a camera slung around her neck. Two men were carrying a giant disco ball between them, fog dulling its silver mosaics.

'What's going on?' said Isaac, narrowly avoiding one of two decorative stone pineapples bracketing the driveway as he attempted to extract a fizzy cola bottle from his pocket while navigating the entrance and the weather.

'Looks like a party,' said Saul, rolling his eyes. He was not the kind of man who enjoyed parties.

They parked and made their way to the front of the grand house. Every window, even those on the two upper storeys, was lavishly festooned with garlands, flowers and hundreds of fairy lights.

Isaac gave a low whistle of surprise. 'There's some serious money here.'

A woman – tall and carrying a clipboard – shrieked at them from across the driveway. 'You can't park there.'

Saul stiffened, his hackles rising, as they always did when being told what to do by a stranger. It didn't bother him that she was a woman. But even though he would never admit to it, he was intimidated by her cut-glass accent and the gloss that seemed to go hand in hand with money and private education. It reminded him of what he'd never had.

Isaac spoke for them both, the mellifluous notes of his accent echoing hers. 'We're from Midtown Police. We're looking for Winter Kellaway.'

Her face softened, the edges of her cheekbones relaxing into prettiness. 'She's inside the house.' She smiled and stuck out her hand. 'Forgive me – I'm Marlowe Butler, Winter's PA.'

Isaac shook it, smiling back. 'I *thought* so. Did you go to school with Patrick Murphy?'

Marlowe beamed at him. 'Yes! How do you know Pat?'

'He's one of my best friends. I played rugby with him for years.'

'Such a good guy. So you probably know Daniel Parker too.'

'Know him? I went to the gym with him last night. And his girlfriend, Sofia Barnes.'

'Sofia lives on my road.' Her voice rose in excitement. 'We were in the same class at Bay College.' They laughed in mutual delight at their shared connections.

Bay College was an academically selective independent school in Midtown-on-Sea. Saul recognized the name because it was the same school that Piper Holden's children had attended. It had been a while since he'd thought about that dysfunctional family, whose disappearance had consumed him two years ago and had led him to Blue, but the dank weather and the excess of wealth reminded him.

Marlowe and Isaac were still laughing and chatting, brimming with a natural confidence that Saul did not – had never – possessed. He envied them, although he might not have chosen that word. The hand that Fate had dealt him had hardened him over the years, physically and emotionally. But cracks were forming in his carefully constructed carapace, and the detective did not enjoy these vulnerabilities because they made him feel.

Saul turned away, always the outsider. It didn't bother him, he told himself. At least, not much. But Blue had unlocked something in him: an unfamiliar desire to belong somewhere or to someone.

'When you've finished listing every person you have in common with Ms Butler, perhaps you could ask her to take us to Ms Kellaway.' His tone was more brusque than he'd intended. Isaac's face fell. Marlowe flushed before her features settled into a professional mask of bland neutrality. 'Of course,' she said. 'This way.'

Isaac couldn't stop staring. Saul had to nudge him into propriety, but he felt a pulse of sympathy for his colleague. It was difficult *not* to stare. Winter Kellaway was unlike anyone he'd met before. Saul felt uneasy about the way that women – and men – could be reduced to the sum of their bodies, the fullness of their lips, the shape of their faces, their height and weight and *desirability*. But while he had encountered beautiful women in the past, Winter Kellaway transcended them all. With money, time and motivation, most ordinary people could attain that glossy put-together look he saw every day on the affluent streets of Midtown. But Winter was so much more than her beauty. Charisma or star quality, or whatever the hell it was called these days, radiated from her.

The entrance hall of Winter Kellaway's home was a hive of activity. Men and women with clipboards and headsets, platters of canapés, silver buckets and armfuls of flowers, scurried back and forth. Marlowe directed them to a quiet corner where Winter was sitting in a low leather armchair, her slim legs crossed. The two police officers introduced themselves. Isaac mumbled his name, blushing as he spoke, but Saul had managed to pull himself together.

'I'm afraid I don't have much time,' she said, straightening an ivory ribbon on a wedding favour, an apologetic note in her voice. 'My sister is getting married in five hours and there's a *lot* to do before then.' She pointed to the rows of tissue-stuffed gift bags on the table in front of her, filled with Gucci cufflinks and Cartier bracelets, individual guests' names inked on each tag with extravagant penmanship. 'I need to check these.'

'It's OK,' said Saul. 'We just wanted to reassure you that we're doing all we can to find the intruder, and we'll need to take a brief statement from you, but we'll be as quick as we can.'

'Is he out?'

Her question caught Saul by surprise with its lack of pre-amble. 'Out?' As soon as the word had left him, he felt like an idiot. Of course he knew who she meant. Everyone did.

She wrapped her arms around herself, and the neckline of her cashmere jumper gaped to reveal a thickened ridge of scar tissue on her collarbone. The imperfection was start-ling. 'Of prison.'

The young detective furrowed his brow. 'If that was the case, you should have been informed of his release by your victim liaison officer, but I can check for you, if you'd like me to.'

Her eyes filled with tears. 'Thank you. Sorry, sorry.' She pressed the tips of her fingers to the undersides of her mascara-coated eyelashes, blinked rapidly and half smiled. 'Prevents smudges.'

Not sure how to respond, Saul shifted awkwardly and changed the subject, his gaze on a distant point behind her left shoulder. 'Do you have any CCTV from this morning?'

'Your colleagues have already downloaded it.'

'Mind if we take a look around your property?'

'Be my guest.'

The two officers wandered back into the grounds, leaving

Winter and the wedding planners to their duties. A vast heated marquee with a tunnel connecting it to the side of the house had been erected, and Saul glimpsed several circular tables decorated with pristine cloths, trailing displays of greenery studded with fat red berries, and antique candelabras that looked as if they cost more than a month's salary.

Within a couple of minutes, the fog had closed off their view of the house. Here, by the bay, it had begun to drift in patches, and Saul, standing at the edge of the estate that led down to the private beach, caught a glimpse of the gunmetal water. He slid his phone from his pocket to check if Blue had called him back, but still nothing.

'Do you believe her?' said Isaac suddenly.

Cold, concerned for Blue, and frustrated at having to go through the motions of what seemed like a public relations exercise, Saul appraised him, a sharp edge to his tone. 'What do you mean?'

'Winter. Did you see her face when you asked about the security footage?'

No. He'd been discomforted by her tears, and had looked away, out of respect and, if he was honest, embarrassment. 'I'm not sure that I did.' He sized up his colleague. 'Walk me through your train of thought.'

Isaac shrugged, nonchalant. 'She's an actor, isn't she? She's *very* good. But it just seemed a bit fake to me, that's all.'

'Go on.'

'Her stalker tried to abduct her a few years ago, right? Broke into her house. Threatened to kill her. Tried to drag her out and almost succeeded. That story made headlines around the world. I was a kid at the time and I can still remember it. If he *had* been released, it would have been big news. It's likely his parole hearing would have leaked. And his release date. All the news outlets both here and in the States would have gone to town on it.'

'Agreed.'

'Winter Kellaway is a household name. She's media savvy. She knows all that stuff better than we do.'

Saul studied his colleague, a reluctant – almost envious – admirer of his logic. 'But why would she pretend the intruder might be her stalker? It doesn't make sense.'

Isaac rummaged in his pocket and pulled out a fizzy sweet in the shape of a baby's dummy. He bit off the end of it. 'Why do you think people lie?'

'For all sorts of reasons.'

Isaac flattened his lips together and gently shook his head. 'I don't agree. When you boil it down to the bones, there are only two reasons.'

'And what might they be?'

He held Saul's gaze for a beat. 'To protect themselves – or someone else.'

17

Deborah

The young woman, cocooned in bed, was pinching the insides of her thighs until the tender patches of skin stung and turned pink. When she grew bored of that, she threw back the duvet, lifted her left leg as high as she could and examined the shape of her calf, repeatedly flexing her ankle.

Dismayed by what she saw, she scrambled to her feet and stood in front of her mirror, half turning left and then right, lifting her pyjama shorts to check for cellulite and its tell-tale dimpling.

Sucking in her cheeks, she pouted at her reflection. Her cheeks were too round and too pasty. Why couldn't she have the sun-kissed freckles and natural slenderness of Kate Moss in that Calvin Klein perfume advert that everyone had been going nuts about for the past few years?

Deborah knew she wasn't ugly because a model scout from one of the big agencies had stopped her outside Dorothy Perkins in the shopping centre last week and given her a business card, and men stared at her all the time when she walked past, which gave her a strange feeling of disgust and power; but she didn't have the edgy look that all the top models seemed to have. Kate Moss was only two years older than she was, and she was famous and dating Johnny bloody Depp, while Deborah was stuck in her boring bedroom in this boring town, her breasts and hips too pronounced to ever be called waifish.

Jen and Alyssa were whispering in the hallway. Those two were thick as thieves. She called out to them, unable to disguise her irritation. 'Shut up, you two. It's too early.' But the girls ignored her and burst, giggling, into her bedroom, piling onto her still-warm bed. 'Happy birthday, Deborah.'

She was celebrating her twenty-first, still living at home, but in her final year at a local university. Jen was fourteen and Alyssa was thirteen. Although she knew it was unkind, sometimes she wished her youngest sister wasn't there. It wasn't that she didn't love her. Because she did. Fiercely. With a protective impulse that comes from being born first. But as the eldest of the trio, Deborah resented the fact that she'd been forced into a position of responsibility by default while Alyssa – and Jen too – enjoyed the kind of idyllic childhood her parents had been too broke to provide when she'd been little. She was jealous, plain and simple.

Personality-wise, Jen had always been the mature one, and she and Deborah shared a lot with each other, despite their seven-year age gap. As for Alyssa, she had grown out of the cuteness that had softened the toddler years, and was now a newly minted teenager with several annoying habits. If Alyssa wasn't being a whiny brat, she was being treated like a princess by the rest of the family. Either way, it pissed Deborah off.

'Congratulations, you can now officially adopt a child. And drive a bus.' Jen put her arms around her elder sister's waist and hugged her tightly. 'What about a tattoo to mark the occasion? You can get one of Mark's face.' She let loose a peal of laughter at the thought.

'Mark and I broke up.'

'When? Why?'

'Last week. He said I was frigid.' Winter snorted. It wasn't frigid not to want to have sex without a condom, although she kept that thought to herself.

Jen placed her hands over Alyssa's ears – she took any opportunity to cement her status as the grown-up one – but her sister, eleven months and a school year younger, squirmed out of her reach. 'What's frigid?'

Both sisters ignored her. Jen folded her arms. 'Mark is an idiot.'

'What about you?' Deborah curled a strand of hair around her finger. 'How's it going with Mr Hot Stuff?'

Jen's eyes sparkled, her tone hopeful but cautious. 'I *think* he might actually like me.'

Deborah plonked herself on the bed and patted the duvet, inviting Jen to join her. Jen had nursed a crush on Dominic Ward since her first year in secondary school. It was the stuff of legend in the Kellaway household. She'd told anyone who'd listen about the time he'd bumped into her in the dining hall while she was carrying her lunch tray, and how he'd righted her bottle of cherry Panda Pops after it had fallen over. Or that morning break in Year 9 when his football had smacked her in the face, and he'd told her to go to the medical room because he could see a bruise forming and she might need an ice pack to take down the swelling. These limited interactions had fuelled Jen's crush until it had become a raging inferno, and she had longed for him to notice her in a more meaningful way, convinced it would happen one day.

At three and a half years her senior, he'd ignored her until a few weeks earlier when they'd bumped into each other at a party, and then she'd chatted to him a few times on the bus after school, and last night he'd called her from a phone box and invited her to the cinema the following week. Dominic had a car – a red Volkswagen Beetle – and a job at one of the fish and chip shops on the bay, and he had long hair that fell across his face like Jordan Catalano in *My So-Called Life*.

Alyssa made kissing sounds and pressed her lips to the back of her hand. Jen thumped her good-naturedly. Deborah grinned. 'When's the big date?'

Jen picked at a thread hanging from her nightshirt and pulled a face. 'I don't even know if Dad will let me go. You know what he's like about us getting into cars with older boys he hasn't met.'

'When are you going to open your presents?' Alyssa tugged at Deborah's pyjama top several times in rapid succession. 'Come on, let's go downstairs.'

Deborah shoved her away, irritated. 'Get off.'

'Is Debs-Debs feeling all grumpy?' She put on a baby voice, stretching out the vowel sounds until Deborah's fingernails curled into her palms, indenting the skin.

'Don't call me that.'

Alyssa repeated the diminutive, chanting it three times in a sing-song voice.

'Shut up, *Looby Loo*.'

Alyssa stuck out her tongue. 'Nope.'

'Then get out of my room.'

'Make me.'

Deborah grabbed Alyssa by her upper arm and began to drag her out. The girl cried out, calling for their mother.

'Mum's not here,' said Jen, the peacemaker, trying to smooth things over. 'She'll be back in a bit.' Deborah smirked at Alyssa, who pinched her arm in retaliation. Deborah bent back her youngest sister's wrist, causing Alyssa to scream. Jen put her hands on her hips, exasperated. 'Stop it, you two.'

'It's *my* birthday.' Although her voice was that of a young adult, Deborah's words were childish and sulky.

'She's thirteen.' Jen spoke softly. 'She's *supposed* to be immature. She doesn't mean it.'

Deborah rolled her eyes. 'Take her side, like you always do.' The accusation spilled from her before she could stop it, envious of the closeness between her younger sisters, and aware of her own immaturity, but unable to stop herself.

Jen was stung. 'I don't.'

Alyssa ran to Jen, and stood behind her for protection. She stuck her head around her sister. 'I do mean it.'

This time, Deborah ignored her, pointedly addressing her next comment to Jen. 'Shall we go out for breakfast? Just you and me. Celebrate my birthday in style.' She waited a beat. 'I'm buying.'

Jen chewed on a fingernail, not meeting Deborah's eye. 'I can't. I promised Mum I'd help Alyssa with her homework.'

Deborah sighed theatrically. She tried not to show how hurt she felt. 'Where is Mum anyway?'

'She had to pick something up. We could go for brunch instead. Or lunch.'

The older girl began to brush her hair. 'Let's not bother. You're obviously too busy.'

Deborah knew she was being unfair. But Alyssa infuriated her. She was always getting in the way, and it was clear Jen doted on her. She tried to dampen down that flicker of jealousy, but it burned, hot and bright.

'Come downstairs, at least.' There was a pleading note in Jen's voice. She had seen her elder sister in this mood before. 'All your presents are waiting for you. I can make pancakes.'

Deborah, too stubborn and too proud, found herself unable to bend at Jen's kindness. 'No thanks.' Tears pricked at her, but she blinked them away. It was her twenty-first birthday. Her father was at work, her mother had gone out without waiting for her to wake up, and her sister was choosing not to spend time with her.

Jen stood awkwardly by the door, waiting for her to change her mind. But Deborah's jaw was set and she turned her back on them both, busying herself with making the bed. Nirvana blasted out from her CD player.

Alyssa tugged Jen's sleeve. 'Shall we go to the library? It's quiet there. We can work on my Kew Gardens project, and buy magazines and sweets on the way back.' At thirteen, she spent her pocket money as soon as she received it.

'Why don't you come with us?' Jen's tone was placatory, warm. 'We could get breakfast at the cafe by the park. It'll be fun.'

But her sister stayed silent, coolly ignoring them.

Bored, Alyssa started to fidget, pulling on Jen's dressing-gown belt. 'Can we go now?'

Deborah waited for Jen to ask again. She'd go with them if she did, she decided, and she turned, anticipating the invitation, heart already lifting. But Jen didn't ask. Alyssa reached out a hand to the middle Kellaway sister, and Jen took it, and the younger girls slipped from Deborah's bedroom without a backward glance.

The nightclub was heaving. Deborah sipped her Bacardi Breezer and observed how the strobe lighting transformed the crowd into a mechanical army with limbs that moved and jerked in slow motion.

Her friends were somewhere on the dance floor, but they'd got separated half an hour ago and she couldn't find them. They were supposed to be getting a taxi home together – her parents would go mad if she left the nightclub on her own as they'd always insisted the girls stick together when they went out – but she was tired. It was noisy and late and she wanted to go to bed.

She sipped her drink. Her friends would worry if she disappeared, especially as this was supposed to be her birthday night out, and she wasn't sure if she had enough money for the fare anyway. She would do one more circuit of the club and toilets, and if she couldn't find them, she would leave. Although he'd be cross, her father would come to collect her if she called him from the phone box on the corner.

Deborah scanned the sea of bodies through the dry ice, music thrumming in her ears, but there was no sign of either Fran or Elspeth, her two best friends. She wandered up the stairs to the next level of the club, which was filled with sofas and dark corners, and had a different vibe. Maybe they'd met some boys and had got distracted.

She was so busy looking for her friends that she wasn't watching where she was going and bumped into a tall boy with a mop of dark hair and a secret sort of a smile, spilling his drink over his pale shirt and chinos.

'Sorry, sorry,' she said, longing for the ground to swallow her up and digging into her handbag for a tissue to offer him.

'No sweat,' he said, 'although it does look like I've wet myself now.'

She covered her face with her hands. To be fair to him, that's exactly what it looked like. It was quieter up here, but she could hear the distant thump of another dance track she didn't like. It had been a mistake to come tonight. This was not her type of place. She risked a glance at him through her fingers.

As soon as she looked at him properly, she recognized him. It was Dominic Ward, her sister's crush. He'd been three years below Deborah at school and she'd never paid him much attention. But he was older now, and standing here, in the dim lights of the club, she saw the attraction.

She smoothed out her gold sequinned dress, straightened her back and smiled at him. 'You know my sister.'

He grinned back at her. 'Jen Kellaway. And you're Deborah.'

'You know who I am?' She tilted her head, a mild flirtatious tone to her voice.

'*Everyone* knows who you are.' He paused for a moment, held her gaze. 'Fittest girl in the school, past or present.'

Deborah considered her position. It would be sisterly to call him out for that.

'I don't think you should be saying that to me. Haven't you asked my sister to the cinema?'

He shrugged. 'Yeah. She's fit too. And funny.'

'And three years younger than you,' she said, an archness to her tone.

'So what?' He grinned again. 'It's only the cinema. We're not getting married. And, like I said, she's cute.'

If Deborah had had a shred of self-respect, she would have walked away at that moment. But like many young women, she lacked confidence in herself. And on that night, on the cusp of adulthood, it felt like Jen was always the one that everyone preferred. Their mother. Alyssa. And now Dominic.

She blew out her lips and crossed her eyes. 'I can be cute too.'

He laughed, a warm sound that made him instantly more attractive. 'Drink?'

'Aren't you underage?' she said in a teasing voice.

'Fake ID,' he said.

'I was on my way home, to be honest. I've lost my friends and I'm tired.'

'Excellent timing. I'm heading off too. Do you want a lift?'

She raised her eyebrows and looked pointedly at the glass in his hand.

'It's lemonade. I'm underage, remember?'

Outside, it was cold, the kind of early spring night that still had bite. Deborah shivered in her thin dress and Dom handed her a hoodie from the back seat of his car. It smelled of deodorant and washing powder. The city lights polluted the night sky but, if she stared for long enough, Deborah could pick out a handful of stars. She was young and beautiful, and her body thrummed with that knowledge.

Dom's car was covered in frost and they sat in the darkness, waiting for the heater to thaw it out. He put on some music, an indie band with jangly guitars she hadn't heard of before, and it made her feel as if the night was full of possibility. She liked that. Deborah closed her eyes and lost herself in it. The song changed, a softer, more intimate track. She shifted in her seat to look at him in profile. In an echo of her movement, he turned and smiled at her, slow and sweet, and her stomach performed a lazy flip. She reminded herself he was Jen's.

But he isn't really, is he? Her inner voice, seductive and dangerous, whispered to her. *They haven't even been on that date yet. Yes, Jen likes him, but what if I like him too?*

'Ready to go?' he said.

Deborah nodded, not trusting herself to speak.

They drove through the quiet streets, past curtains-closed lights-out houses folded up for the night. In the moonshine, the icy pavements glinted, and Deborah thought she might remember this journey forever. In the closeted privacy of this car with a boy on the cusp of manhood, she was aware of every moment, every breath, every word not spoken.

Too soon, they were pulling into Deborah's road.

'Can you drop me off here?' she said, several houses away from her own. 'My parents don't like me getting into cars with boys they don't know or trust.'

'Sounds sensible.' He grinned, and it struck her again how handsome he was. They sat in silence for a moment. Deborah took off his hoodie and handed it back. 'Keep it,' he said. One of the straps of her dress slid down her shoulder, exposing her skin, but she made no move to put it back.

'When are you going to the cinema with Jen?'

He shrugged, his expression neutral. 'Not sure I want to now.'

'What? Why?'

But she knew. She just wanted him to say it.

Dominic tapped his fingers against the steering wheel. He peered at her sideways from beneath his long fringe. 'I didn't know you when I asked her out, did I?'

'No,' she said, her eyes locking with his. 'You didn't.'

Everything stilled apart from her heart, which beat harder and faster than it had done all night. She was aware of every sound and sensation, especially the charge in the air between them. She knew what was coming and so did he.

Dom reached out and lifted the strap back onto her shoulder. He traced the ridge of a childhood scar. Stroked the soft hollow behind her ear. The touch of his warm fingers against her skin thrilled her.

She didn't think about the friends she had left behind in the nightclub, or the fact she had broken two of her parents' rules in the last half an hour, or about the consequences of any of those actions.

As for Jen, she didn't think about her at all, except for a fleeting moment when she acknowledged to herself that although Dom was handsome, he was a bit too young and not her type. But she enjoyed the attention, especially as Jen had ignored her that morning in favour of Alyssa, and she wanted to punish her for that, and, in an odd way, protect her too, from a boy who could trample on her heart with such ease.

Deborah Kellaway leaned across the handbrake and kissed him.

18

Blue

Five men. Two by the door. Two by the window. One standing at the top of the stairs. Blue estimated it would take her thirteen seconds to evade them, if necessary. The one by the stairs was at least twice her weight. He might prove difficult. But she was nimble enough to duck under his arm and could probably outrun him if she needed to. She was faster now. Much faster.

'Are you going to be long?'

The woman with the bleached ponytail and hard face inspected her nails while she waited for Blue to answer.

'Yes, actually. I am.'

A pair of perfectly arched eyebrows lifted but the woman's forehead did not move. She huffed, uncertain, as if she wasn't used to others pushing back, especially a slight twenty-something with a flash of hair the colour of a summer sky. When it was clear that Blue had meant what she'd said, the woman stared her down as she swigged from her water bottle, then turned and walked across the gym towards the battle ropes without another word.

But Blue didn't care. She tightened the buckle on her thick leather belt, widened her stance and bounced on the balls of her feet, adjusting her frame. Then she bent over the metal bar and gripped it with her gloved hands. A couple of days ago, she had dead-lifted a hundred kilos. Today, she was attempting to beat her own record.

She breathed in, a deep intake of air that swelled her lungs and sent the blood spinning through her. Pushing through her legs, bracing her back, using her feet as twin anchors, she gave herself over to the hidden well of strength in her body, the muscles working as one, a kind of poetry in motion. Everything felt loose, powerful. Earlier, she'd strapped up her hands with tape and pulled on boxing gloves, drumming them against the punchbag until exhaustion forced her to stop. She'd run on the treadmill until sweat poured from her. She'd done press-ups and sit-ups, handstands and lunges. But now it was time for the battle between her body and her mind.

Sometimes it was easy, the lifts as smooth and comfortable as she could hope for, and she went home with a sense of pride, of progress being made.

Sometimes, even if she had lifted the same weight the previous week, her body refused to comply.

Except it wasn't the fault of her body, lean and powerful now, but the dark spaces in her mind that whispered she didn't deserve to be strong, that she was weak and wanting, and that police officer, a stranger who had forced himself on her, was the first of many who would sniff out her vulnerabilities and use them to destroy her.

This was why she knew the position of every man in the gym. Who had arrived and who had left. She knew the men who lingered by the female changing rooms, trying to engage in conversation, and those who watched women as they worked out, eyes sliding over their bodies. She did this to empower herself, to console herself with the knowledge that she would never again be unprepared. But still the two-headed monster of shame and disgust taunted her. Despite her physical transformation, the muscles that were now hard and defined, the legs that could outrun almost anyone, it would never be enough to erase the memory of what he had stolen from her.

Blue closed her eyes, shut off her thoughts and focused on the barbell in front of her. She thought only of the challenge ahead, clearing her mind of everything but the feel of the metal beneath the exposed tips of her fingers, the cut of Velcro into her wrist.

But as she prepared to lift, something stalled her. A change in the texture of the air. A quietening of the low-level chatter to a pause, the throb of music filling the empty space left behind.

She opened her eyes, hands still gripped around the bar.

Three uniformed police officers were standing in front of her, their expressions grim. Time slowed. Her surroundings blurred in the way a photograph might lose its background focus until the central image was pinpoint sharp. She could pick out the shaving rash on the chin of the first officer, scabbed over where he'd nicked himself that morning, and the open pores on his nose. The other constable was taller than she was, and she was briefly distracted by a ketchup stain on his shirt collar and the smell of sweat beneath the chemical artificiality of his body spray. The third officer – a woman she recognized, with sharp features that lent her a murine appearance – was unsmiling, lacking in warmth.

Her heart rate climbed.

When Blue was seven, the police had arrived at their family home in the middle of a perfect summer's night. She'd been asleep, but the windows were open, and she'd woken to the scent of jasmine and the echoing slam of a car door. Through a crack in the curtains, the moon had pooled on the carpet and she'd jumped over it, like she did when her mother told her to mind the puddles.

She'd known she wasn't supposed to be out of bed. But she'd heard voices at the bottom of the stairs, and she'd crawled across the landing, comfort blanket in hand, even though her mother had warned her she was too old for such babyish things and threatened to put it in the bin.

The house looked different at night. The familiar shapes became monsters in the dark. When the cat landed with a soft thud behind her, she'd let out a scream and then covered her mouth with her hand. She'd held her breath, expecting her mother to run upstairs and chastise her, but it was her sister who'd dropped to the carpet beside her, older by two years. 'What's happening, Lucky?'

She'd whispered back, breath hot against Macy's ear, 'I don't know.'

The girls had lain side by side, faces pressed against the spindles that ran the length of the hallway. A male voice, low and sombre, asked if he could come in. The girls caught a flash of their mother's towelling dressing gown as she stepped aside to let him enter, followed by the squeak of the sitting-room door. Mrs March had complained only that morning that its hinges needed oiling.

The air was cloying, heavy with heat, the kind of night without a breath of breeze. The girls waited, chins resting on their folded arms, straining for the slightest hint of voices, some indication of the reason for this nocturnal visitation. One after the other, they nodded off, the late hour and the stifling temperature making it impossible for them to resist the lure of sleep.

Some time later, Blue stirred, her left arm buzzing with pins and needles. The back of her hand was wet with drool. She blinked, not sure where she was. Macy was next to her, dark hair falling over her face, knees curled into her night-shirt. Their mother was standing above them.

Blue did not move, holding her breath. Mrs March stared down at her daughters, but Blue had the sense that she wasn't seeing them. That vacancy of expression frightened her. She stretched out her foot until it was digging into Macy, willing her to wake up.

The upstairs landing was filled with grey light, the begin-nings of a new day. In the dawn, her mother was pale, the colour drained from her. A high-pitched noise was coming from her mouth.

Macy sat up, hair sticking out at angles. A man – tall, that's all she remembered, and uniformed – ran up the stairs, two at a time, followed by a woman. Police.

'Why are you here?' Macy looked from the man to her mother. Mrs March closed her eyes and tears spilled down her face.

The man crouched next to the girls. Blue never forgot that. He made himself as small as they were.

'I'm sorry,' he said.

Their father – Jonathan March – had been killed in a helicopter crash that evening as he made his way back from a business meeting in Germany. Engine failure was the most probable cause, but the recovery mission had been hampered by bad weather, loss of light and the inaccessibility of the crash site in a mountainous region of dense forest. All three passengers had been killed: the pilot, their father and family friend Dina Wright.

'Why was Dina there?' As soon as Macy said those words, Blue knew it was a mistake. Her mother, instead of comforting her daughters, let out a sob and ran into her bedroom, slamming the door.

The police officers stayed with the girls until their grandmother arrived. Seventeen years had passed since that night, but Blue still remembered, with vivid clarity, the expression on their faces – grim and unsmiling – when they'd appeared at the top of the stairs.

The officers standing in front of her now were wearing the same expression.

Her first thought was that someone had died. Her mother, who had recently been diagnosed with rapid-onset dementia and was now in a home, or Macy, halfway across the world. She waited for them to break apart her life, to dismantle it with words yet to be spoken, and they did, but not in the way she was expecting.

'Dr Clover March?'

She nodded, looking from one face to the next. She unstrapped her gloves, trying not to display her trepidation, her usual sarcasm deserting her. 'What's this about? It's my day off.'

The officer with the ketchup stain introduced himself as PC Mike Bell from Suffolk Police. A thousand thoughts – some of them treacherous – raced through her brain. Her sister was working in South America for a year, and Blue's thoughts kept returning to her. *Whatever else has happened, please let Macy be OK.*

He stepped forward then, formal, as if he was about to ask her to dance or to take a bow. But instead he looked her in the eye and his words fell upon her like tiny bombs.

Afterwards, in the back of a patrol car, she did not think about the rights she'd been read, or what her family might say, or whether Saul, lost somewhere in his own pain, was facing the same horsemen of the apocalypse. She couldn't. The cool-headedness she was known for had vanished. Panic held her in its grip. Instead, she replayed his first sentence – damning, terrifying, life-changing – over and over again.

'Clover March, I'm arresting you on suspicion of the murder of Detective Constable Douglas Lynch.'

19

Deborah

Every house was in darkness on Deborah's road except for her own. Her digital watch told her it was creeping towards 4 a.m., two hours past her allotted curfew, and she knew before she'd even turned her key in the lock that she was in serious trouble.

Her parents were sitting on the sofa in the living room in their dressing gowns, each clutching a mug of tea. A bottle of wine was open on the table, two empty glasses with a ruby residue at their base. Her mother's eyes were red and swollen. Her father's face was grim.

'Where the hell have you been?'

'Clubbing. I *told* you where I was going.'

'The club shut two hours ago. You weren't in it. Elspeth's mother rang to tell us the girls couldn't find you anywhere. They were distraught. They thought something had happened to you.' A pause filled with the fears and heartbreak of parenthood. 'We all did.'

For years, Deborah had convinced herself that her parents

didn't love her as much as they loved her sisters. And, even now, she lacked the emotional maturity to recognize their concern came from a place of tenderness and care. Instead of trying to placate them, she bristled at the criticism, as she'd done since she was a child.

'I'm here now, aren't I? My friends went off without me and I couldn't find them. As you can see, I'm absolutely fine. Now if it's all right with you, I'd like to go to bed.' Her words dripped with sarcasm.

'Don't be so bloody rude.' Her father's cheeks reddened. 'We've been worried sick. An apology wouldn't go amiss.'

'Sorry.' But she didn't sound it.

Her mother spoke for the first time since Deborah had walked in. 'How did you get home?'

'I used some of my birthday money to get a taxi.'

Her father softened, shaking his head. 'Don't do that, love. Next time, call me and I'll come and pick you up.'

She folded her arms, always on the offensive. 'Of course I will, Dad.' She gestured at the table. 'That's if you haven't been drinking, or you're not at work, or too busy with Alyssa and Jen to bother about me on my twenty-first birthday.'

She flounced out of the living room, aware she was in the wrong but unable to admit it, and paused outside the door to eavesdrop on the conversation she knew would follow. Inevitably, it was about her behaviour.

'She's so selfish,' her father said. 'As cold as ice.'

Her mother murmured in agreement. 'Our girls are as different as the seasons, Geoff. And we love them for it.'

He grunted. 'Some are easier to love than others.'

'She's testing boundaries, love. That's all. Finding her place in the family. We've always encouraged them to stick up for themselves and each other, to celebrate their differences and to be their own people. We can't complain when they do what we've asked.'

Deborah climbed the stairs to her bedroom, shivering in her thin dress and Dom's hoodie. She lay awake, wide-eyed in the darkness, boiling with resentment towards them all. Not for the first time, she longed for different parents. A different life.

She wondered how it would feel to come home to a mother who didn't make her feel guilty and a father who wasn't angry. To feel loved and wanted and special.

Hurt, she replayed the words her father had spoken about her. *As cold as ice.* If Jen was the summer sun and Alyssa the autumn rain, then she, Deborah, would become a winter storm.

20

Jen

Winter's make-up artist was transforming Jen into a stranger.

'I don't usually wear smoky eyeshadow. I prefer a more natural look.'

'Trust me,' said the woman, who was called Katya. 'I will turn you into a goddess.' Jen didn't want to be a goddess. She wanted to be Jen Miller.

Katya applied a layer of Espresso Night to her eyelids, followed by several coats of mascara. She stood back, appraising Jen, a make-up brush tucked behind her ear. 'Maybe we should try some false eyelashes. Do you agree?'

'No.' If Jen sounded short, she intended to. She wanted to look like a better version of herself, not someone who Phil wouldn't recognize. He preferred it when she didn't wear any make-up at all. 'And no red lipstick either. Something neutral. A rose pink, if you have it.'

Katya tutted, but she did as Jen requested and wiped away the dark eyeshadow, which Jen had found unflattering and ageing.

A few minutes later, Winter appeared in the cottage wearing a silk dressing gown and carrying two glasses of champagne. She placed one on the table for Jen, handed one to Katya and fiddled on her phone for some music. A song about going to the chapel and getting married blared out of the expensive sound system.

Jen noticed that her sister's make-up had already been done: a soft cream eyeshadow and a pale glossy lip. It looked classy and sophisticated, and exactly what she'd wanted. There wasn't a false eyelash in sight. It was also a remarkable turnaround from that morning when she'd been red-eyed and distraught. But it made sense. Her sister was an actor, adept at putting on a mask.

'Now,' said Winter, perching on a stool next to Jen and crossing her legs. 'We have a little surprise planned for you.'

Jen groaned inwardly, but mustered a smile. It was too late to do anything about it now, so she might as well allow herself to be swept along with it. 'That sounds exciting. What kind of surprise?'

'I can't tell you *that*.' Winter shrieked with laughter at her audacity. 'You'll love it, I promise. But it does mean Alyssa and Mum won't be getting ready here, I'm afraid.'

Jen was ambushed by a profound sense of disappointment. She'd been looking forward to that part of her wedding day more than she'd realized. She'd wanted to see Teddy in his suit, and help Iris put flowers in her hair, and show off her dress before the ceremony when there'd be too many guests to concentrate on her family for more than a few minutes. She'd wanted to drink too much champagne, and dance around the cottage, and distract herself from her nerves. She'd wanted to be with her sisters. She didn't doubt that Winter meant well but she had badly misread the situation. Not for the first time today, it appeared that no one cared about what the bride wanted.

Her face must have betrayed her because Winter's expression clouded. 'Don't be like that, Jen. It will be worth it, honestly. And I thought you'd appreciate some time alone on such a manic day.'

Jen swallowed down her feelings. It was something she was used to doing, especially where her eldest sister was concerned. She wanted to say, 'It's kind of you, Winter, and I do appreciate it, but next time, can you run it past me? Of course I don't want to be by myself.' But instead she said, 'OK, thank you. I'll look forward to it.'

'Right, I must dash now.' Winter kissed her on the cheek. 'Everything looks fabulous, so don't worry about anything except drinking that glass of champagne.'

'Have you heard from Phil?' Jen was surprised she hadn't heard from him all morning, especially today of all days.

'Why? Are you worried he's not going to turn up?' Winter laughed at her joke, but stopped when she saw Jen's face.

'Hilarious.' Jen was deadpan. 'No, it's just unusual, that's all.'

Winter busied herself with Jen's bouquet, a clutch of cream roses which had been placed in the cottage in a small vase of water by the florist earlier that morning. 'These are stunning.' A pause. 'Do you want me to ring him for you? Perhaps he got drunk at his stag do and has been tied to a lamp-post with his eyebrows shaved off.'

'Don't say that. Can you try Federico too?'

'On it, sis.' Winter blew Jen a kiss. 'The hairdresser will be here in half an hour, OK?' She gave an excited squeal. 'See you at the altar.' She turned to Katya. 'Ready to go?'

Katya, who had been silent throughout this exchange, spritzed setting spray on Jen's face and drained her champagne glass. 'All done.' She gathered together her brushes and cosmetics, and the two women left.

The cottage felt empty after that. Jen wasn't sure what to do with herself. She'd anticipated a busy morning with people coming and going, music and laughter. But she was sitting here on her own and getting maudlin. She hoped Phil was having a better day than she was.

Her phone buzzed with a WhatsApp message. Her mother had sent a video of Teddy and Iris, and her heart swelled with love. She gave herself a mental shake. This was her – *very expensive* – wedding day, courtesy of Winter, and she was going to enjoy it. She would see them after the ceremony and give them a cuddle then.

Iris was already in her party frock, and she was solemnly showing off her white tights and black patent Mary Janes. At eight, she looked so grown-up and Jen's eyes filled with tears. Those years had passed in a flash.

Teddy was buzzing with excitement, hopping from one foot to the next. 'Happy wedding day, Mama!' he shouted into the screen. Iris put her fingers to his mouth to shush him and imitated her mother's voice when she was trying to be stern. 'Say it properly.'

The little boy leaned forward, put his hands on his knees and whispered so that she could barely hear him, 'Happy wedding day, Mama.'

Iris tutted and elbowed him out of the way. 'Hello, Mum. Teddy and me wanted to say have a lovely day and we will see you later.'

'On the boat!' Teddy shouted again.

Iris turned to him, furious. 'Be quiet. That's supposed to be a surprise.' She turned back to the camera. 'Forget he said that. Bye, Mummy.'

That made Jen snort with laughter. 'Goodbye, you two.' She pressed her fingertip to their freeze-framed faces. A boat? She wasn't sure how she felt about that. But that explained why Winter had been so insistent on erecting a floral arch at the end of the jetty. It might be fun. A flicker of excitement replaced her nerves.

Her wedding was going to be a spectacle that no one would ever forget.

21

Alyssa

Alyssa slammed her mug of tea onto the table and swore under her breath when its contents sloshed everywhere. She loved her sister, but this was peak Winter. The idea of bundling herself and the baby into their wedding finery in order to catch a specially chartered pleasure boat on a freezing cold afternoon was less appealing than piercing her eyeballs with a rusty knitting needle.

What on earth had Winter been thinking? Even though the journey was short, their hair would be ruined. And possibly their shoes.

On reflection, it didn't take a genius to deduce why Winter had arranged for them all to arrive in such a theatrical manner. She'd *told* them it would be a wonderful surprise for Phil and Jen, but Alyssa knew that Winter thrived on being the centre of attention. With a grand entrance like this, there was a strong chance they'd outshine the bride on her own wedding day.

Oh, stop being such a bitch. She's only trying to be nice. Alyssa disliked this trait in herself, an instinct to seek out the negative. Jen always gave everyone the benefit of the doubt. She would try to be more like her.

She glanced at the clock on the kitchen wall. She ought to head to Jen's house now. She was meeting her mother there, so they could all get ready together, and then Winter was going to pick them up in her chauffeur-driven car and take them to the pier in town to catch the boat.

Her mobile phone rang, making her jump. She picked it up and stared at the screen. *Private number.* A rush of cortisol, and then she buried the handset at the bottom of her bag. This was not an issue she wanted to deal with today. Or any day.

As a general rule, she didn't answer numbers she didn't recognize or callers who withheld their identity. If they wanted to reach her, they could leave a message. But she'd received a similar call a couple of weeks ago, when she was babysitting Teddy, and her desire to silence the ringing before it woke up the four-year-old had compelled her to answer that time.

'Hello?'

'Can I speak to Ms Matthews, please?'

The colour had drained from her face. She'd run her tongue around her lips, trying to moisten them. 'I'm afraid you've got the wrong number.'

The voice, male and well modulated, did not falter. 'I don't think that's the case. We've conducted some thorough and extensive enquiries.' His voice softened. 'We've spent a long time looking for you. Several years. There's nothing to worry about, I promise.'

'Who's calling?'

'My name is Stephen Pearson. I'm a solicitor at Pearson, Parker and Walker. Do you have a few minutes to talk? I can explain everything.'

'You've got the wrong number,' she'd said again, but her voice lacked her earlier conviction.

'It would be in your best interests,' he'd said. 'I'm going to text our number to your phone, and when you're ready, please do give me a call.'

Alyssa hung up.

22

Saul

Back at Midtown police station, Saul sent a couple of emails to the relevant authorities, enquiring about the whereabouts of Winter Kellaway's attacker. It was Saturday lunchtime, so he didn't expect answers. Weekends were notorious for that. But he was certain that Isaac's hunch would prove to be correct, and the man in question was still in prison.

He'd tried to call Blue again, but she hadn't responded. A stone settled in his stomach. He couldn't ask too many questions without arousing suspicion, but he listened for whispers that might prove useful until he could bear the tension no longer. In search of distraction, he slipped out of the station and walked until he reached the wide expanse of the salt marshes, which were shrouded in fog. The cold air cleansed him.

As he arrived back at the coastguard's lookout for a quick bowl of soup, his mobile rang. The number was unfamiliar, but instinct nudged him to pick up.

'Saul?'

He'd known it was her before she'd even had a chance to finish speaking his name. She sounded distant, but her voice was striated with an undercurrent of fear. A burst of cortisol flooded his system, and he felt his concentration sharpen, as it did whenever he was in her orbit.

'Is everything OK?'

'I've been arrested.' Blue's voice cracked as she said it. Three words freighted with catastrophe. Even though it felt like he'd been holding his breath for months, even though he'd been waiting for this to happen from the moment he'd driven the metal tip of his cane into the skull of the police officer who'd raped Blue, her words were a punch to his stomach. He doubled over, his breath snatched from him, blindsided by the physicality of his shock.

'Saul?' Her voice was small, afraid, no hint of the defiant and sarcastic young woman he was used to. 'Are you still there?'

He forced himself upright, to think. She was ringing him to warn him, he was certain of that, and the irony didn't escape him, but it occurred to him that he had no idea how she would react under this kind of pressure. She was cool, yes. Quick-witted. But both of them were implicated in the murder of Detective Constable Douglas Lynch. Both of them were guilty. Under police questioning, would her nerve hold? Or would she feed him to the wolves?

'I'm here.' Synapses firing, he made himself steady his voice and interrogate his reactions. He needed to act as if he was in the dark, as if he had no idea why she'd been detained. 'On what grounds have they arrested you?'

She whispered the word to him, confirming his worst suspicions: 'Murder.'

A harsh bark of laughter from Saul. He forced himself to sound surprised. 'Murder? That's ridiculous.'

'I know.' He wasn't sure if it was his imagination, but her voice seemed stronger, more determined. This was the Blue he knew and loved. His brain went into overdrive, trying to think of the questions that an innocent party would ask, but his tone was restrained, knowing he needed to protect them both.

'You need legal representation.'

'I know,' she said again. 'The duty solicitor is on his way.'

'Where are you?'

'The station in Midtown. But I think they might move me soon.'

He wanted to tell her that everything was going to be OK. But words failed him. Because Saul was a truth-teller when it came to those he loved, and he couldn't promise her that. They'd been so careful. Meticulous, even. But Saul knew that a clock had been set from the moment the Chief Constable had asked him to secretly investigate the woman he loved.

No one at Midtown Police knew about his intimate relationship with Blue. If they had been discovered, he had planned to lie, to insist it had been part of his plan to extract a confession. But the truth was this: he had done as he'd been ordered because he'd recognized that knowledge was power, that he would be better placed to protect her from suspicion if he was inside this clandestine circle of trust.

But a stray piece of evidence had connected Blue to the scene of Lynch's death, and although he had methodically destroyed anything incriminating that his own enquiries had uncovered, he could not protect her from the wider investigation.

It had been almost a year since DC Lynch, profoundly frightened of birds, had been found in bed at his home, a blunt force injury at the back of his head and multiple lacerations across the upper half of his body from being attacked by a seagull. The official cause of death had been Takotsubo cardiomyopathy, a thickening of the heart muscle induced by fear. But investigators had been perplexed by the presence of a large seabird inside Lynch's home when all the windows had been locked from the inside and the chimney was blocked up.

With every day that passed, Saul had discovered that instead of breathing a little easier, a tension had crept into his bones, waiting for the axe to fall. Now it had. But it was Blue's neck on the executioner's block instead of his own.

'I have to go now,' she said. 'But I wanted to let you know what was happening, OK?'

An impulse to tell her that he was wildly in love with her consumed him. He wanted to say everything that had been left unspoken between them. These last few months, he had given her space because she had needed it, letting her take the lead in their friendship – *relationship* – or whatever it was, especially when it came to the intimacy that had once been so natural between them. An insular man, slow to open himself up, he had found in her a sanctuary he had never expected, but she was harder to read. Sometimes, with her eyes closed and her skin pressed to his, that exhalation of breath as he touched her, he recognized she needed him as a route to oblivion, and sometimes, when she looked at him across the table, that smile playing across her lips, or when she rested her head on his shoulder, or fell asleep in his lap, he thought she might love him back. But now was not the time to find out.

'Take care,' he said. 'The solicitor will sort things out. You'll be home before you know it.'

'If you need to collect your things from mine, you know where the key is. Goodbye, Saul.' She hung up.

A click, followed by the sound of dead air. He frowned, stung by the abrupt end to their call, the lack of even a hint of affection, even though the rational part of his brain told him that the custody sergeant was probably signalling at her to finish up, and her instinct was to protect him.

He stood at the window, watching the tide push against rocks clad in seaweed, clusters of barnacles like hundreds of watchful eyes. In the distance, a patrol car drove along the coast road and he froze for a moment, convinced it would turn left, crossing the salt marshes to the coastguard's lookout, but it drove onwards towards the beach huts at the edge of the bay.

Saul replayed the last words of their conversation. *If you need to collect your things from mine, you know where the key is.* As far as he was aware, he hadn't left any of his belongings at her flat. He travelled light, an old habit from his patchwork childhood. She knew that too, so why had she said that?

A thud startled him, and he turned towards its source. A gull, lost in the fog, had flown into the small sitting-room window that looked sideways, not across the water, but towards Midtown's church, a white clapboard structure. An imprint of its outstretched wings, left by the dust that waterproofed its feathers, curved across the glass, an angel's calling card.

And then Saul was running, faster than he had done in months, ignoring the protest of pain in his back, out of his front door and down the shingle path towards his car.

The traffic was heavy, the cloak of fog slowing the progress of the afternoon shoppers. Saul cursed as he drove towards Blue's flat, forced into a detour by the 'Closed Road' signs that seemed to have multiplied since he'd been there the previous night, watching over her.

He drummed his fingers against the steering wheel, frustrated by the delay, but accepting of it. A sprawling badger sett had undercut the cliffs at the far end of town, causing them to become dangerously unstable, leaving cracks in the tarmac of some residential roads. Although badgers did not hibernate, they spent much of their waking hours underground during the winter months and were protected from the council suits who wanted to evict them. Saul enjoyed this fact. He preferred animals to most people and it amused him that they could traverse their habitat, that network of tunnels beneath the ground, without interruption while humans were forced into diversions and queues.

Blue's flat was on the ragged edges of Midtown. Fast-food joints and overflowing wheelie bins replaced the artisan bakeries and chocolatiers where tourists spent their holiday money and affluent locals posed for their Instagram shots. This was the hidden underbelly of the town, that leaking overspill beneath the rubbish sacks, crawling with vermin. Even the most beautiful places had them.

He drove past a house where a known paedophile lived, the bus stop opposite teeming with schoolchildren every morning and afternoon, and there wasn't a damn thing Saul could do about it. Past a bail hostel and past a run-down bungalow where the remains of an elderly woman had lain undiscovered for months until the neighbours had complained about the smell. He knew the addresses of the headteacher who'd defrauded his school of funds and of the mother who sold her secret self while her baby cried in the room next door as punters paid to choke her in the dark. In some ways, the detective felt more at home amid the moral decay. It was familiar, like a well-thumbed book. The bayside of Midtown-on-Sea might be close to paradise, but everyone knew about the serpent in the Garden of Eden.

The key was hidden in a nesting box, discreetly nailed to a tree close to the entrance of Blue's flat. He removed the lid and there it was, a silver secret, hidden among the debris of leaves and twigs. His fingers brushed the tiny skeleton of a chick that must have died before it fledged, left behind by its brothers and sisters to decompose in a wooden grave.

He hung back for a beat, concerned about what he might find, gauging his position. But if there was a warrant to search the premises, it hadn't been executed yet. The key slid into the lock and opened the front door with a sharp click.

Her flat was in silence, undisturbed by even the mewl of her cat. But he could smell traces of her perfume, and her breakfast plate was still on the table, a pair of uneaten crusts hardening as the hours passed.

Saul prowled from room to room – the kitchen, the compact bathroom, her bedroom – opening drawers and searching for a sign. But everything was as it should be.

He stood in the hallway, perplexed. He was certain he hadn't imagined the coded message she had voiced over the phone, but he doubted himself. And then he saw it. The portmanteau tucked by the side of her wardrobe.

When he was a boy, Saul had once unzipped a suitcase belonging to his father. His mother, Gloria, drunk and incautious, had told him that Solomon had been across the sea on a boat to buy cigarettes to sell in the pub. It had sounded impossibly exotic to Saul, who hadn't travelled further than Ruislip to visit his paternal grandparents one ill-fated Christmas. Saul, looking for a matchbox to store a dead wasp beetle he'd found by the bins at the back of their flat, had assumed he would find one in his father's case. In his nine-year-old mind, cigarettes and matches went together like Batman and Robin.

The suitcase hadn't contained cigarettes but clear bags of powder packed together like bricks. Saul had gently placed the beetle – scientific name *Clytus arietis* – next to him, marvelling at its glossy black body with neat yellow banding that mimicked its namesake. He picked up one of the bags, curiosity overcoming his fear of his father, but caught the edge of it on the teeth of the zip. Through the tear in the plastic, a fine white snow sprinkled the carpet and Saul's bare legs. To him, it looked like sherbet, but it smelled both bitter and sweet, like kerosene with a floral undercurrent. Years later, he would discover that drug canines were trained to detect the odour of methyl benzoate because of its similarity to coca leaves, their alkaloid extracted to make cocaine. But the boy he was didn't know that.

Instead, he sucked his finger and dipped it into the powder, a generous helping, wrinkling his nose at its pungency, so different from the Dip Dabs he bought from the sweet shop on the rare occasions his mother gave him twenty pence. He repeated the motion, to see if anything had changed, but it tasted odd, unlike anything within his realm of experience. A minute or two later, the front door slammed. Saul's knees loosened, as if they could no longer hold him up. When his father appeared in the bedroom and took in the scene, his roar of fury reminded Saul of the boiling waves of the estuary in the eye of a hurricane.

He came for Saul then, punching him in the stomach, the ribs, the side of his head. 'Stupid fucking idiot. Do you know how much that's worth?' The beating might have killed him, but the boy stiffened and started to seize uncontrollably, and even Solomon wasn't cruel enough to hit a child in the midst of a fit.

Solomon refused to take him to hospital, and Gloria was too drunk. They waited until he was still again and put him to bed, hoping he might sleep it off. From his work as a detective, Saul knew that parents whose children had ingested illegal substances rarely shared this information with the doctors trying to save their lives. These days, hospital emergency departments will test a fitting child's urine for drugs if they don't have a fever or a history of seizures, but it wasn't so clear-cut when Saul was a boy. Still, neither parent was prepared to risk it, especially not Sol.

'Should we take him?' Gloria's speech was slurred, the consonants rolling thickly from her in a cloud of vodka fumes. She answered her own question. 'We *should* take him.'

Solomon shook his head, a vehement, slicing motion. 'Don't want social services or the police sniffing around.'

'But what if he doesn't improve?' Sol didn't answer. Gloria, made foolish by alcohol, grabbed his arm and tried to shake a reply from him. 'What if he dies from an overdose?'

He swatted her away, as if she was an irritating fly. 'He shouldn't have touched what wasn't his.'

'He didn't know, Sol. He's just a baby.'

His father gave a half-shrug. 'He'll learn now, won't he?'

Saul shook the memory from him. Even now, all these years later, he remembered the exchange between his parents, their furious whispers, and the strange manic energy and headache that consumed him for days afterwards. He had buried it, deep in the silt of his past, and it surprised him the way it flooded back to him now, a deluge of feelings and sensations, and his hesitation – an unfamiliar reticence – at the sight of Blue's suitcase.

Giving himself a stern talking-to, he lifted it onto the bed, careful not to dislodge its contents, and unfastened the buckles, which were tarnished by age. A flush of guilt stilled his hand – he hated the idea of someone in his home, rooting through his personal belongings – but then he remembered her warning. She was sharp, smarter than he was, and her words held a meaning he'd be ill-advised to ignore.

The suitcase lay in front of him like an open book.

His eyes scanned the treasures it held. A journal, battered by time, its pages, some loose, held in place by a thin piece of leather cord wrapped around it. A ring box, red flocking, marked by what looked to Saul like candle wax. The seagull feather he'd given her after they'd murdered Detective Constable Douglas Lynch, stained with his blood. A collection of letters, kept together by an elastic band. A piece of charred clothing, an acrid smell rising from it, part chemical, part woodsmoke, stirring in him that centuries-old instinct to make fire. A carving knife he didn't recognize, edged with dark matter that had dried onto the blade.

He swore under his breath. He didn't know what any of it meant, but he knew he would have to hide it.

Saul closed the suitcase and carried it through to the hallway. Then he returned to the kitchen and stood for a moment before opening a tin of cat food and spooning it into Miss Meow's bowl. He rinsed out the tin, locked the door, slid Blue's key into his pocket and walked briskly up the path.

As he prepared to drive away, a police patrol car appeared in his rear-view mirror. He slid further down into his seat, holding his breath. It pulled up outside Blue's flat and two uniformed officers got out.

How long would it be before they came for him?

23

Deborah

Jen was sitting on the stairs, waiting for the phone to ring. She was dressed in her favourite jeans and a Bikini Kill T-shirt, and she was wearing hairspray and lipstick, which was a first. Deborah almost tripped over her.

'What are you sitting there for?'

Jen scuffed the toes of her slippers against the carpet and pointed to the rotary telephone on the stand in the hall. 'I thought Dominic might ring me. We're supposed to be going to the cinema this afternoon, but I haven't heard from him. I've hardly seen him at school all week.' Her expression was agonized. 'Do you think he's gone off me?'

Deborah chewed her lip. The magic of that night had faded, leaving her with a feeling of tawdriness, and she didn't like thinking about it because it made her feel guilty. 'I don't know, sis. Can't you ring him?'

'I don't have his phone number.'

Deborah thought about the folded-up piece of paper he'd given to her at the end of the night, her guilt intensifying.

'Why don't you go with your friends instead? Don't let some stupid boy ruin your day. Girl power and all that shit.'

But Jen didn't smile as she usually did. 'Maybe. Can I borrow your jacket? The denim one with the rips in it.'

It was Deborah's favourite, but she said yes because her sister seemed so sad, and she felt responsible. Two minutes later, she regretted it.

Jen came tearing down the stairs, Dom's hoodie over her arm. Her cheeks were flushed with emotion. 'Why have you got this?'

She didn't see the point in lying. 'He gave it to me.'

Jen's tone was incredulous. 'When?'

'The other night when I went out for my birthday. He was at the nightclub too. I was cold. He lent me his top. No big deal.'

'You didn't say.' Jen frowned, pacing the hallway. She stopped suddenly and buried her face in the fabric, inhaling the faint but lingering scent of cigarette smoke and Lynx. 'Why didn't you say?'

'It didn't seem important.'

Deborah bent to tie up her trainers, hair falling over her face. She had an appointment in the city in a couple of hours, and she'd need to leave soon to catch the train. She didn't have time for this conversation.

Jen clutched at her sticky fringe, making it stand on end. 'He doesn't give his hoodies to anyone unless he's dating them.' She started pacing again and then turned to face her sister, her expression lightening. A thought had occurred to her and it made her grin like a Cheshire cat. 'Did he give it to you to pass on to me?' She sat cross-legged next to Deborah. 'He did, didn't he?' She rolled her eyes and gave her sister an affectionate nudge. 'You forgot. Bloody hell, Deborah.'

Deborah removed a rollerball of gloss from her handbag

and applied it to her lips. She wasn't usually lost for words, but she didn't know what to say.

'Can I keep it, do you think? Or does he want it back?' Jen mused on it. 'I suppose you give it back if you split up.' Her eyes widened. 'Does this mean I'm his girlfriend?' She pressed the hoodie to her chest and cradled it like a baby. 'I think it might.'

Deborah didn't have the heart to correct her.

The agency was chrome and glass, and the most imposing building that Deborah had ever seen. It felt a million miles from their four-bedroom semi in the middle of suburbia. She swallowed, nerves biting as she walked through the revolving doors.

A young woman – gamine, edgy – looked up from her computer. As soon as she had ascertained that Deborah wasn't famous enough to concern herself with, she went back to what she was doing, which didn't seem to be very much.

It had been snowing outside and Deborah brushed the flakes off her jacket, waited for a few moments and then cleared her throat. 'I've got an appointment with Maxine Duvall.'

'Name?'

Deborah didn't think it was possible for a person to sound any more bored. The woman printed out her badge without looking at her once. When she handed it over, she'd spelt Kellaway wrong.

Maxine Duvall's office was vast, bigger than Deborah's living room and kitchen put together.

Her hair was slicked back, and she wore an oversized suit with a tie, which Deborah found fascinating, the androgyny of the fashion magazines she voraciously consumed brought to life.

Black and white photographs of some of the most famous models in the world plastered the walls. A fruit basket, bursting with grapes, bananas, apples and exotic produce Deborah had never seen before, sat on a low glass table next to a water jug with slices of lemon floating in it. For a girl from the suburbs, it felt exciting and glamorous, and Deborah wanted to be a part of it.

Maxine grabbed Deborah by the chin, not roughly, but her grip was firm, and she looked at her appraisingly from both angles, moving her face from left to right. From the top of her desk, she retrieved a tape measure and wrapped it around Deborah's waist, her thighs and the tops of her arms, writing the numbers in black ink in a small notebook she carried in her pocket. She weighed her (8 stone) and asked for her shoe size (7), if she'd consider nudity and if she had completed her studies (no, on both counts).

'Stand by the window.'

Deborah obliged, and Maxine fired off several Polaroid shots, one after the other. When she had finished, she directed Deborah to sit down, on a sofa, and she did the same herself, albeit on the chair behind her desk.

She stayed there for several minutes, flicking through the photographs, and at one point pressed an intercom and asked for the agency's co-director and the Head of New Faces to come through.

The three of them huddled in the corner, discussing her. For some girls, this might have felt humiliating, being assessed and prodded like cattle for sale at a meat market, with the risk of being found wanting. But Deborah thrived on this pressure.

'Walk for us,' said Maxine, handing her a pair of heels and folding her arms.

Deborah knew this was the biggest moment of her life.

She pushed back her shoulders. Focused her gaze. She walked with attitude, keeping her hips straight and allowing her arms to sway naturally. Delicate hands. Straight head. With as much confidence as she could muster, she squared up in front of them and then turned and walked back, clean and strong. Her inner voice soothed her. She was going places, even if this agency lacked the foresight to see it.

'You're a natural,' said Maxine Duvall, smiling for the first time that day. 'We'd like to sign you. But you'll need to change your name. Deborah is too plain. Can you think of something else?'

Through the glass windows, she watched the snow fall onto London's skyline and thought about what her father had said about her. 'Winter.'

Twenty-four hours later, Deborah was on a flight to France for Paris Fashion Week, walking for fashion colossus Vivienne Westwood. One of the models had pulled out at the last moment and the agency had promised their clients a replacement, except Westwood's team had rejected every one of their suggestions.

By chance or serendipity, the gods of good fortune were smiling on Deborah that day. She possessed that unique and indefinable look the model bookers were seeking and was summoned to the Grand Hotel for a casting call.

Hours later, after a breathtaking whirlwind of fittings and appointments with hair and make-up, she found herself on the catwalk with international supermodels Helena Christensen and Naomi Campbell.

If Deborah had messed up her debut, it was likely she would never have worked again. It was a risk for all of them. The fashion house. The model agency. And Deborah herself.

But Deborah knew that she could do this. She was at home in this world of haute couture. She could handle the competitiveness, the work ethic, the long days and longer nights, if only she was given a chance.

Her appearance on the runway – and the rags-to-riches story behind it – coupled with the freshness of her look and the novelty of this student-turned-supermodel made head-lines around the world. The high-money offers came rolling in and Deborah never went back to university to finish her degree.

Once she had tasted the sweetness of success, once she had achieved the first of many dreams, Deborah Kellaway knew she wouldn't stop until she had everything she had ever wanted.

24

Winter

Winter slipped her dress over her head and smoothed the silk against her curves, admiring her reflection in Jen's bedroom mirror. Was she imagining things or did it feel a bit snug? She decided it was her imagination. The scales this morning had recorded a half-kilo weight gain. It was probably water retention. She'd avoid salt and carbs for a week once the wedding was over.

In the few hours since she'd taken the test, her mindset had shifted and she knew with absolute certainty that she wasn't giving this baby up. She pressed her palm against her still-flat stomach and allowed herself to daydream about the life beating inside her.

At nine weeks, it was not a pea or a bean, but the size of a strawberry. That fact made her smile. *Strawberry*. Her baby.

She could hear her mother and Alyssa chatting to each other in the sitting room. Teddy was tearing around, bored out of his mind. Iris was reading her book. She couldn't decide if she'd like a boy or a girl. In her fantasy life, she'd have one of each.

It felt strange but not unpleasant to be getting ready in her sister's house while Jen was tucked away on Winter's estate. Although stylish and comfortable, it was a quarter of the size of her own property, but hearing voices from downstairs gave her a warm feeling that she hadn't experienced for so long. Her own place was too vast – the rooms were spaced out and some distance from each other – to ever run the risk of overhearing conversations. But not for the first time, she recognized there was a sterility to her existence.

She sat on the edge of the bed. Jen's side had a scented candle and some pillow spray, and a soft toy that Iris had bought one year in a Mother's Day sale at school. Phil's side had a glass of water, a book on the solar system and a picture of Jen and their two children. One day, Winter hoped, someone would have a picture of her on their bedside table.

She slipped on her cashmere bolero and went downstairs to gather the others. Finally, it was time to head to the pier and catch the boat.

'Come on,' she said, clapping her hands to gain their attention. 'Let's get your shoes on.'

Alyssa, who had been playing trains with Teddy, stood up. She'd turned down Katya's offer to have her make-up professionally applied, and she looked wrung out, dark shadows beneath her eyes. She appeared to have chosen a dress that looked like a potato sack, although Winter, who was already mentally shopping for a maternity wardrobe from her favourite designers, didn't think it would be prudent to mention that.

It was a shame that her youngest sister could not extend her the same courtesy.

'You can't wear that,' she said to Winter before crawling under the sofa to help Teddy look for his lost shoe.

'What do you mean? This is Alexander McQueen. It cost six grand.'

'It's not the cost.' Alyssa was disdainful. 'Everybody knows you can't wear white to a wedding unless it's your own.'

'Jen won't mind. Her dress is ivory.'

'Semantics.'

Winter turned to her mother, who was sitting in one of Jen's armchairs, cradling Claudia. The baby was dressed in a frothy pink concoction that Alyssa had stress-bought on the internet two nights earlier during that half-crazed exhaustion of a 4 a.m. feed. 'What do you think?'

Carol, a queen of diplomacy, eyed her daughter. 'It looks beautiful, darling. The shape really suits you. But I'd say the paler shades are traditionally reserved for the bride.'

'Dad?'

Geoff Kellaway, who had remained silent throughout this exchange, put down his newspaper and peered at his daughter through his reading glasses.

'I've always let you girls sort this stuff out among yourselves. But as you've asked for my opinion, I'll give it to you. You look like you're the one who's getting married, love.'

Winter gestured at her floor-length structured gown and enlisted the opinion of Iris.

'And what do you think, sweetie?'

'You look like a princess, Auntie Winter. Mummy won't mind if you're both wearing the same colour. I think you look very pretty.'

Winter beamed at her niece. She had always said that Iris

was more intelligent than the average eight-year-old and here was the proof. 'That's decided, then.'

Federico was pacing up and down the jetty when the Kellaway family arrived en masse in two chauffeur-driven Mercedes Benzes. He kissed Alyssa dutifully on the cheek, touched a finger to the baby's cheek and greeted his soon-to-be mother-in-law with a grin, but it was Winter he complimented.

'You look sensational.'

Winter was so used to adulation that sometimes it didn't register, but this kind of ego-stroke never got old. She didn't mean to be unkind, but Alyssa ought to make more of an effort. With Federico's career on the rise and his abundant Anglo-Italian charms, he was something of a catch.

'You're looking sharp yourself.' She lowered her voice, so that the others couldn't hear. 'Have you seen Phil? No one's heard from him all day.'

Federico's expression turned sheepish. 'There's a reason for that.'

'Which is?' Her voice was dangerously calm.

'Don't lose your shit, Winter, he's safe and sound. I dropped him at yours twenty minutes ago. But we've been in A&E for most of the morning.'

'Oh God.' She threw her hands skywards. 'What's happened?'

'Too many beers last night. He tripped over his shoes this morning and broke his wrist.'

'Who's broken their wrist?' Alyssa appeared next to them, shivering in the cold. 'Not Phil?'

'The same,' said her fiancé.

'For Christ's sake. I told you not to let him get too pissed.' Alyssa's lips were pressed into a line. 'Jen will be so upset.'

'I'm not responsible for policing how much my brother-in-law drinks. He's a grown man.' He threw a glance at Geoff. 'And *he* buggered off to babysit, and left me to deal with it.'

'Let's not get upset,' said Winter. 'It's done now. Although the photographs are going to look awful.'

'We'll laugh about it in the future,' said Federico with a grin. 'It'll be the talk of the wedding. And at least nothing else can go wrong.'

The jetty was quiet. All of the pleasure-boat services had stopped running the previous month and the fog had deterred even the most hardened sailors. The wooden planks were slippery and damp. In a ramshackle prefab office in the corner by a pile of old fishing nets, a light burned at the window.

'I'll just find out what's going on.' Winter sounded bright, but her voice had a brittle quality. She walked carefully in her heels. The wind carried with it the voice of her sister.

'She's not used to slumming it these days,' murmured Alyssa to Federico.

'Jealous?'

'No.' Alyssa was emphatic in her denial, but Winter knew that she was. She just wouldn't admit it. 'Are you?'

'If this music stuff continues, I'll be almost as rich as she is.'

Winter noted the use of *I* instead of *we*.

The captain had a weathered look about him but was younger than Winter had expected. He was reluctant to skipper them in the fog, but the sight of Winter's thick envelope of cash changed his mind. He locked up his shed and hung a CLOSED sign on the door.

'Let's go.' He was a man of few words.

Teddy was skipping around the jetty, excited by the proximity to water and the knowledge that he'd be reunited with his parents within the hour. He was going to be the ring-bearer again. Winter had promised him the first taste of the chocolate river once he'd performed his duties.

'Keep him under control,' said the captain. 'It's not a playground.'

Alyssa pulled a face at her mother, but Carol called out to her grandson. 'Come and hold my hand.'

The wind had picked up, a freshening north-easterly, and Winter's hair, which had been expensively styled and blow-dried, was beginning to go limp in the fog. She was not one to concede defeat, but even she was starting to regret this gesture. It had seemed like a good idea from the comfort of her home, when she'd imagined Jen's wedding day as cold and crisp with a winter sun that glinted against the waves.

The Kellaway family trooped up the gangplank and onto the specially chartered pleasure cruiser.

Above their heads, the seabirds wheeled and shrieked, and the fog hung heavy, a portent of doom.

25

Saturday, 18 November 2023

Saul

He was almost back at the coastguard's lookout when his mobile phone rang again, a jarring sound in the depths of the misty silence. His heart betrayed him. For a fleeting moment, he allowed himself to hope that it might be Blue, and that she was calling to tell him that there had been a terrible mistake. With cold hands, he fumbled for the handset, praying she wouldn't hang up before he answered. But it was DC Isaac Hunter and the bitterness of disappointment flooded his mouth.

'Where are you? This is the longest lunch break known to humankind. You're needed back at the station.'

Saul's plan had been unformulated, nothing more than a loose awareness, but now he was here, within sight of the place that had been his home for the last two years, he recognized that he'd come here for a reason, intending to pack up his belongings and leave Midtown by nightfall. Before they came for him.

He ran his tongue around his teeth, trying to rid himself of the taste of his misery. A wave of tiredness overcame him and he steadied himself against the fence that bordered the lookout and prevented its occupants from falling into the sea. 'What's going on?'

'You remember the CCTV footage that was recovered from Winter Kellaway's property this morning?'

He grunted his assent, weary and uninterested. He shouldn't have answered. He didn't care. He wasn't going back.

'I've just been reviewing it. It's a state-of-the-art system, so the quality of the images is pretty fantastic. We could do with something of this calibre in the town, to be honest, although I suspect there'd be as much chance of that as hell freezing over.'

'Get to the point, Isaac.' He didn't have the energy to feign enthusiasm, although he was impressed by Hunter's diligence. Before he'd resigned last year, Angus O'Neill, his former DI, had talked to Saul about the possibility of applying for promotion. With an instinctive gift for policing, for navigating dark spaces and spotting connections that others had missed, the young detective's career advancement had been a near certainty. Since his injuries, that had been on hold, but if he was ever in the position to put his own team together, Isaac would be a contender.

'Well . . .' He could hear the detective tapping away at a computer. Across the bay, the denseness of the fog had thinned, and he could make out the bright lights of Winter Kellaway's vast estate. He wondered if the wedding had started yet, and how much money it had cost. 'Take a look at your phone.' Isaac's voice held that note of excitement he'd often heard in police officers on the cusp of a breakthrough. 'I've sent you something interesting.'

Saul looked down at his phone, curious in spite of himself. Isaac had sent two images. One was a freeze-frame from the CCTV, a man's face clearly visible. He was outside her property and it looked as though he had tried to gain access without permission.

But it was the second photograph that interested him most of all. It was a screenshot taken from Winter Kellaway's Instagram account, a group of people with their arms around each other. Saul's gaze flicked between both images, checking and rechecking to make sure they hadn't made a mistake.

'Do you see it?' said Isaac.

'I see it.'

'Are you coming back to the station now? We need to decide what to do about it, and whether it's a coincidence or if we need to take it any further, and if so, how to do that.'

'There's no "we" about this,' said Saul. 'It's your discovery. You deserve the credit for it.'

'No way. We're a team, and we need to talk to the boss as a team. Two heads are better than one, etcetera.' He lowered his voice, conspiratorial. 'Also, she scares me a bit.'

Isaac's generosity surprised Saul. He'd suspected his colleague to be ruthless, career-driven and self-obsessed, but it appeared he was wrong on all counts, and not for the first time.

'I don't know. I've got things to do now.'

'Come on, Saul. You can't leave me on my own with this. I might get paired with DC Williams.' Isaac went up another notch in Saul's estimation. After a brief cessation in hostilities, Saul and Eliot were at loggerheads again, arguing about the calibre of tea and coffee in the canteen and whether women should have their right to vote rescinded.

'We can get a pint later, if you want.' Isaac sounded hopeful.

'No.'

The young detective stood on the promontory and watched the lighthouse beacon flash on and off. He shivered, chilled to the bone, but still reluctant to seek out the comforts that might ease him. Terrible things had happened in this town, and Saul had been part of them. He wanted to run, but he could not bring himself to abandon his lover.

While Saul was many things – a thief, a liar and a killer – he was not a coward. He thought about PC Talbot, the bravest police officer he'd known, and DI O'Neill's unswerving conviction of his talents, even when he'd made misjudgements that had turned out to be deadly.

For his whole life, Saul had been seeking something for himself. He had always thought it was a need to be loved, but, standing here with a decision to be made, he wondered if it might go beyond even that. Perhaps he was wrong. Perhaps this job – this place – this sense of belonging – was it.

He weighed up the choices before him, unsure of what to do next. Could he trust Blue to protect him? Because he would rather die than go to prison. If he stayed, the risk of discovery would inflate with each passing day. And he feared the responsibility would sit heavily on Blue's shoulders. But if he left without warning, he would have no job, no home, no lover and, worst of all, no future.

A black-tipped feather drifted in front of him, the downy underside of a kittiwake's wing. He bent to retrieve it, his fingers brushing its softness. He examined the shaft and the quills. Marvelled at its symmetry. Black and white, the starkest of contrasts.

He had always been a man of absolutes. But perhaps there was a middle ground. He did not need to decide now, he told himself. He could go back to the station and finish this job with Isaac, and then he would make his decision. If he needed to run, he could. And there were always other, darker choices.

In any case, the mechanical part of Saul's brain had begun to whirr and tick, piecing together bits of information and theory, his instincts as sharp and brilliant as honed steel.

'Give me ten minutes,' he said. 'I'm on my way.'

26

Deborah

She dropped her suitcase in the hallway and eased off her trainers. She was so tired she could hardly stand, but her parents couldn't collect her from the airport as they were both at work, and she had taken two trains and a bus on top of her flight from Charles de Gaulle airport.

She could probably have afforded to pay for a taxi. Maxine had called her at the agency's flat in the French capital the previous night to talk through her options.

'The phone has been ringing off the hook, darling,' she'd said, excitement bubbling over in her voice. 'Fuck Kate Moss, you are the model *du jour*.' Offers had been pouring in from fashion houses, magazines and perfume companies in the last couple of days. Deborah's head was spinning with it all. 'We need to capitalize on the interest.' Maxine was brisk. 'Are you planning to leave university?'

Deborah knew what her parents would say. It was only a couple of months until she was due to finish her degree, and then she'd be free to pursue her modelling career. But, as far as she was concerned, it was too much of a risk. The interest might wane. And she was an adult now. It was her decision.

She had assured Maxine that she would be ready to work as soon as she needed her to, which turned out to be in two days' time. She just needed to square it with her parents first.

Geoff and Carol Kellaway were opposed to Deborah's plan.

'Finish your education, love. It's only a couple of months. I'm sure the agency could line you up some work for the summer.'

'It needs to be now. Everyone will have forgotten about me by then.'

'I sincerely doubt that.' Geoff was washing his hands at the kitchen sink. It was the first thing he did when he came in from his job as a bus driver. He said handling coins all day made his fingers smell like the Royal Mint. 'If you've made as big a splash as this Maxine says you have, the offers will still be waiting.'

'It doesn't work like that, Dad.' She was pleading, but she had to make them understand.

'The answer's still no.'

Two days later, she moved out. Maxine Duvall sent an agency car to collect her and said she could live in one of the agency's flats in central London, and they would deduct the rent – along with their commission – from her earnings.

Alyssa cried for five minutes. Then she said, 'Can I have Deborah's bedroom now that she doesn't live here anymore?'

Jen sat on her sister's bed and watched her fold and pack her clothes into the small suitcase she was taking with her.

'You're really doing this?'

'Be happy for me, sis.'

'I am. But I'll miss you.'

She was stuffing her hair straighteners and spare knickers into a holdall when the doorbell rang. A few moments later, Carol called up the stairs.

'Deborah, there's a young man here to see you.'

Jen raised her eyebrows and giggled at her sister's expression. 'Whose heart have you broken this time?'

Deborah gave a nervous laugh. 'No idea, but I'll go and get rid of him. Can you sort out some of my CDs and put them with my Discman? I won't be long.'

Although frustrated by her daughter's wilfulness, Carol Kellaway was a firm advocate of the twin bastions of middle-class life: good manners and frugality. Not wishing for the heat to escape through an open door, she'd invited him in from the cold, and the young man was now standing in their hallway with a bunch of flowers wrapped in cellophane from the BP garage down the road.

'What are you doing here?' she hissed at him, drawing him away from the bottom of the stairs to the dark corner next to the dining room.

'I came to see you. You haven't been at the nightclub for two weeks.'

'I've been busy.' She couldn't meet his gaze. Dominic Ward had always emanated a vibe of cool nonchalance, but he had brushed his hair, and even she could sense the neediness in him.

'You didn't call.'

'I've been to Paris.' She couldn't stop herself from smiling. 'Modelling. On the catwalk.'

He smiled back at her. 'I know. I saw you on the telly last night. Everyone's talking about it.' His voice softened. 'Didn't I say that you were the fittest girl in school, past or present?'

'Is that so?' Jen's voice floated down the stairs.

By instinct, Deborah and Dominic lifted their heads at the same time to look upwards. Jen was leaning over the top of the banister, hands gripping the wood, knuckles white. She disappeared for a moment and then Deborah heard her middle sister thundering down the stairs.

She stood between them, her hands on her hips. 'When were you planning to tell me?'

'I . . .' Deborah couldn't bring herself to say that she wasn't interested in him because that would destroy Jen. In any case, she was leaving town. It was over between them. Dom just didn't know it yet.

'Sorry, Jen.' Dom was gruff. 'But I like your sister.'

'Is that why you didn't take me to the cinema?'

He looked sheepish. 'Yeah.'

Jen turned on Deborah, eyes blazing. 'When?' Deborah was taken aback by the look of fury and disgust on her sister's face. Dom looked at his trainers.

'My birthday.'

Jen moaned, as if she was in physical pain. 'And you didn't tell me? You let me think I was still in with a chance.' She smacked the heel of her hand against her forehead. 'Everything makes sense now.'

'We didn't mean to hurt you.' Dominic was wearing that foolish expression again, as if he really liked her. 'But me and Deborah clicked, didn't we?' He held out his hand, but Deborah ignored him. She could tell she had wounded her sister deeply. Regret pulsed through her. 'We're going out with each other now.'

This was news to Deborah. As far as she was concerned, she was no more his girlfriend than Jen was. 'I think it's time for you to go.'

'Don't worry about it.' Jen held up a palm, saving them both, her voice heavy with sarcasm. 'I'll leave you lovebirds to it.' She narrowed her eyes, detonating a bomb of her own. 'Deborah's moving to London tomorrow, so I expect you'll want to say a romantic goodbye to each other.'

Dom looked crestfallen, visibly crushed. 'You're moving to London?' He ran his fingers through his long hair. 'When did you decide that?'

'It all happened so quickly. I was going to tell you, I promise.'

'Were you? When exactly?'

She was shocked to see he had tears in his eyes. He thrust the flowers at her, colour staining his cheeks. 'You don't care who you hurt, do you?'

There was no answer to the truth in that.

Jen was halfway up the stairs. She pretended she wasn't listening to their exchange, but Deborah could tell by the tautness of her pose that she was drinking in every word.

'I suppose I'd better let you get on with your packing then.' He was awkward now, embarrassed, but it didn't take long for the cocky teenager to replace the wounded boy. He puffed out his chest and dug his hands into his pockets. 'Can I have my hoodie back? It's my favourite.'

'I'll get it,' said Jen. Deborah guessed it was because her sister would rather die than let him know that she'd been sleeping in it every night.

'You can call me, if you want,' he said gruffly. 'From London. Or wherever you are.'

'I'm not sure if I'll have time.' She stared at the carpet. 'My schedule looks pretty busy.'

'Fine.' He stood by the doorway, jiggling his leg, as if he couldn't keep himself still. His eyes ran over her, appraising her face and her body. It made her want to squirm.

'What is it?'

He shrugged. 'You're not that pretty anyway.'

Jen appeared at the top of the stairs, carrying the hoodie over her arm. When she passed it to Dom, he offered her a maximum-kilowatt grin. 'Thanks, babe.'

The younger girl blushed and it made Deborah want to shake some sense into her. 'See me out?' he said.

Deborah willed her sister to say no, but instead Jen turned to her with a pointed look that said *You owe me*. As sisters, they had learned, over the years, to read each other's expressions, and so she disappeared into the living room, although she made certain that she didn't shut the door.

'Please tell me *you're* coming back to school after the holidays,' he said, and Jen giggled in a way that made Deborah feel sick. Jen murmured something that she didn't catch, but Dom's voice was deeper, more resonant. 'Sweet. I'd hate it if you weren't there.'

Deborah clutched the frame of the door and leaned her head around it, willing Jen not to see. Her sister was standing too close to Dom, her face upturned, and the boy reached for one of her hands, holding it loosely in his own.

He held Jen's gaze, a moody and intense expression that Deborah had seen before. 'I asked you out first, remember? Because I always liked you best.'

Jen looked away, the colour rising in her face. 'Why did you kiss her then?'

He shrugged again, that devil-may-care nonchalance. 'It was a mistake. She made a move on me first, and I was an idiot.' He looked at her from beneath his fringe, a boyish grin on his lips. 'Could you ever forgive me?'

She didn't answer at first, but he pulled a hangdog expression, and it made her laugh. 'I dunno.'

'Don't decide now,' he said, 'but if you're free, I was wondering if you'd still like to go to the cinema with me next week?'

Hours later, when Jen was reading in bed, Deborah knocked on her door. A lamp cast shadows on her sister's face, making her seem older than her fourteen years.

'The car's coming to pick me up early tomorrow morning. I'll be gone before you get up, so I wanted to say goodbye.'

Jen didn't look up. 'Bye.'

'I'm sorry, OK? It was crappy of me.'

Jen put down her book. There was a hardness in her eyes that Deborah had never seen before. 'You're my sister. My relationship with you will always be more important to me than any boy. Always. But you knew how much I liked him and you did it anyway. I'd never do that to you.'

Deborah tried to find a way to articulate that her pursuit of Dom had been driven by her own lack of confidence. It was a weakness in her, that relentless need to be wanted, like a flaw in a diamond. It overrode everything. She understood why she behaved in the way that she did, but she didn't know how to explain that to Jen. 'He's too old for you, anyway.'

'Promise you'll never do that to me again.' Jen sat up in bed, held out her little finger and waited for Deborah to interlock it with her own.

'Pinky promise.'

With solemn expressions, the girls shook on it. Then they hugged, neither wanting their farewell to be soured further still.

As she left the bedroom, Jen called out to her, and she turned, half expecting to be asked for another hug or one last kiss, but her sister had a curious expression on her face, part anger, part distress, and Deborah went to her, gathering her in her arms.

Jen's face was damp against her shirt. She could hardly make out what she was saying, but later that night, lying in her own bed when sleep wouldn't come, she replayed the shape of those words and it came to her with startling clarity. It was so unlike Jen, but she was sure she hadn't misheard.

'If you ever do anything like that to me again, I'll make sure I destroy you.'

27

Blue

The walls of the interview room were the same sour-milk colour as the toilets at her former secondary school. These ones might be missing the explicit graffiti and teenage angst, but like many tax-funded buildings past their prime, the paint was peeling off like blistered skin. Blue stared at a spot above the clock and bit her lip.

A detective she didn't recognize sat opposite her, a table topped with cheap brown Formica between them. A recording device – an ungainly lump of metal from the Dark Ages – squatted on the shiny resin surface pockmarked with coffee-cup rings, but it was switched off.

Blue still had no idea what evidence they had or on what grounds they had arrested her, but she knew they must have *something*.

Her mind ran through that night. She must have left some forensic trace at the house. It was the only explanation. In a lecture she'd attended by a highly respected forensic scientist, the woman, who owned her own company specializing in this field, had insisted it was impossible to leave a crime scene free of evidence: cleaning with bleach didn't remove blood, even though it might look like it on the surface, it simply moved it around; every human contact left micro-scopic traces of skin cells or hair or fibres from clothing, however much care had been taken. Blue knew that even saliva from a sneeze could link her to Lynch's murder. They should have burned his house down.

A knock at the door, two sharp and unapologetic raps.

The detective cleared his throat and shuffled a bundle of paperwork between two hands. 'That will be the duty solici-tor. I'll leave you to it for a few minutes, and then we'll begin the interview, OK?'

A young man marched into the room. If Saul's hair was white-blond, his was as dark as a winter's night, and his eyes a startling green. He was wearing a suit but no tie, and a pair of scuffed trainers. He was confident, Blue could tell that from the way he carried himself, but he spoke with a quiet authority, as if he knew his words would be taken seriously, no matter what.

He looked at her and smiled. 'Murder, eh? That's some accusation.'

Her mouth dried. His eyes were sharp but friendly. She didn't know what to say. He held out his hand to introduce himself. When she took it, it was warm and dry. He had a powerful grip but he didn't use it to assert his dominance. 'My name's James Warburton.' He couldn't have been older than twenty-seven, but she was glad her legal representation was almost the same age as she was. She'd never had much in common with grey-haired middle-aged men. She thought about the way the detective had rolled his eyes when the solicitor had walked in, and the salute the young man had offered him in return. In the time these interactions had taken place, no longer than a minute or so, she'd decided she liked him.

He scanned the documents the detective had left on the table. Blue's eyes flitted to the CCTV camera in the corner. 'Are they recording this?'

He laughed. 'No chance. That camera hasn't worked for months. I can ask for us to be moved to another room if you'd prefer, though. But I'd take it as a good sign. If they had an open-and-shut case, we'd be in Interview Room Two with all the bells and whistles.'

Blue felt the muscles in her shoulders loosen for the first time in hours.

'Are you part of a union or professional body?'

She nodded. 'Why do you ask?'

'Because they might help you with the legal side of things.'

'Aren't you a solicitor?'

'Yes. But some clients prefer to engage the services of a private law firm.' He looked up and grinned at her. It felt a bit like sunshine breaking through the rain. 'But then they're not always lucky enough to get me.'

Blue had heard the sniggers about duty solicitors, and the fact that getting a decent one was like a spin of the roulette wheel. But James seemed to know what he was doing. He spoke again, his focus on the paperwork in front of him. 'I assume you have some idea of how this works, given your job?'

She shrugged. 'Yes. But I've never been arrested before.'

'Listen carefully,' he said. 'I don't expect you to tell me everything, but before we go any further, let me explain something to you. If you are absolutely certain that you can't be incriminated in any way, I would advise answering the good detective's questions frankly and honestly. Anything else, I'd suggest no comment.'

'I—'

He held up his hand. 'Hear me out, OK? According to this documentation, your mother's car was caught on CCTV in the vicinity of Douglas Lynch's home on the night he died. But, according to border control, your mother was in France at that time. They could not pull a clear image from the CCTV cameras, given the weather and the late hour, but it appears to be a woman driving. Was it you?'

Blue's stomach fell away. They'd been so careful, taking the back roads, avoiding the city centre. But it hadn't been enough.

James narrowed his eyes. 'I mean, it could be anyone, I suppose. But your mother hadn't reported the car as stolen.' He read on. 'It says here that Lynch sent a derogatory message to several fellow officers about a woman he'd apparently been intimate with.' Blue stilled, wondering if her personal shame – the dark secret that had festered inside her since the night he'd attacked her – had been broadcast to all in Essex Police and beyond. 'It doesn't say who the woman was – just that she was a colleague – but he speaks about her in a demeaning and inappropriate manner.' James folded his hands and looked at the young forensic linguist's hair, and then back to the file. 'It says, "I don't think she enjoyed it. She seemed a bit **blue** when I left."' He said the word blue had been highlighted in bold and followed by three laughing emojis.

Blue leaned over and threw up in a small wastepaper bin under the table.

James didn't fuss over her, but opened his leather satchel and passed her an unopened bottle of water and a packet of tissues. When she had finished wiping her mouth and drunk some of the water, he said, 'This doesn't prove anything, of course. But there's an inference to be drawn that you had a motive to do him harm.' He paused. 'Understandably. He sounds like a prick.'

A silence settled over the room. Blue's head swam. She was in turmoil, uncertain how much she could trust James – and with what. But the words wouldn't form in her mouth, that instinct to protect herself and Saul as strong as it ever was.

The solicitor cleared his throat. 'In all honesty, the evidence – if they can even call it that – is thin. They're fishing, pushing their luck. I've seen it a thousand times. My advice is to say nothing – don't even confirm your name – and I'll have you out of here in a couple of hours.' He smiled at her then, and the part of her that was so tightly wound she was struggling to breathe eased a notch.

James Warburton was as good as his word. When the detective came back into the interview room, his questions were met with polite rebuffs. As instructed, Dr Clover March declined to answer anything, and even though she knew this would count against her if investigators uncovered concrete evidence in the future linking her to Lynch's murder, they were forced to let her go.

'You can hold her for twenty-four hours or thirty-six or even ninety-six, if you want to be ridiculous.' James raised an ironic eyebrow, glanced at Blue and said, sotto voce, 'Good luck with that, pal.' He leaned back in the chair, steepled his fingers under his chin and spoke directly to the detective. 'Look, all of us in this room are familiar with the law. But on what grounds are you holding my client? It seems to me you're attempting to put words into her mouth. As far as I can tell, you have no definitive evidence, and unless you're going to charge her, which I think seems highly unlikely, you'll need to let her go home. So we can twiddle our thumbs for another twenty-two hours – or you can release her now.'

Outside the police station, Blue blinked into the greyness. The afternoon fog had a touch of frost about it. James watched her, concern in his eyes. 'Do you need a lift home?'

She shook her head. 'I can walk.'

'You've had a shock and, well, think of that poor bin.' He grinned to show he was teasing, and then flicked a glance at his watch. 'I'm happy to drop you back. As of five minutes ago, I'm no longer on call.'

Blue, still in her gym kit, sagged, exhaustion threatening to overwhelm her. She thought about phoning Saul, consumed by a flash of guilt at ignoring his calls, but she didn't want to linger outside, fielding curious stares from nosy colleagues. The idea of being driven home was more appealing than she cared to let on. 'If you're sure.'

His Audi Q5 was parked in a designated spot in the police station car park, sleek and expensive. As they walked towards it, Blue stumbled and tipped into him, hit by a sudden but brief narcolepsy attack known as a microsleep. Startled, James reached out to steady her, his arm snaking around her waist to hold her up.

The attack was short-lived, lasting no more than a few seconds before Blue was conscious again, and she smiled up her thanks to James, who was at least a foot taller than she was and broad as a church. She liked the fact he didn't bombard her with questions, demanding to know what had just happened. Instead he removed his arm, conscious to avoid any risk of impropriety, and smiled back.

SOME OF US ARE LIARS

It was a simple and functional exchange between almost-strangers, but Saul Anguish, who'd just arrived back at the station, saw it all.

He stilled, lonely in the afternoon shadows, full of the hurts of his past, and watched them walk to James's car, Blue's name dying on his lips. There was a lightness to her he hadn't seen since the events of the previous year.

He watched another man – young and handsome – open the door for the woman he loved, and jealousy, that devil on his shoulder, sank her teeth into him, drawing blood.

28

Saturday, 18 November 2023

Jen

The guests were gathering for the ceremony. Wedding planners had supervised the building of a bespoke marquee with wooden struts and windows that offered sweeping views across the bay. Several heaters had been strategically placed throughout to offset the autumn chill, and an abundance of white flowers filled every corner. Tasteful drawstring linen bags filled with confetti made from freeze-dried rose petals had been placed on each seat. A gold carpet ran through the centre of the marquee and all the way down to the end of the jetty, framed by a dramatic floral arch that overlooked the water.

Jen was relaxed about her guests' attire. As far as she was concerned, she wanted everyone to feel warm and comfortable. But Winter had insisted on a strict dress code. Black tie for the men and cocktail dresses for women – or evening dress, if they preferred a more formal approach. Some had taken Winter at her word and were wearing floor-length gowns accessorized with sweeping cloaks or fake fur wraps. As a consequence, the assembled crowd looked like a flock of birds, spanning every species from monochrome magpie to the jewelled colours of a hummingbird.

Jen was not supposed to be there. But she had grown so bored and hungry on her own that she'd wandered up to the main house, looking for company. She peeped through a side entrance, catching occasional snatches of conversation, and wondered why Winter had invited so many of her own friends when it was neither her wedding nor her fortieth birthday or golden anniversary celebration.

She spotted her parents' old neighbours in the crowd, a couple from Alyssa's yoga class and one or two mothers from pre-school and Iris's primary, but they seemed ill at ease with the extravagance, wide-eyed at the arrival of the three or four household names that Winter had insisted attend. 'I've been to their families' weddings. It's a bit polit-ical. You don't mind, do you?' And what else could Jen do but agree?

One of the wedding planners spotted her standing outside the marquee and consulted her clipboard. She rushed towards her, wearing a stricken expression.

'You're not supposed to be here.'

'I know, but—'

'You need to be on the jetty in' – she consulted her watch – 'five minutes. Where's your bouquet?' She didn't wait for Jen to answer, but spoke into her radio. 'Can someone collect the bride's bouquet from the cottage? You'll need to run there. It's five minutes until We Are Go.'

Jen stifled an urge to laugh. The woman was not being ironic, but deadly serious. She must have seen something in Jen's face, though, because she said, 'The timing's strict. I'll get into trouble if you're not in position for the surprise.'

'You mean the boat?'

The woman was aghast. 'You're not supposed to know about that.'

'I won't tell if you don't.'

Jen allowed herself to be guided around the side of the marquee and through the grounds towards the jetty. The grass was damp and she felt moisture seeping through her satin shoes.

'The guests won't be able to see you,' said the woman. She pointed to the floral arch. 'You and the groom will stand hidden behind this, and when the surprise arrives, the wedding ceremony can get underway.'

The air had bite, but Jen did not feel the cold. She'd glimpsed Phil waiting for her, and those butterflies took flight again, that delicious kind of excitement that was part nerves, part anticipation. He was standing, straight-backed, in his wedding suit, and he was clean-shaven and handsome, and she couldn't believe her luck.

It was just as well she was not a stickler for convention. It didn't matter that she wasn't being escorted down the aisle by her father, or that her bridesmaids were nowhere to be seen, or that she was essentially living Winter's vision of a perfect wedding. When all was said and done, this moment in time was about no one but Jen and Phil Miller.

She felt a million dollars in her dress, and judging by the grin on Phil's face, she looked it too.

He gave a slow whistle of appreciation and his lips brushed her cheek. 'Bloody hell. You look spectacular, sweetheart.'

'I could say the same about you, Mr Miller.' She noticed the cast on his arm for the first time. 'What on earth have you done to yourself?'

He rubbed his nose twice with the heel of his unplastered hand. 'One beer too many last night.'

'Did it hurt?'

'Only my pride.'

The floral arch was oversized and lavish, and sizeable enough to conceal them both from the view of their guests. The greenery tickled her face. Behind them, the bay was cloaked in the fog that had plagued the town for days. She glanced down at the gold carpet beneath their feet. Winter had fussed about the shade for days, but everything looked grey in this light. A sudden urge to laugh at the absurdity of the set-up spilled through her. 'This whole thing is ridiculous.'

'It's very Winter.'

Jen shivered, the feathery shrug she was wearing over her dress too flimsy to keep out the wind. She wrapped her arms around herself to keep warm and snuggled into Phil, relishing his solidity. He offered her his jacket, but she declined, determined to show off her finery. 'How is it that I'm waiting for *them* to arrive? Surely it's the bride's prerogative to be late on her wedding day, not the wedding party.'

She laughed, enjoying the irony, and glanced at Phil to share the joke, as he often did. She'd lost count of the times they'd poked gentle fun at Winter's excesses. He wasn't smiling, though, which surprised her. He was one of the smiliest men that she knew. His face was drawn, but it wasn't from his hangover. She knew him better than that.

The woman with the clipboard materialized next to them and murmured an instruction. 'If you turn around now, you should see your family arrive. We'll start moving the guests into position on the waterfront. ETA is three minutes.'

The couple spun around in unison, scanning the bay for signs of their 'surprise'. Through the gloom, Jen glimpsed the lights of the pleasure cruiser, tiny beacons of joy through the grey.

'There they are,' she said, her voice excited, rising a notch. She craned her neck for a better view. 'Can you spot the kids?' But Phil, whose eyes always lit up when he saw his children, was uncharacteristically subdued.

'Are you OK?' she said, assuming he was tired from the previous night's overindulgence, but mildly irritated that he couldn't manage to summon up even a pretence of enthusiasm on this special day.

He gazed at her, and, for a moment, she thought she saw something in him break. The fairy lights strung around the jetty caught the film of tears in his eyes, but then he pulled himself together, composing his features. Jen felt the first stirrings of anxiety. 'What is it?'

The fog shrouded them, and the sounds of the wedding guests faded, and their world was reduced to the space between them. She thought about how much she adored him. Their family. The home and life they had built together. He swallowed once, his Adam's apple bobbing in his throat, and his expression was grave.

She had known and loved this man for years. She had seen the best and worst of him. And standing here, on their wedding day, she sensed that something was very wrong indeed.

But Jen never got the chance to press him for answers because a flicker of movement across the water caught her eye, and her life, as she knew it, ended.

29

Teddy

Teddy Miller was four years old when death made its first attempt on his life. Except there was no cloaked figure with a scythe and hood from one of his storybooks, but a woman in a party dress who loved him with all she had.

It was supposed to be a surprise for his mother and father: Teddy, his sister Iris, his aunts and uncle, baby cousin and grandparents, arriving at the party to end all parties by specially chartered pleasure boat, decorated with fairy lights and flowers.

He was dressed for a wedding: white shirt and tie; a pale blue suit with a rose in his buttonhole; Teddy-sized trainers with Velcro fastenings, because he hadn't yet mastered tying his laces.

The patchy fog had almost grounded them, but his aunt had pleaded with the skipper, and because he was so familiar with the caprices of the bay, he'd agreed to set sail, albeit with some reluctance.

Their course had been steady, a twenty-minute trip from Bell Wharf to the private jetty that belonged to the elegant waterfront residence hosting the celebration. It was a simple journey, and one the skipper had travelled thousands of times over the years. But the weather had worsened, even during that short Saturday afternoon period, and the fog now obscured the welcoming lights on the wooden walkway. For that reason, the pleasure cruiser was closer to the shoreline than usual when the anchor was dropped.

Teddy and his sister ran to the side of the boat, peering through the murk for their parents, who'd been primed to stand beneath the decorated arch at the end of the jetty.

Iris was taller than her brother, her chin resting on the high side of the boat. She waved energetically, her voice rising, full of anticipation. 'There they are.' She called out to their mother and father. Once. Twice. Three times.

'I can't see them,' said Teddy, standing on his tiptoes, leaning into his sister. His lower lip trembled. He said it again, soft but urgent. No one heard him.

His aunts had gathered on the deck behind the children, an unusual stiffness between them, champagne flutes already in hand. One of the adults exclaimed in delight as guests lined the waterfront to welcome them in. The skipper directed his mate to disembark and fix the mooring ropes around the cleats on the jetty

Teddy jumped up and down, trying to get a better look. A woman's voice, warm and loving, remonstrated with him. 'Hold your horses, young man.'

'But I can't see anything.'

Two hands – strong and familiar – slipped beneath his armpits and lifted him into the air. He caught the scent of his Auntie Lyssa's perfume and, for a moment, he cuddled into her, relishing the softness of her coat and hair, before turning back to scan the shoreline for his mother and father.

But he still couldn't see, and so he squirmed in his aunt's arms, his trainers seeking a foothold on the lip of the upper side of the boat. He held himself rigid, in that way stubborn four-year-olds can, until he was standing upright on the gunwale, and his aunt's hold had slipped down his body from his waist to his knees.

'Keep still, you little monster,' she said, but there was laughter in her voice, and Teddy, on hearing it, continued to wriggle, trying for extra laughs and a better look.

'I see them.' His shriek of excitement made the rest of the family laugh too, apart from his grandfather, who called a warning from inside the cabin. 'Be careful with Teddy. Get him down from there.' From his perch on the bench, the older man lit a cigar and blew out the smoke, appealing to his wife, who was standing by the window, holding the baby. 'Give her a hand with him, Carol.'

Even then, it might have been OK, but three things happened: Alyssa, relaxed and in a teasing mood, lifted Teddy higher into the air than she ought to have done. Theirs was a playful relationship, full of rough and tumble, and joyous spontaneity, and she was fully intending to swing him back to the safety of the deck. But with a flash of impetuosity she would forever regret, she dangled him over the side of the boat, just for a moment, pretending she was about to drop him into the sea.

It was a silly, badly thought-out joke, with no malice or ill intent, but with serious and unintended consequences. Her actions prompted the boy to buck more violently than she'd anticipated, startling her post-partum body with his strength. At the same time, a large wave crashed against the hull, jolting even the most sure-footed of passengers and causing her grip on him to slacken.

She tried to readjust her hold on him, but something hard knocked into her, propelling her forward.

In that split second, Teddy slid from her grasp, falling through the air, not in cinematic slow motion, but before she'd even had a chance to register what was happening. Her fingers reached for him, brushing the soft cloth of his jacket, but she was too late. In another life, she would have grabbed his arm and pulled him back from the brink of danger, a story to be told and retold until memory softened its edges and they laughed about his near miss, that visceral sense of fear lost to time, passing into family lore. But this was not another life.

Teddy's arms pinwheeled, a look of almost comical surprise on his face. Years later, his sister Iris would tell their mother that Teddy had cried out for her, a single, desperate plea, but the sound was torn from him by the wind and the waves. As the fog closed around him, the boy – a much-loved son, brother, nephew and grandson – didn't make another sound before he hit the water, slipped beneath the surface and was gone.

PART THREE

AFTER

30

Sunday, 19 November 2023

Blue

Blue hadn't contacted Saul for twenty-four hours, but she knew she ought to. She was being unfair. It was time to tell him the truth.

After James Warburton, the duty solicitor, had dropped her home yesterday, Blue had climbed into her bed with Miss Meow, and she hadn't moved from there until hungry mewling had forced her to this morning.

She'd wanted to believe him and his parting words. As she'd thanked him for the lift, he'd lingered on her doorstep and smiled at her, warm and reassuring. 'Try to relax. They don't have the evidence to hold you, Clover. They can't charge you with anything.'

He wouldn't say that if he knew what they'd done. She couldn't tell him the truth though, even if she'd wanted to. And a self-destructive part of her did. The knowledge she carried inside her was poisoning everything.

At first, the full force of her fury had been directed at the police officer who had raped her, and her focus had been on making sure that no man could ever brutalize her in that way again. But as the months had passed, the gravity of his murder had begun to weigh heavily, pressing down on her until she struggled to breathe, haunting every waking moment and seeping into her dreams until they became nightmares.

She felt tarnished, dirtied by their actions, and a tendril of resentment took hold and wrapped itself around her so tightly that she felt no relief or chance of escape.

When she and Saul had met, as new recruits on their first day in the job, they had bonded over their nerves, and the thunderbolt of attraction that existed between them. Their relationship had been like no other she'd experienced. The heat that burned between them had consumed them both. He had been non-judgemental about her narcolepsy, and both of them had admired the brilliance of the other's mind, piecing together the complexities of their cases in synchronicity.

But everything had changed.

Day by day, hour by hour, she'd begun to blame Saul Anguish, this stranger who'd appeared in her life one day and ruined everything, not least her job as a forensic linguist, which she loved and was now out of bounds. She had asked James Warburton about her professional future, but his answer had been unsatisfying, with no clear guidance and no roadmap for her return.

'In these circumstances, it's customary for you to remain off work on indefinite leave while they complete their enquiries. If we haven't heard anything in a couple of weeks, I'll chase them to find out what's happening and when you might be able to return. If things are still proving difficult, we can get your union involved. Does that sound OK to you?'

She'd nodded, but in truth, it did not sound OK to her at

all. Without her job, she didn't know who she was and how she would fill her time, and she watched James drive away from her flat, envious of his liberation, his sense of well-being. She had not realized how important those things were to her until she had lost them.

But now she had to deal with Saul. Part of her was concerned about his reaction: she knew what he was capable of, and she worried that the darkness she'd seen inside him would not turn itself inwards, but towards her. For months, their relationship – their sense of kinship – had afforded her an element of special protection, but that would no longer exist if she decided to walk away from him. He had always been solicitous, almost courtly towards her, and she had enjoyed being the focus of his intensity. She knew he was a good man with shadows in his heart, but what did that mean for her? Would he let her go? Or would he see her as a threat to be eliminated?

But she could not share her dilemma without divulging their secret.

She forced herself to eat a piece of toast. She'd lost weight and her reflection in the mirror was pale and wan. She considered pretending a bit longer, until the immediate threat to her liberty had passed, but she knew she could not bear him to touch her, and as that had always been a fundamental part of their communication, she recognized that she had no choice now but to tell him it was over.

It was just a question of when.

31

Winter

Come on, Teddy. Hold on. This is a family of fighters. We won't let you leave us.

32

Sunday, 19 November 2023

Alyssa

Don't die. Please, don't die. Please.

33

Sunday, 19 November 2023

Jen

Goodbye, my baby boy.

34

Monday, 20 November 2023

Saul

Midtown was full of Monday shoppers. He bought himself a sandwich and took his solitary lunch to a bench on the cliffs that overlooked the bay. The damp clung to him. Across the water, he could guess the rough direction of Winter Kellaway's estate, but the fog was still impenetrable.

Although he could not spot them today, he knew the mudflats would be dotted with hundreds of black specks, spread across the horizon as far as the eye could see. The brent geese travelled to Midtown from Siberia every winter, and from his bed in the coastguard's lookout, he could sometimes hear their cries, drifting across the tide. They reminded him that despite the tragedy of the weekend, the world would always turn.

The boy had died. He was four, a year younger than a girl called Clara he'd once saved from the arms of a serial killer with a whisper and a pipe-cleaner doll. Absently he rubbed his forearm, which still bore the faint scar of her teeth. This was one of the reasons he did not believe in God. Children, whether innocents or those hollow-eyed scraps whose upbringing had turned them towards darkness, never deserved to die.

A wind with a brisk edge blew in from the bay, and it chilled him, but not enough to move him on. Saul was at home in the elements. The salted freshness of the seascape was energizing, and it kept him alert. His kayaking had trained him to withstand all weathers, and he found that he preferred the cold secrets of the winter sea.

'Mac told me you'd be here.'

He recognized her voice before he turned around, and sent up a silent prayer of thanks to the nosy sergeant on duty at the front desk. She was wearing a hat pulled over her ears, but the flash of blue fringe was impossible to disguise.

'I went to the lookout first,' she said. 'But your kayak was leaning against the wall, and no one was home, so I guessed you were at work.'

He shrugged, not sure whether to be flattered at the effort she had taken to track him down or concerned that she had something to say to him that couldn't wait.

'I didn't have anything else to do.' He regretted those words as soon as he'd said them. It made him sound like he had nothing but work in his life. Which was true. But still, she didn't need reminding of that. And he didn't want her to think he was rebuking her, although the fresh mango and yoghurt he'd bought for their breakfast two days earlier was still in the fridge, waiting to be eaten.

She took a deep breath. 'I'm sorry I didn't call yesterday.'

'It's OK,' he said, even though it wasn't.

He watched her carefully, trying to gauge where this conversation was leading. Blue had always seemed so robust, despite her diminutive stature, but she had lost weight and her coat, already oversized, almost drowned her. She bit her lip. He waited, but she didn't speak. He could read her well. There was an edginess about her, in the way the words tumbled out of her mouth, faster than usual, and she fiddled with her buttons, gloved hands fluttering like brightly coloured butterflies.

'Sit down.' He patted the bench as an invitation. She hesitated, but conceded, perching herself at the far end, creating a distance between them. He remembered the days when she would sling an arm around his shoulder and sit on his lap, her face shining up at him. But now she could barely meet his gaze. He'd thought she might find it easier to sit down next to him because then she could speak to the wide expanse of the bay instead of looking at him.

'I don't want to do this anymore.' The words spilled from her without fuss or preamble. There was no dressing it up in platitudes, or declarations of ongoing love and friendship. She'd stated it calmly and simply. It was over between them.

He didn't say anything. Later, he would wonder if he should have fought harder for her, or tried to change her mind. But he was a proud man who could not bring himself to beg for anyone's love, not even Blue's.

At his lack of reaction, she turned to look at him. Her sea-mist eyes were full of sympathy, and that riled him. He could not abide being the subject of anyone's pity. He stood up, afraid this sudden burst of anger would take him to places he did not want to go. She reached for the sleeve of his coat, but he shook her off. 'Get off me.' His tone was hard, clipped.

Her eyes filled with tears. In the past, that would have been enough to soften him, but an irreversible shift had occurred. He stared at her without compassion. She looked away, an expression of confusion on her face.

'Don't you want to talk about it?'

'What's the point? You've already made a decision.'

Her hands were in her lap, still fluttering. 'Why did you call me five times? Before I was arrested.'

He stilled. He could tell her the truth. That the Chief Constable had ordered him to investigate Dr Clover March under the radar, and he'd agreed to do so in order to protect her. That police officers from the Kent arm of the Serious Crime Directorate were closing in on her. That he'd destroyed or hidden every scrap of evidence he'd unearthed that might have incriminated her. That he'd called to warn her they were coming to arrest her. But her betrayal turned those words to dust in his mouth.

When he did not answer, she spoke again. 'Do you want to know what happened at the police station?'

'I know you haven't been charged.'

'Don't you want to know what I said?'

'Why? I can't change it.'

He knew he was being difficult, deliberately obstructive even, and to his own detriment. It was important to know what she had said in her interview, and whether she had implicated him. But a numbness had set in, spreading through his head and his heart. Seven simple words, and the wall that Blue had taken apart, brick by brick, was back in place. Except this time, he was building himself a fortress, and no one would get inside it. He would never make that mistake again.

'I didn't say anything about you,' she said. 'I wouldn't. But I don't know how long I can carry this secret, Saul. It's eating me up inside. I can't sleep. I can't eat.' The tears were spilling down her face now. 'I can't live with what we've done.'

Saul crumpled up the paper wrapper from his lunch and threw it in the bin. He walked a few steps away from her, to the cliff edge. The fog was drifting, thicker in some places. If he narrowed his eyes, he could make out the dark shape of the rocky outcrop, close to the lighthouse. He wanted to step off the edge and disappear into its nothingness. He couldn't decide whether feeling pain was worse than feeling nothing at all.

She appeared at his side, a will-o'-the-wisp in the November murk.

'I'm sorry.' He had to strain to hear her. 'But I can't help the way I feel.'

Saul wasn't sure if she was referring to him or to what they had done, but the distinction felt important. He willed her to separate their relationship from their crime.

'Confessing isn't a choice. It's a suicide mission.'

'It's not your decision.'

'You'll go to prison.'

She shook her head, her voice rising. 'I'm *in* prison. Can't you understand that?'

'It might feel that way. But the alternative would be so much worse.' He could be persuasive if he wanted to be. Some might say manipulative, even sly. 'Think about the repercussions. The effect on your sister. Your mother. You'll lose your job, your flat, your reputation. Everything you've worked for. There'll be no going back from this.'

'It's not your decision,' she said again, mouth set in a stubborn line.

It wasn't. Of course not. But her actions would impact him. His liberty. The life he had carved out for himself. He could move on from Midtown without a backward glance. Pack his bags and be gone tonight. But he did not relish the prospect of looking over his shoulder for the rest of his days.

Blue might think she was intelligent enough to obfuscate the truth, but the police and barristers were skilled interviewers. Her lies would be difficult to maintain under intense scrutiny. In time, they would wheedle the truth from her. His name. His part in the murder of Douglas Lynch. And that would be catastrophic for him.

In the past, when Saul had been confronted by a challenge to his will, he had influenced the outcome by whatever means necessary. He had not balked at physical violence, no matter who it was.

He knew that about himself. And Blue knew it too. But she'd taken the risk anyway.

Silence hung between them, and it was painful and loaded. It wasn't the electrically charged tension of sexual attraction or the comfortable intimacy of that late-night drink that required no conversation. There was knowledge in this silence. Both of them recognized that. Blue was braver than he was, he realized. She'd had the courage to bring this to him. If his heart hadn't turned to a splinter of ice, it might have made him weep.

'I have one request,' he said eventually.

She tipped her head to one side, and he noticed that her eyes were the same colour as the fog that surrounded them. He thought, for the thousandth time, how beautiful she was.

'What is it?'

'If you're serious about making a confession, give me enough time to get away.'

Her face crumpled then, and he almost felt his own composure slip.

'What about telling the truth?' Her voice was low, but persuasive. 'You can't outrun your past forever.'

'No.' An emphatic shake of the head. He would rather die than spend years locked up in a cage.

'Then I'll warn you, I promise.'

She stood on her tiptoes and kissed him softly on the side of his mouth. He closed his eyes and allowed himself to commit to memory the feel of her skin, the scent and taste of her.

Perhaps, in time, they would be friends, although he doubted that. He could not conceive of a time when friendship would ever be enough.

He broke away from her touch and allowed himself one last glance at the woman he loved. Then he walked away and he didn't look back.

In his mind's eye, he would forever see her standing on the cliff edge, her blue hair lifting in the wind, the distinctive black and white pattern of her houndstooth coat. Perhaps, in time, he would recognize that this was the right decision for them both.

For now, it felt like the end of everything.

35

Alyssa

It was the children who undid her. Bundled up in their coats and scarves, they lined the streets, an imperfect and fidgeting guard of honour for Teddy Miller, each clutching a winter-flowering daffodil in their small gloved hands.

The cold had pinked their cheeks, and they spoke to each other in whispers, but sometimes they forgot why they were there, and their voices escalated, excited about the holidays, the forthcoming festivities, and their teachers and parent-volunteers would hush them into silence.

Uncertain of her welcome, Alyssa Kellaway had not joined the funeral cortège that was departing from Jen's house, but walked with Federico to the church on the clifftop, over-looking the bay. They had barely exchanged a word, but Alyssa noticed the glances that came her fiancé's way. His fame was spilling beyond their small corner of Midtown-on-Sea and into national – *international* – consciousness. Someone was filming him with their camera-phone. In less than five minutes' time, that footage would find its way onto the internet.

One or two of Iris's classmates recognized her, smiling shyly as she passed them, and a little boy from the pre-school, who had cried during pass the parcel at Teddy's fourth birthday party, waved at her. 'It's the lolly lady,' he said, and she tried to smile back, recalling how she'd placated him with a plastic-wrapped lollipop, sticky and artificially red.

All these children had come to pay their respects. But her nephew, who should be among their chattering brightness, was in a four-foot box in the back of a hearse.

'Did you speak to Phil?' She had asked Fed this question many times over the preceding few days, but had so far failed to elicit an answer.

He'd half shrugged, not meeting her eye. 'He hasn't been at work.'

'I know, but I thought . . .' She didn't know what she thought. Except this. *He's your best friend, you must have spoken to him.*

'I don't want to intrude.' His tone was irritated. 'He'll be in touch when he's ready.'

Although he'd been careful not to throw accusations in her direction, it was clear that Fed blamed her for exploding this grenade in their lives. It radiated from him, a blast wave of disgust and disbelief.

At first, he'd tried his best to be kind, comforting her when she collapsed into sobs on the bathroom floor and encouraging her to eat, feeding her bland spoonfuls of porridge, the only food she could stomach.

But as the days rolled on, she sensed a shift in his attitude towards her. He'd asked her again and again to replay Teddy's final moments. When she'd explained, that first time, he'd pressed a hand to his mouth and pulled her to him, a fierce hug filled with compassion. But four weeks on, that sentiment had hardened into contempt.

She could read it in the sharp way he spoke to her, and the shape of his body, stiff with shame. Although he didn't say the words outright, it felt to Alyssa as if he was constantly asking her a question that she would never be able to answer. *How could you be so stupid?*

In the immediate aftermath of Teddy's accident, she'd spent as much time with Jen as their lives had allowed. Their family – tight-knit and loving – had turned inwards, leaning on each other for support. But over the last fortnight, her sister had distanced herself from Alyssa, and her messages had been left unread, her phone calls not returned. Determined to respect their grief and to give the Millers all the space they might need, Alyssa had hesitated to push herself forward and had instead tasked Fed with finding out about the funeral arrangements from his brother-in-law. But it was Carol who had eventually shared those details, and when Alyssa, worried, had queried Jen's silence, her mother had soothed, 'She just needs a bit of time.'

Outside the church, the vast crowd of mourners had spilled into the graveyard, a flock of crows among the lichen-covered headstones and memorial crosses. Alyssa recognized many of the same guests who'd gathered for the party a month earlier, but she did not talk to any of them. Instead, she and Fed stood a distance away, heads bowed against winter's cruelty.

At 11.12 a.m., the minister conducting the service announced, in his low voice, that the cortège was due to arrive and ushered them inside.

At 11.15 a.m., the polished hearse containing Teddy's remains made its slow progression up the drive, followed by three black cars: the first containing Jen, Phil and Iris;

the second, Carol, Geoff and Winter; and the third, Phil's sister and parents, who had declined Winter's invitation to join them on the pleasure boat and now carried themselves with an air of sanctimoniousness.

Alyssa had not entered the church with the other mourners, but had hung back, intending to welcome, to comfort her family. Before she'd had a chance to greet any of them, Phil had climbed out of the car and strode across the gravel until he was standing in front of them. Fed pulled him into a hug, and Phil let him, but Alyssa sensed the resistance in him, their physical contact brief.

'Why are you here?' His question was addressed to Alyssa, no bend in his tone, no warmth at all.

The answer was so obvious that she almost laughed, but the expression on Phil's face stopped her. She faltered, the creep of shame rendering her inarticulate and clumsy. It took her three attempts to get her words out, and even then, her voice cracked. 'To say goodbye.'

But Phil, who she had known for most of her life, who had once been so loving and gentle towards her, was unmoved. 'We don't want you here. Please go.'

Tears, hot and stinging, sprang to her eyes. She thought of all the things she could say to him, to wound him as he was wounding her, but she couldn't bring herself to utter the words. Jen had got out of the car too, but was standing back, holding Iris's hand. *Iris.* Her hair was neatly brushed. Black tights. A new coat with a velvet collar and the same shiny patent Mary Jane shoes she'd worn as a bridesmaid. The girl's lower lip was trembling and her instinct was to enfold her niece within her arms, to protect her from the violence of her loss, but she feared Phil's reaction.

A part of her knew she should leave without causing a

scene, but she couldn't find that dignity within herself. She appealed to her sister. 'Jen?'

Jen, too thin from weeks of not eating, met her sister's gaze. Grief scarred her face, its deep lines bracketing her mouth, hollowing her out. A range of emotions flitted across her features, like fast-moving clouds on a wind-blown day. Sorrow. Uncertainty. A glimpse of something harder.

Phil again. 'You need to leave.'

Alyssa waited for her sister to speak up for her, but Jen's silence said everything. A tear tracked its way down Iris's cheek. Tiny flakes of snow began to fall, making the air whisper.

The undertaker, in his funereal finery of top hat and tails, reminded her of a black peacock. He cleared his throat, a gentle reminder that he was waiting for Phil to join the rest of the pallbearers.

Winter, in dark glasses and an elegant black cape, and mindful of the photographers gathered at the bottom of the church grounds, tried to intervene. 'Perhaps—' But Phil, brusque and rough, cut her off. 'Stay out of this, Winter.'

Carol and Geoff stood back awkwardly, caught in a trap of divided loyalties, but neither spoke, not wishing to upset the bereaved parents, whose feelings took precedence over everything on that cold December morning.

A stone lodged itself in the back of her throat. She wanted to scream at them. *It was a stupid accident. It wasn't my fault. I didn't mean for him to die.* But instead Alyssa, excluded and unwelcome, gave a sharp nod of defeat. She moved backwards, half turning towards her fiancé.

'Are you coming?' The rising heat of her grief at the back of her throat almost strangled her words. Federico took a step closer to Phil. 'No, I'm going to stay.'

At that final betrayal, Alyssa turned her back on them all.

Cut adrift from those she loved most, it was a lonely walk from the church entrance, past the cemetery and towards the grey wash of the bay. She felt as frozen inside as the earth beneath her feet. As she reached the gate that separated the churchyard from the frost-tinged salt marshes, the sound of running footsteps caught her attention.

Iris slammed into her, crying and hysterical, her arms around her aunt's waist, burying her face in her chest, squeezing her close until there was no space between their bodies, no room to breathe.

The girl's distress was palpable. She mumbled into Alyssa's buttons. 'Please don't go. I won't let you.'

In the near distance, Jen was running back down the drive towards them, her heels too high for any kind of speed. Alyssa smoothed the child's hair from her hot, damp face. There was so much she wanted to say, but there was no time, and instead she cupped Iris's cheeks between her palms.

'I have to, sweetheart. For Mummy and Daddy's sake. But whatever happens next, I love you, OK? Always will.'

Iris cried harder. The crack in Alyssa's heart widened. Not for the first time in her life, she felt her world tip on its axis. But she felt an inner compulsion to do the right thing by her sister and her eight-year-old niece. What was her shame and humiliation when compared to their loss?

She wrapped her niece in a fierce hug, murmuring into her ear. 'Remember what I said?' Iris sniffed and rubbed her eyes with the heel of both hands. 'Yes.'

'I love you, Iris.'

'Love you too.'

The snow was heavier now, settling on Iris's hair and her coat, as if Teddy himself was shaking it out from the clouds.

Her aunt gave the girl a gentle nudge in the direction of her mother, who was now standing a short distance from them both, anguish twisting her features. 'It's time to go now. Say goodbye to your brother for me.'

For the briefest of moments, Jen glanced at Alyssa. The younger woman searched for a hint of connection, for some sense of their shared love and sisterhood that had spanned decades, but Jen's eyes were glittering and hard, and still she did not speak. Jen took Iris's hand and the pair of them walked back up the incline towards the church.

Alyssa watched them until the church doors opened, and Teddy's family and his coffin disappeared into its depths, the strains of music drifting across the morning air.

She waited in the cold for a few minutes longer, hoping that the Millers might experience a change of heart, until the urge to hold her infant daughter became too powerful to ignore, and she began to run, suddenly desperate to get home.

Tears wetted her cheeks. As she crossed the path that cut across the salt marshes and joined the road back to Midtown, she replayed the memory of her sister and her niece again and again, those two figures clad in black, leaving her behind, not knowing that the next time she would see them would be seven months later across a courtroom.

36

Sunday, 24 December 2023

Jen

Jen sat in the cold sitting room, wrapped in a blanket, watching videos of Teddy on her phone. The heat had gone from the fire, but she couldn't be bothered to move. If Phil was here, he'd have thrown another log on by now, but he'd gone to bed hours before and was snoring in the embrace of his new mistresses, whisky and gin.

Christmas Eve was a night for children, but her youngest was lost somewhere to the ether. Part of her longed to believe in heaven, to find solace in the fact of its existence, but instead she tormented herself with thoughts of Teddy wandering in the darkness, lost and alone.

After his funeral, the family had attended a brief committal service at the crematorium and her son's ashes were now in a cardboard box in his bedroom. The funeral director had warned her not to make any hasty decisions about what to do with them next. Phil had talked about scattering them at the beach or in the bluebell wood, but that didn't feel right to Jen. Teddy wouldn't want to be apart from them and she couldn't bear the idea of letting him go. It comforted her, knowing he was at home with his parents and sister, the place where he belonged.

One of her friends had asked why they had chosen not to bury him. They had considered it, but she couldn't bring herself to lower him into the damp earth. The nurse at the hospital had understood. Jen had noticed the tender way she'd tucked a blanket around Teddy, and sent him to the morgue with a pillow, and warmed the water for his wash, even after he'd taken his last breath.

Tomorrow – or was it today now? – was Christmas Day. She did not want to celebrate, but her mother had gently encouraged her into action. 'Iris still believes, my love. Don't ruin the magic for her yet.'

While she had bristled inwardly at Carol's interference, she'd followed her advice and wrapped a small pile of gifts for her daughter, waiting until she was asleep before tiptoeing into her bedroom to fill her stocking. Jen could still remember the childish joy of waking in the night to an unfamiliar weight at the end of her bed, sleepily patting the packages and snuggling back beneath the covers, knowing Father Christmas had been. Her mother was right. She couldn't deny Iris that pleasure.

After that, she'd stood in Teddy's bedroom, a quiet, empty place, lit by the moon. She couldn't get used to its tidiness, the unwrinkled duvet, his toys put away in their baskets, his books waiting for him on the shelf. It felt wrong to leave him out, but she didn't want Iris to ask awkward questions. Instead she placed a new die-cast train she'd bought for him under his pillow and whispered into the silence, 'I miss you.'

At 3 a.m., she forced herself off the sofa and went to bed, driven upstairs by exhaustion and the chill that had settled into her bones. The room smelled of stale alcohol. As she got into bed, Phil stirred and then woke up. He switched on his bedside lamp.

'You're freezing.'

'Sorry. The heating's gone off.'

His breath reeked and stubble shadowed his chin. In the dim light, he looked ten years older than he had a few weeks ago. For one awful moment, she thought he was going to wish her a happy Christmas, but instead he said, 'Are you hungry?'

She hadn't eaten properly for weeks. 'Maybe. I don't know.'

'Wait there.'

A few minutes later, he was back with a plate of hot buttered toast and two mugs of tea. She bit into a triangle, the taste of comfort. 'Thank you.'

Although she was dog-tired, she knew she would struggle to sleep. It was the same every night. The GP had suggested medication, but she hated the way it deadened her senses and turned her into a stranger, sluggish and slow.

'What do you want to do tomorrow?' Phil sipped his tea.

Spend the day in bed by myself watching videos of Teddy. Cry until my eyes are swollen and raw. Try not to think about how much I want to follow my boy into death. Remember to breathe.

But she wouldn't wound him by saying those truths out loud.

Her elder sister had invited them for lunch, but she wasn't sure how she felt about that. A part of her couldn't face it without Teddy, but Iris needed to eat, to lose herself in the distraction of family. In these endless dark days, her daughter, who had become worryingly quiet, deserved some normalcy. Perhaps she and Phil did too, just for a few hours. She missed being ordinary. 'How do you feel about going to Winter's for lunch?'

Phil placed his mug on the bedside table with deliberate care. 'Are you being serious?'

Her hackles rose, but she kept her voice steady. 'Yes. It might be good for all of us.'

'Fed and Alyssa are going.'

'I know.'

'I can't be around your sister.'

She didn't know what to say to that. She was angry with Alyssa too. Incandescent at times. But it wouldn't bring Teddy back. They had to find a way to manage their hurt before it destroyed all of them. Her mother was shattered by the death of her grandson, and the rift it had caused between her daughters. Iris hadn't seen her cousin for weeks. She asked every day if they could visit baby Claudia. How could Phil continue to work with Fed if he refused to see his sister-in-law? But it was complicated. She acknowledged that. Her own feelings could not be parcelled into a neat little package, so how could she expect that of Phil? It was messy and confusing. Phil did not share the same emotional bonds with the Kellaways as she did. He was in pain, and he needed someone to blame. She tried to explain, but words were inadequate. 'I understand how you feel, but I need my family.'

'Iris and me, *we're* your family.'

'You know what I mean.'

Phil's voice was hard. 'The police called me a couple of days ago. A file has gone to the Crown Prosecution Service. If they agree there's enough evidence to support a case, she'll be charged with gross negligence manslaughter.' He wouldn't look at her. 'I'm fully behind them.'

'I don't know, Phil. It's—'

'No less than she deserves.' The venom in him was unmistakeable.

Jen closed her eyes. She knew this had been a possibility since their nightmare began. But she had pushed it to the back of her mind, unable to cope with the ramifications on her marriage and extended family.

'She killed him, Jen. It's as simple as that.'

And how could she argue with that?

The toast had gone cold now. It tasted like cardboard. She placed the plate on her bedside table, next to her undrunk tea. Phil pulled the duvet over him and switched off the light. He rolled away from her, his back a wall.

She lay unmoving in the darkness, wide-eyed and heartsore, until the thin light of Christmas morning washed the night away, and another day of a life without Teddy began.

37

Saul

He walked for miles until his hip was singing with pain and he found himself on the eastern edges of the salt marshes at the far end of Midtown.

He crouched down into the tussocky grassland, wet mud seeping into his shoes, and sought out the comforts of his childhood, grubbing through the tidal debris and vegetation for the gifts hidden among nature for those who knew where to look.

He found one near the shore on the underside of a piece of driftwood. He picked it up and examined its beauty, marvelling at the soft incline of its antennae and the feel of its sole against his palm. He observed it for a couple of minutes, considered the miniature heart and stomach and kidneys that were concealed within its calcareous covering, and the outgrowths at its opening which protected it from predators. It was a beautiful specimen, rich in colour and lacking imperfections.

But Saul did not take living creatures, and so he placed it back where he had found it and walked a few steps further, casting around in the dune slacks until he found an empty shell, its brown spiral gleaming in the dampness. The narrow-mouthed whorl snail, Latin name *Vertigo angustior*. He tipped it over, examining the interior, but he could not see its body and therefore did not know whether it had shrivelled to nothing, dying within its home, or if it had detached itself, its muscular stickiness decomposing somewhere among the coastal turf.

He put the shell in his matchbox, but habit propelled him onwards, seeking other treasures in the landscape, eyes sharp, fully focused on his task. Eutrophication – an increase in nutrients that led to the deterioration in water quality of these coastal seepages – was decimating the snail population in this corner of the county. It saddened him that humanity had sacrificed the natural world on the altar of convenience and excess.

When he was a boy, no more than six or seven, his father had told him that no one would ever love him. Saul had no reason to disbelieve that. His mother was a drunk, detached and angry, and his father had hit him many more times than he had kissed him. 'There's a sickness inside you. You're all twisted up.' His father had crouched next to him, a sneer on his face. 'Remember, Saul, if your parents don't want you, no one will.' He had carried those words with him all of his life.

Blue had been the first woman that Saul had loved. She had redefined its meaning for him, and for a while, in the white heat of their lust and their friendship, he had allowed himself to imagine that she might love him back. That had turned out to be a brief but futile hope.

Since that bleak November Monday, he had buried himself in work, taking extra shifts on his rest days and volunteering for the grunt jobs that no one else wanted.

Almost every night, he had driven to her flat and sat outside in the darkness, trying to steel himself for what might come next.

He was haunted by memories of his happiness, but he understood that it was the loss of all those possibilities, of his future with the girl with the sea-mist eyes, that would plague him. He wanted to leave Midtown, as Blue had left him. There was nothing to keep him here anymore.

But something stayed his hand.

As he trudged through the salt marshes, the walls of the fortress he had built around himself growing taller, that instinct towards darkness sharpening with every step, he mused that while there had been many flaws in Solomon Anguish's character, on this occasion, his father had been proved right.

38

Carol

It was not yet 7 a.m., but her youngest two girls were already in the garden, searching for the brightly painted wooden eggs she had hidden among the daffodils and crocuses, behind the shed and underneath the trampoline.

Carol smiled to herself at the childish exchanges between Jen and Alyssa, and their shrieks of excitement at each new discovery. It was the first Easter in their new home – the family had only moved in six weeks earlier – and she wanted it to be special.

Each child – even Deborah – had a soft bunny embroidered with her name, and Carol had hand-sewn triangles of bunting and strung it through the trees. Even at this early hour, it was too warm to hide the chocolate eggs she'd bought. Later, they would decorate hard-boiled eggs and eat hot cross buns and the simnel cake she'd made for tea.

She sipped her coffee, relishing a couple of minutes' peace. Sometimes it felt absurd to her that she was deemed responsible enough to be a mother of one, let alone three.

231

Deborah appeared behind her, blinking into the sunshine. She was wearing pyjamas with acorns on them, but her wrists poked from the too-short sleeves like newly sprung twigs and her bottoms were threadbare in places.

'You're growing so quickly,' said Carol, touching her on the shoulder. 'We'll have to buy you a new set.'

The girl shook her head, a refusal. 'I like my old ones.'

Alyssa raced into the kitchen, her basket full to the brim with wooden eggs. 'Look, Mummy.'

A disconsolate Jen trailed behind, her lower lip trembling, and she ran to her mother, grabbing her hand. '*My* mummy.' She pointed to her almost empty basket. 'I only got two.'

Deborah, eyes flashing, snatched some from Alyssa's basket and put them into Jen's. Alyssa let out an ear-piercing scream and tried to snatch them back. 'Mine!'

'It's nice to share.' Deborah hissed the words at her youngest sister. 'Be a good girl.'

'There's plenty to go round.' Carol was patient. 'If you wait a little while, I'll hide some chocolate eggs in the house. We can count them up at the end and share them out. Does that sound fun?'

But Alyssa wouldn't stop crying. Deborah sighed, then picked her up until her tears softened into hiccups.

Solemn-faced, Jen carefully placed all the eggs back into Alyssa's basket, including her own. 'Yours,' she said.

Much later, when the girls were full of too much chocolate and tired from a day playing outside, their mother gathered them to her for a story. Deborah curled up at one end of the sofa, pretending not to listen. On either side of Carol sat Jen and Alyssa.

'Once upon a time, there were three sisters who ruled

over Evermore. One was just and fair, one was kind and generous, and one was as wild as the wind. It was a happy and thriving place.

'One day, a stranger visited their kingdom and offered each of the sisters a deal. To the sister who was just, he offered the chance to be selfish; to the sister who was kind, he offered great personal riches; and to the sister who was wild, he offered freedom from responsibility. The only conditions were that each sister must make her decision alone and, if she accepted his offer, she must leave the kingdom she called home.

'Two of the sisters accepted his deal and one chose to remain in Evermore. Years passed. And, on a spring day very much like this one, the two sisters returned. But the kingdom was not the thriving place it had once been. The houses were crumbling and run-down. The fields, once filled with crops that fed a whole kingdom, were nothing more than blackened stubble. And the castle that had once been their home was a shambling ruin. All hope had been forsaken in Evermore.

'The sister who had once been as wild as the wind opened the door to them. She was old and grey, bent with the burden of responsibility. "Sister, what has happened?" they cried.

'She paused for a moment to admire their expensive gowns, embroidered with the finest gold thread, and the jewels they wore on their fingers. "Tell me," she said, "are you happy?"

'The sister who had once been just and fair shook her head. "My selfishness has made me lonely." The sister who had once been kind and generous shook her head. "My wealth has come at the expense of our kingdom."

'The remaining sister replied, "As a three, we are stronger together than apart."

'And the sisters reunited and rebuilt Evermore until it thrived once more.'

Deborah stretched out her legs and snorted. 'I think I'd still take the money.'

Carol smiled at her. 'Money does smooth the pathway in life, there's no doubt about it. But I think there's a moral in that story too.'

'What's a moral?' The ends of Jen's hair were in her mouth, blurring the four-year-old's words.

'It's a lesson,' said Carol. 'You girls are all different, and your dad and I want to celebrate those differences, to enjoy your individuality, but you're a family too. And the thing about families is that we always look after and protect each other. Whatever else happens in life, never forget that.'

39

Thursday, 16 May 2024

Alyssa

MIDTOWN-ON-SEA CROWN COURT (3764)

To: Miss Alyssa Grace Kellaway   Date: 16 MAY 2024
    14 Springvale Rise   ASN: 173462917
    Midtown-on-Sea
    MS4 3RG

You are hereby summonsed to appear on Monday, 22 July 2024 at 10.00 a.m. before the Crown Court at High Street, Midtown-on-Sea to answer the following information:

Alleged offences:
FOR THAT, you Alyssa Grace Kellaway (DOB: 06/12/83) of 14 Springvale Rise, Midtown-on-Sea did on Saturday, 18 November 2023, at approximately 15.02 hrs drop a child overboard a vessel, culminating in his death.
SUCH THEREFORE, you are being prosecuted for GROSS NEGLIGENCE MANSLAUGHTER.

Fiona Cummins

Prosecutor: David Jarvis, KC

Address: Radcliffe Chambers, LONDON, GENEVA, BRUSSELS

Date of Information: 16 MAY 2024

Pamela Graham
Clerk of the Court

PART FOUR

NOW

40

Monday, 22 July 2024

Saul

The sun was rising when the young detective finished his circuit of the bay. He steadied his kayak and watched the ball of fire hover above the horizon and then crawl upwards, a cruising flock of cormorants cutting across its surface.

In the past few months, the parameters of his life had shifted once more. He had lost Blue – his heart was still bruised by that – but at least he'd regained his place in the Murder Club.

The seascape was a painting, the brushstrokes of dawn revealing the day in all its glory. Aside from the birds and fish, and an occasional seal, Saul was the only living creature as far as the eye could see. Even at this hour, he could feel the promise of the record-breaking heat predicted by forecasters. The sweat was beading on his forehead, and he swiped his wrist across his mouth, tasting salt on his skin. He wished he could spend his day on the water instead of in the stuffy confines of Court Two.

The detective had given evidence in the past a handful of times, but he was nervous today. Alyssa Kellaway's defence barrister, Trudi Baxter, had the reputation of being a

Rottweiler. Saul had spent the previous night rereading his statement, and the notes he had taken in preparation for his appearance in the witness box, but he knew how combative counsel could be, and this time, it would be in the full glare of the media spotlight.

At the coastguard's lookout, he showered and dressed, and drank a mug of coffee, scalding and strong. In his left pocket he carried a silver button that had come loose from Teddy Miller's jacket, weakened by its submersion in seawater. His thumb pressed against its rutted surface, tracing the shape of a letter. Saul had collected it from the jetty in the aftermath of that day. He would carry it as a talisman, a reminder to do his best for the boy who could no longer speak for himself. Accident? Gross negligence manslaughter? The court would decide.

Through force of habit, he checked his phone. Eight months on, and he still missed her, although he'd now accepted that reconciliation was not on the cards. He locked his door and headed into town.

The metal barriers positioned outside the courthouse were barely enough to contain the scrum of journalists, camera crews and photographers. They stopped talking when they saw him, but they let him pass without comment as they didn't yet know who he was. As soon as proceedings were underway, they'd find out exactly how significant his role had been in building this court case.

Even so, when Saul walked past them, he was aware that he was being filmed. He didn't blame them. They needed the footage, just in case he turned out to be newsworthy. He suspected the end of the day would bring a marked difference, but for now, he was unmolested.

He found his way through the maze of corridors to the relevant witness waiting room. It was empty apart from a court official with a grey buzz cut and no-nonsense attitude. She ticked him off her list and directed him to the toilets and the vending machine. He'd already been warned that he might not be called to give evidence today. But if the judge was satisfied, and there were no last-minute hiccups with the jury or representations from the respective legal teams, he would be due to take the stand after the prosecution and defence barristers had delivered their opening statements.

His mind drifted to the events of that fateful afternoon. They were still pin-sharp in his mind, and he would be asked to go over his honest recollections. But he was torn by what he knew. Would it be so bad if he distorted the facts? Yes, he had a legal obligation, but what about a moral one?

Saul understood that he was bound by law to tell the truth. He knew from experience that lawyers were skilled at bending those truths to fit their own narratives. But he also knew that he was prepared to lie to save his own skin, and that of those in need. *So help me, God.*

41

Monday, 22 July 2024

Alyssa

Even though she was the youngest of the three sisters, her hair had grey streaks in it that she couldn't be bothered to colour, and her body, still recovering from her baby's birth eight months earlier, was softer now than in the days immediately post-partum.

There was a stain on her skirt – possibly Claudia's baby rice – and the armpits of her blouse were already dampening in the heat. Unironed clothes littered the house in haphazard piles. Muslins and babygros were drying on the airer. In the kitchen, a row of sterilized bottles sat near the microwave. However often she cleaned them, she could never manage to erase the milk residue that lent the plastic an opaque appearance. She sat on the sofa in her sitting room, Claudia on her lap, and watched Sky News report on the case, live from outside the court.

Jen looked tired. Careworn. Ravaged by grief. Guilt sluiced through her. As it did every day. Every hour. Every minute. It was a crown of thorns on her head. Nails through her hands and feet. A spear buried in her chest. She hadn't seen her sister for months. Or her niece. She'd been asked to stay away after Teddy's funeral, and she'd respected that. But she missed him. She missed them all.

She glanced at her watch again and rose, setting the baby on the floor among her toys. Federico would be here soon, and he would tut and sigh if Claudia's overnight bag wasn't packed and ready, even though he was already late, but heaven help her if she mentioned that.

The doorbell rang, but she checked the camera before she went to answer it. In the immediate aftermath of Teddy's death, she'd been targeted by ghouls and grief tourists, and it wouldn't surprise her if that happened again, given the publicity the trial would spark. But a familiar face greeted her. It was still strange to her that he didn't have a key anymore. But their old house was sold now, and they were living in separate places and leading separate lives.

'You look knackered.'

'Thanks, Fed. I'll be sure to take that on board.'

'You need to make a bit of an effort with your appearance. You can't turn up at court looking like that. Everyone will judge you before you've even had the *chance* of a fair hearing.'

Her laugh was hollow. 'I've already been judged. Some grey hair and a few extra pounds isn't going to make a difference.' She smoothed the creases in her skirt. 'Trudi told me not to wear make-up or look too polished because it would show I didn't care. The jury need to see the impact this has had on me too.' She cringed, aware of how calculating she sounded, even though it was true.

She handed him the bag and the baby. She didn't know what was going to happen next. Her lawyers had fought tooth and nail for her to be released on bail, and she'd been lucky to spend the past few months in relative freedom. She could easily have been remanded in custody, waiting for the trial from prison. Social services were involved, but she hadn't been forced to relinquish care of Claudia, although there was regular supervision. Federico would care for their daughter for the duration of the court case. And beyond, if required. Although she couldn't bear to think about that.

'Good luck,' he said, but he couldn't bring himself to look at her. This was one of the more humbling elements of finding herself in the eye of the storm. Almost everyone had deserted her. All of her friends. Most of her family. She guessed that Fed had only maintained contact with her because of Claudia.

'How's Phil?'

He shrugged, reluctant to speak honestly. 'Angry. Struggling.'

She bowed her head, hardly daring herself to ask. 'And Jen?'

'I've hardly seen her.'

She knew then that there was more he wasn't saying, but she understood his dilemma, his divided loyalties. Her daughter reached for her and Alyssa kissed her chubby fingers, one by one. She smelled sweet, of baby lotion and freshly laundered clothes. 'If I get home in time, I'll drop by tonight and see her, OK?'

'I don't think that's a good idea. It might unsettle her.'

She didn't have it in her to fight him. Her shoulders slumped and she nodded once, defeated.

'The weekend, then.'

'Let's wait and see.'

As if she sensed her mother's distress, Claudia offered Alyssa a sunbeam of a smile that lifted the rounded pouches of her cheeks. She would carry that smile with her through the next few hours, drawing upon the memory of her daughter to give her strength, a reason to fight and survive.

Stomach tight with nerves, she checked her watch for a final time. She ought to have left ten minutes ago, but Fed had been late, and, even now, she felt no compulsion to rush. Her gaze flicked back to the television screen, and the footage of the courthouse and the security barriers, imposing even in the bright sunlight. There, in a matter of days, her fate would be decided.

She grabbed her cycling helmet and blew her baby a kiss goodbye, not knowing when she might see her again.

42

Monday, 22 July 2024

Jen

A deep breath, and she stepped from the taxi, running the gauntlet of the assembled press. They swarmed around her like flies on a carcass, but she didn't want to hide away, today of all days, and so she squared her shoulders and gazed steadily ahead of her. Let them feast. Meanwhile, she would attempt quiet dignity in memory of Teddy. She had always admired parents who had managed that when most days she wanted to tear the face off the world.

Voices from all directions called her name, but she didn't answer any of them. She wasn't allowed to sit in the courtroom and watch the trial until she had given her own evidence, but it was important to her to be here.

And so she submitted to it. The cameras. Shouted questions. The knowledge that she and her family were fodder for rolling television footage beamed across twenty-four-hour news channels. She wondered how these journalists would cope if the tables were turned and they found themselves and their lives interrogated in the midst of personal tragedy. But she would never know. This was her cross to bear.

Away from the journalists' pen but still relatively close to the courthouse, and behind a metal barrier of their own, a group of superfans had gathered, waving placards decorated with hearts and photographs of Winter Kellaway. Jen ignored them too.

The courthouse was cool compared to the sun-baked streets of Midtown. It had been built at the same time as the town hall and the church, and it smelled of old wood and history. She saw the detective arrive, but she shrank against the wall, not ready for conversation.

She wondered if her father was in the public gallery yet, and one or two of her oldest friends, who had promised to support her.

Her mother would be at home. Or at yoga. She was obsessed with yoga these days. As a witness, she'd been called to give evidence by the defence, but would not be needed until the end of the week at the earliest. Not for the first time, this fact enraged Jen. She knew it was due process – or whatever David Jarvis, the prosecution barrister, had called it – but it still felt like a betrayal, as if her mother had chosen a side.

Her eyes flicked to the courthouse door. David had told her that witnesses for the defence and prosecution would be kept in separate rooms, and that she could choose to give evidence from behind a screen if she preferred not to see Alyssa, but she half expected her sister to walk through the entrance at any moment. A part of Jen wanted her to.

Even though she'd tried hard not to listen to it, she could not ignore the voice inside her head that whispered her younger sister's name over and over again.

Despite everything, she missed her. She hadn't seen her for months, except on the television or through the pages of a newspaper or updates from her mother and Winter. She hadn't seen her baby niece either. She wondered if Claudia was crawling yet, and if her hair had lightened in colour, and if she shared a likeness with Iris, her cousin, or was paler, like Teddy.

In the past, she had always turned to her sisters for support, but in recent years, she had grown much closer to Alyssa than Winter. Her elder sister was always away from home, but Alyssa lived around the corner and was almost the same age. They had fallen into the habit of coffee, or wine, or casual dinners. And now, more than anything, she wanted to lean on her. To tell her all about the gulf that grief had wrought on her life, and her marriage to Phil, and how, even though it wasn't Iris's fault, sometimes it was hard to listen to her talk about school and her friends and birthdays because she wasn't Teddy. She missed Alyssa's spikiness and her sense of loyalty, and even though she hated her and wanted her to pay for her stupid mistake that had cost them so much, she loved her too. She was desperate to see Alyssa and she never wanted to see her again, and managing both of those feelings was complicated and painful.

For weeks she had been both dreading and anticipating this day, but now it was here, Jen didn't know what to do with herself. Her fingers found the pendant around her neck, and she squeezed it in her palm until it was warm and the rhythm of her pulse made it seem as if it had its own heart-beat. It had been made from Teddy's ashes and she wore it every day. She didn't want to go to the witness room. She couldn't face getting coffee from one of the cafes outside because it meant walking past the journalists again. Tears threatened to spill from her.

A woman with dark hair and glasses was sitting on a

bench and she made a show of moving up. 'Room for one more.'

'No.' Jen shook her head. 'Thank you.' She turned and walked briskly to the ladies. Inside the cubicle, she locked the door and sat on the closed toilet seat, and then she cried as if her heart might break.

43

Monday, 22 July 2024

Winter

Her stylist had arrived at dawn, followed by her hairdresser and make-up artist. They had all agreed that powerful but demure was the look. They spent almost an hour debating whether her hair should be up or down, and if she should wear a trouser suit, or settle for a simple shift dress with a jacket to conceal her post-pregnancy tummy. An appearance in court was still a public appearance, after all.

The car arrived at 9.15 a.m. It was a ten-minute drive to the court building, but Winter was determined to give the photographers what they wanted. She was used to attention, and although she felt adrenalized, she knew that her nerves would give her an edge. If there was ever a moment to put on an Oscar-worthy performance, it was now.

What had happened to Teddy, and to Phil and Jen and Iris and their extended families, was a tragedy of unimaginable proportions, truly devastating, and she could never say this aloud to them, of course, but the events of last November had seen a huge impact on her profile.

In a recent strategy meeting, her team had explained that

Google searches of her name were up by 23,500 per cent since the wedding that never happened, and she had given several high-profile interviews to talk shows both here and in the US, and was being considered for roles that would previously have been reserved for triple A-listers.

A noise on the stairs made her turn. The nanny was bringing her baby down for a bottle, and she handed the four-week-old to Winter for a good morning kiss.

'I'll see you soon, sweetie,' said Winter, nuzzling her nose into the baby's soft hair. To the nanny, she said, 'Call me if there are any problems. If you can't get through to me, try my mother. Failing that, call my assistant.'

She gave her reflection a final once-over. Her make-up was subtle but arresting, and she pouted at herself in the mirror, checking the placement of her blusher, the perfection of her lipstick. Her hair, smoothed back into a sleek bun, lent her an elegance that suited her. Despite intense societal pressure, she had so far resisted plastic surgery, but could see the beneficial effects of the non-surgical facelift her beautician had recommended. Her skin glowed. She spent a lot of money and time on skincare to stave off the effects of ageing. The front page of every newspaper would use her photograph tomorrow, and she was damned sure she was going to look good.

It was almost as exciting as a red-carpet premiere.

The car dropped her outside the entrance to the court. A witness care officer had been primed for her arrival, and he was waiting to escort her through the crowds to the front door. Winter had briefly considered the merits of hiring a security team, but she had always enjoyed the footage of celebrities being mobbed by journalists and fans – it lent them a certain vulnerability which would play well with her audience – and so it was agreed that she'd walk herself in.

Since the attack earlier in her career, she'd always been wary that it might happen again, but her therapist had helped her to realize that she couldn't spend the rest of her life in a state of hyper-vigilance. Court officials had offered the opportunity to use a door at the back of the court, but she had declined.

Look grief-stricken and fragile, Winter. She dipped her head and dropped her shoulders, so it appeared as if she was carrying the weight of the world on them. She stopped in front of the court building and posed, one leg in front of the other to slim them both, and a hand on her hip. In her other hand, she carried a folder containing a printed copy of her statement, which she used to cover her post-pregnancy stomach. She needed to be careful that it didn't look too contrived.

'How are things with your sisters?'

'How's motherhood?'

'Is it true that you're going to play Elizabeth Taylor in a new biopic of her life?'

Winter sent a gracious smile in the direction of that journalist. 'My lips are sealed, I'm afraid. I can't tell you anything about that.' She wasn't, but a little fevered speculation didn't hurt. 'As for the previous two questions, I would like everyone to know that I love my family very much. All of them.'

44

Sunday, 21 July 2024

Jen

It surprised her to see it written down. She didn't use that name now, except on official documents, though she supposed they didn't come any more official than this.

CERTIFIED COPY OF AN ENTRY: DEATH. DATE AND PLACE OF DEATH: NINETEENTH NOVEMBER 2023 MIDTOWN HOSPITAL, MIDTOWN-ON-SEA. NAME AND SURNAME: TEDDY MILLER. (A) NAME AND SURNAME OF INFORMANT: GENEVIEVE MILLER (B) QUALIFICATION: MOTHER.

She traced her finger over his name and put it back into the memory box that was full of important things, like his hospital wristband, a lock of his hair and his first pair of shoes. People rarely talked about the administrative tasks surrounding death, but it felt like she'd barely had time to draw breath before she'd been expected to talk to the coroner liaison officer, and give a statement to the police, and confirm permission for his tissue samples to be kept for medical research after the post-mortem examination.

She wasn't supposed to be in here, going through these belongings that had held meaning in life, but had now assumed an almost mythic status as her most precious of all possessions. She was supposed to be spending quality time with Iris before the trial started, and so she quickly packed the box away and went in search of her daughter.

Iris was curled on the beanbag in her bedroom, thumb corking her mouth, holding her battered bear by its arm and staring at the ceiling.

'What are you doing, sweetheart?'

Iris removed her thumb and pressed a bitten-down finger to her lips. 'Trying to listen.'

Jen smiled, bemused. 'To music?'

'No, to Teddy.'

Poleaxed, Jen felt tears prick the back of her eyes, but she blinked them away, not wanting her daughter to see her crying again. 'What's he saying?'

'It's not what he's saying, Mum. It's what he's doing.' Jen's confusion must have shown on her face because Iris, exasperated, went on, 'He's not *saying* anything. But we're playing hide-and-seek and I'm trying to work out whether he's under the bed or in my wardrobe.'

It was not unusual, Jen had discovered since Teddy's death, for children to instigate make-believe games with their deceased sibling. But hearing Iris articulate her play shattered the pieces of Jen's heart that weren't already broken.

She sat on the edge of Iris's bed. 'Do you remember the time Teddy hid in the cupboard with the broken handle and had to be rescued?'

Iris giggled. 'You and Daddy were in the garden, and he was roaring his head off. He was all red in the face, and you gave him ice-cream to cool him down, but it melted over his T-shirt, and his hands and face were so sticky that you had to hose him down.'

That Sunday returned to Jen with pin-sharp clarity. The low groan of a lawnmower from a house up the road. The sound of birdsong, uplifting and joyous. Teddy's shrieks. Iris stripping down to her knickers and leaping through the arc of water, the spray glinting in the sun.

Those memories both sustained and destroyed her. Experts talked about the five stages of grief, but Jen knew there were only two: who she was before Teddy died, and who she was afterwards.

It was difficult to isolate Iris's loss from her own. Although she appeared to be coping on the surface, going to school and playing with her friends, her daughter struggled every day. Sometimes she was rude and angry, but mostly she was quiet and subdued. But her own grief made her selfish. Jen was lost to it, and even though she recognized her daughter needed her, she could not find the strength to climb out of the trough she was in, but longed to wallow in it forever.

'Do you play with Teddy much?'

'Every day.' Iris held up her soft toy and waggled its legs. 'I used to talk to this teddy all the time. But I can't hear him anymore. So I talk to my brother instead. My other Teddy. His favourite games are jumping on the bed and hide-and-seek.'

A lump of hurt lodged itself in Jen's throat and she struggled to get her words out. 'Yes, and I interrupted your game, and I'm sorry for that.'

'Teddy won't mind, Mummy. It was his turn to hide and it always takes him ages to pick a spot, just like when he lived here with us.'

In that moment, Jen loved her daughter more than she

ever had. Like her mother, Iris was fighting hard to keep Teddy's memory alive. She bent over and tucked a strand of hair behind Iris's ear.

'It would take him forever. Do you remember? He'd run in circles while you were counting to twenty, and your dad always had to tuck him under his arm and run with him during the last few seconds.' Jen was warmed by this recollection. 'Tell me, has he chosen a hiding place?'

Iris cocked her head, as if listening to an invisible voice. 'He has.'

Jen smiled and held out her hand to her daughter. 'Do you want me to help you find him?'

Iris shook her head from side to side, deep in thought, and when she spoke again, Jen glimpsed the gap where she'd lost her tooth the previous week. 'He's not hiding from *us.*'

Jen was confused, convinced she had missed something. 'What do you mean, pumpkin?' Iris's gaze flicked between the door and her mother, and back again, clearly uncertain. Jen tried to reassure her. 'It's OK, it's just you and me. No one else is here.'

The little girl came and stood in front of her mother, resting her small hands on Jen's knees. Before Teddy died, her daughter had never bitten her fingernails, but now the skin around them was pink and raw. She leaned into her mother, breath hot against Jen's ear.

'He's hiding from Auntie Winter.'

45

Monday, 22 July 2024

Saul

When an usher informed Saul it was time to give his evidence, the detective swallowed the dregs of his coffee and followed her to the side door that led into Court Two.

He had stood in the witness box at Midtown Crown Court before. The last time had been for a case concerning domestic abuse, where his account of events had been disputed by the accused. The accused had been right. But no one had believed him. They'd believed the young police officer with the earnest face and the weight of the Establishment on his side. This felt different, though, as if what he was about to say might not only alter the verdict of the jury, but the lives of the families involved in this tragedy.

The prosecution and defence barristers had finished their opening statements and every juror had been given a paginated bundle including police interview transcripts and photographs. Mouth dry, Saul moistened his lips and glanced around the court.

Alyssa Kellaway was sitting in the dock. Up until this morning, he'd wondered if she'd change her plea to guilty, but it was apparent she had not. Her face was free of make-up and she looked almost childlike to Saul. When Teddy Miller had been fished from the water, the sound she had made was unearthly, according to statements from Winter Kellaway's staff.

The public gallery was full, crammed with Winter's fans, and friends and relations of the families involved. Due to exceptionally heightened levels of media interest, news organizations had been invited to apply for 'tickets' to attend, and extra press seats had been allocated in the courtroom, as well as the remote streaming of proceedings in the media annex.

The presiding judge – the Honourable Mrs Justice Lambert – was sitting at the bench, making notes, while the prosecution and defence counsels, and their legal teams, occupied the front two rows in the well of the court.

The clerk of the court, who sat below the judge, acknowledged the police officer and rose to hear his oath.

Although he did not believe in God, Saul chose to swear on the Bible. While the law would dispute this, in Saul's mind it meant his oath did not stand, although he was shrewd enough to keep that thought to himself.

David Jarvis, KC, walked the detective through the events on the date of Teddy Miller's death, indicating he planned to return to this later. For now, he was interested in what had happened two days previously.

'Is it true that on Thursday 16 November of last year, you were out in your kayak in the stretch of water in front of Winter Kellaway's house?'

'Yes, I try to go out most days, if I can.'

'Can you tell the court what you saw on that morning, as you were planning to head back to shore?'

'I saw a woman in a rowing boat.'

'And what was she doing?'

Trudi Baxter, the defence barrister, leapt to her feet. 'If I may, my learned friend, this is not relevant to the facts of this case.'

Mr Jarvis was smooth in his rebuttal. 'If you permit me to continue, my lady, I will explain to the jury why it is.'

Mrs Justice Lambert nodded. 'Continue.'

The prosecution barrister turned his attention back to Saul. 'Can you tell us what this woman was doing, Detective Constable Anguish?'

'She was throwing a bloodstained dress into the water.'

'How did you know it was bloodstained?'

'Believe me, I've attended enough crime scenes to know what blood on clothing looks like.'

Trudi Baxter was on her feet again, words like bullets strafing the courtroom. 'Speculation. And if I may, prejudicial—'

One or two of the jurors looked at each other. The journalists scribbling shorthand into their notebooks paused to look up at the barristers and police officer.

The judge nodded. 'I'll allow.' She directed the jury to strike the detective's answer from their evidence.

David Jarvis reframed his question. 'She had a dress?'

'Yes.'

'How do you know this?'

'Because I saw it in the water.'

'Where is that dress now?'

'The tide took it before I had a chance to retrieve it.'

'And this woman – she was a stranger to you?'

'At the time, yes.'

'But you know who she is now?'

'That's correct.'

'Can you tell us?'

Saul Anguish drew in a breath and gazed across the court, an almost apologetic expression on his face. 'It was the defendant, Alyssa Kellaway.'

46

Monday, 22 July 2024

Alyssa

All those faces, staring right at her. Alyssa lifted the glass
of water to her lips, her hand trembling. She tried to read
their expressions, but it was impossible. If she had been a
member of this jury, she would have judged herself harshly,
so she could expect no less from them.

Gross negligence manslaughter. An ugly term for an ugly
crime. But there was no punishment this court could inflict
that would be worse than the one she flagellated herself
with every hour and every minute of every day.

She tried to catch her breath, panic beating its wings in
her chest. When that proved impossible and ragged hitches
spilled from her into the silence of the courtroom, she used
techniques the family therapist had suggested until she had
calmed herself.

She noticed that one or two members of the public looked
at her with compassion, but most of them, especially the
journalists, stared at her as if she was a specimen on a glass
slide under the microscope.

Her palms were slick with sweat. She'd been warned it

might feel cool in Court Two, but she felt as if she was being cooked. The air-conditioning unit had chosen the hottest day of the year to break down. Her barrister, Trudi, was covered in a sheen of perspiration, her wig and robes trapping the heat against her skin.

Alyssa watched the detective, knowing as soon as he'd arrived at Winter's house that he would recognize her. It had been a struggle out on the water that day, less than a week after having a baby. But Claudia's birth had been uneventful and she hadn't needed to row out far, just to the shallows. At sunrise, she'd fed the baby and left Federico in charge, telling him she needed a breather, and to give Claudia formula milk if she was hungry again.

But she had no intention of sharing that with the court.

She didn't know why she'd agreed to travel, heavily pregnant, to meet that solicitor and collect the dress, which she'd immediately stuffed in a plastic bag at the back of her wardrobe. Curiosity, she supposed. A reminder of what she'd escaped. But as soon as her daughter was born, she'd been driven by this compulsion to rid herself of the past, to wash clean the stains of her family's history.

Federico knew nothing about it. The only person she'd confided in was Phil, but he hadn't talked to her since the accident. She wondered if he'd broken the pact they had made. Everything had changed now. He owed her less than nothing – she had killed his son.

A sob rose inside her and she gulped it down. The judge frowned at her. The prosecution barrister was talking but she wasn't listening to his words, just the rise and fall of his speech, as rhythmic as music. It was impossible to concentrate and remain fully focused. Distracted by the pins and needles in her right foot, she flexed it, an attempt to ease the tingling.

Her father was in the public gallery; she could see his shock of white hair. Her stomach unclenched a fraction. She'd spoken to him last night. He'd been civil to her since that day, but she'd sensed his distance, especially in recent weeks.

'Are you coming to court, Dad?'

'I don't know.' A pause. 'I want to support you, but I need to think about Jen and what's best for her.'

She imagined him standing in the darkened hallway of their home, clutching the telephone receiver in his hand, dressed in his uniform of pullover and slacks. Grief had savaged him. It rode on his back, bending his spine beneath its weight, and had scored lines into his face. His divided loyalties had come at great cost. He loved her, she understood that. But Jen needed him more. Always Jen.

She'd wanted to yell at him that she needed the comfort and support of her parents more than anybody in the world. But instead she had said, 'I understand.'

She didn't ask him if he wanted her to be found guilty. She couldn't bear to know the answer to that question. She knew what Jen and Phil wanted, though. Justice for Teddy. And prison for her.

If she was honest, she didn't blame her sister. It had been a stupid mistake. One of her own making. And she deserved to pay for it. But it was much more complicated than that.

Her gaze flicked back to the public gallery. No sign of her mother or Winter, but that was not a surprise. Both women were giving evidence later in the week.

She didn't know if Fed would come, even for a bit. Today was one of Claudia's nursery days, but she suspected he would rather work than watch his ex-fiancée stand trial. As for Phil, she had no idea. He wasn't on the witness list, as far as she was aware, but he wasn't here either. Her mouth dried. It was all such a fucking mess.

The prosecution's line of questioning had moved on. David Jarvis was now asking the detective about his first meeting with the Kellaway family, and the intruder in the grounds of Winter's house on the morning of the wedding.

An unexpected name caught her attention. She stiffened, adrenaline pumping through her system. Her tongue felt thick in her mouth and she reached for her water, palm slippery against the glass.

The journalists were scribbling in their notebooks. Her father was listening, focused and with intent, his head cocked to one side.

Alyssa's gaze flicked back to the detective. He was softly spoken and she leaned forward to listen to what he had to say, her heart stuttering in her chest at his revelation.

47

Monday, 22 July 2024

Jen

The witness waiting room was sweltering. After exchanging a few pleasantries with the court official, she sat on a chair in the corner and pulled out her book, but she couldn't concentrate and read the same page three times before she gave up and put it back into her handbag.

The door opened. A woman wearing a black suit and sensible heels, and with a tightly woven French braid, hurried over. Jen recognized her as a junior member of the prosecution's legal team, although she'd forgotten her name.

The young paralegal introduced herself as Emma Jones and sat on the chair next to her, relief lighting her features. 'You're here.'

Jen gave her a level look. 'So it would seem.'

'We didn't know if you'd come.'

'Neither did I, to be honest.'

Emma smoothed out the creases from her pencil skirt. She was about thirty and wore an expensive-looking diamond ring on her engagement finger. A cynical observation about how marriage was more than material goods floated into

Jen's mind, but she kept it to herself. 'Do you want to explain that voicemail you left us last night?' The paralegal's pen was poised above her pad.

'No.'

Emma wrote something down. 'You do realize we're compelled to disclose any new information that arises to the defence?' She waited for a beat without looking at Jen. 'Is there anything you want to share?'

Jen considered the question, replaying the previous night's conversation with Iris. In the cold light of morning, what had the child actually said? Nothing concrete. Everyone on that boat had seen Alyssa drop Teddy into the water. *She* had seen her do it with her own eyes. All the time and money and emotional energy that had gone into preparing this trial. She couldn't – wouldn't – risk the chance of a successful conviction.

She shook her head, suddenly so exhausted by lack of sleep that she could not speak. She closed her eyes and struggled to organize her thoughts, trying to isolate the truth from emotion.

Bereavement was an odd animal, especially as a parent. She often felt handled, as if her feelings were too raw and intrusive for polite company. Choices were removed. Assumptions made. *Jen won't want to come to that party. Don't invite Jen, it's not appropriate, she's still grieving.* Friends and family meant well. But the lack of autonomy was suffocating. Losing a child was like forgetting how to breathe every day and being forced to relearn.

She couldn't bring herself to speak to Alyssa, even if she wanted to. Her mother was struggling with her own feelings of grief, torn between her daughters. Phil had become so distant from her that she was unsure if there was a way back for them. They had argued constantly about the trial. How many times had she wished to roll back the hands of time? To remake that day in a different way. The world had tipped on its axis and everything had changed. No matter what else happened, it would never be right again.

Her confusion must have shown because Emma, in a moment of empathy, reached out and squeezed her hand. 'I know you'll do the right thing.'

But how could she know what that was? For so long, Jen had been driven by a desire – scalding, white-hot – to seek justice for Teddy. Alyssa must be made to atone for his death. She deserved to be punished for her recklessness. The sheer idiocy of her actions. Her negligence, even if it had been unintentional, had wrought devastating consequences upon their family. This was an unassailable fact.

In the immediate aftermath of the accident, Alyssa had written them a letter, full of remorse and guilt and self-loathing. Phil had read it, but Jen had refused to, and it had lain in the drawer of the bureau in their hallway until a few weeks ago when it had passed into evidence. David Jarvis had thought its existence might convince Alyssa to change her plea to guilty, but her younger sister was stubborn, determined to convince the jury that while she had been stupid and thoughtless, she hadn't been negligent.

This refusal to admit responsibility, publicly at least, had incensed Jen, fuelling her determination for justice to be served. But in her bleakest moments, those hours lost to the dark, wrestling the demons of *if only* and *what if*, a flicker of doubt had kindled. Even if Alyssa was convicted and sent to prison, it wouldn't bring Teddy back. The death of her son – the unforgettable sight of his pale, limp body pulled from the waves – played on a constant loop, haunting her days and her nights. But if Alyssa went to prison, she would be depriving her sister's child of a mother as she'd been deprived of a son. And there would be no winners in that scenario.

'David will come and talk to you when the court breaks for lunch, OK? For now, sit tight and we'll let you know when you'll be called to give your evidence.' Emma's smile was brisk and professional, an anxious-to-get-back-to-work kind of smile.

'Who's giving evidence now?'

'Detective Constable Saul Anguish.'

'What's he saying?'

'I'm afraid I'm not allowed to tell you that. You have to give your own evidence first.'

She'd known about that rule, but had forgotten it. She forgot about lots of things these days. They slipped from her memory without a murmur. Shock and trauma, the gifts that kept on giving.

When Emma had left, Jen prowled the waiting room, restless and keyed up. None of the other witnesses were here. Those appearing for the defence were directed to a separate room, but she'd half expected to see Winter, who'd been summonsed to give her own evidence for the prosecution and had offered to keep her company.

In the far corner of the waiting room, tucked out of sight, Jen glimpsed something shiny, out of place. A lost piece of jewellery, perhaps. Or a coin. She glanced over to see if the court usher had noticed it, but she was busy, head bent. She crouched down, perplexed by its familiarity, to pick it up.

It was a silver button, slightly tarnished. A button made specially for a wedding suit, distinctive by its customization. Heart thumping, she turned it over, searching for clues that did not exist, and as she did so, her finger brushed its raised surface, an engraving in the shape of the letter T.

48

Monday, 22 July 2024

Saul

He had been in the witness box for almost forty-five minutes, but it felt like a lifetime. The heat in the courtroom had intensified, if that was possible, and sweat gilded the back of his neck.

It was difficult not to be impressed by David Jarvis, KC. The prosecution barrister was not what Saul had anticipated at all. He'd imagined a restrained but savagely intellectual man, bespectacled and serious. But Jarvis was a showman, given to extravagant flourishes that bewitched both the public and the jury, although Saul found his tactics distracting and wondered if others felt the same way.

As far as Saul was concerned, he was not expecting questions about the intruder at Winter Kellaway's home on the morning of the accident, but at the barrister's request, Saul recounted what he and his colleague had encountered when they had arrived at The Beach House, culminating in DC Isaac Hunter's decision to review the CCTV footage himself.

'And he called you, didn't he?' Jarvis's voice echoed with

authority around the court. 'Can you tell us what he'd discovered?'

'Part of our investigation into any crime is to consider motive, and so we'd looked at Winter Kellaway's social media accounts to see what they might yield. If she was being trolled or targeted, and so forth.'

'And they yielded something important, didn't they?'

Saul was uncomfortable under David's intense gaze, even though they were seemingly on the same side, and fought with himself to stay controlled and unreactive.

'That's right.'

David gestured at Saul to continue with a slight impatience that made the detective bristle. 'Can you tell us what that was?' The mild tone of sarcasm irritated him.

'We came across a photograph of Winter Kellaway and her extended family that she had posted on her Instagram account.'

'And there was someone in that photograph you recognized, wasn't there?'

Trudi Baxter, who had objected several times since David had begun his examination-in-chief, citing compound or leading questions, was on her feet again, appealing to the judge. 'Respectfully, he is leading the witness.'

The judge waved a dismissive hand. 'Continue.'

Saul took a long pull on his glass of water. 'Winter Kellaway was concerned that a man who had attacked her as a younger woman had somehow gained access to her property.'

'But it wasn't that man. He's still in prison.'

'That is correct.'

'Who *was* the man you saw running on the CCTV footage?' David turned and addressed the jury. 'If you would like to see visual confirmation, the stills are on page thirteen of your evidence bundle.'

Saul waited for the inevitable flurry of rustling paper from the twelve members of the jury to cease. He wasn't sure if the Kellaway family were privy to this information or if Winter had kept it to herself. The court was silent, as if every person in the room was holding their breath.

His fingers groped blindly for Teddy's silver button, but it was gone, fallen through a hole in his pocket, somewhere unknown. Its loss saddened him. Although he had no children of his own and Solomon Anguish had been a poor excuse for a parent, Saul felt an overwhelming compulsion to seek justice for the four-year-old boy at the centre of this case.

He drew in a breath, his gaze fixed on the defendant in the dock.

'The intruder was Teddy Miller's father and Winter Kellaway's brother-in-law, Philip Miller.'

49

Jen

'Why would Teddy want to hide from Auntie Winter?'

Iris shrugged, the too-loose straps of her sundress rising with her shoulders. 'She can be mean sometimes.'

'What do you mean?'

'She pinched Teddy once. It left a mark on his leg. He showed me.'

A memory came rushing back to Jen, one she hadn't thought about for years. Alyssa had been no older than ten. Jen, who was in her first year at secondary school, and Deborah, as she was called then, had been listening to music in Jen's bedroom. Alyssa had wanted them to play with her, and when they'd refused, she'd snatched at the arm of the record player. Jen could still hear it – it had made an ugly sound, like a zip being fastened – and when they had checked, the needle had left a deep scratch in the vinyl of Deborah's favourite album.

'You little bitch.'

Deborah had grabbed Alyssa by the arm and bent it behind her back. She had pinched and pinched her until the girl cried out in pain, and Jen had intervened. 'Stop! You're hurting her.'

Alyssa had never told their parents. Jen had given Deborah her own birthday money to buy a new album. And when their mother had asked about the ladder of bruises climbing all the way up Alyssa's wrist, forearm and tricep, all three of them had feigned ignorance.

'Why did she pinch him?'

'He said he wasn't allowed to tell me.'

Jen thought for a minute. 'Has she ever pinched you?'

Iris's eyes were wide. 'No.' But her expression said something different.

Jen drew her daughter onto her lap and held her. Her little body was hot to the touch and clammy, not surprising on the fifth day of this record-breaking heatwave. Jen had opened the upstairs windows, but it had been a mistake. With the absence of a breeze, the air was stuffy, uncomfortably so. They sat like that for several minutes, Iris's thumb in her mouth and head on her mother's shoulder. Jen rocked her gently, as she might rock a baby. Both drew comfort from the other.

Eventually, as the sun dipped beneath the horizon and shadows crept their way across Iris's bedroom, the little girl said, 'I'm sorry that Teddy died, Mummy. I wish it could have been me.'

Jen squeezed her as tightly as she dared. 'Never say that. You're just as precious to me as Teddy was.'

'But I'm his big sister. Big sisters look after their little brothers. I should have protected him.'

'I think we all feel that way, sweetheart. Daddy and I certainly do. But it was a terrible accident.'

'Will Auntie Alyssa go to prison?'

'I don't know. Possibly.'

'But you said it was an accident.'

Jen inhaled and exhaled, trying to calm her breathing, the rush of adrenaline that threatened to overwhelm her when she talked about Teddy's death. She had tried to avoid these conversations with Iris, not only because she didn't want to colour her daughter's view and deprive her of a relationship with her cousin, but because she was frightened that her own bitterness and bile would poison her eight-year-old's sweetness.

'It was an accident, yes. But Auntie Alyssa did something very stupid. If she hadn't done that, Teddy would still be with us.'

The young girl's face grew serious in the half-light. She blew out a breath, extending her bottom lip and sending the air upwards, so that her fringe lifted in the artificial breeze she'd created.

'But what if Auntie Alyssa didn't do the stupid thing?'

'What do you mean, honey? We witnessed it ourselves.'

Iris didn't answer, but picked up her teddy and sat on the floor. She danced him around the carpet, singing to herself. After a minute or so, she turned to her mother. 'But what if what you saw wasn't what you thought?'

50

Winter

Even the security guard who manned the scanner at the entrance to the court couldn't stop staring at her and whisked her to the front of the queue.

'I'm a huge fan of yours,' he murmured, a blush spreading over his cheeks. 'I've seen everything you've been in.'

Although his lack of subtlety irritated her, a significant part of her enjoyed this kind of adulation. The stares. The need for extra security. The flash of the cameras. After all these years, she couldn't imagine life without it. Because it meant that she was treated as a goddess rather than as a mere mortal, and who wouldn't prefer that?

It had been gratifying to see her fans gathered outside court to lend their support to both her and her family. Correction: *some* of her family.

While there had been endless talk shows in the US discussing the rights and wrongs of what her younger sister had done, and a handful of commentators had expressed compassion, she had been careful not to ally herself too closely to Alyssa, particularly as conservative America was her biggest market.

But when she was alone, lost in those rare moments of reflection, of unvarnished honesty, she admitted to her secret self that she had always resented Jen for taking Alyssa from her, and Alyssa for loving Jen best.

Although they had argued as children, she had been close to both her sisters, but it was difficult to maintain an emotional connection when her job took her all over the world. Winter had struggled through adulthood to form lasting relationships, but her sisters had been her constant. Until now.

Of course, she had noticed her siblings had grown closer before the accident, and she had tried not to mind. She knew that they loved her, even if they didn't see her all the time.

But while Winter's wealth had improved everybody's life in a material way, it was Jen who held the sisters together. She was the light in their lives, offering a steadiness that the others were unable or unwilling to provide. Although Jen had considerably less wealth than she did, Winter had always envied the richness of the life she'd created – a loving husband and two beautiful children.

She wanted something like that for herself. And what Winter wanted, she usually got. She was ruthless that way.

But Jen had fallen apart in the weeks and months since Teddy's death. All she did was talk about her son. She didn't want to do anything or go anywhere. She'd become so self-absorbed that she had even forgotten Winter's birthday. She cried all the time. Her grief was exhausting – boring, even – although she kept that nugget to herself because even Winter recognized she was not supposed to think something as awful as that.

Take last night, for example. She'd called Jen to make plans for today, but her sister had been clipped and keen to get off the phone. That wasn't unusual these days, but she wasn't often so short with her. She'd thought her sister would want to ask about the baby and see how they were both getting on, and frankly, show a bit more gratitude that Winter had offered to sit with her in court, but she'd barely had a chance to confirm she was coming before Jen was gone.

She'd half considered not turning up. Jen had let her down badly the previous month when she'd declined to be her birth partner, and she'd had to ask their mother to step in instead. Admittedly, Jen had never wholeheartedly committed to it. 'I'm not sure it's a good idea, Winter. I think I'd find it pretty difficult, to be honest.' Her voice had cracked. 'It will remind me of Teddy's birth – and when he died. Phil thinks that being in a hospital setting will be bad for my emotional well-being.'

She'd wanted to shout, *What about* my *emotional well-being?* As for Phil, his attitude had infuriated her. But nothing trumped Jen's grief. It sounded bitter and selfish, but it was the truth.

And so her mother had come with her. Carol, who had never stopped talking, even when she should have known better.

They'd sat in the hospital together. Not Midtown General, but a private one in London that cost a bloody fortune, even to a woman of Winter's means. She had her own suite with Egyptian cotton linens on her bed and the baby's crib, and extra security, and afternoon tea served on a silver stand to celebrate his birth.

Her mother had cradled the baby, stroking his cheek. She didn't ask questions about his parentage, but said simply of her fourth grandchild, her second grandson, 'What a beauty.' And then, 'He looks a lot like Teddy.'

Winter had dug her fingernails into her palms. Fucking Teddy again. Why did everything come back to Teddy?

'What are you going to call him?' Her mother was looking at her with something akin to anticipation. For one horrible moment, Winter realized that her mother was expecting her to name the baby after her deceased nephew. Her eyes dropped to the baby's face, his dark eyelashes and rosebud mouth. 'Alexander Nico.'

Carol's face fell, but she recovered quickly. 'That's a lovely name, darling.' She frowned a little. 'Nico sounds Italian.'

Anxious to change the subject, Winter had smothered jam and cream on her scone, and poured herself and her mother some tea. There had to be some perks to paying for maternity care.

Her mother must have read her mind because she began to reminisce about her own experience of labour. 'Didn't even get a slice of toast when I had Jen. The midwife forgot all about me. I was so hungry your dad had to nip home and make me a sandwich.'

Winter shoved in another mouthful, crumbs falling onto the sheets. The post-partum diet she'd devised with her nutritionist was starting tomorrow, so she intended to make the most of today.

A soft knock at the door interrupted them. Winter's private suite was already filled with flowers from her celebrity friends. But it was not another delivery. It was Jen, carrying a small stuffed duck.

'May I come in?'

She didn't wait for a reply, but headed straight for the baby. 'He's beautiful. Well done, Winter.'

Despite her earlier annoyance, Winter felt herself soften and poured Jen a cup of tea. She knew this wasn't easy for her sister. Once she was seated, she directed her to the cake stand. To ease any awkwardness, she picked up her conversation with their mother, giving Jen a moment to compose herself. 'How did you feel about becoming a mum? You were pretty young.'

Carol smiled. 'I was so happy to meet you all at last. My beautiful girls.'

Jen nibbled on a biscuit. 'What about Alyssa? She must have come as a bit of a shock to the system so soon after having me?'

Carol dropped a kiss on Alex's head. 'But she slotted right in, didn't she?'

'It's a shame you and dad lost all our baby photos when we moved into Kendal Road.'

'We made up for it, though.' The older woman laughed. 'I don't think there can be any children in the world more photographed than you and your sisters. Your dad was a demon with that camera.'

Winter studied her mother. She was busying herself with the baby, fussing over his sleep-suit and adjusting the scratch mittens on his tiny hands. Winter wondered if Jen sensed Carol's evasiveness. She gave her a chance to tell the truth.

'Did we all look alike when we were little?'

Her mother gave her eldest daughter a surprised look. 'You had your father's colouring. You were the spitting image of him when you were a baby. Jen was more of a mix of me and Dad.' A teasing smile in Winter's direction. 'You should consider yourself lucky you didn't inherit the Kellaway nose.'

Jen swatted at her mother with faux outrage. 'People pay fortunes for a nose like mine.'

Winter sipped her tea. A casual question. 'And Alyssa?'

'I always thought she had a touch of your great grand-mother about her, but your father could never see the resemblance.'

Winter narrowed her eyes and placed the bone china cup carefully on the table of her hospital bed. Her mother wouldn't look at her. When it came to discussing their child-hood, her mother was skilled at swerving questions. It was a pattern that Winter had noticed over the years. She let the matter drop.

But one thing was crystal clear. Carol was not prepared to be honest about the secret she'd been hiding for almost forty years.

51

Monday, 22 July 2024

Saul

At the mention of Philip Miller, he watched the colour drain from Alyssa Kellaway's face, but the prosecution's barrister had moved on, as fluid as the tides.

Although it had been months since he'd seen her, Saul felt such a longing for Blue that he was forced to look away, to swallow down the needle-sharp pain that remained raw and unhealed. Some days, hours could pass when he didn't think about her, but reliving that November day last year when she had been arrested reminded him of all that he had lost.

'And so you were sent back to Winter Kellaway's estate after the emergency services were called for a second time that day?'

David Jarvis's question pulled him back into the past, and he left the heat and expectation of the courtroom and travelled to that afternoon when the sky was colourless, and the damp clung to his clothes and hair, and chilled his shattered heart.

The ambulance was already there by the time DC Hunter and Saul arrived, its blue lights spinning in the darkening.

Dozens of wedding guests huddled in knots, speaking in quiet voices, throwing glances in the direction of the jetty. Some of the chauffeur-driven cars were not due to return until much later, and the valet parking was in disarray, but the woman with the clipboard, her voice high-pitched and strained, was directing everyone to leave until Saul stopped her. 'We'll need to talk to them. Potential witnesses.'

He asked DC Hunter to start taking down names and statements, and called DI Elena Nunn, requesting extra manpower. Then he squared his shoulders and walked with trepidation towards the water's edge.

Teddy Miller was prone on the wooden walkway, two paramedics bent over him, administering CPR. On reflex, Saul ran through his first-aid training in his head. It was different for children. A lighter touch was required due to the differences in the physiology, musculature and bone density of their smaller bodies. Open the airway. Five initial rescue breaths. Thirty chest compressions. Two rescue breaths. Rinse and repeat until a defibrillator arrived.

In films and television, the act of resuscitation was sanitized. In the real world, it was brutal, violent and often – heartbreakingly – too late. The boy had no pulse. No heartbeat. No signs of life at all.

The waves lapped against the struts of the jetty, strong and rhythmic. To Saul, it felt like a taunt. Through the fog, he could hear the call of the last shearwaters as they set off on their epic trans-equatorial migration. In a stroke of nature's cruelty, these seabirds mimicked the cries of a baby.

Under the gleam of the fairy lights, the boy's face and lips held a bluish tinge. His eyes were closed and his wet fringe had formed kiss curls on his forehead.

Saul turned away, a lump in his throat, unable to watch.

Instead he busied himself with the family. Jen Miller was on her knees, one hand splayed on the jetty, the other gripping Teddy's hand. The hem of her wedding dress was streaked with mud and dirt, the roses in her hair askew. She bent her head towards her son and one of the petals fell away, spinning and drifting on the wind until it was lost to the murk. Her lips were moving, and although he wasn't close enough to hear what she was saying, her anguish was evident in the slump of her shoulders and the deadness of her expression. He could see no spark of hope at all. She knows, he thought.

Alyssa Kellaway stood motionless, her hand clamped over her mouth, as if that physical act would hold back the scream he could sense rising within her. He watched her, curious, for a moment, recognizing her as the woman with the child's white dress, the synapses of his brain whirring and clicking with mechanical precision.

She caught the detective's eye. Her face was pale and her whole body was trembling. It was clear the woman was in shock.

'Are you OK?'

'I dropped him.' Her voice cracked. 'I killed him.'

Phil Miller, the boy's father, marched up to Alyssa and wheeled away from her again before circling back, his body vibrating with aggression; bewilderment and pain and fury jostled for dominance. 'What did you do?' he was shouting, too close. 'What the fuck did you do?'

Saul didn't hesitate, but stepped between them, resting a hand on Phil's shoulder to create distance, a warning, albeit a compassionate one. The anger left Phil in a heartbeat, and he slumped against the detective, coughing out his grief until tears took hold.

'Take your time,' said Saul. He didn't ask him why he'd been running through his sister-in-law's property at 5.30 a.m. on his wedding day or if that was how he'd got his broken wrist. There would be time for that later.

Family dynamics were important in the aftermath of tragedy. It was when people gave themselves away. Saul observed their tiny interactions. Made mental notes and filed them away. He noticed that Federico, Alyssa's fiancé, did not comfort his own partner, but repeatedly checked on the well-being of Winter Kellaway. The boy's grandparents, Carol and Geoff Kellaway, were huddled together, cradling their infant granddaughter. Every now and then, they sent a glance in the direction of Alyssa that was freighted with a meaning Saul did not understand.

But, most pertinently of all, he noticed that Iris Miller was standing alone in the fog, watching the paramedics fight to save her brother's life. Her thumb was in her mouth, eyes wide and frightened. Not one of the adults in her family was paying attention to the girl, locked in their own unfolding horror stories, and he moved towards her, angered by their selfishness and determined to distract her from witnessing what might be Teddy's last breath, if he wasn't gone already. But before he had a chance to talk to her, Iris had wandered further down the jetty to where Winter Kellaway was crying into her hands.

Iris stopped by her aunt, and said something to her, but there was too much background noise for Saul to hear. He was close enough to observe Winter's reaction, though. Her eyes narrowed, and she bent down to the child, whispering something into her ear. Iris flushed and took a step backwards, shaking her head. Winter reached for her niece, pulling her into an embrace that lasted no longer than a few seconds until the girl pushed her away and ran, not to her mother or father or grandparents, but into the arms of her aunt, Alyssa.

The family stayed that way, frozen in a tableau of helplessness, until one of the paramedics let out a cry. At last, a heartbeat. A flurry of action. Teddy transferred to the ambulance. His mother, gathering up her wedding dress and climbing into the back with her son. Blue lights flashing in the darkness until all that was left was their imprint in the air, like the trail of a sparkler.

The courtroom was silent apart from the sounds of journalists taking notes. Saul's words, powerful but neutral, had made an impression.

'Thank you,' said David Jarvis. 'That must have been difficult to witness.'

'Police officers see lots of awful things,' said Saul. 'It's part of our job. But this case will stay with me for a long time.'

'Did you speak to the defendant, Alyssa Kellaway, once Teddy had been taken to hospital?'

'I did.'

'And what did she say to you?'

Saul glanced at the young woman in the dock. Her head was bowed. He felt a pulse of sympathy for her, but was compelled to tell the truth. '"I deserve to be punished for what I have done."'

52

Monday, 22 July 2024

Phil

When Teddy was born, Phil had taken three weeks off work. He'd changed all his new baby's nappies, sterilized every bottle and, each morning and afternoon, he'd proudly pushed Teddy's pram through the park while his wife had slept.

On his first day back in the office, Jen had called him, half laughing and half crying. 'I don't know what I'm doing.'

Now, eight months after Teddy's death, Phil didn't know what he was doing either.

He went to work. He drew up paperwork. He talked to clients. He attended bereavement counselling once a week and tried to support his wife and daughter. But he could not grieve.

His therapist had tried to get to the root of why this might be, but Phil knew she would never succeed. Because he hadn't told her the truth. He hadn't told anyone the truth.

His secret ate away at him, corroding everything, even his ability to mourn for his son. He couldn't confide in Jen, which would have been his natural instinct, or his friends, even Federico. He had pushed everyone away. His parents.

His in-laws. Unforgivably, his wife. They lay in bed night after night, not touching each other. Not kissing or comforting or holding hands. Not even talking. As each day passed, Phil's sense of guilt and regret grew heavier until he thought he might collapse under its weight.

'Dad?' Iris was squeezing his hand. 'Can I have an ice cream? Please.'

He blinked into the sunshine. The boutique cafes of Midtown-on-Sea were teeming with tourists. Children in swimsuits were everywhere, carrying buckets and spades or brightly coloured crab lines and nets. Shrieks of laughter drifted up from the bay, distant but unmistakeable. It was the start of the summer holidays and the mood was one of festivity. But Phil could not imagine being part of it. It seemed like an alien planet to him.

Unable to concentrate on work, he'd collected Iris from friends and taken her for a walk by the beach to distract them both. He hadn't been called as a witness. *Thank fuck for that.* But Jen had expected him in court, to watch from the public gallery, and for moral support.

'And because you want to, surely?' Her tone had been almost contemptuous.

'I don't know if I can bear to sit through it. I don't need to hear the medical details of how Teddy died or be reminded that I wasn't there to protect him.'

If he'd hoped for understanding, he'd been mistaken. Jen had been horrified, aghast that he could even consider not attending. 'You pushed for this as much as I did. *More* than I did. It's not easy for me either. I know what she did was wrong, but Alyssa is still my sister.'

His face had hardened, his anger, always close to the surface these days, spilling over. 'Your *sister* killed our son.'

'Yes, *our* son.' She emphasized their joint responsibility. 'You owe it to Teddy to be there. How could you live with yourself if you look away now?' She'd almost spat the words at him.

His eyes had met hers, but the fight had left him. 'I can't live with myself, Jen. A court case won't change that.'

It was true. Although he'd voiced it to no one, Phil had contemplated taking his own life. He longed for the respite that death would bring. When a child died, it wasn't the past, or even the present, that was lost. It was the future. He was haunted by the swimming lessons he would never take him to, and the holidays that wouldn't happen, and the exams and first dates and driving test that Teddy – and, by extension, Phil – would never have the chance to experience. He felt cheated. He wanted to switch himself off. He wanted to be with his son.

Iris tugged his hand again. *Dad.* He forced himself to focus on his daughter, the here and now instead of ghosts. 'Yes, sweetheart. Sorry.'

She chose mint chocolate chip with a flake, Teddy's favourite, and they sat on a wooden bench with a silver memorial plaque and watched other children unburdened by grief running in and out of the sea.

'Are you nervous about speaking in court?'

Phil and Jen had argued about whether Iris should be expected to endure that kind of trauma in a public setting. Surprisingly, it had been Jen who had pushed for it. *She'll be fine. She's a smart kid.*

'I'm not allowed to talk about that, Daddy.' She gave him an arch look, one that reminded him of her mother.

'That just means you shouldn't discuss your evidence with other witnesses, sweetheart. You can talk to me, especially if you're worried.'

Iris concentrated on her ice cream. The heat was making it melt and she spun the cone in her hand to catch stray drips with her tongue.

'Do you go to prison if you tell a lie?'

'If you lie under oath in a court to a judge and you get found out, then possibly. But not if you're eight.' He wanted to reassure her.

'What about if you're not in court?'

'Sometimes people tell lies to protect the feelings of others. Or they pretend to eat all their carrots when they've secretly put them in their pocket because they want to have cake for dessert.' Iris grinned at him, recognizing Teddy in his story. 'But no one should tell big lies. They'll always get found out in the end. You know it's wrong to lie, Iris.'

The girl was wiping her sticky fingers with the serviette that had been wrapped around her cone. Iris liked to be neat and tidy. A smudge of ice cream had found its way to the tip of her nose, but Phil couldn't bring himself to tell her because it made her look adorable. Iris crossed her ankles and swung her legs back and forth, watching the boats. 'If you know someone has told a big lie, should you tell the truth?'

Phil gazed at the horizon, the light catching the waves like shards of broken glass. A father was playing tag with his young son, and when he caught him, he picked him up and spun him in dizzying circles until the boy collapsed into laughter and begged him to stop. It was a difficult question, one of morality and nuance. 'I think so, yes.' He acknowledged the irony. His was not an honest answer, but an ethical one.

'Even if it might hurt someone you love?'

'Even then.'

She gazed up at him then, and he saw the worry in her face transform into something like conviction. She gave a little nod, as if he had satisfied her, and they sat together in silence until the midday sun drove them to seek shade.

As they prepared to leave, Iris turned to the plaque nailed to the bench and planted a soft kiss on it. Phil swallowed down the lump in his throat, as he did every time Iris brought him here.

Teddy Miller, forever four. May he play in the sea always.

53

Saul

As soon as David Jarvis informed the court he had no further questions, the defence barrister, Trudi Baxter, rose to her feet to cross-examine Saul.

A diminutive woman, no taller than five foot, her reputation was considerably larger than she was. Some of his police colleagues had been the victim of a Baxter filleting, and had warned him to be prepared. 'She'll gut you faster than a fishmonger,' said one of the uniforms.

She was considerably younger than Jarvis, but Saul was not fooled by her stature or her smile.

'Detective Constable Saul Anguish, you mention that you saw the defendant, Alyssa Kellaway, rowing a boat two days before Teddy Miller's death?'

'That's right.'

'It was foggy?'

'Yes.'

'She was some distance away?'

'Yes.'

Her tone was respectful but her words were not. 'You do

realize that she'd given birth one hundred and forty-four hours previously.' She glanced at the jurors, especially the female ones, and laughed, a tinkle of bells. 'I mean, we all know we have to be superwomen every single day, but I suspect that would be a push for even the most athletic of us.' Her smile was saccharine-sweet.

Saul didn't answer.

'Are you sure it was Alyssa Kellaway?'

'Yes.'

'Even though there are no other witnesses, and Alyssa says it wasn't her.'

'I'm sure.'

David Jarvis smiled, and Saul relaxed a little. Trudi Baxter wasn't as scalpel-sharp as he'd been led to believe.

'Interesting. Because according to Winter Kellaway, who is due to give evidence later in the trial, Alyssa Kellaway was with her eldest sister at The Beach House at the precise time you claim to have seen her.'

Saul blanched. 'That's not possible.' His mind was racing, seeking a flaw in his memory or an error he may have made, but he *knew* he was right. It had been Alyssa Kellaway at sea that day.

Trudi Baxter smiled at him. A junior member of her legal team passed her a sheaf of printouts with a time-stamped image of the defendant arriving at her sister's estate. 'You're welcome to view the footage, DC Anguish.' She walked slowly up to the jurors and placed a copy in front of each of them before turning back towards Saul, the sounds of her footsteps echoing through the court.

'My point is this. Detective Constable Saul Anguish would like us to believe that Alyssa was reckless. That she was out in a boat six days after giving birth, doing God knows what.

But she wasn't in that boat. She was at her sister's home. If a police officer, a figure of authority and respect, can't be trusted to get this right, how can we believe him when he tells us that Alyssa admitted to killing Teddy Miller?'

54

Jen

'There was a boy in America. A baby.' Jen fought to keep her voice steady, overcome by the enormity of the occasion. It was harder out here than she'd expected, all those faces staring at her, including her younger sister. *Don't look at Alyssa.* She swallowed down the burning sensation at the back of her throat. This was another element of bereavement that no one talked about. The physical manifestations of suffering a traumatic loss. In her case, it was the onset of acid reflux. So mundane that it felt almost stupid. A broken heart or a missing limb would have been more fitting.

'They called him the Lazarus child. He was twenty-one months old, and he was found face down in a ditch, pinned by a log. His heart stopped beating for an hour.' Her eyes travelled to the public gallery, seeking out her husband, but he wasn't there. When she spoke again, the jurors had to lean forward to hear her whisper. 'An hour. Can you believe it?'

She shook her head, as if she couldn't believe it herself. 'His family fought with everything they had to revive him,

294

but they couldn't do it. He was taken to hospital in an ambulance and everyone thought he was dead.'

She sipped her water and didn't even try to wipe away the tears that were spilling down her cheeks. 'At the hospital, they restarted his heart. Three days later, he woke up. No brain damage. As good as new.

'It was a miracle. A bona fide miracle. He came back from the dead. And when I was at the hospital that night after Teddy's accident, I was scouring the internet for these stories, hoping against hope the same thing would happen to my own baby.'

The courtroom was silent, breathing in her testimony.

'But he died. Because my sister dropped him. And my family have to live with that every single day.'

David Jarvis and Trudi Baxter gave her space to speak. And she knew why. Both were shrewd enough to recognize that she, Jen Miller, could win or lose this case for either of them. If the jury felt that pull of sympathy for a grieving mother – and how could they not? – it might sway them in her favour, even if they believed their verdict was evidence-based and the bias happened on a subconscious level. Both barristers had seen it before.

But Alyssa was a mother too.

Jarvis approached the witness box. 'I appreciate this must be difficult for you, Mrs Miller. Can you tell us what you saw when you were standing on that jetty, waiting for the pleasure boat to arrive? Take your time. There's no rush.'

Jen gave a faraway smile, lost in the memory of the wedding day that never happened. 'I could see them, but not clearly. It was a foggy afternoon and it was difficult at first. But as the boat got closer, I could make out Teddy's head poking over the rail. Iris was smiling and waving.'

Her boy. Cheeks rosy in the cold. He was the ring-bearer. The box had still been in the pocket of his jacket when they pulled him from the water.

'Did you know they would be arriving by boat?'

'No, I had no idea. Actually, that's not strictly true. One of the children let slip, but as far as my family were concerned, I didn't.'

'What did you think about it?'

She paused, shifted in the witness box. 'I thought it was a stupid idea. I don't mean to sound ungrateful, but I don't know what Winter was thinking. It was cold. The kids can swim, but I didn't love the fact they weren't wearing life-jackets, and neither Phil nor I were on board.'

The barrister nodded. 'Then what did you see?'

'Alyssa, my younger sister, lifted Teddy up. I've since learned it was so he could get a better view.'

'Hearsay.' Trudi Baxter appealed to the judge. 'She wasn't there. She doesn't know that.'

The judge nodded. 'Allowed.' She smiled at Jen, her tone gentle. 'Try to stick to what you personally witnessed.'

'I was waiting on the jetty, and I saw Alyssa pick Teddy up.'

'Where was everyone else?' David picked up the thread of his questioning.

'Iris was standing next to them. I couldn't see my mother or father.'

'What about your other sister?'

'She was standing behind Alyssa. She had a glass of champagne in her hand and she was laughing at something. They all looked happy. That's what I remember most of all. Because I *wasn't* happy.'

It might have been sweltering in the courtroom, but Jen

could taste the salted air and feel the cold surprise of the fog in her chest as she inhaled sharply. 'I shouted at Alyssa to put Teddy down, but she was too far away to hear me. Iris was waving like a mad thing.' She choked back the lump in her throat. 'She had this nervous energy about her, and I could tell she was excited, but all I could focus on was how close Teddy was to the edge.'

'And then?'

'Alyssa lifted Teddy, and I could see he wasn't comfortable. He doesn't like it when he's surprised by something, and he was wriggling and squirming, and I was worried he was going to kick her.' Her laugh turned into a sob. 'He was always such a determined boy.'

Jen closed her eyes, but it was a pointless gesture. It didn't matter whether she was in bed or at the supermarket or in the bath, she replayed that moment over and over again until it was burned into her memory and her dreams.

'The wind was picking up. It was cold and Phil offered me his jacket, but I refused to wear it because I was being vain and I didn't want to spoil the way that either of us looked, but I was getting cross because the weather was ruining my hair.

'I said something to Phil and then I looked back at the boat. Alyssa was dangling Teddy over the edge and there was this strong gust and the boat seemed to lurch and I saw Alyssa and Winter – they stumbled, tipped forward – and then Alyssa lost hold of Teddy and . . .'

The courtroom was silent. One of the jurors – a woman in her late thirties – dabbed at her eyes with a tissue.

'I saw him fall.' She enunciated each word and the effect was electric. 'Can you imagine that? I watched my boy, who loved trains and bananas and custard and giraffes and building sandcastles, spin through the air and hit the freezing water.'

'I appreciate how difficult this must be.' David Jarvis was standing close to the witness box. 'Do you need a break?'

'No. Thank you.'

'And you're certain that Alyssa was the one who dropped Teddy.'

'One hundred per cent.'

'Can you tell the court what happened next?'

'I think I screamed. In fact, I know I did because the celebrant who was conducting the service heard me, and came running down to the jetty, but it's all a bit of a blur. I wanted to jump in the water, but I can't swim, and she had to hold me back. Phil was already taking off his shoes and jacket, and I didn't want him to go into the sea in case he drowned, you know, like those terrible stories you read in the newspaper, but at the same time I wanted him to hurry up, throw himself in and rescue Teddy. Does that make sense?'

'Perfect sense. Can you tell us how Teddy was recovered from the water?'

'One of the crew from the boat jumped in. He was a strong swimmer. There's a protocol – I didn't know that at the time. *Stop the propeller. Throw in the lifeline to mark the spot. Use a flashlight.* It took him a while to find Teddy, but when he did, he swam to him and managed to get hold of him. He was struggling himself in the cold, but he managed to keep Teddy afloat until the lifeboat arrived and pulled them both out of the water.'

Jen began to cry again, the trauma of reliving that day hitting her with blunt force. When she had gathered herself, she addressed the jury. 'By the time that Teddy was carried to the jetty, he'd been in the water for twenty minutes. The paramedics were waiting and they administered CPR until they restarted his heart.'

'What about the pleasure boat, the *Dawn Treader*?'

'As soon as Teddy was out of the water, it moored at the jetty and everyone got off.'

David Jarvis asked a few more questions. About the logistics of getting Teddy to hospital. The hours spent in the paediatric intensive care unit. How twenty-four hours after Phil and Jen should have exchanged their wedding vows, each of the family came to say their goodbyes.

'Including Iris?'

Jen nodded. 'Iris was the last in. She didn't want to leave him. She tucked his favourite train into his hand, and she lay on the bed next to him, and she sang him a lullaby, and read to him from his favourite book.' Teddy's mother shared those words with the court, a rhythm to her sorrow.

'And then we kissed him, and they turned off his ventilator, and he died.'

Several jurors were in tears. Jen needed a few moments to compose herself, but she felt strangely calm, as if a great burden had been eased from her shoulders. Some of the journalists were making furious notes, due to file their copy. She glanced at her watch. The hours had flown by, and she knew the court would be adjourning soon until tomorrow, but the prosecution team had explained court protocol, and the defence barrister could choose to cross-examine her now, if she wanted to.

Trudi Baxter wanted to.

'Please accept our condolences for your terrible loss, Mrs Miller. Your evidence has moved us all.'

Jen inclined her head. 'Thank you.'

'You mentioned the family came to say goodbye to Teddy. Was the defendant included in that?'

'Yes, Teddy was very close to his aunt, and it didn't feel right to exclude her. Not then.'

'Even though you were' – Trudi Baxter consulted her notes – 'quote "*one hundred per cent*" sure that Alyssa had dropped Teddy in the water.'

'I was in a mess. I didn't have any capacity to make decisions at that time. Alyssa wanted to say goodbye to her nephew, and both Phil and I accepted that.'

Baxter locked glances with some of the jurors. 'I'm not sure I would have been so magnanimous.'

She turned from them and softened her tone. 'I don't feel it's right for me to keep you in the witness box for too long after such an emotional day, Mrs Miller, but there is one thing I'd like to check, if that's OK with you?'

Jen nodded.

Baxter consulted her notes again. 'Earlier, when my learned friend was asking you to recall what happened on that awful afternoon in the moments before and after Teddy's accident, you said, "*It's all a bit of a blur.*" That's right, isn't it?'

Jen's voice was small. 'Yes.'

Baxter turned back to the jury, conversational, inviting them in, as if their opinions mattered more to her than anyone else's ever could. 'It's no surprise that in the shock and horror of that moment, everything became *all a bit of a blur*. But, and I'm sure you'd agree, Mrs Miller, any recollection that is *all a bit of a blur* is not enough to convict my client. No further questions.'

55

Saul

If he thought it would be a relief to escape the stultifying atmosphere of Midtown Crown Court, Saul Anguish was mistaken. As he stepped out of the building, driven to feel fresh air in his lungs, a wall of heat hit him.

He needed to escape from the noise and dirt of the urban sprawl. A rubbish truck rumbled past, the stink of rotting food exaggerated by the weather. The odour made him gag. But even without that encouragement, he felt sick to his stomach. He'd been bested by the defence barrister and his cheeks burned with confusion at the memory.

He needed to unpick what had just happened away from the scrutiny of others. With that in mind, he left the town behind him and walked for an hour or more, seeking sanctuary in the place that offered him space to think without judgement – the salt marshes.

Even on an afternoon as warm as this one, the coastal wetlands were almost deserted. In the far distance, he spotted a couple walking hand in hand, a pair of dogs running ahead of them, sniffing at the salt-crusted earth. Behind them, the bay rose like a painted canvas, a promise of peace, if only he knew how to find it and keep it. The sight of the water calmed him as he navigated his way across the mud and peat to a sun-bleached hideout, hidden among the dense stands of shrubby sea-blite and the succulent prickly saltwort, long abandoned to the elements.

Saul had stumbled across it by accident a few months before, seeking out insects in the samphire-rich saltings. The entrance had been camouflaged, but he'd caught his foot against the lip of a barely exposed semi-circle of corrugated iron and fallen, sprawling across the ground.

Fascinated, he'd explored further, uncovering a tunnel of curved corrugated-iron sheets beneath the surface, dug into the earth and disguised from view. A hidden trapdoor thirty metres away served as a second entrance.

The shelter was rudimentary and in a state of disrepair, but perfect for Saul's purposes. Despite its marshy location, the interior was dry and sandy, and solidly constructed. He guessed it had once been a bunker set up by the British resistance to disrupt a potential German occupation of the Essex coast.

As soon as he was able, Saul had concealed that first entrance with several layers of shrubbery. Easy work. While the trapdoor entrance was impossible to see from above unless its location was known, Saul was fearful of discovery. One rainy afternoon, when his chances of being interrupted were at their lowest, he carried his tools and a spade over the salt marsh and secured it with a padlock and chain, disguising it beneath a scattering of freshly dug peat.

It was the key to this padlock that Saul now slipped from his pocket and slid into the mechanism, unlocking it with an audible click.

A stepladder was positioned beneath the trapdoor, and Saul climbed down awkwardly. Although the shelter must once have been packed with grenades and ammunition and non-perishable foodstuffs, it was empty when he'd found it, save for a couple of kerosene lamps hanging from hooks.

Over several weeks, he'd transferred his collection of insects and crime scene trophies from the coastguard's lookout to this place of secrecy, buried deep beneath the marsh. It was here where he'd hidden Blue's seagull feather and her suitcase, and the other treasures he'd magpied.

But he was careful.

No personal effects. No correspondence or hand-written notes. Several mahogany boxes. Two display cabinets. A stool and workbench for painstakingly recreating the crime scenes he visited. Nothing to connect Saul to this place except his DNA.

The detective was a self-aware young man, but he was so lost in himself that he did not recognize he was mimicking what the serial killer Mr Silver had shown him a decade earlier. A museum, of sorts. A collection of his special interests.

He unhooked the catch on one of the boxes and withdrew the dress he'd claimed from the sea on that afternoon Alyssa Kellaway had discarded it. It was stiff with salt, but pliable in his hands, and he examined the stubborn traces of blood that remained around the neckline. The sea had almost rinsed them away, but not quite, and the rusted imprint of someone else's pain had become part of its history.

Saul knew it mattered, but he didn't know how or why. He turned the dress over in his hands, examining it, as he had done many times before. He did not doubt himself. The woman rowing that boat had been Alyssa. He had wanted to challenge her, to produce this evidence that might prove what he'd said. But he could not. Because he'd stolen it, and he did not wish to relinquish it. But why had she and Winter Kellaway constructed a lie to conceal this truth?

Saul turned the dress inside out, searching for the answer to that question. It was a child's white summer dress with blue and yellow flowers, dated in style, and from a clothing store that had closed down years before.

There was a label on the inside seam. *Age 10–11.* Nothing out of the ordinary or untoward. The same printed care instructions that were included on every garment of clothing, faded but still readable.

A name had been hand-embroidered on a thin strip of white fabric, neatly sewn to the care label. The letters were italicized, tiny stitches of blue thread that spelled out another life.

Hannah Matthews.

He hadn't paid much attention to it, that first time he'd noticed it. He'd been busy with other, more important things. And then it had slipped his mind. But now it had taken on a significance he could not ignore. He had no idea who she was. But a name meant a place to start.

In the late-afternoon sun, he wandered back to the coast-guard's lookout by the path that hugged the headland. A breeze was coming in from the sea, and Saul enjoyed the relief from the unrelenting heat. The bushes were bursting with berries, plump sloes and the shiny invitation of rose hips, and he allowed himself a moment to admit that he was right to have stayed in Midtown in his cottage on the cliffs.

Not surprisingly, he'd heard nothing from Blue for months. He'd kept his ear to the ground, alert to any rumours of her whereabouts. But none of his colleagues had seen or spoken to her. Occasionally, her name would come up in relation to a case, but there was a vagueness to it, as if no one was sure where or whose responsibility she was. Every now and then, he thought about calling her, but then he remembered, and he would carefully put his phone back into his pocket. But he missed her.

In happier times, he would have dialled her as soon as he'd left the courthouse, railing against the barrister and his own tongue-tiedness, the shame of being exposed as a liar in front of everyone, and she would have calmed him by listening and talking it through, laughing it off until the sting had eased, and he could laugh too.

But that was all gone now.

By the time he'd walked home, the sun was beginning to wane, a low-slung ball of fire in the sky that kindled in him a yearning for long summer evenings, spent in the company of friends. He imagined sitting in a beachside bar somewhere with Blue, the feel of heat on his skin, and the promise of the night, their bodies slick with sweat and arousal.

He bit his lip, allowed his hand to drift back to his phone. One message wouldn't hurt.

56

Winter

She was showered by 6 a.m. Then straight into hair. Make-up. The right kind of clothing. Winter's stylist had spent weeks putting her court outfits together and today's look was a show-stopper, which was just as well because Winter Kellaway, the Emmy-Award-winning star of stage and screen, was due to give evidence in less than an hour.

She kissed Alex on the top of his tiny head and handed the baby to the live-in nanny. Her car was waiting outside the gates to take her to the second day of the trial. Technically, she was not supposed to discuss her evidence with anybody else, but she'd looked up the news stories on the internet when she'd woken up at stupid o'clock, and was delighted to see the detective had been challenged by Trudi Baxter.

The prosecution's legal team had left several messages for her the previous night, ostensibly to confirm timings and to run through her statement, but she had not answered her phone. She wasn't an idiot. They were worried she was going to go off-piste and ruin their carefully constructed case. A part of her enjoyed that power. But she wasn't going to let

Jen down. She smiled to herself. Some might find it strange, but she was looking forward to taking centre stage.

Outside the court building, the same crowd of fans with their placards and posters had gathered, some with garden chairs and flasks and foil-wrapped sandwiches, but if she wasn't mistaken, their numbers had swelled to almost twice as many as the previous day.

'Shall I nip you round the back?' her driver Arthur enquired.

'It's fine.' She waved to the crowds as the car pulled in. 'I can get out here.'

While she waited for Arthur to open the rear passenger door, she checked her make-up in the compact mirror she kept in her handbag, and smoothed the fabric of her designer jumpsuit. Then, with an elegant swing of her legs, she slipped out of the back seat and catwalked up to the court as if she was on the red carpet.

Court Two's air conditioning had not been fixed. For the public, press and court officials, it was like stepping into the humid atmosphere of a swimming pool. The Honourable Mrs Justice Lambert, red-faced in her robes and wig, was not amused.

'Get on with it,' she said to both legal counsel, and her exasperation was still evident when Winter Kellaway took the stand.

David Jarvis didn't waste his breath on good mornings – this particular judge found them irritating, a waste of everyone's time – and addressed the jury instead. 'You may recognize our next witness from films and television, but I would urge you to put aside any preconceptions you may have, and listen only to the evidence you will hear in court today. Ms Kellaway is not one of the characters she plays, but a loving aunt who has lost a nephew in tragic circumstances. This will be the first time we hear from a witness who was on the *Dawn Treader* at the time of Teddy Miller's accident, so please pay particular attention.'

Winter glanced at the jury to assess their reactions to the barrister's opening salvo. Eight women and four men. One of the men – slight, clean-shaven – was staring at her, his mouth slightly open. Two of the women were stone-faced and impossible to read. A third was flushed and fidgeting, a sign to Winter that she was a fan, even if she was trying hard not to show it.

When he'd talked briefly to her in the witness room that morning, David Jarvis had explained the gender split of the jury. This was an advantage, he'd said, because the prosecution team believed the female jurors were more likely to sympathize with Jen and Winter than with Alyssa.

'No surprises today, please. Stick to the facts. Jurors warm to witnesses who are approachable and likeable, so be yourself. Good luck.'

Winter was an actor. She was so used to pretending to be somebody else that being herself was more difficult than it sounded. 'I'll do my best.'

And she intended to. It was odd, the sight of Alyssa in the dock. She'd put on weight. Her hair was a mess. It needed a decent cut and colour. Why wasn't she wearing any makeup? She looked washed out and sallow, and she couldn't have chosen a more shapeless and unflattering dress.

Subconsciously, Winter sucked in her post-partum stomach. The courtroom sketch artist was making notes on her appearance and she angled herself to present her best side. She'd seen those illustrations on the *Ten O'Clock News.*

To her eye, the portraits rarely captured the people they were supposed to denote, but resulted in potato-shaped caricatures. She pouted slightly, to accentuate her cheekbones, and hoped the woman would make a half-decent job of it. Her make-up artist had used liberal amounts of setting spray and she prayed her foundation wouldn't slide off in the heat of the courtroom.

Jen, who had given evidence yesterday, was now sitting in the public gallery with their father. She resisted an impulse to wave at her. No sign of Phil. She flicked another glance at Alyssa. She must not allow emotion to get the better of her. With effort, she forced herself to detach from her younger sister, as if she were a stranger.

'You had a glass of champagne in your hand during the short pleasure-boat trip to your estate. Your sister Jen saw you drinking it from the jetty.'

'Absolutely. We were excited. It was a wedding, and weddings mean bubbles, right? So, yes, I did have a glass on the boat. Two, actually.'

'Were you the only one?'

'God, no. We were all in high spirits. Our gorgeous Jen was getting married and it was a cause for celebration. We'd been toasting her all day.'

'Was Alyssa drinking?'

A shadow crossed Winter's face. She arranged her features into an expression of concern. Lowered her voice to a suitably sombre tone. 'She was, yes. I saw her with at least one glass of champagne on the boat, and I heard her ask for a top-up.'

'Even though she had a new baby?'

'She'd decided not to breastfeed that day, so she thought it would be OK. As it was a special occasion.'

'Presumably, she'd abstained from drinking for most of

her pregnancy. Do you think it's possible that the alcohol had gone to her head?'

Trudi Baxter was on her feet, appealing to the judge. 'This is outrageous speculation. Alyssa's choices throughout her pregnancy are not the business of the court, and, in any case, Ms Kellaway couldn't possibly know the answer to that question.'

The judge shook her head. 'But it *is* relevant if she was drinking on that day. Go on.'

David Jarvis was succinct, to the point. 'I suppose another way of phrasing it would be this: from what you witnessed that afternoon, Ms Kellaway, would you say the defendant was drunk?'

Winter rifled through the mental filing cabinet of facial expressions that she regularly used to manipulate others, although she preferred to call it acting. She stopped at *sorrowful dismay*. She did not look at Alyssa as she betrayed her.

'That's exactly what I'd say.'

Trudi Baxter did not mince her words. Winter knew that she would be in damage-limitation mode, and she readied herself to face her adversary. She'd met women like this before. Baxter was intelligent but plain. In Winter's experience, these types of women often had a common trait. They were jealous of her breathtaking looks but pretended they weren't.

For an uncomfortable few moments, the court waited in silence while the defence barrister had a whispered conversation with Alyssa. Then her cross-examination began.

'Ms Kellaway, your reputation as a household name precedes you. I believe you've starred in several films and television shows that observers in this courtroom will have seen.'

Winter gave a modest incline of her head. 'It's possible.'

'And you're a full-time professional actress?'

'Most of us prefer the term "actor" these days. It's more inclusive.' Her smile was the embodiment of *sweetly forgiving*. 'But yes, that's right.'

Baxter waved an impatient hand. 'But you're paid huge sums of money to pretend.'

David Jarvis stood up with a bark of indignant laughter. 'Oh, come on. That's irrelevant. The witness's salary has no bearing on this case.'

The judge overruled him and Baxter continued. 'Plays, movies, the latest Netflix series – whatever medium, they're all make-believe, yes?'

One of the jurors rolled his eyes at Winter, and she struggled to hide a grin. 'I suppose you could say that.'

Baxter's tone was cool. 'But you do realize that this is a courtroom, Ms Kellaway, and not a film set?'

'Of course.'

'Then can you explain why what you shared with the jury about Alyssa's drinking is a work of fiction?'

Four or five of the watching journalists laughed and Winter blushed. 'It isn't.'

'How much champagne did you drink that day, Ms Kellaway? You've already admitted to having two glasses on the boat, and you said, I quote, "We'd been toasting her" – that's Teddy's mother, Jen Miller – "all day." Did you have a glass or two while you were getting ready? Perhaps more?'

When Winter didn't answer, Baxter raised an eyebrow. 'Ms Kellaway?'

'I had some, yes. But so did everyone, including Alyssa.'

Baxter addressed the jurors. 'We'll hear more about this from the defendant when it's her turn to give evidence later this week, but I can tell you that I've consulted my client, and I'm confident she wasn't drunk. Ms Kellaway has clearly spent too much time in the Land of Make-Believe.'

Despite her vow to remain poised and in control, Winter was goaded into retaliation. 'With all due respect, you weren't there.'

Again, Baxter raised an eyebrow. 'With all due respect, perhaps the copious amounts of champagne you'd consumed has clouded your recollection of events.'

A ripple of amusement spread throughout the court. Winter squirmed with embarrassment, but she kept it hidden. Yes, she'd had a few glasses, but she hadn't been drunk. She'd just found out she was pregnant, and the party had been her last hurrah. Determined not to let this bitch of a barrister get the better of her, she narrowed her eyes.

'I attend around fifty or sixty film premieres, award ceremonies, industry parties and so on each year. I can cope with a few glasses of champagne.' A well-timed pause. 'But perhaps you can't handle *your* alcohol, Ms Baxter,' she said, *smoothly patronising*, 'and that's impaired your ability to understand the nuances of this case.'

Everyone, even the judge, laughed. 'Touché,' said Baxter, holding up her hands in a gesture of surrender.

The barrister paced the floor, allowing the public gallery to settle down. When the court was silent again, she turned to Winter, her voice dangerously quiet.

'Winter isn't your real name, is it?'

Winter paled, ambushed by the question. She glanced at Alyssa, but her younger sister was looking down at her lap, her hair falling in lank strands around her face. David Jarvis watched them both, his eyes narrowed.

'No.'

'What is it?'

Winter mumbled her answer. Some of the jurors turned to each other and frowned, unable to hear what she'd said.

'Can you speak a little more loudly, please?' said Baxter.

Alyssa lifted her head and watched her sister, an expression of agony on her face. Winter stared back at her and a wordless communication passed between them.

'Deborah.'

It had been a long time since she'd spoken that name. The vowels and consonants felt lumpy on her tongue, as if her mouth was filled with wet sponge. Winter imagined the magazine headlines it would spawn in the next few weeks, misquoting the lyrics of that hit song by Pulp. *Her name was Deborah.*

'Not quite as glamorous as Winter,' said Baxter.

'No.'

'Tell me, were the three of you close, growing up?'

'We were normal siblings. We loved and hated each other. But we stuck together. Always.'

'Would you say that's the case now?'

Winter gave a helpless shrug. The circumstances spoke for themselves. Alyssa was looking at her hands again. Jen was watching her intently. She swiped her hand across her upper lip to disappear the beads of sweat. 'It's not as simple as that, is it?'

'I think it is. Three's a crowd, isn't it?'

'I don't know what you mean by that.'

'Come on, Ms Kellaway. It's fair to say that you've always been closer to your middle sister, Jen. You spend a lot of time with her. Your relationship is more distant with Alyssa. You have less in common.'

'That's not true. Jen and I are close, yes. My relationship with Alyssa is different, but still close.'

'*Different?*'

'The dynamic within our family has changed since Teddy's death. I don't think anyone would expect otherwise.'

'But if you were forced to choose, say, one sister over the other, you'd always choose Jen.'

She hesitated, uncertain how to respond, but before she'd had a chance to speak, Baxter turned to the jury, her palms open to convey truth and honesty. 'I think we can all agree that her silence speaks volumes.'

And what could she say to that?

When David Jarvis re-examined his witness, he pointed out to the jury that Winter had been equally generous to both her sisters, that she had provided an alibi for Alyssa which countered the detective's evidence, and that her recall for events would be better than most ordinary people's because of the number of scripts she'd had to memorize over the years. But all of them – Jarvis, Trudi Baxter and Winter – knew that the damage had been done.

57

Carol

The days dragged by. Geoff came home every night, wearing his sadness like a second skin. He didn't repeat the evidence he'd heard in court that day – he was a stickler for following the rules – but he talked about who had been in the witness box and how they'd conducted themselves. The consultant paediatrician from Midtown Hospital who'd treated Teddy during his final hours: articulate and compassionate. An official from the Health and Safety Executive: diligent but dull. The skipper of the *Dawn Treader* and his crew-mate: evasive. He offered Carol a daily update on the air conditioning. And their daughters. But it was difficult for both of them. Geoff and Carol loved their children equally. The death of their beloved grandson had been a terrible accident, nothing more than that, but the consequences had been catastrophic. Carol couldn't see how the schism could ever be repaired.

'Do I look OK?' She was wearing a short-sleeved cotton dress with daisies on it.

'Fresh as a daisy, love,' said Geoff, and laughed at his own weak joke. 'Ready to go?'

Carol's stomach was full of butterflies. She hadn't wanted to give evidence because it felt like she was choosing sides, but the defence had subpoenaed her on the strength of her statement, and both Jen and Alyssa had said they understood.

And now that moment had arrived. She'd kissed her husband goodbye, knowing the next time she saw him, she'd be standing in the witness box and he'd be in the public gallery in the same seat he'd occupied every day. Jen was sitting next to him, but there was no sign of Winter.

'Thank you for being here today,' said Trudi Baxter, smiling at her witness. She turned to the jury. 'This is Teddy Miller's grandmother.' Back to Carol, her tone warm. 'Can you tell us a bit about your grandson?'

Carol's voice was shaking, like her hands. She swallowed, trying to control her nerves. 'He was a pickle. Full of energy. Cheeky, and ever so affectionate. He loved cuddles with me and his grandpa.'

'We've already heard from several witnesses about what unfolded on the pleasure boat that afternoon, but I'd like to hear it from you.'

'That's my point,' said Carol. 'I told the police this. I didn't *see* anything. Geoff called out to me to help Alyssa with Teddy – he could be a bit of a handful, at times – and the next thing I knew, he was over the side.'

'Was Alyssa drunk?'

'No. She's not a big drinker at the best of times. In any case, she was a new mother and she was breastfeeding. A few sips of champagne at most, I'd say.'

Alyssa shot her mother a grateful look. The prosecution barrister, half out of his seat, looked as if he had something to say, but changed his mind and sat back down again.

'It must have been a challenge bringing up three daughters, Mrs Kellaway.'

'I loved it. I'd always wanted to be a mother.'

'What was Alyssa like as a baby?'

It was an innocuous question. Neither Trudi Baxter nor her opposing counsel had the faintest idea of the Pandora's box those seven words were about to unlock. A wave of nausea hit Carol. She didn't want to tell the truth, but she was bound by law not to lie. She had sworn an oath, and to her, that was sacrosanct. Her eyes found Geoff, seeking his guidance. He gave a slight nod, and she exhaled, knowing what had to be done.

'I don't know.'

Baxter, who liked to pace the courtroom, stopped in her tracks. She was rarely surprised, her arguments and her witnesses well prepared, but this was unexpected. 'What do you mean?'

'Alyssa came to us when she was two and a half.'

'You adopted her?'

'Later, yes. We fostered her first.' Carol let out a rush of breath. 'I've never told anyone that before.'

Jen's mouth was agape. Carol longed to comfort her, willing her kind-hearted but emotionally restrained husband to be proactive for once, and do what she wasn't able to. They should have told her the facts a lifetime ago, but the past was a polluted place, and she'd fought with all her maternal instincts to preserve the sanctity of their home from its harmful effects.

'Does Alyssa know this?'

'Yes,' said Carol, sending a loving look in her youngest daughter's direction.

'But you kept it a secret from everybody else?'

'With the odd exception, yes.'

'Why?'

If Trudi Baxter had expected David Jarvis to challenge such a personal question of this witness, she'd misjudged him. He wanted to know the answer as much as she did.

'We were determined to protect her from the scrutiny and judgement of others.'

'Go on.'

Carol paused, unsure of how much more to say. From across the courtroom, Alyssa half smiled at her mother, as if to reassure her, and Carol read that as permission to continue.

'My daughter witnessed an extremely violent and disturbing incident as a young child. Her biological father murdered her birth mother and siblings, and then took his own life. Alyssa survived this attack and managed to get away.' Carol fumbled in her sleeve for her handkerchief, then dabbed at her eyes. 'We didn't want her life to be shaped by this awful tragedy. We never talked about her past. As a little girl, she had extensive therapy and, believe it or not, forgot about it – or blocked it out, we're not sure – for a long time. We moved to a new town for a fresh start as a family of five.

'But when she became pregnant, not surprisingly, she wanted to know about her medical history. I told her she was adopted, and when she asked me for information about her biological parents, I couldn't, in all conscience, deny her that.'

The courtroom erupted into chatter. The judge called for order, and both counsel requested the court to rise, so they could seek an adjournment to examine the significance of this new information.

Carol's gaze flicked between Alyssa and Jen. Her youngest

daughter looked as if a great burden had been lifted from her shoulders, the strain easing from her face for the first time in months. Carol had no idea if this revelation would help or hinder her case, but it was the truth, and there was a courage and nobility in that.

Jen was a different matter. She ran from the public gallery, and Carol was relieved to see that Geoff had gone too, presumably to explain everything to their middle daughter. It was a shock. No one could deny that. Another loss for Jen to process. But she was sensible and pragmatic. In time, she would come to understand. At least, that's what Carol prayed for as she stood in the witness box, awaiting further instructions.

As for Winter, her mother knew that her eldest daughter, ambitious, often selfish, and deeply concerned with her global profile, would be incensed that this information had been made public without prior knowledge or warning.

She steeled herself for the incoming storm.

58

Wednesday, 31 July 2024

Alyssa

The Honourable Mrs Justice Lambert had granted a two-day adjournment, but made it clear to counsel that she'd been reluctant to allow even that. No extensions would be permitted. With that schedule in mind, the trial in Court Two of Midtown Crown Court resumed at 10 a.m. on the following Wednesday.

The courtroom was packed. Not a single spare seat remained. The defendant, Alyssa Kellaway, was due to give evidence that morning, and the starry nature of this trial, coupled with the moral conundrum at the heart of Teddy Miller's death and the dramatic revelations about her childhood, ticked every box in every newsroom across the country.

Alyssa had been awake since 4 a.m. She had spent a few days with Claudia after the unexpected adjournment, but Federico had resumed fatherly duties the previous night, and the house was strangely silent. Even so, she awoke with a start at dawn, listening for the familiar wail of her daughter. Her curtains were open and the sky was filled with a bronze haze, the bright jewels of Jupiter and Venus still visible above the horizon.

Trudi Baxter had impressed on her the importance of making a positive impression on the jury, and she walked herself through what they'd practised until her eyes felt gritty and her bedroom was flooded with the light and birdsong of a summer morning. Groggy from lack of sleep, she sat in the garden and drank a mug of strong, hot coffee, and dressed with more care than she had for the previous ten days.

She hadn't spoken to Winter or Jen, but her mother and father – she couldn't remember her birth parents, except through faded newspaper articles of a time and place that no longer existed for her – had impressed upon her how much they loved her, and how special she must have been, because they had *chosen* her. Her place in the Kellaway family was not an accident of fate, but an act of careful deliberation. The rational part of her brain recognized this was a calculated attempt to make her feel better about the tragedy of her past, but the frightened child that still lived within her was comforted by their assurances.

Although she tormented herself by imagining the reactions of her sisters, particularly Winter, she didn't ask what they had said, and Carol and Geoff didn't volunteer it. But her parents had promised her they would be in court today, and she drew strength from that.

'Do you know what it feels like to stare at your newborn daughter, to examine every inch of her skin to determine whether she carries a physical trace of her murdering grandfather? To wonder if the genetic traits that made him kill his family exist within this tiny scrap of life?'

Alyssa fought to compose herself and the courtroom held its breath. 'To wonder if they exist in *me?*'

Her mouth was dry. Her parents watched from the public gallery, but she couldn't see Jen or Winter, Phil or Federico. Her family – her support system – had all but collapsed, and, bereft, she struggled to catch her breath, trying to quash those first familiar flutterings of a panic attack.

'When I was eight months pregnant, I had an appointment to see my midwife. She was running late, and so I picked up a magazine in the waiting room, and there, sandwiched between a feature headlined "My Daughter's Affair with My Boyfriend" and "How to Dress a Decade Younger", was an article about my father, and the terrible things he had done to my family. Every excruciating detail. There was even a grainy photograph of him on a beach in his swimming trunks, waving to someone in the water.

'And *that* is exactly why Carol and Geoff Kellaway have worked so hard to throw a protective ring around my life. My past is not a salacious titbit of water-cooler gossip, to be dissected and pored over and written about by strangers. It *is* me. All of us in this courtroom are shaped by events that happen to, or around, us. They become a part of who we are. So please don't judge my mother and father, or me, for keeping it a secret. Especially as I have a daughter now. A niece. And a nephew.' Her voice wobbled. 'Two nephews. I'd do anything to protect them, and I regret what happened to Teddy every single moment of my life.'

Trudi Baxter turned to the jury, appealing to the humanity in them. 'I think we'd all agree that Alyssa Kellaway is a compassionate woman, a loving sister and aunt, and an empathetic mother. The events of her past make that achievement all the more impressive, wouldn't you agree?'

The defence barrister reached across the dock to squeeze Alyssa's hand in a gesture of solidarity. In truth, Alyssa's words had moved the advocate, and the sympathy in her face was not for show, but reflected genuine sorrow.

'But I suppose we must address the elephant in the room. Teddy died when he fell from your arms. *We* know it was an accident. The prosecution say it was negligence. The armchair critics – and there will be many – might suggest that the apple doesn't fall far from the tree. That your father was a killer, and so are you.'

One or two members of the public gave an audible gasp, and there was a rustle of paper as several journalists made a shorthand note of the controversial statement that would undoubtedly lead that night's TV coverage of the trial, but Alyssa wasn't surprised. Trudi had explained the reasoning behind this shock tactic, and it made sense to her. 'We need to claim ownership of your past before the prosecution does,' her barrister had said over breakfast. 'We want to hand the power back to you.'

'I can understand why people might say that.' Alyssa's voice was calm. 'But it's not true. If we were all judged by the sins of our fathers, none of us would be exempt. Doing wrong is not a contagion. We might share DNA, but we are not the same. We will never be the same.'

Baxter allowed a moment for the weight of Alyssa's words to sink in. The courtroom was almost too cool now that the air conditioning had been fixed. For the first time, two female jurors smiled at Alyssa, and she offered a tentative smile in return. Her gaze returned to the public gallery. Her sister Jen had attended every day of the trial so far, and she was surprised not to see her. But the comforting flash of white hair from two heads in the front row steadied her.

Alyssa inhaled deeply. She knew what was coming next.

Briefly, Baxter outlined the *agreed evidence*: the morning

of the wedding, the run-up to the boat trip. As she asked Alyssa to tell the courtroom what had happened during that heartbreaking afternoon, Jen slipped into the public gallery, sitting beside her parents in a seat they had saved for her.

'Teddy was in high spirits, bouncing about like a jumping bean.' She softened at the memory. 'He wanted me to play with him.'

'And you did?'

'For a bit. He had a couple of Thomas the Tank Engine trains in his pocket, those small metallic ones, and we played with those, running them along the grab rail of the boat.' She laughed. 'He said I could be the Fat Controller. I was a bit sensitive about my tummy after having a baby, so I told him that wasn't a very nice thing to say, but I realize now he didn't mean it in an unkind way.'

'And when you stopped playing?'

'One of the crew poured me half a glass of champagne. A sip, really.'

'So why do you think Winter Kellaway told the court that you were drunk and asked for more?'

'I *did* ask for more. But only because the sea was choppy, and I'd spilled most of my first glass when I lost my balance.'

'And the drunkenness?'

'I wasn't drunk. At all. I had a taste. And I was excited about the wedding, so perhaps I was a little giddy. But that was it.'

'What made you pick up Teddy Miller?'

'He couldn't see. I could tell he was getting upset, and I didn't want that, not on Jen's special day. I lifted him up so he could get a better view of his mother and father, standing on the jetty.'

'He was stronger than you expected?'

'Yes, he was wriggling about all over the place, and he put

his feet on the railing of the boat. I told him to keep still or I'd put him down, and he did as I asked.' Her heart raced as she recalled the sequence of events of that tragic day.

'Why did you dangle him over the side of the boat?'

'It was a split-second decision. I was trying to make him laugh, and it was for no more than seven or eight seconds, but it became apparent to me very quickly that I'd frightened him instead, and so I tried to get him back on deck as soon as I realized that.'

'What stopped you?'

'The sea was choppy. It was hard to find my balance. The boat lurched, and he was like a slippery little fish, and my grip on him weakened.'

'And you dropped him?'

'Not quite.'

'Go on.'

The jury was listening intently. This was the evidence they had been waiting to hear first-hand from Alyssa since the Health and Safety investigator had reported his findings the previous week.

'An object thumped me on my back and knocked me forward. That's when I lost my hold on him.'

'Do you know what it was?'

'Possibly one of the stowage compartments swung open, and the door hit me, or its contents did, but it's hard to tell as it came from behind, and I was taken by surprise. In the furore that followed, it went out of my head, and the compartment was latched by the time the Health and Safety Executive began their investigation.'

'Yes, their findings concluded that while these stowage compartments were not built into the boat but free-standing, and they were in a location that was too close to the guard rail, there was no fault with the mechanism of the compartment in question.'

'I don't know what happened, but something did. I would never have dropped Teddy if I hadn't lost momentum like that.'

'Thank you, Alyssa. And since your nephew's accident, you've been estranged from his mother and father?'

'That's right. They don't want to see me, which I understand, of course. But I miss them.' The tears that she had been holding back all morning trickled down her face. 'I miss my sister. I miss Iris.' She shivered, as if a goose had walked over her grave. 'But most of all, I miss Teddy.'

After a break for lunch, David Jarvis began his cross-examination and went straight for the jugular.

'My learned friend was correct when she said the Health and Safety Executive could find no fault on the part of the boat's operators. The overboard procedures were robust and effective. The guard rail was at an appropriate height. The stowage compartments were latched and working as they ought to. No one else on the *Dawn Treader* witnessed any object falling and hitting you that afternoon. We only have your word that this happened.'

Alyssa shrugged. What else could she say? 'That might be the case, but it's true.'

His expression suggested otherwise. 'Ms Kellaway, you told the court that you weren't drunk and you spilled your champagne because you lost your balance, not because you'd consumed too much alcohol?'

'Yes. That's exactly what happened.'

'And later in your evidence, you said, "The sea was choppy. It was hard to find my balance." That's right, isn't it?'

'Yes.'

'If the boat was so unbalanced, what on earth possessed you to lift up your four-year-old nephew and *dangle him over the side*?' His tone of patronizing incredulity made Alyssa's insides shrivel up with shame.

'I don't know,' she whispered. 'It was an accident.'

'An accident that happened because you didn't think, Ms Kellaway. An accident that happened as a result of your stupidity. An accident that happened because you were grossly negligent.' He waited a beat before delivering his final, damning line. 'An accident that killed a child.'

The sound of quiet sobbing could be heard from the public gallery. Alyssa bent her head, unable to look at her sister or parents, or to face the condemnation of the jury.

Trudi Baxter rose to re-examine her client. She could not leave those eight women and four men with the memory of the prosecution's powerful parting shot.

'Alyssa, you were invited to say goodbye to Teddy at the hospital, weren't you?'

'Yes.'

'Can you, if you're able, tell us a little bit about that?'

Alyssa's words were halting and sounded as if they came at great cost. 'He looked like he was sleeping. There was a bruise on his temple where he must have bumped his head, but otherwise, he was Teddy. Not a mark on him. I kissed his forehead, and I told him I loved him.' She was crying now, the tears spilling down her cheeks. 'I said I was sorry.'

'And Teddy's mother, your sister Jen, she came in with you, didn't she?'

Alyssa nodded, wiping the sleeve of her top across her nose. 'She did.'

'Can you tell us what she said to you?'

Alyssa bit her lip. This was deeply personal. Private. A marker of how everything had changed. But perhaps the jury needed to know. Her memory threw her back to that Sunday in November when time had stopped still for them all.

Walking down the sterile corridors of Midtown General Hospital to the paediatric intensive care unit, she had felt the bite of disinfectant in her nose and throat. Torrential rain had soaked her hair and cold rivulets of water trickled down the back of her neck, but she scarcely noticed. Sleep-deprived and grief-torn, her focus was on reaching her sister.

Jen was standing outside the unit, waiting for her. She'd refused to leave the hospital, even for half an hour, and was still in her wedding dress, an expression of dazed shock on her face.

Alyssa held out her arms and Jen collapsed into them, her body wracked with sobs. The women stood together for several minutes until Jen pulled away. Her skin was blotchy with distress, and by some miracle, that rose was still in her hair, its few remaining petals bruised and discoloured, but clinging on. When others had gently suggested she remove it, she'd reacted with anger, insisting it was a talisman to be removed only when Teddy opened his eyes. Jen took Alyssa's hand in her own.

'They can't do any more for him.'

Alyssa had sunk to her knees then, repeated apologies spilling from her, mumbled and indistinct. She had cried until her face was raw, her guilt pinning her to the floor. Her voice held a pleading note. 'No, no, I don't believe that. Poor Teddy. Surely there's something they can do? There must be. What about a second opinion? Or a private hospital?

I'm sure Winter would help with that.' She looked up at her sister, the horror of her actions dawning on her, desperate and selfish. 'I don't want this to come between us. I couldn't bear it.'

Jen shook her head vehemently. One of the petals fell to the floor. 'It will never come between us, I promise.' She hugged her youngest sister. 'Teddy loves you so much. You always find time to play with him and tell him stories.' She used the present tense, even though they both knew he was dying. 'I know it was an accident and you'd never do anything to deliberately hurt him.'

The two women sat with Teddy as the rain drummed against the skylight. Phil had gone home to change and collect Iris, and the rest of the family were due to arrive imminently. But for now it was Jen and Alyssa, and they watched the rise and fall of Teddy's chest as the machines kept him alive for their last goodbyes, knowing that, whatever else happened, their bond of sisterhood would see them through.

59

Jen

But what if what you saw wasn't what you thought?

Jen replayed that sentence in her head, trying to make sense of it. It was clunky and opaque, but Iris was eight and grieving, and she wasn't about to correct her grammar. She sat, cross-legged, next to her daughter on the carpet in her bedroom.

'Can you explain to Mummy what you mean?'

Iris danced her teddy around for a bit longer. 'What I said.'

'But Mummy doesn't understand what you said, Iris.' Jen sent up a silent prayer for patience. 'Please can you try to explain again.'

Iris gave a theatrical sigh, stood up and tucked her teddy into her bed, pulling the duvet up to the bear's chin and resting its furry arms over the cover. She turned her back on Jen and began to play with the ridiculously extravagant three-storey doll's house that Winter had commissioned for her last birthday, complete with cinema room, a wardrobe of miniature designer outfits and a doll-sized grand piano.

She was muttering to herself, dressing and undressing

her dolls, and moving them between rooms, but Jen couldn't make out what she was saying. 'Iris?'

The girl turned back to her mother, an expression of irritation on her face. She was holding three of her dolls, two in her right hand and one in the other. With a sudden rush of anger, she mashed their faces together, surprising Jen with the violence of her actions, and then threw all three of them onto her carpet before bursting into tears.

Jen was shocked but tried not to show it. She drew her daughter in for a cuddle and waited for her to calm down. Iris's face was pressed into her mother's shoulder, and when she began to speak, her voice was muffled.

'Do you remember when Calypso broke her arm at school?'

'Yes, sweetheart. Didn't she fall off the monkey bars?'

Iris pulled away and Jen's heart lurched at the sight of her tear-stained cheeks. Her daughter gave a solemn nod. 'Yes. Maddie was messing about with Calypso, being all annoying to her, and then Harriet kicked Maddie into Calypso, which knocked her off the monkey bars.'

Jen gave an encouraging smile. 'Go on.'

'Maddie was the one who hurt Calypso, but it was an accident and it only happened because Harriet kicked Maddie. So whose fault was it?'

Jen's blood ran cold. In the darkest reaches of herself, she knew it wasn't a coincidence that Iris was asking this question. But what exactly was Iris trying to tell her? She needed to be sure.

'Are you saying that someone other than Auntie Alyssa hurt Teddy?'

Iris's eyes filled with tears. A whisper. 'Yes.'

A volcano of acidic fury burned its way from Jen's stomach to her throat. An urge to scream consumed her, but she didn't want to frighten Iris, or cause her to clam up. She forced herself to control herself, but names ran through her head like ticker tape and she could think of only one.

She remembered what Iris had said about Winter pinching Teddy, and her eldest sister's ruthless streak, and how she tried, even now, to push Alyssa out, and all those times in the past when she had taken precious things that had belonged to Jen.

'Can you tell Mummy who it was?'

Iris, wide-eyed, put her finger to her lips. 'It's a secret.'

'If you won't tell me, will you tell the judge?'

Iris gave a sulky shrug. Jen gripped her daughter's shoulders and gazed straight into her eyes. 'You must always tell the truth, Iris, however difficult or painful it is.' Iris's eyes filled with tears again, and the penny dropped for Jen. How could she have been so blind?

'Are you worried about getting into trouble? That me and Daddy won't love you anymore?'

Iris nodded, her bottom lip quivering. 'Especially Daddy.'

'We will always love you, no matter what, OK?'

Mother and daughter clung to each other in the dying light of a summer's evening, both in need of comfort. They stayed that way until the stars lit up the night sky and both fell asleep, knowing that this would change everything.

60

Wednesday, 31 July 2024

Saul

DC Isaac Hunter placed a mug of coffee on Saul's desk. It was too full and slopped over the corner of the detective's mobile phone. Saul swore softly under his breath. Isaac blushed and mopped up the mess with his sleeve. As an apology, he offered him a sour cherry sweet, which Saul declined.

'You look like you haven't slept for days, chief.'

Saul hadn't, but he didn't feel like sharing that with his colleague, who was bursting with energy that afternoon, his leg constantly jigging until Saul wanted to ask him to stop. He did, however, like the sound of the moniker Isaac had jokingly used. *Chief.* He wondered again what it might feel like to progress his career, to seek promotion where he could hone his natural instincts to lead, not follow. But he said none of this. Instead, he thanked Isaac for the drink he would almost certainly forget about until it was cold and had acquired a film of scum.

'It arrived, then.'

Saul nodded. 'Finally.'

The file was thick, stuffed with pieces of paper that appeared to be in no particular order. With so much of the world computerized and digitized these days, it was almost a relief to resort to old-fashioned methods.

It had taken four days for West Midlands Police to locate the original file and courier it to Saul. Four days during which he had turned the revelations over and over in his head, reaching the same conclusion every time.

He rested his hands on the file and waited for DC Hunter to leave. He liked Isaac, but he wanted to uncover its secrets alone and confirm his suspicions.

The detective constable took the hint. 'I've got to write up a statement now, but do you fancy grabbing some dinner later?'

Saul considered the request. He wanted to say no. He always said no. But he was lonely. He missed O'Neill and PC Talbot and Blue. He'd messaged her earlier in the day, but she hadn't replied. This had not come as a surprise, but still. He longed for her to answer, even once.

He'd thought again, as he often did, how incriminating mobile phones could be. How those who did wrong tried to use them as an alibi to cover their tracks. How many criminals had he and other police officers caught by using cell-tower triangulation or tracking their GPS? He'd arrested countless perpetrators who'd thought that switching off their handset, or flinging it into a river, or messaging their victim, knowing they weren't alive, would save their skin. It never did.

'Go on,' said Isaac, interrupting his train of thought with a laugh. 'It might even be fun.' He nudged Saul. 'I thought Vietnamese. Or maybe Mexican. But if you say you'll come out with me, you can choose.'

And Saul found himself agreeing to meet his colleague downstairs in a couple of hours.

The office was quiet, punctuated by the occasional ringing

telephone, but Saul wouldn't have noticed even if every desk had been occupied.

He opened the file and lost himself in the summer of 1986. He'd already gleaned the basic facts from a search of the internet, but as he read through various witness statements, he pieced together the rest of the story.

It had been a hot afternoon in late June. Aaron Matthews was an alcoholic who'd been sacked from yet another job after a complaint of sexual harassment, and faced losing his home and his family. He was often bad-tempered, and when he was drunk, he had a mean streak that occasionally resulted in violence. On that particular day, he'd spent three hours in a pub downing neat vodka before driving himself back to their rented accommodation.

Helen Matthews had been at home with her two-and-a-half-year-old daughter Louise, preparing an early tea of new potatoes, cold ham, hard-boiled eggs and salad. When the rest of her children were back from school, they were planning to eat around 4 p.m., and then drive to British Home Stores to buy swimwear for their forthcoming summer holiday.

Michael, who was thirteen, arrived first. According to the pathologist's post-mortem report, he had a glass of orange squash and a Garibaldi biscuit. Eight-year-old Paul was dropped home five minutes later and ate a quarter of a leftover cheese sandwich from his lunchbox.

Their father's van pulled up outside the house one minute after that.

Saul bit his lip. He knew what was coming next but, thirty-eight years on, the mundanity of these details floored him.

Helen and Louise were upstairs in the girls' bedroom, putting laundry away. Michael and Paul were in their own bedroom, getting changed out of their school uniforms.

Aaron Matthews parked his car, went into the small back garden and retrieved a hammer from the shed, then returned to the kitchen, where he withdrew a knife from the cutlery drawer and slid it into his left sock. He attacked the boys first – Michael, who was bigger, and then Paul – and when their mother ran to defend them, he attacked her too. All three of them died within five minutes of that initial blow.

At the sound of the first screams, Louise had crawled under her cot, as instructed by her mother, and stayed there, *quiet as a mouse.*

Hannah Matthews, wearing the white summer dress that was now hidden in Saul's lock-up on the salt marsh, arrived home roughly two minutes after he'd slaughtered half of her family.

According to the senior investigating officer, her decision to go upstairs saved the life of her little sister. While Hannah was stabbed multiple times by her father, Louise was able to escape next door and raise the alarm.

By the time West Midlands Police arrived at the house, Aaron Matthews was found hanging in the garage, having taken his own life. On his body were scratches consistent with DNA material found beneath the nails of thirteen-year-old Michael, who fought until the end to defend his brother and sisters, and his mother.

Saul closed his eyes, heartsore at the tragedy of this innocent family. He couldn't shake the mental picture of Helen Matthews preparing dinner, unaware of the fate that awaited them all. Or of ten-year-old Hannah arriving home from school to a scene of such devastation.

He wondered about the effects on Louise – *Alyssa* – of witnessing the murder of her family. It was well documented that adults who were exposed to violence in the home as children were at higher risk of continuing the cycle of abuse themselves. Was there a kernel of evil within Alyssa that made her complicit in the death of Teddy Miller?

But there was something else that stunned him, which hadn't been made public yet, certainly not in court. He suspected the press was already onto it and it would leak in a matter of days, if not before.

When police first arrived at the Matthews home, they had discovered the bodies of Aaron, Helen, Michael, Hannah and Paul.

But when a forensic pathologist had arrived an hour later to examine the victims and their killer, she'd noticed that although Hannah's clothing was heavily bloodstained and her injuries were severe, she was moving slightly and had a faint pulse.

He sifted through the remaining paperwork and picked up a photocopy of a report from the regional social services department.

Louise Matthews was placed into emergency foster care before finding a permanent placement with Geoff and Carol Kellaway (and their three-year-old daughter Genevieve), who later went on to adopt her.

It was the recommendation of the local authority panel meeting that the sisters stay together, if possible. After several weeks in hospital and a rehabilitation unit, against all odds Hannah Matthews was able to join her sister in the Kellaway family. She, too, was later adopted by them.

61

Iris

Jen and Phil had argued for months about whether Iris should give evidence at the trial of her aunt. Her father was adamant that she was too young and too traumatized. Her mother insisted that Iris had a voice and she wanted to use it. In the end, the decision was made for them. The defence called Iris as a character witness.

After a brief break following Alyssa's testimony, the court resumed its afternoon session. After much discussion, it had been decided that Iris would give her evidence in Court Two rather than via a live TV link. Cynically, this pleased Trudi Baxter. Iris would appear small and vulnerable in the witness box, and she had a natural charm. If she spoke glowingly about her aunt, as she was expected to, this could land well with the jury.

A few weeks earlier, Iris had attended a court familiarization visit with her mother. She was offered the opportunity to give her evidence from behind a screen, and for the courtroom to be emptied of all but judge, jury, counsel and defendant, but she had declined, her curiosity

338

about the mechanics of justice more appealing than hiding from view.

In a concession to her age, the judge and both barristers had removed their wigs, and Iris, always independent, and who had insisted she did not want to exercise her right to have a supporter sit with her during her examination, was allowed to bring in her teddy.

Her eyes were wide as she stared around the packed courtroom. Her mother, who had been granted special permission to sit in the well of the court, waved at her, and Iris waved back, causing most of the jurors to smile. Her father, who was in court for the first time since the start of the trial and sitting next to her mother, gave her a thumbs up.

Baxter did not waste time. 'Can you point to your auntie?'

Iris lifted her hand in the direction of the dock. Alyssa smiled at her niece, and Iris's mouth twisted upwards a quarter-turn.

'Good girl,' said the defence barrister 'Can you tell us a bit about her, Iris?'

Iris's voice rang out as clear as a bell. 'She's kind and funny and plays with me, but I haven't seen her for a while. Not until today.'

'Do you have a favourite memory of something you've done with your aunt?'

Iris's face lit up. 'Yes! One day, when Mummy and Daddy were working, Auntie Lyssa took me and Teddy to the zoo. It was cold and rainy, but she didn't care. She said, "There's no such thing as bad weather if you have the right clothes." We put on our wellies and our wet-weather trousers, and she let us jump in puddles as many times as we wanted to, and we fed the giraffes, and then there was a thunderstorm and the three of us ran to the cafe, and she said we could have anything we wanted from the menu, and we had hot chocolate and ice cream and chips, and Teddy dipped his chips in his ice cream, and pretended the strawberry sauce was ketchup, and we laughed so much our tummies hurt.' She stopped, out of breath.

'That sounds like a lovely day.' Trudi Baxter's voice was soft.

Iris nodded eagerly. 'It was.'

'You have an excellent memory, Iris. Can you remember what happened the day of Teddy's accident?'

The change in Iris was abrupt. Her face clouded over, and she chewed on her bottom lip. 'Yes.'

'Were you excited?'

'Yes.'

'And what about Alyssa? Was she excited too?'

Iris flicked a glance at Alyssa, and then her father. She knew this wasn't what the police lady had written down in her statement after Teddy died, but both parents had insisted on the importance of telling the truth. 'I don't think so.'

Baxter frowned. Iris could tell she was annoyed. She didn't have the words to articulate what the barrister was thinking, but she could guess. She'd heard her talking to the legal team earlier. *Children could be unpredictable witnesses.*

'Why do you say that, Iris?'

'They were cross.'

'Who was?'

'My aunties. Lyssa and Winter. They were arguing.'

'Where was this?'

'On the boat. At the start of the journey. Grandma and Grandpa were below deck with Teddy and Claudia and me, but I wanted to see if I could see any seals on the rocks, so I climbed up the stairs, but they didn't know I was there.'

'Do you know why they were arguing?'

Iris glanced at her father again. He was sitting upright in his chair, stiff and still. Alyssa slumped in her seat and closed her eyes, as if she knew what her niece was about to reveal, and couldn't bring herself to watch the car crash unfold in slow motion.

'Yes.'

'Can you tell the court, please?'

Iris licked her bottom lip. She squeezed her teddy to her chest. 'The baby.'

The air in the courtroom seemed to hum with electricity. The journalists were alert, scenting a headline. Baxter glanced at Alyssa and raised her eyebrows in a questioning manner. But Alyssa didn't react.

'Alyssa's new baby? Your cousin Claudia?'

Iris shook her head several times, and her bunches moved with her. 'No, Auntie Winter's baby.'

'Go on.'

'I heard Auntie Winter tell Auntie Lyssa she was pregnant, and at first Auntie Lyssa was excited, and she hugged her, but then she asked about the baby's father.'

Baxter didn't speak, but Iris could tell she wanted her to continue. Her mother's face was pale but intent. The girl ran her thumb over the black glass of her teddy's eye, drawing comfort from it.

'Then Auntie Lyssa got angry and she was shouting at Auntie Winter, and Auntie Winter was shouting back. I was scared they were going to hurt each other like that time Teddy ate my cupcake and I was so upset I bit him.'

'Why was Auntie Alyssa so cross with Winter?'

For the first time, Iris appeared to lose her composure, irritated by what she considered to be an obvious question. 'I told you. Because of the baby's father. Winter's baby.'

'And who is the baby's father?'

The girl licked her bottom lip again, but her voice was strong and clear. 'My daddy.'

62

Wednesday, 31 July 2024

Jen

The courtroom gave a collective gasp, but Jen, rigid with shock, did not react at all. She was aware of the babble of voices, and of Iris's anguished face, and the mechanical thrum of the air conditioning, but she couldn't move.

Her parents had lied to her. And so, it turned out, had her husband, her sisters and her daughter.

Her vision swam. She dug her fingernails into her thighs and waited for the feelings of dizziness to pass. A metallic taste flooded her mouth. If she threw up in court, would the judge adjourn the case? A high-pitched giggle rose from somewhere inside her and she pressed her palm against her mouth to stifle it. Her body was filled with unfamiliar sensations. Her knees felt as if they might give way. But her brain felt detached from her corporeal self, as if a stranger was observing her from afar.

'Do you want to go outside?' Phil, familiar, solid and treacherous, whispered to her. She could not find her voice, and instead shook her head, refusing his offer.

It was true they'd grown apart in the months since Teddy's

death, and she anticipated they would divorce, probably soon. One of the secondary tragedies of child loss was marital breakdown. It was not uncommon for bereaved parents to lose themselves in their grief and anger, and separate, unable to find their way back to each other. She found she didn't mind that idea. Phil had been a peripheral presence in her life for too long when she'd needed him most. But it was the knowledge that Winter's baby had been conceived before they'd lost Teddy, when she'd still believed in love and the sanctity of marriage, that floored her.

'Is it true?' She murmured the words, aware of the eyes of the media upon her.

'Let's go outside.'

His lack of denial was all the confirmation she needed.

Oddly, though, she didn't feel anger towards Phil or Winter. She tried to summon up some kind of self-righteous fury, but all she could think of was how difficult it must have been for Iris to keep that secret inside her for all these months. And Alyssa. All of them.

If she felt anything at all, it was humiliation. Her cheeks burned with it. She hated the idea that her husband, her sisters and even her daughter had known the truth about Winter's pregnancy, but she understood why they hadn't told her. In the aftermath of losing Teddy, she had barely been able to function. This might have tipped her over the edge.

In her fog of grief and heartbreak, she had never pressed Phil on why he'd seemed so upset on that cold November afternoon, standing on the jetty, waiting to exchange their vows. But somewhere inside her she'd suspected it all along.

As for her parents, she had no idea what she felt. Her sisters were not her sisters. At least, not in the biological sense. Even in her state of shock, she understood why her parents had concealed the truth. But what kind of life was one built on a lie?

She was aware of Phil's eyes upon her. He would be mortified that he'd hurt her in such a public way. Of the damage that he'd wrought upon Iris. They would need to talk about what happened next. To try to reframe their relationship. But she would survive this. The most catastrophic thing in her life had already happened to her.

It would never be worse than losing Teddy.

63

Trudi

After the furore from Iris's revelations about her father and Winter Kellaway had died down, Trudi Baxter resumed her questioning of the eight-year-old girl.

She had explained to Iris that although she had been called as a character witness, her testimony could be of relevance to the criminal case, and she must continue to answer questions truthfully.

The irony had not been lost on the defence barrister. Shocking as it had been, Iris's evidence had shown her client to be an honest and loyal sister. The girl seemed bright enough. Despite her young age, she seemed to understand what was required of her. Children were unpredictable. They could go off-script, but this was not unexpected. Trudi was keen to see what else she could draw out of the child that could benefit Alyssa's case.

'Your aunts were angry with each other.'

'Yes. But they stopped shouting when I came up onto the deck, and Auntie Winter had a glass of champagne and she got me some apple juice.'

The girl was fidgeting and Trudi knew that she would struggle to keep her attention for much longer.

'What happened next?'

'It was freezing. We were waiting for the boat to get to Mummy and Daddy, and I could see them in the distance, and Teddy wanted to see too, so Auntie Lyssa picked him up.' She danced her teddy around the witness box, but resumed her testimony after a gentle reminder from Trudi.

'I was standing a little bit away from them, but I could hear her whispering to Auntie Winter about the baby. Auntie Winter was crying because Auntie Lyssa said she had to get rid of it and pretend it never happened, and then Auntie Winter said that she'd saved her life when she was a baby, and that she could never hurt the one that was growing inside her.'

Two high, bright dots of colour had appeared on Iris's cheeks. Her voice trembled as she shared the final moments of her brother's life.

'Auntie Lyssa said that if Auntie Winter didn't do as she said, she would tell Mummy about the baby. And then Teddy was falling into the water, and everything ended for us.'

Everything ended for us. Such a sorrowful conclusion from one so young. The sound of Jen Miller's soft crying echoed around the court, and Trudi felt a pull of compassion, but forced herself to concentrate.

She locked eyes with Iris. 'This next bit is very important, and I want you to try your hardest to remember what happened next. Did you see any kind of equipment fall from the boat, hit your aunt on the back and knock her forward while she was holding Teddy?'

'Not equipment, no.'

But her sentence felt unfinished, as if she had something more to say.

'OK, Iris. You didn't see any falling equipment, but . . .'

Iris cuddled her teddy. Even though the court usher had placed a cushion on the seat, she looked small and fragile in the witness box. The girl's eyes filled with tears.

'Someone pushed her.'

A hush descended over the court. In her thirty-year career, Trudi had prosecuted and defended too many trials to count, but she could not recall a moment like this. Her mouth was dry, her own heart knocking in her chest. Alyssa was sitting forward, her eyes fixed on her niece. The jury was statue-still. Even the judge was watching intently. With a surge of adrenaline, Trudi Baxter asked the most important question of all.

'Can you tell us who that someone was?'

Iris Miller appeared wretched. Her gaze flew from her parents to her aunt, and back again. Her mother was holding a hand over her mouth, eyes liquid with sympathy.

With a shuddering breath, Iris let go of the secret she had been keeping inside her for eight months, fourteen days and fifty-one minutes.

'It was me.'

64

The eve of the trial

Winter

The summer house by the lake was tucked away in a corner and obscured by the branches of the weeping willow, which swayed in the dusk with a fluidity that was mesmerizing.

Winter was certain that no one had seen her cross the lawns of her vast estate. All her staff had left for the day except Alex's nanny, who was upstairs giving him a bath when she'd slipped out into the softening light.

It wasn't that they were forbidden from seeing each other, as long as they didn't discuss the trial and their evidence, but given that was exactly what they planned to do, Winter thought it was best that their rendezvous was in secret.

A shadow at the door startled her. Alyssa slipped into the cool of the summer house, which smelled of wood and fresh paint and long, hot evenings watching the sun fade from the sky.

Winter studied her sister. The toll of the previous few months was evident in the new lines bracketing her mouth and the streaks of grey in her hair. There was a flatness in Alyssa's expression that pained her.

'You don't have to do this. There's still time to tell the truth.'

Alyssa gave a vehement shake of her head. 'It's too late now. In any case, I don't want to.' She let out a sigh that was lost to the dance of the willow's branches. 'How could I?'

Winter gathered her youngest sister into her arms as she had done since she was a baby. Alyssa's tears soaked through the thin gauze of her shirt. She felt it was her duty to warn her sister again what she faced.

'You could go to prison.'

'I know.' Alyssa closed her eyes, and Winter could see the teardrops at the edge of her lashes, like a string of glass beads.

A deep breath. The most painful part of it, bar losing Teddy. 'You won't see Claudia.'

Alyssa's face crumpled. 'It won't be as bad as that.' Winter thought it sounded like she was trying to convince herself. But she needed to know that Alyssa was sure about what she was doing.

'It might be.'

'They have mother-and-baby units.' Her voice dropped a notch. 'If the worst happens, I suppose I could apply to take her with me.'

'And if Fed objects?'

Alyssa didn't answer, but turned her gaze to one of the summer-house windows. The lake was undisturbed, its surface as flat and polished as a mirror. The spell was broken by a flash of azure and rust. A kingfisher on its eternal quest for supper. She locked eyes with Winter.

'You must have been so frightened.'

Alyssa didn't need to spell it out. Winter knew exactly what her sister meant. Some nights, she awoke drenched in sweat, the whine of the hammer slicing through air ringing in her ears. Some nights, she visited the bodies of her mother and brothers in her dreams, every injury recalled in photographic detail.

'But you still put me first. Even though it cost you so much.' She reached for Winter's hand. 'I want to do the same for Jen and Iris.'

And what could Winter say to that?

The truth was that Alyssa and Jen and her adoptive parents could and would never know what she had suffered as a ten-year-old girl.

For Alyssa, the memory of what had happened in that cramped house in the corner of suburbia was garnered from fragments of newspaper articles and old photographs, and the recollections of her sister, sanitized and designed to protect. She had been a young child. Too young to remember much of her past.

Winter's story was different.

She was old enough to remember her real parents. Old enough to remember the agony of her wounds. Old enough to remember the months and months it took for her to trust Carol and Geoff, and to allow them even to touch her. To go to bed without pushing a chair against her door. To learn how to sleep again without screaming. To worry, relentlessly, about the safety of her sisters, biological or not.

Days like this one – sun-baked and full of summer flowers and iced drinks in tall jugs – were not to be enjoyed, but endured. For Winter, even after all these years, they were threaded with fear and recrimination, and tasted of copper.

Because Winter had a secret.

On the afternoon of the murders, she had returned to the house after school, yes. She had told the police that, and had signed her statement in a childish print. *Hannah Matthews*. She had talked to social workers and police officers, a child psychologist and a coroner, and countless other faceless adults. But she had not told a single one of them that she had first gone home at lunchtime that day. *Home lunch*. Her favourite. A chance to see Mum and her baby sister.

When Miss McGovern had announced it was time for lunch, she had run all the way, not wanting to miss a single minute. Her mother had promised a picnic in the garden with iced fingers from the bakery and orange squash.

When she'd arrived at home, her mother wasn't back from the shops. But her father, in his work overalls, was standing in the hallway, banging a nail into the wall with a hammer.

'Where's that bitch?'

She'd assumed he was talking about her mother. 'I don't know. I haven't seen her.'

'Well, if you *do* see her, tell her I'm going to fucking smash her brains out.'

His breath smelt of stale coffee and, when he'd lunged towards her, there was the threat of violence in his movements, and she'd turned and run back down the path, across the fields to school.

She didn't know it at the time, but her father had climbed into his van and driven off, scouring the streets for his eldest daughter, before ending up in the pub and downing the vodka that would lead him to kill most of his family in a drunken rage.

Her mother had called the school, concerned that she hadn't come home, and when Mrs Potter, the lady on reception, had found her climbing a tree in the playground, she'd told her that she'd decided to stay at school for lunch after all.

'Do you want a quick hello to Mum?' Mrs Potter had been all smiles. 'I won't tell if you don't.'

Playing with her friends and halfway up the tree, she'd shaken her head. *No, thank you.*

She'd never spoken to her mother again.

Neither had she warned her about her father's threat.

That failing had haunted Winter for almost four decades. Never mind that her father had often voiced dark intentions. Never mind that she was ten and frightened, and had no concept that grown-ups were capable of such unspeakable deeds.

She had carried that failure to protect her mother and brothers like a millstone around her neck. The scars from the attack – vivid and ugly – had eventually healed, but the mental ones had not. For the rest of her life, she'd been driven by a compulsion to atone for what she had done. To protect her family at all costs. Even from the truth.

At times, the events of her childhood made her spiky and reckless, and caused her to behave in a manner that was reprehensible. She remembered, with shame, the jealousy she'd felt towards Alyssa, growing up in a happy home without the torment that she'd been subjected to. Towards Jen, too, and the perfect husband she'd borrowed for one night to satisfy her weakness of needing to feel wanted, and her perfect children and her perfect life.

Except poor Jen's life wasn't so perfect anymore.

Iris was eight years old.

Winter remembered what it felt like to carry a secret as a child. The acid burn of conscience. The burden – relentless and unforgiving – of guilt.

It was her duty – Alyssa's too – to protect this little girl, whatever it took. Which is why they were going to lie through their teeth. As far as she was concerned, she would go to any lengths necessary to protect those she loved most of all. If ever an untruth was justified, it was now.

Winter had fame. Impossible wealth. But, she had realized, those things didn't matter. For the first time in her adult life, Winter felt cleansed, as if she and Alyssa were going to repay a debt they had long since owed – their survival – in an act of selfless love.

She kissed her sister goodbye and wished her luck, and stepped into the night, the lights of the house and the town beyond shining in the distance like so many constellations.

65

Three weeks after the trial

Jen

The pile of newspapers had faded in the sun, but Jen hadn't got around to filing them away yet. At some point, she would take a pair of scissors to the dozens of articles and cut them into neat rectangles, ready to stick into Teddy's memory book, but for now they lay discarded in the conservatory, the headlines already slipping from the national consciousness as the ever-changing news agenda was dominated by the new Labour government and conflict in the Middle East.

It was the first time in several days that Jen had found herself alone. In the fall-out from the collapse of the trial, she and Phil had whisked Iris away to a rural getaway owned by friends, and tried to put their daughter back together again.

Iris had not spoken a single word on the journey from Midtown-on-Sea to the Peak District. It was only when they had driven down the dirt track to the farm and a rabbit surprised them by running in front of the car, the flash of its bobtail silhouetted in the headlights, that she had cried out a warning.

That act unlocked something in the girl, and, as her father

navigated the potholes under a night sky, the words fell from her without guile or artifice, but with an edge of panic.

'It was a stupid accident. I didn't mean for it to happen. I didn't know that if I pushed her she would drop Teddy. I didn't know that, or I would never have done it. I promise, Mummy. I promise.'

Jen, who was sitting in the back seat next to her daughter, reached out a hand to calm her, finally asking the question that had tormented her since Iris's confession. 'Why did you push her, sweetheart?'

'My friend Kyra's daddy had a baby with someone who wasn't her mummy, and she says he's her half-brother now, and she gives him baths and pushes his pram at the weekends.

'I wanted a baby brother or sister so badly, but you'd said no, and I was mad with Auntie Lyssa because she was telling Auntie Winter that she shouldn't have my baby brother or sister, and I pushed her to make her stop saying it.' A storm of tears consumed Iris.

Jen didn't know how or what to feel. But she knew she loved her daughter, no matter what she'd done. She waited for the red mist of her anger to descend, to rail at Iris's carelessness and Alyssa's stupidity, at Winter's greed, at Phil for his weakness and cowardice, and at her mother and father for unleashing two girls damaged by their father's killing spree into their family like a wrecking ball. And, yes, at Teddy for demanding to be picked up in the first place.

She ran a finger along the sharp blade of revenge, testing her desire for retribution, her resolve to take Alyssa's and Winter's babies from them as they had taken her child and her future. But her heart wasn't in it. Instead she felt a profound sense of sadness for them all.

As soon as Iris was in bed, she and Phil had talked in a way they hadn't for years. A stripped-back and honest communication. He wanted to try again. To rebuild their family. And, with her blessing, to step up and care for his newborn son.

He had tried to talk Winter out of the pregnancy. That's why he'd gone to her house on the morning of their wedding. But Winter, not expecting him, had panicked at the sight of a hooded figure at her door, and had locked herself in her safe room, alerting the police. In his rush to get away before he was discovered, Phil had slipped and fractured his wrist.

'Nothing like this will ever happen again, I promise.'

His face, so familiar, was one she had loved for such a long time, but Jen wasn't sure. What was a marriage without trust? Dust and broken promises. She was too raw to make a decision. But she held herself – her family – together for Iris, temporarily at least. There was no rush. The three of them spent their days walking in the lush green hills, and the evenings cuddled up on the sofa, watching films. A few days later, they travelled home, and Iris was now at a holiday summer camp with her friends.

Jen tidied up the breakfast things, made herself a cup of tea and turned on the television. Her mother had texted her, urging her to watch. Winter's face filled the screen, a guest on a popular morning show.

With her hair and make-up done, she was breathtaking. But she was naturally beautiful too. Jen could see why Phil had been drawn to her. He'd insisted it had been a moment of weakness for both of them, a drunken one-night stand while he was on business and she was filming in Texas, which they'd had no plans to repeat. He'd kept the details brief. Both homesick and lonely, they'd agreed to a friendly dinner. Too much tequila. A kiss that had turned into something it shouldn't have done. She believed him. But she didn't want to be reminded of their dalliance at every family gathering and occasion, to worry that they might experience another 'moment of weakness'.

Inside her secret self, she recognized that, if forced to choose, she would rather have her sister in her life than her husband. Some women would feel differently, she didn't doubt that. But it had always been that way for Jen. Phil was a good father; she had no desire to cut him loose. But his infidelity had shown her that he was not a good husband. In time, she hoped they would co-parent their daughter in an amicable way.

As for Winter, her sister was capricious and disloyal, but she was bound to Jen in a way that Phil was not. She'd forgiven her countless betrayals. In time, she could forgive this one too.

Some might say she was a pushover, too passive and accepting, but Jen was a realist. Forgiving Winter was not the same as trusting her. But her childhood had left more than physical scars on Winter Kellaway, and Jen was compassionate enough to recognize that. Self-important and fierce and loving and complicated, Winter had known all along who she was, but had never breathed a word to Alyssa, a big sister still protecting her sibling all those years later.

Jen's family had been torn apart by losing Teddy. She didn't have it in herself to widen that rent further still. When the initial shock of discovering their brutal and bloody past had eased, Jen understood that it did not matter to her. Families came in all shapes. They were still her sisters. In truth, her heart broke for those frightened girls, Hannah and Louise Matthews. She imagined Iris living through the horrors they had done, and it knocked the breath from her. They'd already lost one family. She would not allow them to lose another.

'This was where my father stabbed me first,' said Winter, pointing to a silvery necklace of slashes on her neck that she'd always covered up and dismissed as the result of a childhood accident. The interviewer, a shiny-haired twenty-something with too-white teeth, asked if there were more. 'On my chest and my lower pelvis.' Winter shrugged. 'They're part of me.'

The public outpouring of love for Winter had been staggering, but unsurprising. Once the truth about her past had been revealed, her fears that she would be shunned had proved to be unfounded. She'd been liberated by the truth. The world had seen who she was, and loved her still. For Winter, who had always been unsure of her place in said world, this validation was life-changing.

'But there's a special reason I've agreed to do this interview today. It's a surprise for my sister, but we're pretty sure she'll support it.' Winter smiled and looked into the camera. 'We love you, Jen.'

Jen put down her mug, her heart thumping. These days, she didn't like surprises. Her eyes were glued to Winter's face, a buzz of adrenaline in her veins.

'We want to announce the Teddy Miller Foundation, which I'm supporting with a three-million-pound donation. In my nephew's name, the foundation will work with children of violent offenders and young people who have been the victims or witnesses of traumatic crimes.'

A photograph of Teddy filled the screen. Stunned by Winter's generosity, Jen released the breath she'd been holding, her son's face blurring through her tears.

A soft knock at the door dragged Jen from the television. Her youngest sister, Alyssa, was standing on the doorstep, nine-month-old Claudia in her arms.

'Hi,' said Alyssa. It was still awkward between them, but they were making headway. She thrust a bunch of sunflowers at her sister. Alyssa was full of regrets, but thankful that Iris had told the truth. In turn, Jen had been grateful for her sister's loyalty to her, and her willingness to protect her young niece at great personal cost to herself.

But it was too soon to think about forgiveness. The loss of Teddy was too messy for that. At times, Jen was convulsed by loss, blinded by fury at her sister's carelessness, her insides aflame with a bitterness that lingered for days. At other times, she was calmer, recognizing the accident for what it was, and that Alyssa, worn hollow by guilt and heartbreak, would do anything to turn back the dial. Their relationship was a work in progress. All that anyone could hope for.

She stepped aside to let Alyssa in, shy in her presence for the first time in decades.

The sisters stood side by side, watching the closing moments of Winter's interview.

'We hope you don't mind that we didn't tell you,' said Alyssa, a note of nervousness in her voice. 'We wanted to surprise you with something that would honour Teddy, and make you proud.'

For the first time in months, Jen had reached for her then, a brief squeeze of her fingers. By chance, baby Claudia had giggled at the same moment, and it had sounded like sunshine. It had felt odd, to feel her sister's skin against hers. And then it had felt like coming home.

Later, Winter arrived at the house, pushing Alex's pram

and carrying a large takeaway bag filled with more lunch than the three of them could eat. She unloaded boxes of salads, bread and cheeses, platters of cold meat, olives, fruit, a cake with fresh raspberries and cream, and bottles of ginger and elderflower cordial.

'A celebration for Teddy's foundation,' she said, 'if it's OK with you.' She eyed Jen warily. 'But I can leave, if you prefer. I don't mind. I just wanted to mark the moment.'

It was the first time that Jen had seen Winter since the courtroom revelation. She took a deep breath. A part of her wanted to close the door in her sister's face. To leave her out in the cold. To make her pay for her betrayal for the rest of her life, in loneliness and misery. But Winter, who had always traded on her beauty, had looked so vulnerable, so desperate for love and acceptance, that something inside Jen loosened, and although she found she could not speak, she stood to one side, allowing the older woman to enter.

The sisters laid out blankets in the garden, and parked the babies under a wide parasol. They filled their plates with food, conversation stilted.

And then Winter, weeping, covered her face with her hands, apologizing over and over again to Jen for all that she'd done and for how the burden of keeping the secrets of her past had corroded her over time.

That simple act of humility unlocked the tension between the sisters, and the three women talked in a way they had never done before.

All of them had cried, and Winter told them she was taking a break from acting to focus on Alex.

'What about you and Federico?' said Jen, passing a bowl of fruit to her sibling. 'Do you think you'll work things out?'

Alyssa bit into a strawberry. 'Not a chance. He's shacked

up with some dancer from one of his music videos. He'd been seeing her for months, apparently, even when I was pregnant.' She gave a rueful grin. 'I sometimes think the only reason he stayed with me for as long as he did was because of you, Winter. He didn't do much to hide his crush, did he?'

'Nothing happened between us, I swear.' Winter looked between her sisters, aghast. 'I always thought of Fed as a brother.' Her eyes filled with tears. 'You were too little to remember Paul and Michael, but I still miss them.'

Alyssa reached for Jen's hand. 'I know you must feel so angry, and I'm not trying to deny what happened was wrong, but Phil was a better friend to me than Fed ever was. After Mum told me the truth about my past, it was actually Phil who helped me to come to terms with it.' She offered Jen a slice of cake. 'I asked him to find a way to share it with you.'

Jen helped herself to a forkful of cream and sponge, remembering and regretting her curt dismissal of her son. 'Teddy told me that Phil was spending time at your house, but I thought he'd made a mistake.'

It felt strange, discussing their partners in this detached way. For so long, it had been *Lyssa and Fed* and *Phil and Jen*, sharing late-night suppers and days at the beach, but both women would need to learn how to remake themselves as independent entities. Alyssa was further ahead in that journey than her sister. But at least they had each other.

Their children meant they would never be truly separated from the men they had once loved, and who had disappointed them so profoundly. But both understood they were right to let them go. While neither sister could conceive of the possibility of a new relationship, in time they would come to recognize that romantic love might visit them again.

The subject of Phil Miller was a thorny one between the women, especially Jen and Winter, and instinctively they shied away from it. A part of Jen was curious, though. Who had made the first move? Did Winter feel guilty? But she didn't ask those difficult questions; there would be time for that another day. But not now.

The sun was high and bright in the sky. Jen's garden was filled with the scent of roses, and the drone of pollinating bees. A pair of butterflies danced above them. Were they Painted Ladies or Red Admirals? Jen could never tell the difference. But for the first time in months, she felt her body and mind relax.

Alyssa leaned back in one of the garden chairs with Claudia on her lap, reading her a story. Baby Alex began to stir and Winter scooped him out of his pram, patting him on the shoulder to soothe his whimpers.

Winter's phone rang, and with her free hand, she dug into her bag and checked the screen. 'Shit, I need to take this. Do you mind?' And without waiting for an answer, she thrust the baby at Jen.

After the trial had collapsed, Jen had deliberately kept her distance from Alex. Now she knew the truth about his parentage, she was afraid of the emotions the baby would stir in her, but Winter, being Winter, had given her no choice.

Stiffly, she cradled him, willing her sister to hurry up. She flicked a glance at Alyssa, who was feeding Claudia a crust of bread. A thought struck her out of nowhere, macabre and ugly.

She could hurt him. Right now. She could press her hand over his nostrils, his hungry mouth, and hold it there until he stopped breathing. Tit for tat. She could take a child from Winter as an act of revenge for taking her husband. Once, a long time ago, she'd promised her sister she'd destroy her if she ever betrayed her again.

Alex gazed up at her. His eyes were deep blue, the colour of twilight. A mewl escaped from him and, instinctively, she rocked him back and forth, quieting his cries. His fingernails were tiny, the same mottled pink and white as the seashells she'd collected the previous week on the beach with Iris. One of his fingers curled around hers. She stroked his cheek. She'd forgotten how soft babies could be.

This was Phil's son. Iris's half-brother. Her nephew. He was part of her family now, whether she liked it or not. An innocent at the centre of turmoil that was not his fault. And Jen Miller was many things, but she was not a killer.

A sob rose inside her. And a longing for Teddy so powerful that her knees almost buckled beneath her. Nine months to grow a baby. Nine months since her boy had died. Some mornings, she got up and dressed herself, and managed to crawl from the start of the day to its end, for Iris, if nothing else. But mostly she could not imagine ever feeling joy again. Her world had been voided of all colour. It was hard to breathe. To exist. To do anything at all.

All of Jen's certainties had been crushed to fragments beneath Fate's heel. Her love for her husband. Her belief in her sisters. Her role as a mother of two. She didn't know who she was anymore. And she didn't know when this would change. *If* it ever would.

Alex stretched into a superhero pose, one arm punching the air. Teddy used to do that. He nuzzled into Jen, his mouth gumming his fist. Teddy used to do that too, especially when he was hungry.

The knot of grief and anger she'd carried inside her since her son's death slackened a notch. His hair was the same golden brown as Teddy's, and he had that same newborn-sweet smell of biscuits and milk.

She stroked his cheek again.

Jen wasn't naive. The road ahead would be difficult, the dark hollows of grief overwhelming at times. She anticipated loneliness. Frequent bouts of anger. A Teddy-shaped hole that could never be filled. She had lost her son. Her husband. The wounds ran deep.

But she wasn't completely on her own. She had the support of her parents. Her love for Iris. And, for better or worse, she had her sisters.

The baby yawned, screwing up his face, and he looked so much like Teddy that her heart soared at this second chance to love a little boy with a dimple on his chin like the half-brother he'd never meet, but would know everything about. The past was a strange place, full of memories she wasn't ready to relinquish and deeds she must try to forgive.

His eyes fixed on hers again.

'Hello you,' she said. 'I'm your Auntie Jen. I hope we're going to be great friends.'

But Jen Miller – mother, sister and survivor – wasn't just saying hello to Alex. She was saying hello to the possibility – one day – of a future where she might smile again.

66

Four weeks after the trial

Saul

The salt marsh was alive with summer. Saul Anguish watched a redshank scramble towards the nest hidden in the tussock, a chorus of piping calls alerting its mate and their chicks to the presence of the sparrowhawk soaring above.

A curlew burst from the lagoon at the edge of the mudflats, startling him, and he laughed to himself as he watched it wade through the sludge. At the upper ungrazed edges of the grassland, a shrew darted into the shadows. With so much wildlife on offer, the marsh was regularly patrolled by birds of prey, the spectre of death ever-present.

Saul understood how it felt to live under threat of discovery.

The detective padlocked the dugout's trapdoor and made his way across the damp peat until he found the coastal path that hugged the edge of the bay. With its unmatched views across the water, the salt marsh was a haven of beauty at this time of the year, but Saul preferred the winter months, when the numbers of wildfowl swelled to their thousands, and the geese returned to roost overnight, flying in skeins across the sky during the quietude of the blue hour.

Saul carried a parcel under his arm, wrapped carefully in tissue paper and tied with reeds, a sprig of sea lavender tucked into its bindings. He'd chosen the fragrant purple flower because it represented healing and peace of mind.

He walked until the path hit a steep set of steps carved into the cliff that led to the beach. His back twinged with pain occasionally, but he no longer needed his cane, and made his way down until he reached the bottom and continued his journey along the wide expanse of shingle.

In the near distance, he could see Winter Kellaway's waterfront estate, but he already knew that she wasn't at home. Following the relentless headlines about her family, she'd been photographed leaving the country earlier that week, flying to a secret destination.

He left the shingle beach and cut through an alleyway that led into town. In the late-summer afternoon, the streets were bursting with tourists, and Saul passed the Vietnamese restaurant where he'd shared dinner with Isaac, before walking up the hill to the conservation area in which Alyssa Kellaway lived.

Saul had deliberately waited for the newspapers to grow bored of this story. When he scanned her street, an affluent private estate of million-pound houses, he was relieved to see it was free from the photographers and journalists who'd waited in their cars from dawn to midnight on the off-chance of a single quote or picture.

Hers was a Georgian double-fronted residence with a teal-coloured door and a silver knocker. He opened the gate and wandered down the path. The front garden was attractive, and contained two chairs and a round table shielded by the box hedge that surrounded the property. A vase of fading roses sat on the windowsill in water that was a brackish green.

He knocked once, and she opened the door immediately, as if she had been waiting for him, although that would have been impossible.

'Oh, it's you.' A fleeting expression of panic crossed her face before she rearranged her features into a mask of neutrality. 'What can I do for you, DC Anguish?'

'This is an off-duty call.'

'Do you want to come in?'

He followed her into a sitting room scattered with toys. Her baby was asleep in her pushchair, still wearing her sun-hat, cheeks flushed in the heat. 'We went for a walk in the park. I decided not to wake her up, so I could tidy up a bit.'

But Saul wasn't interested in the baby or in household chores.

'Why did you and Winter lie in court?' He watched her carefully to gauge her reaction, but to her credit, she didn't evade his question.

'To protect ourselves. And our family. We didn't want anyone to know about our past.'

'Why?'

'Shame. Judgement. We all have our secrets, don't we?'

Yes, thought Saul, *we do*.

She misread his silence as anger. 'I'm sorry that it discredited your evidence. When my mother told me what Aaron Matthews had done, we all agreed that even if the truth came out about me, we would always protect my sister, if that's what she wanted. Winter has made something of herself, in spite of everything. She didn't deserve to lose that.' She paused. 'Are you going to make a complaint? Will we be charged with perjury?'

Saul shook his head. This was not the kind of vengeance he sought. But he was curious. He had questions. 'Why was there CCTV footage of you at Winter's house when you were out in the boat?'

'Because I *was* at her house. I launched the boat from her beach.'

Occam's razor. *The simplest explanation is almost always the right one.*

'Why did you throw away the dress?'

'A couple of weeks before Teddy died, I was contacted by a solicitor who'd been looking for us for a long time. They'd found me first. The house and its contents had been sold years earlier, and a small box of belongings had been left in the care of his legal firm. Paperwork. My mother's wedding ring, that sort of thing. But it was so long ago that most of it had gone missing. The dress was the only remaining item of the personal effects that the police had returned to the estate.

'I didn't know what to do with it. I didn't want Federico to find it, or for Winter to be reminded of that horrific day. She'd carried the huge burden of our family's secret on her own for so long.' She smiled sadly. 'It probably sounds silly to you, but I'd just had a baby, and it was all about new beginnings. I didn't want her to be tainted by those murders. And so I thought I'd get rid of it where no one would ever find it.'

She looked away, regretful. 'Stupid, really. It was our last connection to the past. My mother hand-sewed those flowers to my sister's skirt. But it's too late now.'

In the silence that followed, Saul handed her the tissue-wrapped package. She turned it over in her hands, a question mark on her face.

'I salvaged it from the water that day,' he said. 'When everything became public, I thought you might like it back, so I had it dry-cleaned. For when you're ready.'

As soon as he'd learned of its bloodstained history, Saul

had burned to keep that dress. But he followed his own code of ethics. He only retrieved mementoes from crime scenes he'd attended himself. This did not belong to him.

'Thank you,' she said, and her eyes shone with gratitude.

There wasn't much else to say. He declined her offer of a cold drink and she walked him back down the garden path to the gate. The air held that golden light of summer, although he knew it wouldn't be long before the first whisper of autumn would make itself heard. As he prepared to leave, a thought occurred to him, and he paused, his hand resting on the gate's metal frame.

'Why did Winter pretend you'd been drinking when you hadn't?'

Alyssa gazed at him, and waited for him to puzzle out the answer to his own question. It didn't take him long. The detective wondered why he hadn't realized it before.

'You *knew* it was Iris.'

'We both did.'

'But why didn't you say anything?'

'And ruin another little girl's life? We needed to protect our niece. And Jen. They'd had so much to cope with already.'

'But you might have gone to prison.'

'It was a risk for me, of course it was. But I was sure I'd be able to convince the jury to find me not guilty.' She smiled. 'I reckon I was almost there. But Iris made up her own mind in the end.'

And he couldn't argue with that.

In the eyes of the law, the detective had an obligation to report this new information, but he recognized a kindred spirit in Alyssa Kellaway, another emotionally damaged survivor of childhood trauma. He would say nothing. This family had been through enough.

He didn't feel like going home, and so he walked back to the dug-out along the cliff path, scanning the rocks for seals. Blue would have approved of his decision to keep this family's secrets. He was the keeper of many secrets. He was not afraid of the dark.

The sun was sinking now, his favourite time of the evening. If he hurried, he might catch the oystercatchers wading through the pools of water on the intertidal mudflats, or the short-eared owl on the hunt for field voles.

Blue had been as good as her word. She hadn't replied to a single message or text or call from Saul. But he couldn't bring himself to let her go. He wanted to hear her voice. He knew she wouldn't pick up, but he would listen to her voice-mail message and draw comfort from that.

He unlocked the padlock and climbed down the ladder into the sanctuary of the shelter, scented with a base note of sand, salt and decay.

His visits had become more frequent in recent months. This place held a stillness and calm for him, away from the demands of his job. It was where he felt most himself.

The detective settled himself into an old chair, found Blue's number and redialled it, as he'd done several times over the previous few weeks. He was used to it by now. An electronic click. Then her voicemail would kick in.

Except this time, a woman answered her phone.

Saul held his breath, his heart thumping.

'Saul?'

Her voice held the same lilt and rhythm, the same distinctive cadence, but even as he asked, he knew it wasn't her. 'Clover?'

'No, it's Macy, her sister.'

Saul had not met Macy before. But Blue had talked about

her a lot during the nights they'd spent together, pressed up close in the dark.

'Have you spoken to her lately?'

He shook his head, even though she couldn't see him. 'No, not for months,' he said.

She swore softly under her breath. 'Neither have I.'

He knew he should ask her questions about this, but his mind was running in frantic circles and he couldn't catch his breath. Before he could form the words, she answered for him. 'I've been abroad, but she dropped out of contact a few months ago. I thought she was busy with work, you know, but I'm at her flat, and some of her stuff has gone. Someone's been here.'

He made a non-committal sound.

'But it's weird. Her phone was by her bed, and her motorbike's still outside. I was thinking of calling the police, but then you rang, and I wondered if you'd mind helping me to look for her.'

Saul's mouth was dry, but what else could he say? 'Of course. I'll come now.'

The detective disconnected the call, placed his phone gently on his work-bench and stood up, flexing the stiffness in his hip.

In the dying light of the day, his collection looked more museum-like than ever. Behind the glass doors of his curio cabinets, his treasures were on display. A bloodied seagull feather. The gold filling he'd stolen from a shooting two years earlier. Countless other mementoes he'd magpied over the years.

And a lock of hair, the colour of a summer sky.

EPILOGUE

Two days later

The Chief Constable

The Chief Constable, a man who had stamped on countless fingers and toes during his scramble to the top, poured two large whiskies into two small tumblers before shoving the bottle back into his desk drawer.

At the sound of soft knocking at his door, he barked at the young detective to enter, and then linked his hands behind his head and leaned back in his chair, his shirt buttons straining under the pressure from his ever-growing paunch.

The golden glow of late afternoon filled the office with a luminosity that seemed at odds with the duplicitous exchange that was about to unfold.

He gestured at his visitor to sit down and pushed the whisky in his direction. The man – twenty-six and already earmarked as a gifted talent within the force – took a sip and grimaced. The distilled peatiness of fermented grain mash held a sour bitterness that he was not used to.

The Chief Constable raised his eyebrows, an unspoken question. The police officer sitting in the chair opposite him adjusted the cuffs of his shirt, and met his gaze straight on, his mouth collapsing into a lopsided grin.

'I think he's starting to trust me.'

The Chief Constable, who had been at public school with the detective's father, rubbed his hands together in undisguised glee, eyes gleaming with excitement. 'Excellent work.'

'What do you want me to do next, sir?'

'Keep doing what you're doing, son. Get as close to him as you can without arousing suspicion. He'll slip up at some point and we'll need to catch him when he does.'

DC Isaac Hunter gave a sharp nod of agreement, picked up his phone and dialled a now-familiar number. His eyes, ruthless and calculating, met the Chief Constable's, and he pressed a finger to his lips.

'Hey, Saul, it's me. Yeah, I'm good. Look, I was wondering, are you free to meet up for a beer and curry tonight?'

ACKNOWLEDGEMENTS

Have you ever read a story in the newspaper about a baby forgotten in the back seat of a car on a sweltering day or a child accidentally run over by a reversing vehicle driven by a loved one? As a part of a close-knit family, I've often wondered how the aftermath of an accidental tragedy might impact on such relationship dynamics, and *Some of Us Are Liars* is the result.

A novel is never written alone. Thanks, as always, to my brilliant and supportive agent Sophie Lambert, agent assistant Alice Hoskyns, and the foreign rights team at C+W; to my fabulous commissioning editor, Trisha Jackson, who, it turns out, is twice the genius in half the time; to the whole team at Pan Macmillan, including Maddie Thornham, Stuart Dwyer, Rebecca Kellaway, Rory O'Brien, Rebecca Lloyd, Leanne Williams, Claire Evans, Lucy Hale, Neil Lang, Gillian Mackay, Andy Belshaw, David Adamson, Kate Bullows, Keren Western, Tom Clancy, Richard Baker and Melissa Bond; to Amber Burlinson and Kate Berens; and a special hat-tip to publicist extraordinaire Laura Sherlock.

Grateful thanks to Helen Fields and Tony Kent for their generous and expert advice on legal matters, and to Graham Bartlett for his brilliant guidance on police procedure. Any mistakes are my own, and deliberate. For those who are familiar with the workings of the court system, I'm aware that I've bent the rules in places – for example, defendants usually give evidence first, and the courtroom would be cleared for a child in the witness stand – using artistic licence for the purposes of the story. The first Paris Fashion Week of 1997 took place earlier than the one mentioned in this book; and, at the time of writing, July 2024 has been full of rain, with no sign of a heatwave.

Thank you to the fantastic booksellers, bloggers, reviewers, librarians and readers. Without you and your continuous enthusiasm, I'd have stopped writing years ago.

Heartfelt appreciation, too, to my friends, both inside and outside the writing community. As some of you know, it's been a tumultuous year. To my family, thank you, always, for your unwavering love and support.

Lastly, this is a book about sisters, who will go to any lengths to protect each other. I've never had a sister, but it doesn't matter because friends can be family too. Keely Buckle was born in the house next door to mine. We went to primary and secondary school together and have shared high days and holidays, heartbreak and sorrow. My mother, Ann, was friends with her late mother, Glynne, and our daughters, Alice and Clemmie, are also friends. There is deep comfort to be found in the continuing cycle of love and kinship between our families, these three generations of girls and women. Keely – mother, daughter, wife, sister, aunt, teacher and friend – is the strongest woman I know. This book is for her.